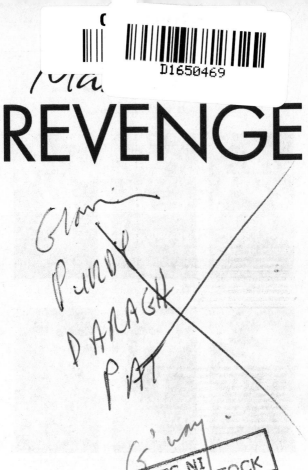

REVENGE

REVENGE

COLLECTION

November 2015

December 2015

January 2016

February 2016

March 2016

April 2016

Married for
REVENGE

Lynne
GRAHAM

Published in Great Britain 2015
by Mills & Boon, an imprint of Harlequin (UK) Limited,
Eton House, 18-24 Paradise Road, Richmond, Surrey, TW9 1SR

MARRIED FOR REVENGE © 2015 Harlequin Books S.A.

Roccanti's Marriage Revenge © 2012 Lynne Graham
A Deal at the Altar © 2012 Lynne Graham
A Vow of Obligation © 2012 Lynne Graham

ISBN: 978-0-263-91787-1

25-1215

ROCCANTI'S
MARRIAGE REVENGE

Lynne Graham was born in Northern Ireland and has been a keen Mills & Boon book reader since her teens. She is very happily married, with an understanding husband who has learned to cook since she started to write! Her five children keep her on her toes. She has a very large dog, which knocks everything over, a very small terrier, which barks a lot, and two cats. When time allows, Lynne is a keen gardener.

CHAPTER ONE

VITALE ROCCANTI was a banker descended from a very old and aristocratic European family. Opening the private investigator's file on his desk, he studied the photograph of four people seated at a dining table. The Greek billionaire, Sergios Demonides, was entertaining Monty Blake, the British owner of the Royale hotel chain, his highly ornamental wife, Ingrid and their daughter, Zara.

Zara, nicknamed Tinkerbelle by the media for her celebrity status, her silver-gilt-coloured hair and fairy-like proportions, wore what appeared to be an engagement ring. Evidently the rumours of a buyout anchored by a family alliance were true. Most probably Demonides' loathing for publicity lay behind the lack of an official announcement but it certainly did look as though a marriage was on the cards.

Vitale, renowned for his shrewd brain and ruthless pursuit of profit, frowned. His lean, darkly handsome face hardened, his firm mouth compressing. His dark gaze flared gold with angry bitterness because it could only sicken him to see Monty Blake still smil-

ing and at the top of his game. For a fleeting instant
he allowed himself to recall the loving sister who had
drowned when he was thirteen years old and his stomach clenched at the recollection of the savage loss that
had left him alone in an inhospitable world. His sister had been the only person who had ever truly loved
him. And the moment that he had worked towards for
the better part of twenty years had finally arrived, for
Blake looked to be on the brink of his greatest ever tri-
umph. If Vitale waited any longer his prey might well
become untouchable as the father-in-law of so powerful
a man as Sergios Demonides. Yet how had Blake contrived to catch a fish as big as Demonides in his net?
Apart from the little known fact that the Royale hotel
chain had once belonged to Demonides' grandfather,
what was the connection?

Were the oft-publicised charms of Tinkerbelle,
whose brain was said to be as lightweight as her body,
the only source of Blake's unexpected good fortune?
Was she truly the sole attraction? Vitale had never let a
woman come between him and his wits and would have
assumed that Demonides had equal common sense.
His mouth curled with derision. If he ensured that the
engagement was broken the business deal might well
go belly up as well and he would bring down Monty
Blake, who desperately needed a buyer.

Vitale had never dreamt that he would have to get
personal or indeed so unpleasantly close to his quarry
to gain the revenge that his very soul craved for closure,
but he remained convinced that Monty Blake's cruelty
demanded an equal response. Should not the punish-

ment be made to fit the crime? This was not the time to be fastidious, he reflected harshly. He could not afford to respect such boundaries. No, he only had one option: he would have to play dirty to punish the man who had abandoned his sister and her unborn child to their wretched fate.

A man who had always enjoyed enormous success with women, Vitale studied his prey, Tinkerbelle. His shapely mouth quirked. In his opinion she fell easily into the acceptable damage category. And wasn't suffering supposed to form character? Huge blue eyes wide in her heart shaped face, Blake's daughter was undeniably beautiful, but she also looked as shallow as a puddle and was anything but a blushing virgin with tender feelings. Undoubtedly she would regret the loss of so wealthy a catch as Demonides but Vitale imagined that, like her glossy mother, she had the hide of a rhinoceros and the heart of a stone and would bounce back very quickly from the disappointment. And if he left her a little wiser, that would surely only be to her advantage…

'I can't believe you've agreed to marry Sergios Demonides,' Bee confessed, her green eyes bright with concern as she studied the younger woman.

Although Bee was only marginally taller than her diminutive half sibling, and the two women had the same father, Bee was built on very different lines. Zara looked delicate enough to blow away in a strong breeze but Bee had inherited her Spanish mother's heavy fall of dark brown hair and olive-tinted skin and she had substantial curves. Bee was the child of Monty Blake's first marriage, which had ended in divorce, but she and Zara were close. Monty had a third daughter called Tawny, the result of an extra-marital affair. Neither girl knew their youngest sister very well because Tawny's mother was very bitter about the way their father had treated her.

'Why wouldn't I have?' Zara shrugged a narrow shoulder, striving for a show of composure. She was very fond of Bee and she didn't want the other woman worrying about her, so she opted for a deliberately careless response. 'I'm tired of being single and I like kids—'

'How can you be tired of being single? You're only twenty-two and it's not as if you're in love with Demonides!' Bee protested, scanning her sibling's flawless face in disbelief.

'Well...er—'

'You can't love him—you hardly *know* him, for goodness' sake!' Bee exclaimed, quick to take advantage of Zara's hesitation. Although she had met Sergios Demonides only once, her shrewd powers of observation, followed up by some careful Internet research on the Greek tycoon, had warned her that he was altogether too tough a proposition for her tender-hearted sister. Demonides had a very bad reputation with women and he was equally renowned for his cold and calculating nature.

Zara lifted her chin. 'It depends what you want out of marriage and all Sergios wants is someone to raise the children that have been left to his care—'

Bee frowned at that explanation. 'His cousin's three kids?'

Zara nodded. Several months earlier Sergios' cousin and his wife had been killed in a car crash and Sergios had become their children's legal guardian. Her future husband was a forceful, sardonic and distinctly intimidating shipping magnate, who travelled a great deal and worked very long hours. If she was honest, and there were very few people in Zara's life whom she dared to be honest with, she had been considerably less intimidated by Sergios once he had confessed that the only reason he wanted a wife was to acquire a mother for the three orphans in his home. That was a role that Zara felt she could comfortably cope with.

The children, ranging in age from a six-month-old baby to a three-year-old, were currently being raised almost entirely by his staff. Apparently the children had not settled well in his household. Sergios might be a very rich and powerful man but his concern for the children had impressed her. The product of a dysfunctional background himself, Sergios wanted to do what was best for those children but he just didn't know how and he was convinced that a woman would succeed where he had failed.

For her own part, Zara was desperately keen to do something that would finally make her parents proud of her. Her twin Tom's tragic death at the tender age of twenty had ripped a huge hole in her family. Zara had adored her brother. She had never resented the fact that Tom was their parents' favourite, indeed had often been grateful that Tom's academic successes had taken parental attention away from her wounding failures. Zara had left school halfway through her A-levels because she was struggling to cope, while Tom had been studying for a business degree at university and planning to join their father in the family hotel business when he crashed his sports car, dying instantly.

Sadly for all of them, her charismatic and successful brother had been everything her parents had ever wanted and needed in a child, and since his death grief had made her father's dangerous temper rage out of control more often. If in some way Zara was able to compensate her parents for Tom's loss and her survival she was eager to do it. After all she had spent her life striving for parental approval without ever winning it. When Tom had died she had wondered why fate chose him rather than her as a sacrifice. Tom had often urged her to make more of her life, insisting that she shouldn't allow their father's low opinion of her abilities to influence her so much. On the day of Tom's funeral she had promised herself that in honour of her brother's memory she would in the future make the most of every opportunity and work towards making her parents happy again. And it was a sad fact that Zara's entire education had been geared towards being the perfect wife for a wealthy man and that the only way she would ever really please her parents would be by marrying a rich high-achiever.

The children in Sergios' London home had touched her heart. Once she had been an unhappy child so she knew something of how they felt. Looking into those sad little faces, she had felt that finally she could make a big difference in someone else's life. Sergios might not personally need her, but those children genuinely *did* and she was convinced that she could make a success of her role as a mother. That was something she could do, something she could shine at and that meant a lot to Zara.

What was more, when she had agreed to marry Sergios, her father had looked at her with pride for the first time in her life. She would never forget that moment or the glow of warmth, acceptance and happiness she had felt. Her father had smiled at her and patted her shoulder in an unprecedented gesture of affection. 'Well done,' he had said, and she would not have exchanged that precious moment of praise for a million pounds. Zara was also convinced that marriage to Sergios would give her freedom, which she had never known. Freedom primarily from her father, whose temper she had learned to fear, but also freedom from the oppressive expectations of her perfectly groomed, socially ambitious mother, freedom from the boring repetition of days spent shopping and socialising with the right people in the right places, freedom from the egotistical men relentlessly targeting her as the next notch on their bed post...freedom—she hoped—that would ultimately allow her to be herself for the first time ever.

'And what happens when you *do* meet someone you can love?' Bee enquired ruefully in the lingering silence.

'That's not going to happen,' Zara declared with confidence. She had had her heart broken when she was eighteen, and, having experienced that disillusionment, had never warmed the slightest bit to any man since then.

Bee groaned out loud. 'You've got to be over that lowlife Julian Hurst by now.'

'Maybe I've just seen too many men behaving badly to believe in love and fidelity,' Zara fielded with a cynical gleam in her big blue eyes. 'If they're not after my father's money, they're after a one night stand.'

'Well, you've never been that,' Bee remarked wryly, well aware that, regardless of the media reports that constantly implied that Zara had enjoyed a wide range of lovers, her sibling appeared to be sublimely indifferent to most of the men that she met.

'But who would ever believe it? Sergios doesn't care either way. He doesn't need me in that department—' Zara would not have dreamt of sharing how welcome that lack of interest was to her. Her reluctance to trust a man enough to engage in sexual intimacy was too private a fact to share, even with the sister that she loved.

Bee froze, an expression of even greater dismay settling on her expressive face. 'My goodness, are you telling me that you've actually agreed to have one of those *open* marriages with him?'

'Bee, I couldn't care less what Sergios does as long as he's discreet and that's exactly what he wants—a wife who won't interfere with his life. He likes it as it is.'

Her sister looked more disapproving than ever. 'It won't work. You're far too emotional to get into a relationship like that at such a young age.'

Zara lifted her chin. 'We made a bargain, Bee. He's

agreed that the kids and I can live in London and that as long as I don't work full-time I can continue to run Edith's business.'

Taken aback by that information, Bee shook her head and looked even more critical. Zara's parents had simply laughed when Zara's aunt, Edith, died and left her niece her small but successful garden design business, Blooming Perfect. The Blakes had sneered at the idea of their severely dyslexic daughter running any kind of a business, not to mention one in a field that required specialist knowledge. Their father had stubbornly ignored the fact that in recent years Zara, who had long shared her aunt's love of well-groomed outdoor spaces, had successfully taken several courses in garden design. Huge arguments had broken out in the Blake household when Zara stood up to her controlling snobbish parents and not only refused to sell her inheritance but also insisted on taking a close interest in the day to day running of the business.

'I want…I *need* to lead my own life,' Zara confided with more than a hint of desperation.

'Of course, you do.' Full of sympathy when she recognised the tears glistening in Zara's eyes, Bee gripped the younger woman's hands in hers. 'But I don't think marrying Sergios is the way to go about that. You're only going to exchange one prison for another. He will have just as much of an agenda as your parents. Please think again about what you're doing,' Bee urged worriedly. 'I didn't like the man when I met him and I certainly wouldn't trust him.'

Driving away from the specially adapted house that

Bee shared with her disabled mother, Zara had a lot on her mind. Zara knew that it didn't make much sense to marry in the hope of getting a new life but she was convinced that, as a renowned entrepreneur in his own right, Sergios would be much more tolerant and understanding of her desire to run her own business than her parents could ever be. He would be even happier to have a wife with her own interests, who had no need to look to him for attention, and her parents would at last be proud of her, proud and pleased that their daughter was the wife of such an important man. Why couldn't Bee understand that the marriage was a win-win situation for all of them? In any case, Zara could no more imagine falling in love again than she could imagine walking down the street stark naked. A marriage of convenience was much more her style because love made fools of people, she thought painfully.

Her mother, for a start, was wed to a man who regularly played away with other women. Ingrid, a former Swedish model from an impoverished background, idolised her husband and the luxury lifestyle and social status he had given her by marrying her. No matter what Monty Blake did or how often he lost his violent temper, Ingrid forgave him or blamed herself for his shortcomings. And behind closed doors, her father's flaws were a good deal more frightening than anyone would ever have guessed, Zara thought, suppressing a shiver of recoil.

A moment later, Zara parked outside Blooming Perfect's small nursery. Rob, the manager her father had hired, was in the cluttered little office and he got up with a grin when she came in. 'I was just about to call you—we have a possible commission from abroad.'

'From where?' Zara questioned in surprise.

'Italy. The client has seen one of the gardens your aunt designed in Tuscany and apparently he was very impressed.'

Zara frowned. They had had several potential clients who backed off again the minute they realised that her aunt was no longer alive. 'What did he say when you told him she passed away?'

'I told him you do designs very much in the spirit of Edith's work, although with a more contemporary approach,' Rob explained. 'He was still keen enough to invite you out there on an all-expenses-paid trip to draw up a design. I gather he's a developer and he's renovated this house and now he wants the garden to match. By the sounds of it, it's a big bucks project and the chance you've been waiting for.'

Rob passed her the notebook on his desk to let her see the details he had taken. Zara hesitated before extending a reluctant hand to accept the notebook. For the sake of appearances she glanced down at the handwriting but she was quite unable to read it. As a dyslexic, reading was always a challenge for her but she had always found that actual handwriting as opposed to type was even harder for her to interpret. 'My goodness, what an opportunity,' she remarked dutifully.

'Sorry, I forgot,' Rob groaned, belatedly registering what was amiss, for she had had to tell him about her dyslexia to work with him. He dealt with what she could not. Retrieving the notebook, he gave her the details verbally instead.

While he spoke Zara remained stiff with discomfiture because she cringed from the mortifying moments when she could not hide her handicap and colleagues were forced to make allowances for her. It took her right back to the awful days when her father had repeatedly hammered her with the word 'stupid' as he raged about her poor school reports. In her mind normal people could read, write and spell without difficulty and she hated that she was different and hated even more having to admit the problem to others.

But Zara's embarrassment faded as enthusiasm at the prospect of a genuine creative challenge took its place. Apart from the designs she had worked on with Edith, her experience to date encompassed only small city gardens created on a restricted budget. A larger scheme was exactly what her portfolio lacked and, handled well, would give Blooming Perfect the gravitas it needed to forge a fresh path without relying so heavily on her late aunt's reputation. In addition if she made such a trip now it would ensure that Sergios and her family appreciated how seriously she took her new career. Perhaps then her family would stop referring to the design firm as her hobby.

'Phone him back and make the arrangements,' she instructed Rob. 'I'll fly out asap.'

Leaving Rob, Zara drove off to check the progress of the two current jobs on their books and found one in order and the other at a standstill because a nest of piping that nobody had warned them about had turned up in an inconvenient spot. Soothing the customer and organising a contractor to take care of the problem took time and it was after six before Zara got back to her self-contained flat in her parents' house. She would have preferred greater independence but she was reluctant to leave her mother alone with her father and very much aware that Monty Blake made more effort to control his temper while his daughter was within hearing.

Her indoor pet rabbit, Fluffy, gambolled round her feet in the hall, welcoming her home. Zara fed the little animal and stroked her soft furry head. Within ten minutes of her return, Ingrid Blake, a beautiful rake thin woman who looked a good deal younger than her forty-three years, joined her daughter in her apartment.

'Where the heck have you been all afternoon?' her mother demanded impatiently and at the sound of that shrill tone Fluffy bolted back into her hutch.

'I was at the nursery and I had some jobs to check—'

'The nursery? *Jobs?*' Ingrid grimaced as if Zara had said a rude word. 'When is this nonsense going to stop, Zara? The nursery can only ever be an interest. The real business of your life is the wedding you have to arrange—there's dress fittings, caterers and florists to see and that's only the beginning—'

'I thought we had a wedding organiser to take care of most of that for us,' Zara responded evenly. 'I've made myself available for every appointment—'

'Zara,' Ingrid began in a tone of exasperation, 'don't be more stupid than you can help. A bride should take a more active role in her own wedding.'

'Don't be more stupid than you can help' was a comment that could still cut deep, like a knife slicing through tender flesh, for Zara still looked back on her school years as a nightmare. Her lack of achievement during that period was, even now, a deep source of shame to her.

'This *is* more your wedding than mine,' Zara finally felt pushed into pointing out, for she couldn't have cared less about all the bridal fuss and frills.

Ingrid clamped a thin hand to a bony hip and swivelled to study her daughter with angry eyes. 'What's that supposed to mean?'

'Only that you care about that sort of thing and I don't. I'm not being rude but I've got more on my mind than whether I should have pearls or crystals on my veil and Sergios won't care either. Don't forget that this is his second marriage,' Zara reminded her mother gently, seeking a soothing note rather than piling logs on the fire of her mother's dissatisfaction.

In the midst of the dispute, Rob phoned Zara to ask how soon she could fly to Italy and he kept her on the line while he reserved her a flight in only two days' time. Too impatient to wait for Zara to give her her full attention again, Ingrid stalked out of the apartment in exasperation.

Left alone again, Zara heaved a sigh of relief. At least in Italy she would have a break from the wedding hysteria. Nothing mattered more to her mother than the appearance of things. Zara's failure to hog the gossip columns with a string of upper class boyfriends had offended Ingrid's pride for years and her mother had revelled in Tom's escapades in nightclubs with his posh pals. Ingrid, however, was determined that her daughter's wedding would be the biggest, splashiest and most talked about event of the season.

Sometimes Zara marvelled that she could have so little in common with her parents. Yet Zara and her father's sixty-year-old unmarried sister had got on like a house on fire. Edith and Zara had shared the same joy in the tranquil beauty of a lovely garden and the same unadorned and practical outlook on the rest of life. Her aunt's death, which had occurred within months of her brother's car crash, had devastated Zara. Edith had always seemed so fit that her sudden death from a heart attack had come as a terrible shock.

Zara dressed with care for her flight to Italy, teaming a khaki cotton skirt and jacket with a caramel coloured tee and low-heeled shoes. She anchored her mass of pale hair on top of her head with a judicious clip and used the minimum of make-up, apprehensive that her youth and looks would work against her with the client. After all, nobody knew better than a girl christened a dumb blonde at fourteen that first impressions could count for a lot. But, at the same time, as she stepped off her flight to Pisa she knew that her brother, Tom, would have been proud of her for sticking to her guns when it came to Blooming Perfect and making it clear how close the business was to her heart.

A driver met her at the airport and she was whisked off in the air-conditioned comfort of a glossy black four-wheel drive. The stupendous rural scenery of misty wooded hillsides and ancient medieval towns soothed nerves left ragged by a last-minute difference of opinion with her mother, who had objected bitterly once she realised that Zara was flying off to Italy for a long weekend.

'And how is your fiancé going to feel about that?' Ingrid had fired at her daughter.

'I have no idea. I haven't heard from him in a couple of weeks but I left a message on his phone to let him know that I would be away,' Zara had countered gently, for Sergios was not in the habit of maintaining regular contact with her and she perfectly understood that he saw their marriage to be staged three months hence as being more of a practical than personal connection.

'He's a very busy man,' Ingrid had instantly argued on her future son-in-law's behalf.

'Yes and he doesn't feel the need to keep constant tabs on me,' Zara pointed out quietly. 'And neither should you. I haven't been a teenager for a long time.'

Ingrid had pursed her lips. 'It's not like you're the brightest spark on the block and you know how dangerously impulsive you can be—'

Recalling that dig as she was driven through the Tuscan hills, Zara felt bitter. Only once in her life had she been dangerously impulsive and had paid in spades for that miscalculation. Even four years on, Zara still burned and felt sick at the memory of the humiliation that Julian Hurst had inflicted on her. She had grown up very fast after that betrayal, but even though she had never been so foolish again her parents continued to regularly remind her of her lowest moment.

The car turned off the road and her thoughts promptly turned to where she was headed, she sat up straighter to peer out of the windows. The lane became steep. If the house stood on a hill, as seemed likely, the garden would have wonderful views. Her first glimpse of the old stone building basking in the late afternoon sunshine made her eyes widen with pleasure. A traditional set of box-edged beds adorned the front of the villa, which was much bigger and more imposing than she had expected. Designing anything for an individual who owned such a beautiful property would be a major creative challenge and she was thrilled at the prospect.

As the driver lifted out her weekend bag the front door opened and a dark-haired woman in her thirties, elegantly dressed in a business suit, greeted her. 'Signorina Blake? Welcome to the Villa di Sole. I'm Catarina—I work for Signore Roccanti. He will be here shortly. How was your flight?'

Ushered into an airy hall floored in pale limestone, Zara smiled and set down her bag. It was obvious that the newly renovated house was empty and she began to wonder where she would be staying the night. The chatty woman showed her round the property. Well over a hundred and fifty years old, the villa had undergone elegant modernisation. In every way it was a stunning conversion. Rooms had been opened up and extended, opulent bathrooms added and smooth expanses of natural stone flooring, concealed storage and high-tech heating, lighting and sound systems added to achieve a level of luxury that impressed even Zara.

Catarina was a blank wall as far as questions con-

cerning the extensive grounds were concerned. She
had no idea what her employer might want done with
the garden or what the budget might be.

'Signore Roccanti has discriminating taste,' she remarked as Zara admired the fabulous view of hills covered with vineyards and olive groves.

Fine taste and plenty of cash with which to indulge
it, Zara was reflecting when she heard the dulled roar
of a powerful car engine at the front of the property.
Catarina hurried off with a muttered apology and moments later Zara heard heavy footsteps ringing across
the tiled entrance hall.

She glanced up just as a man appeared in the doorway and her breath tripped in her throat. Sunshine
flooded through the windows, gleaming over his black
hair and dark curling lashes while highlighting the stunning lines of his classic bone structure and beautifully
modelled mouth. He was smoking hot and that acknowledgement startled her—it was rare for Zara to have such
a strong, immediate response to a man.

'A business appointment overran. I'm sorry I kept
you waiting, *signorina*,' he murmured smoothly, his
dark reflective gaze resting on her.

'Call me Zara, and you are…?' Zara was trying not
to stare. She picked up the edge of strain in her voice
and hoped it wasn't equally audible to him. She extended her hand.

'Vitale Roccanti. So, you are Edith's niece,' he remarked, studying her from below those outrageously
long lashes, which would have looked girlie on any less
masculine face, as he shook her hand and released it

again, the light brush of those long brown fingers sending tingles of awareness quivering all over her body.
'Forgive me if I comment that you don't look much like
her. As I recall she was rather a tall woman—'

Zara stilled in surprise. 'You actually met Edith?'

'I was living at the Palazzo Barigo with my uncle's
family when your aunt was designing the garden,'
Vitale explained, his gaze momentarily resting on her
slender hand and noting the absence of an engagement
ring. Had she taken it off?

As he made that connection with the woman who
had taught her almost everything she knew Zara relaxed
and a smile stole the tension from her delicate features.
'It is the most wonderful garden and in all the professional design books…'

When she smiled, Vitale conceded, she shot up the
scale from exceptionally pretty to exquisitely beautiful. The photos hadn't lied but they hadn't told the
whole truth either. In the light her pale hair glittered like
highly polished silver, her velvety skin was flawless and
those eyes, lavender blue below arched brows, were as
unusual as they were gorgeous. He reminded himself
that he liked his women tall, dark and curvaceous. She
was tiny and slender as a ribbon, her delicate curves
barely shaping her T-shirt and skirt, but she was also,
from her dainty ankles to her impossibly small waist,
an incredibly feminine woman. As for that mouth, unexpectedly full and rosy and ripe, any man would fan-
tasise about a mouth that alluring. Vitale breathed in
slow and deep, willing back the libidinous surge at his

groin. He had not expected her to have quite so much appeal in the flesh.

'Have you been outside yet?' Vitale enquired.

'No, Catarina was showing me the house when you arrived—it's most impressive,' Zara remarked, her gaze following him as he pressed a switch and the wall of glass doors began to slide quietly back to allow access onto the terrace. He moved with the silent grace of a panther on the prowl, broad shoulders, narrow hips and long elegant legs defined by his beautifully tailored grey designer suit. She found it difficult to remove her attention from him. He was one of those men who had only to enter a room to command it. Even in a crowd he would have stood out a mile with his exceptional height, assurance and innate sophistication.

'The garden should complement the house with plenty of outside space for entertaining,' he told her.

'I see there's a pool,' she remarked, glancing at the feature that was at least fifty years old and marooned like an ugly centrepiece in the lank, overgrown grass.

'Site a replacement somewhere where it will not be the main attraction.'

Zara tried not to pull a face at the news that that landscaper's bête noire, the swimming pool, was to feature in the design. After all, every job had its pitfalls and there was plenty of space in which to provide a well-screened pool area. 'I have to ask you—is this going to be your home? Will a family be living here?'

'Aim at giving the garden universal appeal,' he advised, his face uninformative.

Zara felt slightly foolish. Of course if the villa was to

be sold which was the most likely objective for a property developer, he would have no idea who the eventual owner would be. As she began to walk down the worn steps her heel skittered off the edge of one and his hands cupped her elbow to steady her. The faint scent of a citrus-based cologne flared her nostrils in the hot still air. When she reached level ground again he removed his hand without fanfare but she remained extraordinarily aware of his proximity, the height and strength of his long, lean frame, not to mention the unmistakeable aura of raw masculinity.

She needed measurements for the garden, all sorts of details, but Vitale Roccanti did not look like the patient type, happy to stand around and wait while she took notes. She would have to contain her eagerness to start work until her next visit. The garden ran right up to the edges of woodland and merged with the dark shade cast by the trees. But the open view to the south was nothing short of breathtaking.

Vitale watched her face light up as she caught the view of the hills with the sun starting to go down, bathing the trees in a golden russet light. Her habitually wary expression was transformed into one of open enjoyment. She was not at all what he had expected, being neither flirtatious nor giggly nor even high maintenance if that plain outfit was the norm for her. No make-up that he could see either, which was an even more unusual sight for a man accustomed to decorative women, who preferred to present a highly polished image for his benefit.

As Zara turned back to him her unusual lavender

eyes were shining at the prospect of the challenge before her. In such beautiful surroundings this was truly
her dream job. 'How much land does this place have?'

The purity of her heart-shaped face, lit up with
the unhidden enthusiasm of a child's, made the man
watching her stare. *Per amor di Dio,* Vitale reflected
involuntarily, what a piece of perfection she was! The
unfamiliar thought jolted him and his hard bone structure tautened and shadowed.

'The land as far as you can see belongs to the house.
It was once a substantial agricultural estate,' he explained. 'You'll be able to come back here to explore
tomorrow. A vehicle will be placed at your disposal.'

Zara encountered stunning dark golden eyes with
the shrewd watchful penetration of gold-tipped arrows.
Dark-hued, deep-set, very sexy eyes surrounded by
inky black lashes and blessed with extraordinary impact. Goose bumps erupted on Zara's arms. Her mouth
ran dry, her tummy executing a sudden somersault that
made her tense and dizzy. 'Thanks, that will be very
helpful,' she responded, striving to overcome the way
she was feeling by making herself remember Julian and
the pain and humiliation that he had inflicted on her.

'Prego!' Vitale answered lightly, showing her back
indoors and escorting her back through the silent house.

In the hall she bent down to lift her weekend bag.

'I have it,' Vitale said, reaching the bag a split second in advance of her.

She followed him outside and hovered while he
paused to lock up. He opened the door of the black

Lamborghini outside, stowed her bag and stepped back for her to get in.

'Where will I be staying?' she asked as she climbed into the passenger seat, nervous fingers smoothing down her skirt as it rose a little too high above her knees.

'With me. I have a farmhouse just down the hill. It will be a convenient base for you.' His attention inescapably on those dainty knees and pale slim thighs, Vitale was thinking solely of parting them and he caught himself on that X-rated image with a frown.

What the hell was the matter with him? Anyone could have been forgiven for thinking that he was sex-starved, which couldn't be further from the truth. Vitale scheduled sex into his itinerary as efficiently as business appointments. He had lovers in more than one European city, discreet, sophisticated women who knew better than to expect a lasting commitment from him. There were no emotional scenes or misunderstandings in Vitale's well-ordered life and that was how he liked it. He had not rebuilt his life from the ground up by allowing weakness to exist in his character. He had no expectations of people and he certainly didn't trust them. If there were no expectations there was less chance of disappointment. He had learned not to care about women, especially not to love them. Life had taught him that those you cared about moved on, died or betrayed you. In the aftermath of such experiences being alone hurt even more but it was safer not to feel anything for anyone. That credo had served him well, taking him from extreme poverty and deprivation to the comfortable cultured life of a multimillionaire, who seemed to make more money with every passing year.

CHAPTER TWO

THE farmhouse sat a good distance from the mountain road, accessed by a track that stretched almost a kilometre into dense woods. Built of soft ochre-coloured stone and roofed in terracotta, the property was surrounded by a grove of olive trees with silvery foliage that seemed to shimmer in the fading light.

'Very picturesque,' Zara pronounced breathlessly, belatedly registering that she had allowed herself to be brought to an isolated place in the countryside by a man whom she knew almost nothing about! She mentally chastised herself for her lack of caution.

As her lips parted to suggest that she would prefer a hotel—at her own expense—a plump little woman in an apron appeared at the front door and smiled widely.

'My housekeeper, Guiseppina, has come out to welcome you. Be warned, she will try to fatten you up,' Vitale remarked teasingly as he swung out of the car.

The appearance of another woman relieved much of Zara's concern, although a stubborn thought at the back of her mind was already leafing through various murders in which the killers had enjoyed female companionship and support in which to commit their crimes. Her colourful imagination had often been considered one of her biggest flaws by her teachers. 'I think I would prefer to be in a hotel—I'll settle my own bills,' she muttered tautly.

In considerable surprise, for he was accustomed to women seizing on every opportunity to enjoy his full attention, Vitale recognised her apprehension and murmured, 'If you would be more comfortable staying in this house alone I will use my city apartment while you are here. It is not a problem.'

Flushing in embarrassment, afraid that she might have sounded a little hysterical while also being soothed by his offer, Zara hastened to recant. 'No, that's really not necessary. I think it's the fact I know virtually nothing about you except that you're a property developer—'

'But I'm not…a property developer,' Vitale confided in a ludicrous tone of apology.

Zara studied his lean bronzed features with a bemused frown. 'You're…*not*?' A helpless laugh bubbled out of her throat because there was something very amusing about the way in which he had broken that news.

'I'm a banker,' Vitale admitted.

'Oh…' Zara exclaimed, nonplussed by that level admission, there being nothing flashy, threatening or indeed exciting about bankers in her past experience.

'The property developing is only a pastime.' Her patent lack of interest in his admission set his teeth on edge a little. Had he been spoilt by all the women who hung on his every word and eagerly tried to find out everything about him?

Bubbling Italian like a fountain, Giuseppina was a bustling whirlwind of a woman and she instantly took centre stage. Although Zara didn't understand much of what she was saying, it didn't inhibit Giuseppina's chatter. She drew Zara eagerly into the house and straight up the creaking oak staircase to a charming bedroom with painted furniture and crisp white bed linen. Zara glanced with satisfaction at the en suite bathroom. The walls might be rustic brick and the furniture quirky and antique but, like the Villa di Sole, every contemporary comfort had been incorporated.

A light knock sounded on the ajar door. Vitale set her bag down on the wide-planked floor. 'Dinner will be served in an hour and a half. I hope you're hungry. I bring guests here so rarely that Giuseppina seems determined to treat us to a banquet.'

Zara glanced at him and for an instant, as she collided with dark eyes that glowed like the warmest, deepest amber in the fading light, it was as though her every defence fell down and she stood naked and vulnerable. For a terrifying energising moment she was electrified by the breathtaking symmetry and beauty of his face regardless of the five o'clock shadow of stubble steadily darkening his jaw line. She wondered what it would feel like to kiss him and the passage of blood through her veins seemed to slow and thicken while her heart banged behind her ribs and her breath dragged through her tight throat.

As Giuseppina took her leave, her sturdy shoes ringing out her descent of the stairs, Vitale held Zara's gaze, his eyes scorching gold, lashes dipping low as though to conceal them. 'I'll see you at dinner,' he told her huskily, backing away.

As the door shut on his departure Zara was trembling. She felt too warm. Unfreezing, she darted into the bathroom to splash her face with cold water. Her hands shook as she snatched up the towel to dry herself again. Never before had she felt so aware of a man. The feelings that had drawn her to Julian as a teenager paled utterly in comparison. She stripped where she stood to go for a shower. What was happening to her? She had decided a long time ago that she just wasn't that sexual a being. Only once had a man made Zara want to surrender her virginity and that man had been Julian, but if she was truthful she had only been willing to sleep with him because she had assumed that it was expected. When in fact Julian had put greed ahead of lust in his priorities, Zara had been left a virgin and a very much sadder and wiser one. So what was different about Vitale Roccanti?

After all, in August she was supposed to be marrying Sergios Demonides and, having thoroughly weighed up the pros and cons, she had reached that decision on her own. All right, she didn't love the man she had promised to marry and he didn't love her, but she did respect the commitment she had made to him. Loyalty and respect *mattered* to her. Was it stress that was making her feel edgy and out of sync? Or was Bee's warning that she might fall for another man after she married working on some level of her brain to make her more than usually aware of an attractive man? Vitale *was* an extraordinarily handsome man and very charismatic. That was fact. Possibly she was more nervous about getting married than she had been prepared to admit even to herself. And for all she knew Vitale Roccanti was a married man. Yanking a towel off the rail as she stepped out of the shower, she grimaced at that suspicion. At the very least he might be involved in a steady relationship. And why on earth should that matter to her? Not only did it not matter to her whether he was involved or otherwise with a woman, it was none of her business, she told herself staunchly. In the same way it was none of Vitale's business that she was committed to Sergios. She thought it was unfortunate, though, that Sergios had chosen not to give her an engagement ring. But there was still no good reason why she should bother telling Vitale that she was getting married in three months' time. Why was she getting so worked up?

Releasing her hair from the clip, she let the silvery strands fall loose round her shoulders and she put on the print tea dress she had packed for more formal wear. Dinner was served on the terrace at the rear of the property. A candle flickered on the beautifully set table in the shade of a venerable oak tree. Her slim shoulders unusually tense, Zara left the shelter of the house.

A glass of wine in one hand, Vitale was talking on a cell phone in a liquid stream of Italian. He was casually seated on the edge of a low retaining wall, a pair of chinos and an open shirt having replaced the suit he had worn earlier. Black hair still spiky from a shower, he had shaved, baring the sleek planes of his features and throwing into prominence his beautifully shaped mouth. Her heart seemed to take a flying leap inside her body, making it incredibly difficult to catch her breath.

'Zara,' he murmured softly in greeting, switching off the phone and tossing it aside.

'I used to hate my name but suppose everyone does at some stage when they're growing up,' Zara confided, aware that she was chattering too much in an effort to hide her self-consciousness but quite unable to silence herself.

'It's a pretty name.'

Madly aware of his intense scrutiny, Zara felt her cheeks warm. For goodness' sake, relax, she urged herself, exasperated by her oversensitive reaction to him. He sprang fluidly upright, his every physical move laced with easy strength and grace, and asked her if she would like some wine. He returned from the house bearing a glass.

It was a warm evening. She settled into the seat he pulled out from the table for her and Giuseppina appeared with the first course, a mouth-watering selection of *antipasti*. Her bright dark eyes danced between them with unconcealed curiosity and romantic hopes.

'I'm twenty-nine. She thinks I ought to be married by now with a family and she keeps on warning me that all the best girls have already been snapped up,' Vitale told her in an undertone, his eyes alive with vibrant amusement.

Surprised by his candour, Zara laughed. 'Have they been?'

'I don't know. The women with wedding rings in their eyes are the ones I've always avoided,' Vitale volunteered.

Zara reckoned that if she was truly the honest person she had always believed she was she would be telling him that she was within a few months of getting married herself. Yet while the admission was on her tongue she could not quite bring herself to speak up. At the same time she could not help wondering if Vitale could actually be warning her off. Was it possible that he was letting her know that he had only ever been in the market for a casual affair?

Whatever, there was no future or sense in succumbing to any kind of entanglement with him and she was far too sensible to make such a mistake. In honour of that conviction and impervious to his polite look of surprise, Zara dug her notebook out of her bag and began to quiz him about his garden preferences and his budget. The main course of steak was so tender it melted on her tongue and it was served with a tomato salad and potato and cheese croquettes. She ate with unbridled pleasure for it was, without a doubt, an exceptional meal, and when she could bring herself to set down her knife and fork she took notes.

'This is not quite how I envisaged dining with you,' Vitale remarked wryly. It hadn't escaped his notice that she ignored any hint of flirtation, preferring to maintain a professional barrier he had not expected. Of course she was clever enough to know that lack of interest only made the average man keener, he decided, unwilling to concede the possibility that she might be genuinely indifferent to him.

Although he was taken aback by her eagerness to work he was pleasantly surprised by her healthy appetite and the way in which she savoured Giuseppina's renowned cuisine, for he was accustomed to women who agonised over eating anything more calorific than a lettuce leaf. 'You should be relaxing. You can work tomorrow.'

'But I'm only here for a couple of days. I need to make the most of my time,' Zara told him lightly as Guiseppina set a lemon tart on the table and proceeded to cut slices. 'And if I do find myself with a spare couple of hours I'm hoping to try and visit the garden my aunt Edith made at the Palazzo Barigo.'

'Have you not already seen it?'

'I've never been to this area before. My parents don't do rural holidays.' Her sultry mouth quirked at the mere idea of her decorative mother in a countryside setting. 'I did ask my aunt once if she would like to come back and see the garden and she said no, that gardens change with the passage of time and that she preferred to remember it as it was when it was new.'

'If I can arrange it before you leave I will take you to the Palazzo Barigo for a tour,' Vitale drawled softly, lifting the bottle to top up her wine glass.

'No more for me, thanks,' Zara told him hurriedly. 'I get giggly too easily, so I never drink much.'

Vitale was sardonically amused by that little speech. She was putting up barriers as prickly as cactus leaves and visibly on her guard. But he was too experienced not to have noticed her lingering appraisals and he was convinced that she wanted him even though she was trying to hide the fact. Erotic promise thrummed through his body, setting up a level of anticipation beyond anything he had ever experienced.

Vitale was as well travelled as Zara and they shared amusing anecdotes about trips abroad, discovering that their sense of humour was amazingly similar. He moved his hands expressively while he talked and slowly but surely she found herself watching him like a hawk. When all of a sudden she collided with his scorching golden eyes, she couldn't even manage to swallow. The truth that she couldn't stifle her physical response to him alarmed her. She was not in full control of her response to Vitale Roccanti and disturbingly that took her back to her ordeal with Julian. She breathed in slow and deep and steady, mentally fighting to step back from her reactions. Vitale was gorgeous but not for her. She didn't want to dip a toe in the water, she didn't want to get her fingers burnt either. Even if it killed her she was determined to retain her self-respect.

'I hope you won't think I'm being rude but I've had a lot of late nights this week and I would like to turn in now so that I can make an early start in the morning,' Zara proffered with a bright smile of apology.

Vitale accepted her decision with good grace, rising immediately to his feet. Her cheeks warmed at the sudden suspicion that he might only have been entertaining her out of courtesy. Not every guy wanted to jump her bones, she reminded herself irritably.

At the foot of the stairs, she hovered, disconcertingly reluctant to leave him even though she had carefully engineered her own exit. 'Will I see you in the morning?' she asked breathlessly.

'I doubt it. I'll be leaving soon after six,' Vitale imparted, watching her slim figure shift restively. His level of awareness was at such a pitch it was not only his muscles that ached.

Still unable to tear herself away, Zara looked up at him, focusing on the irresistible dark glitter of his stunning eyes and his perfect lips. He was downright drenched in sex appeal and she wanted to touch him so badly her fingertips tingled. The hunger he was suddenly making no attempt to hide made her feel all hot and shivery deep down inside.

'But before we part, *cara mia*...' Vitale purred, purebred predator on the hunt as he closed long, deft fingers round her arm to ease her closer.

He took Zara by surprise and she froze in dismay, nostrils flaring on the scent of his cologne. 'No,' she said abruptly, planting both her palms firmly to his broad chest to literally push him back from her. 'I don't know what you think I'm doing here but I'm certainly not here for this.'

Ditching the smile ready to play about his beautifully sculpted mouth, Vitale lifted a sardonic brow. 'No?'

'You have a hell of an opinion of yourself, don't you?' The tart rejoinder just leapt off Zara's tongue, fierce annoyance rattling through her at his arrogant attitude. Evidently he had expected her to succumb rather than shoot him down and the knowledge infuriated her, for she had met too many men who expected her to be a pushover.

His dark, heavily lashed eyes flashed with anger and then screened. 'Perhaps I misread the situation—'

'Yes, you definitely did,' Zara retorted defensively. 'I'm grateful for your hospitality and I've enjoyed your company but that's as far as it goes! Goodnight, Vitale.'

But as she hastened up the stairs and hurriedly shut her bedroom door she felt like a total fraud. Exit shocked virginal heroine stage left, she mocked inwardly, her face burning. He had not misread the situation as much as she would have liked to believe. She *did* find him incredibly attractive and clearly he had recognised the fact and tried to act on it. She was not the undersexed woman she had come to believe she was. But what a time to make such a discovery about herself! Why now? Why now when she was committed to marrying another man? Even though her bridegroom had no desire to share a bed with her, her susceptibility to Vitale Roccanti's lethal dark charisma made her feel guilty and disloyal.

She lay in bed studying the crescent of the moon gleaming through the curtains. Vitale was simply a temptation she had to withstand and maybe it was good that she should be reminded now that being a married woman would demand circumspection from her. In the future she would be more on her guard. But she could not forget that even in a temper she had still not told him that she was getting married that summer.

CHAPTER THREE

AT WAR with herself, Zara tossed and turned for a good part of the night, wakening to a warm room bathed in the bright light filtering through the thin curtains. Seating her on the terrace, Giuseppina brought her a breakfast of fresh peaches, milky coffee and bread still warm from the oven served with honey. Birds were singing in the trees, bees buzzing and golden sunshine drenched the country valley below the house. It was a morning to be glad to be alive, not to brood on what could not be helped. So, a handsome Italian had made a mild pass at her, why was she agonising over the fact? The attraction had been mutual? So, she was human, fallible.

Giuseppina brought her keys to the car and the villa and Zara left the house to climb into the sturdy pickup truck parked outside. In the early morning quiet the garden of the villa was a wonderful haven of peace. Grateful that it was still relatively cool, Zara took measurements and sat down on a wrought iron chair in the shade of the house to do some preliminary sketches. She chose the most suitable site for the pool first and, that achieved, her ideas were free to flow thick and fast. For the front of the house she wanted a much more simple and soft approach than the current formal geometry of the box-edged beds. So engrossed was she that she didn't hear the car pulling up at the front and she glanced up in surprise when she heard a door slam inside the house.

Vitale strolled outside, a vision of sleek dark masculinity sheathed in summer casuals, a sweater knotted round his shoulders with unmistakeable Italian style. She scrambled up, her heart going bang-bang-bang inside her chest and her mouth dry as a bone.

'Time for lunch,' he told her lazily.

Zara glanced at her watch for the first time since she had arrived and was startled to find that the afternoon was already well advanced. It had taken his reminder for her to notice that her tummy was hollow with hunger. 'I lost track of time…'

Vitale moved closer to glance curiously at the sheaf of sketches she was gathering up. 'Anything for me to see yet?'

'I prefer to submit a design only when I'm finished,' she told him evenly, accustomed to dealing with impatient clients. 'I've been working on some options for the hard landscaping first.'

He studied her from beneath the dark lush screen of his lashes. Even without a speck of make-up and clad in sexless shorts and a loose shirt, she was a true beauty. Tendrils of wavy silvery hair had worked loose from the clasp she wore to cluster round her damp temples and fall against her cheekbones. Her lavender eyes were wide above heat-flushed cheeks, her temptress mouth lush and natural pink. The tightening heaviness at his groin made his teeth clench. She looked very young, very fresh and impossibly sexy. He remembered the rumour that Monty Blake had paid a fortune to suppress pornographic pictures taken by some boyfriend of hers when she was only a teenager and he reminded himself that it was quite some time since Zara Blake was in a position to claim that level of innocence.

Disturbingly conscious of his measuring appraisal, Zara packed away her sketch pad and pencils. The coarse cotton of her shirt was rubbing against her swelling nipples. As was often her way in a hot climate she had not worn a bra and in his presence her body was determined to misbehave and she was insanely aware of those tormented tips.

'I'm taking you to the Palazzo Barigo,' Vitale volunteered, walking her back through the house and out to the Lamborghini.

Edith's garden, he was taking her to see Edith's garden! Zara almost whooped with delight and a huge grin curved her soft lips; she turned shining eyes on him. 'That's wonderful—is it open to the public, then?'

'Not as a rule.'

'Of course, you said it belonged to your uncle,' she recalled, reckoning that, had she been on her own, she might not have been granted access. 'Thank you so much for making this possible. I really appreciate it. Should I get changed or will I do as I am? I haven't got many clothes with me. I like to travel light.'

'There is only staff at the palazzo at present. You can be as casual as you like,' Vitale responded lightly.

'What will we do about the car I drove here?' she asked belatedly.

'It will be picked up later.'

The Palazzo Barigo lay over an hour's drive away. Zara used a good part of the journey to sound him out on different kinds of stone and then she discussed the need for a lighting consultant. She found him more silent and less approachable than he had seemed the night before. Had her rejection caused offence? It was probably her imagination, she thought ruefully, but once or twice she thought he seemed distinctly tense. His lean, hard-boned face was taut in profile, his handsome mouth compressed.

'How did you spend your morning?' she enquired when she had failed to draw him out on other topics.

'At the office.'

'Do you often work at weekends?'

'I was in New York last week. Work piled up while I was away.' His fingers flexed and tightened again round the leather steering wheel.

'This landscape is beautiful. No wonder Edith felt inspired working here.'

'You talk a lot, don't you?' Vitale sighed. The views she was admiring were painfully familiar to his grim gaze. He felt as though his world were turning full circle, bringing him back to the place where the events that had indelibly changed his life had begun. Yet conversely he was conscious that only two years earlier he had taken a step that ensured he could never hope to escape that past.

Zara could feel her face reddening. She did talk quite a bit and it wasn't exactly intellectual stuff. Perhaps he found her boring. Annoyance leapt through her as she fiercely suppressed a sense of hurt. He wasn't her boyfriend, he wasn't her lover, he wasn't anything to her and his opinion should not matter to her in the slightest.

'I'm sorry, that was rude,' Vitale drawled softly, shooting the powerful car off the road and below a worn stone archway ornamented with a centrally placed Grecian urn. 'I'm afraid I've had a rough morning but that is not an excuse for ill humour. I find spending time with you very relaxing.'

Zara wasn't quite convinced by that turnaround and when he parked she got out and said stiffly, 'You know, if there's only staff here, you could leave me to explore on my own for an hour. You don't need to stay—'

'I want to be with you, *angelina mia*,' Vitale intoned across the bonnet, whipping off his sunglasses to view her with level dark golden eyes. 'Why do you think I arranged this outing? Only to please you.'

As Zara could think of no good reason why he should have bothered otherwise, the anxious tension fell from her heart-shaped face. 'I'm no good with moody guys,' she confided with a wry look. 'They make me uncomfortable.'

'I'm not moody.'

Aware of the powerful personality that drove him, Zara didn't quite believe him on that score. He might

not be subject to moods as a rule but he was definitely
a very driven and strong individual. She was convinced
that he could be stubborn and tough and a bit of a maverick but she had no idea how she could be so sure of
those traits when she had only met him the day before.
And yet she *was* sure. In much the same way she read
the strain in his dark golden gaze and realised for the
first time that he wasn't just flirting with her, he wasn't
just playing a sexual game like so many of the men she
had met. Vitale Roccanti was keen to soothe the feelings he had hurt. He sincerely cared about her opinion.
Heartened by that conviction, she tried not to smile.

Vitale lifted out the picnic basket Giuseppina had
made up and tossed Zara a cotton rug to carry and extended his free hand to her. 'Let's find somewhere to
eat…'

'The orchard,' she suggested dreamily, already mentally visualising the garden design she had often studied.

In the heat of the afternoon they strolled along grav-
elled paths. The clarity of her aunt's talent as a designer
was still as clear as it must have been forty years earlier when it was first created. 'The garden's been re-
planted,' Zara registered in surprise and pleasure, for
she had expected to see overgrown shrubs and trees,
the once noticeable lines of her aunt's vision blurred
by many years of growth.

'Eighteen months ago.' Vitale's explanation was
crisp, a little distracted. As she stood there against the
backdrop of a great yew tree he was remembering his
sister dancing along the same path in a scarlet silk gown

for a fashion photographer's benefit, her lovely face stamped with the detached hauteur of a model, only the sparkle of her eyes revealing her true joyous mood. 'For a while the house and garden were open as a tourist attraction.'

'But not now,' Zara gathered.

'The owner cherishes his privacy.'

'It's almost selfish to own something this beautiful and refuse to share it with other people,' Zara contended in a tone of censure, lavender eyes darting in every direction because there was so much for her to take in.

His handsome mouth quirked as he watched her clamber unselfconsciously onto a stone bench in an effort to gain a better overall view above the tall evergreen hedges. 'The temple on the hill above the lake offers the best prospect.'

Zara's fine brows connected in a sudden frown. 'There was no temple in the original scheme.'

'Perhaps the owner felt he could add a little something without destroying the symmetry of the whole,' Vitale murmured a tinge drily.

Zara went pink. 'Of course. I think it's wonderful that he thought enough of the garden to maintain it and secure its future for another generation.'

Vitale shot her a searching glance, much amused against his will by her quick recovery. She was a lousy liar, having something of a child's artlessness in the way that she spoke and acted without forethought. She had no patience either. He watched her hurry ahead of him with quick light steps, a tiny trim figure with silvery pale hair catching and holding the sunlight. When he had seen the photos of her he had assumed the hair was dyed but it looked strikingly natural, perfectly attuned to her pale Nordic skin and unusual eyes. He would have to get her clothes off to explore the question further and that was a prospect that Vitale was startled to discover that he could hardly wait to bring about.

Monty Blake's daughter had an unanticipated charm all of her own. Even in the casual clothes her quintessential femininity, dainty curves and deeply disconcerting air of spontaneity turned him on hard and fast. It was years since any woman had had that effect on him and he didn't like it at all. Vitale much preferred a predictable low level and controllable response to a woman. He did not like surprises.

Beyond an avenue of cypresses and the vista of a picturesque town clinging to the upper slopes of a distant hill, the garden became less formal and a charming winding path led them to the cherry orchard. Wild flowers laced the lush grass and Zara hovered rather than spread the rug because it seemed almost a desecration to flatten those blooms. Vitale had no such inhibitions, however and he took the rug from her and cast it down. He was wondering if she could possibly have chosen the private location in expectation and encouragement of a bout of alfresco sex. No way, absolutely no way, Vitale decided grittily, was he sinking his famously cool reputation to fool about in long grass like a testosterone-driven teenager.

Seated unceremoniously on her knees and looking not remotely seductive, however, Zara was already dig-

ging through the basket and producing all sorts of goodies. 'I'm really hungry,' she admitted.

Vitale studied her and decided that he was becoming too set in his ways. Maybe he could bite the bullet if the only option was making out in the grass. He
poured chilled white wine while she set out plates and
extracted thin slices of prosciutto ham, wedges of onion
and spinach frittata, a mozzarella and tomato salad and
a bowl of pasta sprinkled with zucchini blossoms. It
was a colourful and enticing spread.

'Giuseppina is a treasure,' Zara commented, digging
in without further ado to a wedge of frittata washed
down with wine from a moisture-beaded glass.

'I'm an excellent cook,' Vitale volunteered unexpectedly. 'Giuseppina is a recent addition to my household.'

'I can just about make toast,' Zara told him cheerfully. 'My older sister, Bee, is always offering to teach
me to cook but I'm more into the garden than the
kitchen.'

'I didn't know you had a sister.'

Zara kicked off her shoes and lounged back on one
elbow to munch through ham and a generous spoonful
of the juicy tomato salad with unconcealed enjoyment.
'Dad has three daughters from two marriages and one
affair. He's a bit of a womaniser,' she muttered, down-
playing the truth to an acceptable level.

'Is he still married to your mother?'

Worrying at her full lower lip, Zara compressed her
sultry mouth. 'Yes, but he's had other interests along
the way—she turns a blind eye. Gosh, I don't know
why I'm telling you that. It's private.'

'Obviously it bothers you,' Vitale remarked percep-
tively.

It had always bothered Zara. Several years earlier,
Edith had gently warned her niece to mind her own
business when it came to her parents' marriage, pointing out that some adults accepted certain compromises
in their efforts to maintain a stable relationship. 'I think
fidelity is very important…'

Thinking of the wedding plans that he already
knew were afoot in London on her behalf, Vitale almost laughed out loud in derision at that seemingly
naïve declaration. He supposed it sounded good and
that many men, burned by female betrayal, would be
impressed by such a statement. More cynical and never
ever trusting when it came to her sex, Vitale veiled his
hard dark eyes lest he betray his scorn.

Zara could feel hot colour creeping across her face.
She believed fidelity was important yet she had agreed
to marry a man who had no intention of being faithful
to her. Suddenly and for the first time she wondered if
Bee had been right and if she could be making the biggest mistake of her life. But then, she reminded herself
quickly, she would not be entering a real marriage with
Sergios. In a perfect world and when people loved each
other fidelity was important, she rephrased for her own
benefit. Feeling panicky and torn in opposing directions
by the commitment she had so recently entered, Zara
drained her wine glass and let Vitale top it up.

'How do you feel about it?' Zara pressed her silent
companion nonetheless because she really wanted to
know his answer.

'As though we've strayed into a dialogue that is far too serious for such a beautiful day.'

Was that an evasion? Vitale was very adroit with words and Zara, who more often than not said the wrong thing to the wrong person at the wrong time, was reluctantly impressed by his sidestepping of what could be a controversial subject. More than anything else, though, she respected honesty, but she knew that some regarded her love of candour as a sign of immaturity and social awkwardness.

'I could never, ever forgive lies or infidelity,' Zara told him.

Watching sunshine make her hair flare like highly polished silver, her eyes mysterious lavender pools above her pink pouting mouth as she sipped her wine, Vitale reflected that had he been the susceptible type he might have been in danger around Zara Blake. After all she was a beauty, surprisingly individual and very appealing in all sorts of unexpected ways. That radiant smile, for instance, offered a rare amount of joie de vivre. But most fortunately for him, Vitale reminded himself with satisfaction, he was cooler than ice in the emotion department and all too aware of whose blood ran in her veins.

Barely a minute later and without even thinking about what he was going to do, Vitale leant down and pressed his sensual mouth to Zara's. He tasted headily of wine. His lips were warm and hard and the clean male scent of him unbelievably enticing. Zara stretched closer, increasing the pressure of his mouth on hers with a needy little sound breaking low in her throat.

Her hands curved to his strong, muscular shoulders and, as though she had given him a green light to accelerate the pace, the kiss took off like a rocket. His hot tongue pierced between her lips and she shivered violently, erotic signals racing through her slight length. A flood of heat travelled from the pinched taut tips of her breasts to the liquid tension pooling at the heart of her. Her heart thumping out a tempestuous beat, she dug her fingers into his silky black hair and kissed him back with a hunger she couldn't repress.

Within seconds she was on her back, Vitale lying half over her with one lean thigh settling between hers. On one level she tensed, ready to object the way she usually would have done if a man got too close, but on another unfamiliar level his weight, proximity and the fiery hunger of his kiss somehow combined in a soaring crescendo of sensuality to unleash a powerful craving she had never felt before.

'You taste so good,' Vitale growled huskily, '*so* unbelievably good, *angelina mia.*'

He was talking too much and she didn't want him talking, she wanted him kissing, and she pulled him back down to her with impatient hands. He reacted to that shameless invitation with a driving passion that thrilled her. His mouth ravished hers, his tongue darting and sliding in the tender interior and the thunderous wave of desire screaming through her was almost unbearable. Long fingers slid below her top, travelling over her narrow ribcage to close round a small rounded breast. He found the beaded tip, squeezed it and she arched off the ground, shattered by the arrow

of hot liquid need shooting down into her pelvis. And
that jolt of soul stealing desire was sufficient to spring
her out of the sensual spell he had cast.

Eyes bright with dismay, Zara had only a split second to focus over his shoulder on the trees around her
and recall where she was and what she was doing. Shot
back to awareness with a vengeance, she gasped, 'No!'
as she pushed at his shoulders and rolled away from
him the instant he drew back.

Still on another plane, Vitale blinked, dazed at what
had just happened. *Almost* happened, he corrected mentally. *Dio mio,* they were lying in an orchard and there
wasn't even the remotest chance that he would have
let matters proceed any further. She was like a stick
of dynamite, he thought next, dark colour scoring his
high cheekbones as he struggled to catch his breath and
withstand the literal pain of his fully aroused body. A
woman capable of making him behave like that in a
public place ought to carry a government health warning. Overconfident, he had underestimated the extent
of her pulling power, a mistake he would not repeat, he
swore vehemently.

'I'm sorry…' Zara's teeth almost chattered in the af-
tershock of having called a crushing halt to that run-
away passion. 'But someone might have come along,'
she completed lamely, wondering if she seemed dread-
fully old-fashioned and a bit hysterical to a guy of his
experience. After all he had only kissed her and touched
her breast and she had thrown him off as if he had assaulted her.

'No, I'm sorry,' Vitale fielded, reaching for her hand,

the nails of which were digging into the surface of the
rug in a revealing show of discomfiture, and straightening her fingers in a calming gesture. 'I didn't think.'

It was an admission that very nearly choked Vitale
Roccanti, who, with the patience and power of a
Machiavelli, had planned and plotted his every move
from the age of thirteen and never once failed to deliver on any count. Zara, however, was soothed by his
apology and his grip on her hand. In her experience not
all men were so generous in the aftermath of thwarted
desire.

In seemingly silent mutual agreement they put away
the picnic and folded the rug to start back to the car.
She had barely seen the garden but it no longer had the
power to dominate her thoughts. Her entire focus was
now centred on Vitale. Was this what an infatuation
felt like? Or was it something more? Was he a man she
could fall in love with? How did she know? Was she
crazy to wonder such a thing? Julian had been her first
love but he had never had the power to make her feel
the way Vitale did. Sadly she had been too young at
eighteen to understand that there should be more said
and more felt in a relationship with a future.

Just before she climbed back into the car, a gardener
working at a border across the front lawn raised a hand
to acknowledge Vitale. Of course, his uncle's employees would know him. She watched him incline his head
in acknowledgement. Her fingers had messed up his
black hair and as he turned his handsome dark head,
stunning golden eyes locking to her as if there were no

other person in the world, she felt a fierce pride in his acknowledgement and refused to think beyond that.

As he drove her back to his house she was in a pensive mood and slightly dreamy from the heat, the wine and the passion.

'You're very quiet,' he murmured.

'I thought you would like that.'

In a graceful gesture he linked his fingers briefly with hers. 'No. I miss the chatter, *angelina mia*.'

Zara thought crazily then that engagements could be broken and weddings could be cancelled. That possibility momentarily put paid to the guilt and assuaged her conscience. It had never been her intention to deceive either man but now it was too late to tell Vitale the truth, that she was supposed to be getting married. She shifted uncomfortably at the knowledge that an honest and decent woman would have spoken up much sooner and certainly before the first kiss. Now she could not bear the idea that Vitale might think badly of her and she hugged her secret to herself in silence.

Not surprisingly, with her unusually optimistic mood interspersed by anxious spasms of fear about the future controlling her, the journey back to the farmhouse seemed very short because she was so lost in her thoughts.

She wandered into the sunny hallway. 'I didn't even explore Edith's garden properly,' she remarked with regret.

'Someday I'll take you back to see it,' Vitale promised and then he frowned.

'I'm leaving in the morning,' she reminded him help-lessly.

His beautiful dark deep-set eyes lingered on her anx-ious face and he lifted a hand, brushing her delicate jawbone with his knuckle in an unexpected caress. 'Let your hair down,' he whispered.

The look of anticipation gleaming in his eyes made her heart race and the blood surge hotly through her body. 'Why?' she asked baldly.

'I love your hair…the colour of it, the feel of it,' he confessed huskily.

And like a woman in a dream, Zara lifted her hand and undid the clip. Vitale need no further invitation, angling his proud dark head down as he studied her and used his hands to deftly fluff her rumpled hair round her shoulders. 'I even like the smell of it,' he admitted, a bemused frown tugging at his ebony brows even as his nostrils flared in recognition at the vanilla scent of her.

He was gorgeous, Zara thought dizzily, the most gorgeous guy she had ever met and he seemed equally drawn to her. It was a heady thought, and not her style, but she was basking in the hot golden glow of his ap-preciative appraisal. It was the work of a moment to mentally douse the sparks of caution at the back of her mind and instead stretch up on tiptoe as if she were free as a bird to do whatever she liked and taste that remarkably beautiful mouth of his again. He lifted her up in his arms and began to carry her upstairs.

CHAPTER FOUR

ZARA surfaced from that kiss to discover that she was on a bed in an unfamiliar room.

It was a larger, more masculine version of her room with bedding the colour of parchment. Unfortunately the last time that Zara had been alone in a bedroom with a man she had been handcuffed half naked to a metal headboard and it was thanks to that terrifying experience that she remained a virgin at the age of twenty-two. Momentarily transfixed by that chilling recollection she turned pale as milk and studied Vitale, reminding herself that she had kissed him, and encouraged him entirely of her own free will. She was not under the influence of alcohol this time around either.

'What's wrong?' His shirt already half unbuttoned to display a dark, hair-roughened wedge of muscular torso, Vitale regarded her with observant eyes, reading her tension and her pallor and wondering at her mood.

He was too clever by half to miss her nervous tension, Zara registered in dismay. A blush of discomfiture warmed her face as she struggled to suppress the apprehension that was a direct result of the betrayal she had suffered. Vitale wasn't a blackmailer, she told herself urgently. He wasn't going to whip out a camera either…at least she hoped not. He was a wealthy successful man in his own right with no need to target her as a potential source of profit.

'It's all right…it's not you,' she told him awkwardly. 'I had a bad experience once…'

Vitale spread his hands in a fluid soothing movement. 'If you want to change your mind I'll understand.'

Her wide eyes prickled with tears at that considerate offer because she knew it could not have been easy for him to make. He was not selfishly putting his own needs first, he *cared* how she felt and that meant a great deal to Zara. After all, in spite of all his protestations Julian had never cared about her, he had only seen her as a means to an end, a convenient conduit to her father's bank account. Her chin came up and she kicked off her shoes in a statement of intent. It was time she shook off the shadows cast over her life by Julian Hurst; it was time that she accepted that not every man was a user or an abuser.

'I'm staying,' Zara informed him unevenly, fighting her nerves with all her might. Twenty-two and a virgin—no, she absolutely was not going to share that embarrassing truth with him. She had read somewhere that men couldn't tell the difference so he would never guess the level of her inexperience unless she made it obvious by parading her insecurity.

Vitale wanted to tell her that she wouldn't regret sharing his bed but he was no hypocrite and he knew that she would. But what was another one-night stand to a woman with her level of experience? Unhappily for him, however, nothing seemed as cut and dried as it had before and he was suffering stabs of indecision directly in conflict with his usual rock-solid assurance and resolute focus. When and how had the business of avenging his sister contrived to become a guilty pleasure?

How could a little pixie-like blonde threaten to come between him and his wits? Vitale always knew what he was doing and controlled his own fate every step of the way. Time after time in his life he had made tough choices and he had never flinched from them. He might loathe the fact but he wanted Monty Blake's daughter much more than he had ever dreamt possible. Even knowing that she was engaged to another man and a heartless little cheat didn't kill his desire for her. Did it matter how he felt though? Surely all that mattered was that he took revenge for his sister's pitiful death at the hands of a filthy coward? And the woman on his bed was the magic key to that much desired objective.

'Take the shorts off,' he urged huskily.

Tensing, Zara was very still for a moment before she scrambled off the bed. It was a modest request, she told herself. He hadn't asked her to take off everything. But she was all fingers and thumbs as she undid the button at the waistband of her shorts and shook her slim hips clear of the garment, finally stepping out of them to reveal a pair of high cut blue satin knickers.

There was something wrong. What, Vitale didn't know, but his instincts were good and he sensed it. Her face was pink, her eyes evasive below concealing lashes and her movements curiously stiff. This was not a woman confident in the bedroom and the suspicion sparked a sense of unease in him for once again she was defying the picture he had of her. Her lavender eyes met his with an unmistakeably anxious glint and her arms were crossed defensively. He recalled that bad experience she had mentioned and wondered just how bad it had been to leave a beautiful young woman so unsure of herself. Disconcerted by the train of his thoughts, Vitale reminded himself that he only wanted to spend the night with her, not step into her mind and psychoanalyse her. He never went deep in relationships, never got involved. He liked his affairs light and easy, with sex the main event and no bitter aftertaste. What was it about her that continually off-balanced him?

Zara had always worried about displaying her body to a man. Unforgettably Julian had laughed at her very slight curves, remarking that she might as well have been a boy as she would never make a centrefold. She had once considered getting a breast enlargement but had feared that with so slim a body she might end up looking top heavy and unnatural. Now all of a sudden she wanted to be perfect—she wanted to be perfect purely for Vitale.

'What *is* it?' he prompted, crossing the floor to grip her taut shoulders.

'I'm feeling horribly shy,' she told him in a rush.

He lifted her off her feet and set her on the side of the bed and then he kissed her, knotting one hand into the soft silky fall of her hair to hold her steady. It was a hungry, demanding kiss, his tongue flicking against the sensitive roof of her mouth to fire a response that raced through her like an explosive depth charge. She forgot who she was, she forgot who he was, she even contrived to forget that she was a virgin. Her palms skated up over the hard muscular wall of his powerful chest and with a groan deep in his throat he caught her hand and, in a stark expression of need, brought it down to the thrust of his erection beneath his trousers.

Pleased to recognise that he wanted her that much, Zara stroked him and struggled to run down his zip. Her slim fingers skimmed beneath the fabric to find the long, thick evidence of his arousal. He pushed against her hand, hard, eager, and hungry for her touch and it fired her up, finally convincing her that in spite of her inexperience she was sexy enough to turn him on hard.

Vitale yanked off her T-shirt with impatient hands and kissed her again while pushing her back across the bed. His urgency, as he dispensed with his trousers while exchanging hard, driving kisses that stoked her hunger higher and higher, was undeniable. He couldn't get enough of her, couldn't get close enough. Zara knew exactly what she wanted for all her lack of experience. She wanted him on top of her, she craved his weight, but instead he found the petal-soft pink tips of her small breasts and used his mouth on those delectable buds with a skill that wrung a gasp from her parted lips.

'You're very sensitive there, *gioia mia*,' Vitale breathed thickly, raking her dainty breasts with eager, admiring eyes.

No longer concerned about the size of her attributes, Zara trembled, insanely conscious of the wet heat building at the heart of her, but for an instant, when he skimmed off his boxers and she saw the powerful upstanding proof of his excitement, her nerves almost betrayed her. Her body craved him but she was afraid it might hurt. Irritated with herself, she suppressed that fear and then all such thoughts fled her mind as he explored her most private place that she was tempted to hide from him. But the desire was too strong, the sensation he gave her too intense to be denied by modesty.

He lay on the bed teasing at her lower lip with tiny little bites that only inflamed her more while he touched her most tender flesh with a skill that made her back arch and her hips lift off the mattress. He eased a finger inside her and groaned against her swollen mouth. 'You're so tight, so wet...'

Her face burned and an ache bloomed between her thighs, an unbearable yearning for much more. With his thumb he found her clitoris and all thought and awareness fell away, reducing her to a much more elemental level. She pushed up to him and kissed him wildly for herself, shivering when the straining buds of her nipples grazed his warm hard chest.

All masculine dominance, Vitale leant over her, dark golden eyes ablaze with desire as he kissed her long and hard. 'I want you so much I'm burning...'

'So what are you waiting for?' Zara urged breathlessly, because he had brought her to an edge of anticipation that was intolerable and without her volition her hips were shifting up to him in tiny needy movements.

He tore the foil off a condom and eased it on while she watched, madly curious about what she had never known but rather apprehensive as well, although she was striving to suppress that feeling. He would fit, of course he would. Nature had designed men and women to fit. He leant over her, strong and sure, and she felt the head of him against her slick, damp entrance. Her body trembled with expectation when he plunged into her.

It hurt and a moan of protest escaped Zara. When he froze, staring down at her, his eyes full of enquiry and confusion, she was mortified.

'Zara?' he began, 'I hurt you. I'm sorry—'

'I don't want to discuss it,' Zara told him hurriedly. She could feel the tension draining away, the pain already receding, and suspected she had made a lot of noise about nothing. 'You can continue…'

It was that prim little command now, in the most inappropriate of circumstances, that nearly sent Vitale into a fit of laughter. With difficulty he restrained his amusement, for her lovely face was a picture of disquiet and embarrassment. 'But I hurt you—'

'Some things are just too private to talk about,' Zara assured him.

'You really want me to continue?' Vitale queried in a strained undertone, wondering why no other woman had ever made him want to laugh as she did.

'You might as well now,' Zara pointed out prosaically, abandoning all hope of receiving much enjoyment from the act now.

Just as she thought that, Vitale sank into her up to the hilt and an erotic thrill sizzled through her like the touch of a firebrand on naked skin. As he began to move she struggled to swallow back a gasp of surprise. She felt truly extraordinary, as if her body were directly attuned to his. A sweet torment of pleasure built as he withdrew and then thrust deep again, jolting a low cry from her. She no longer had the ability to rein back her response. Intense, all-consuming pleasure gripped her and she panted for breath, her urgency rising in exact proportion to her need. Her excitement climbed higher and higher, spiralling through her like a bright light fighting to escape. Then, just when she thought she couldn't bear it any more, she reached a peak and fell apart in an exquisite agony of sensation, eyes opening, lips parting in wonderment as he shuddered over her in the throes of his own climax.

Eyes brilliant with gratification, Vitale claimed her mouth one more time. '*Ebbene*…now then, you amazing woman,' he growled hoarsely. 'That was a worthy continuance.'

Feeling wonderfully at peace, Zara pressed her lips gently against his satin-smooth shoulder. He lifted her wrist and let his tongue glide along the pulse there, making her quiver helplessly. She glanced up at him from below her lashes, recognising that this was a guy who knew every button to push. He kicked back the sheet and got up to stride into the bathroom, and she turned over onto her side, still stunned by the power of what she had experienced in his arms.

The aftermath of that wondrous pleasure was still engulfing her. Great sex, she labelled dizzily, but she wanted more and was already wondering if Vitale planned to continue what they had begun. Or was she

just a little weekend distraction? That humiliating possibility had to be considered. After all, theirs had been a
chance attraction, rather than a more conventional one.
Ironically she had sacrificed so much more to be with
him, she recognised ruefully. There was no question of
her marrying Sergios Demonides now. Furthermore she
could barely believe that she had been so blind to the
risk of temptation when she agreed to marry a man she
neither loved nor cared for simply to please her parents.
How immature and foolish was that? Oh, how much
easier life would have been now had she paid more heed
to Bee's warnings and told Sergios that she was very
sorry but she had changed her mind!

Well, she supposed wryly, a change of heart weeks
before the wedding invitations even went out was better
than a marriage that failed. No doubt Sergios would be
annoyed with her for wasting his time. She had wasted
everyone's time and no doubt the cancellation of all the
wedding arrangements would cost her parents a great
deal of money. She had been very foolish and short-
sighted about her own needs. But what was done was
done and now everything had changed. There was no
going back to the mindset she had cherished before she
came to Italy and met Vitale Roccanti. He had blown
everything she thought she knew about herself to smith-
ereens. She wanted more from a marriage than Sergios
could ever have given her.

'Join me in the shower,' Vitale husked from the doorway.

She slid out of the bed as though he had pulled an
invisible piece of elastic that had her attached to one

end. Being naked without even the coverage of a sheet or his body was a challenge for her, but already the demeaning memories of what Julian had done to her were being replaced by more positive ones. What went without saying was that she wanted to be with Vitale and felt as though she had waited all her life to feel as strongly about a man as she felt about him. Moreover she was overpoweringly conscious that she was flying back to London in the morning and that then the ball would be in his court as to what—if anything—happened next. There was no way she would chase after him—she had way too much pride for that.

Having finally shed his shirt, Vitale caught her up in the doorway and lifted her high against his lean bronzed body. 'I could easily become accustomed to a woman your size, *gioia mia*. You're so easy to move around!'

A smile as bright as a solar flare lit across her face and all thoughts of the future fled to the back of her mind. Right now she would live for the moment. Why not? She was young, she was, if not technically free, morally free in her own mind to enjoy herself. The only cloud on the horizon was the fact she dared not be honest with Vitale for fear of how her explanation about Sergios might alter and indeed destroy his good impression of her.

The shower was already running and Zara gasped as the cascade of water hit her, then Vitale kissed her and nothing else mattered but the need to get as close to him as possible. He sank his hands below her bottom and hoisted her high so that she could wrap her arms round his neck and kiss him back with passionate fervour. As her fingers moved across his strong back she felt the surprising roughness of his skin there and wondered if he had been in an accident, for she was sure what she was feeling was some sort of scarring. But her curiosity was soon overwhelmed by the heat of his mouth on hers. Just as quickly she discovered that she wanted him again for her nipples instantly pinched into prominent aching beads and the slick heat pooled between her legs again.

'You are so hot you burn me,' Vitale rasped, lowering her back onto the tiles again, his strong erection brushing her stomach.

Shower gel foamed between his hands and he transferred it to her sensitised skin. His expert fingers glided over the pouting mounds of her breasts, lingered over her straining nipples, toying with them before slowly delving lower to graze the most tender bud of all in the most indescribably arousing way. Trembling, she leant against him for support, making no attempt to pretend that she was still in control, surrendering entirely to the tingling, taunting need pulsing through her. With a hungry groan, Vitale hoisted her up against him again and swung round to brace her spine against the tiled wall.

'I can't wait,' he breathed, spreading her thighs and bringing her down on him so that her lush opening sheathed his shaft in a single stunning move.

Hands anchored to her hips, he drove deeper into her and then lifted her to withdraw again before thrusting back into her quivering body again. It was incredibly exciting. She couldn't think, couldn't speak, she just hung onto his broad shoulders for what felt like a wildly exciting roller-coaster ride. At some stage he lifted her out of the shower and laid her down on the floor so that he could continue to pleasure her there with tireless vigour. She writhed in a frenzy of abandon and hit another breathtaking climax that sent her spinning off into the stars.

'Wow...' she whispered weakly in the aftermath, belatedly aware of how hard the floor was below her and how heavy he was.

'That wasn't very well planned,' Vitale breathed abruptly, freeing her from his weight and pulling her up with him.

'Planned?' In a sensual daze, Zara blinked and reached for one of the towels on the rail. 'How... *planned*?'

'I forgot to use a condom. Do you take contraceptive pills?'

Zara froze and looked up at him. His devastatingly handsome face was suddenly very serious. 'No,' she said, the size of the risk they'd just taken slowly dawning on her. 'And I'm about halfway through my cycle.'

'I'll be more careful from now on...I promise,' Vitale asserted, running a fingertip caressingly below her sultry lower lip, swollen from his kisses. 'But I do find you incredibly tempting. You make me dangerously impulsive.'

Meeting the urgent appeal in those stunning golden eyes, Zara could barely put one foot in front of another, never mind think logical thoughts. 'I'm sure I'll be fine,' she muttered, suppressing her concern that she might fall pregnant and thinking that if she took after her mother, who, in spite of her longing for more children, had only ever conceived once in her entire life, she probably had nothing to worry about.

As he turned away to reach for a towel she saw his back and her shocked breath caught in her throat. Line after line of raised scars like welts criss-crossed his long, muscular back and there were little round darker marks as well across his shoulders and spine. 'What on earth happened to your back?' she asked abruptly.

Momentarily, Vitale froze in the act of towelling himself dry and shot her a glance over one broad shoulder. 'Ancient history,' he said dismissively.

And he did not offer to share it.

He pulled on boxers and a shirt to go downstairs with her to raid the fridge. It was Giuseppina's day off but she had left the cabinet packed with goodies. They were both very hungry. He lit a candle on the terrace and they sat eating cold spicy chicken and salad washed down with wine and lively conversation. She wanted to ask him about his back again but was reluctant to snoop. Somehow he manoeuvred her back onto his lap and his hands travelled below her tee to cup her breasts. She stretched back against him, helpless in the grip of her instantaneous hunger and they went back to bed where he made love to her twice more. Afterwards, she lay spent on the bed watching Vitale sleep and feeling ridiculously happy.

Even in the moonlight he had the most amazing bone structure, from his high cheekbones to classic nose and his hard, angular jaw line. She wanted to touch him, trace the winged ebony brows, the sensual firmness of his mouth, but she curled her hands into fists of restraint instead. She was thinking and acting like a teenager, a lovesick teenager, she scolded herself impatiently, deliberately turning away from him and lying back again. Somehow she had never got to play it cool with Vitale the way she usually did with men and that made her feel very insecure. They had bypassed the calm getting-to-know-you phase and plunged straight into meaningful looks and passion. He was as attracted to her as she was to him, she reflected wryly, so at least the spell she was under was a mutual one…

Vitale couldn't sleep. When he woke it was still dark and he reckoned that it was the awareness that he had company that had made him feel uneasy. After all, he always slept alone. He never stayed the night with anyone. He didn't like that kind of closeness. By nature he was a loner and after the childhood he had endured he thought it was hardly surprising that he should be uncomfortable with any form of physical intimacy that went beyond sex. But she was very affectionate, hugging and kissing and snuggling into his lean hard frame. His eyes bleak, he eased away from her, resisting that togetherness. It would soon be over. He couldn't work out why he didn't feel happier about that. But then he had never been given to introspection.

'You should have woken me up sooner!' Zara complained several hours later as she struggled to close the zip on her case.

While Vitale had risen early, he had let her sleep in

and it had been a rush to get dressed and packed ready for the time he had said they had to leave. At first it had pleased her that he was making the effort to personally drive her to the airport, but even the most insensitive woman could not have missed out on noticing how polite and almost distant Vitale seemed to be acting all of a sudden. Zara had never had a one-night stand but it struck her that her vision of how a morning after such a night would feel best described Vitale's behaviour. The awkwardness in the atmosphere was not solely her fault. And maybe she *had* just enjoyed a one night stand, she reasoned painfully, maybe this was it for her and Vitale Roccanti.

What were the chances of him trying to conduct a long-distance relationship with her? Did he even visit London in the course of his work? For the very first time she acknowledged that the odds were that she might never see Vitale again.

Her potential client had become a lover and that could well have destroyed any chance of him seriously considering her for the job.

'Do you still want to see a set of plans for the villa?' she enquired stiffly.

'*Si*, of course,' Vitale confirmed, shooting her a muted glance, his tension palpable as he swept up her case in a strong hand and carried it downstairs for her.

All Zara's suspicious antennae were on alert. Had Vitale already toyed with the idea of telling her not to bother with the plans? Wouldn't that provide a neat end to a potentially embarrassing situation? *I'm never going to see him again. I'm never ever going to see him again.* The conviction cast a pall over Zara's spirits. She told herself she didn't care, that it didn't matter to her, that a few days ago she had never even heard his name before. And while those thoughts whirled round and round in her mind, pride forced her head higher. With brittle efficiency she discussed arrangements for submitting plans for his inspection while ascertaining the exact level of detail he required. As he seemed to have little to say on that score she was convinced that he would reject the plan, but as Blooming Perfect always charged for putting in a basic design her time would not have been entirely wasted.

His lean, strong face set in forbidding lines, Vitale opened the front door and took her small case out to his car. Standing in the porch, she donned her jacket, her delicate features blank as she fought for composure and blamed herself bitterly for having abandoned her professionalism in the first place. This sense of discomfiture, this sharp sense of loss were the payback for her reckless behaviour.

'Zara…' And as she looked up she was taken aback when Vitale closed his arms round her and bent his head to kiss her, because the way he had been behaving actual physical contact had to have been about the last thing she expected from him.

But in the emotional mood Zara was in, his carnal mouth had only to touch hers for her hands to delve possessively back into his black hair. In fact she held him to her for a split second before she yanked her arms away again and angled her head back, having finally recognised in some disconcertion that he had offered her more of a peck than a passionate embrace.

But even as she released him it seemed all hell broke loose. She stared in shock and flinched at the sight of two men wielding cameras only yards away from them. The men leapt up from crouching positions, clearly having taken photos of Vitale and Zara in each other's arms, and tore off into the trees surrounding the property to speedily disappear from sight.

'Where on earth did they come from? Who are they, for goodness' sake?' Zara demanded angrily. 'Why the heck were they taking pictures of us?'

CHAPTER FIVE

'PAPARAZZI. They must've staked out the house to await their chance.' It was the incredible calm with which Vitale made that explanation that first alerted Zara to the idea that something was badly wrong. He didn't seem surprised by the invasion of their privacy or even particularly bothered by it, which shook her.

'But what on earth for?' Zara queried, marvelling at his seemingly laid-back attitude when everybody she knew in the public eye hated the intrusion of muckraking journalists into their private lives.

'Obviously you know *why* the paps would find photographing you with another man worth their while,' Vitale countered with a harsh edge to his dark deep drawl, his intonation cold enough to make him sound momentarily like a stranger.

Taken aback by that tone, Zara frowned up at him. 'If they were paps, how would they know I was here with you? *Another* man? What are you saying?'

Vitale quirked a derisive brow, stunning eyes dark as pitch and harder than she had ever seen them. 'Have you forgotten your Greek fiancé? The fact that you're marrying Sergios Demonides this summer? In the light of that, proof of your obvious intimacy with me is more than sufficient to sell a grubby tabloid story for a profit.'

Air rasped in Zara's throat and the muscles there tightened, making it hard for her to catch her breath. She was deeply shaken by the level of his information. 'You *know* about Sergios?'

'Obviously,' Vitale admitted drily.

'We're not engaged,' she said limply, not really even knowing why she was troubling to make that distinction since it was painfully obvious that Vitale Roccanti had already judged her badly for her silence on the score of her marital commitment. 'There was no ring, no engagement…it's not like Sergios and I are in love with each other or anything like that—'

Vitale shifted a silencing hand, his lack of interest patent and like another slap in the face. 'Whatever—'

'No.' Zara refused to be silenced, determined to defend her behaviour as best she could. 'As soon as I got back to London I was planning to tell Sergios that I couldn't go ahead and marry him. I wasn't fooling around behind his back. I'm not like that. I had already decided that I couldn't go ahead and marry him after meeting you—'

'It's immaterial to me—'

'You knew about Sergios and yet you said nothing?' Zara pressed, struggling to understand and not linger on that last lethal statement, for nothing positive could be gained from the words, 'It's immaterial to me.' He didn't care that she was supposedly marrying another man? Didn't care in the slightest? That was a declaration of towering lack of interest that cut her to the quick.

'If you're to make your flight, we have to leave now.' Vitale delivered the reminder without any emotion at all.

'I'll catch a later flight at my own expense,' Zara fielded with a slight shake in her voice. 'I'm more interested right now in finding out what's going on here. I went to bed last night with one guy and this morning it's like I've woken up with his nasty identical twin. If you knew about Sergios why didn't you mention it?'

Vitale resisted a strong urge to ask her why she hadn't mentioned it. Why should he care? She was faithless, pleasure-loving. She meant nothing to him, less than nothing. He breathed in deep and slow, suppressing any hint of an emotional reaction. He was keen to be done with the dialogue and it struck him that honesty was probably the best policy in the circumstances. It would draw an efficient line under their entanglement as nothing else could do. 'I was willing to do whatever I could to ensure that your marriage plans fell through as I believe it will have a detrimental effect on your father's hopes of selling the family hotel group to Demonides.'

Zara was so startled by that explanation that her legs wobbled beneath her and she sank down heavily on the low wall surrounding the shrubbery beside the porch. Her lavender eyes narrowed in bemused concentration when she stared up at him. 'What on earth are you talking about?'

'I set you up,' Vitale volunteered grimly, spelling

out the facts without hesitation. 'From start to finish. Contacting your design firm, bringing you out here—'

In receipt of that admission, Zara had slowly turned white as snow. 'Sleeping with me?' she interrupted jerkily, distaste scissoring through her like a blade. 'Was that part of the set-up? If you wanted Sergios to dump me, ensuring embarrassing pictures of his future bride misbehaving appear in some tabloid rag would be a good start.'

'I thought so too but, believe it or not,' Vitale imparted grittily, 'I had no wish to hurt you personally. Your father has always been my target—'

'My father?' Zara could feel her muscles stiffen in shock as she sat there, spine rigid, feet set as neatly together as a small child told to sit still at church, her hands so tightly clasped together in an effort at self-control that her fingers ached. 'Why would my father have been your target?'

A bleak expression entered his eloquent gaze. 'Sixteen years ago, your father took my sister, Loredana, out on a sailing weekend and when the yacht got into trouble he saved his own skin and left her to drown. She was twenty years old and pregnant with his child.'

In shock at that horrible story, Zara slowly shook her head as though to clear it. Sixteen years ago her father had been divorced from Bee's mother but still a single man. Zara had been born quite a few years before her parents actually wed, but then a wedding ring or indeed a child had never kept the older man faithful. She did actually remember something happening, some kind of an upheaval, which had resulted in rows between her parents... What was it? What had happened? Her smooth brow furrowed. But no, her memory seemed to have packed up and gone home. Sixteen years ago, after all, Zara had only been a child of six. Yet Vitale had still targeted her for something he believed Monty Blake had done to his sister?

'So now you know the truth.'

Her teeth set together so hard that her jaw thrummed in punishment but she did not want to break into impulsive speech. Yes, now she knew that once again a man had made a colossal fool of her. Maybe all the people, including her parents, who had called her dumb were right—she had not had the slightest suspicion of Vitale while he had been executing his charm offensive.

Not until this very morning, at the last possible moment, had she recognised his change of mood and attitude. So what did that say about her? That when it came to men she was criminally stupid and blind and ought not to be let out on her own, she thought painfully. To follow a Julian Hurst with a Vitale Roccanti suggested seriously bad judgement. Twice she had fallen headlong for the flattering approaches of men programmed to hurt and use her for their own purposes. And now she felt as if the bottom had fallen out of her world, as if she had been deserted and left utterly lost in alien territory. This guy, who had shamelessly used and abused her, was the guy she had actually believed she might be falling in love with? That was the lowest blow of all and it decimated her pride.

'Call me a taxi to get me to the airport,' Zara told him curtly.

'There is no need for that.' Vitale flung wide the passenger door as if he expected that she would still scramble into the car like an obedient dog.

The delicate bones of her face prominent below her fine skin, Zara fixed scornful lavender eyes on him and ignored the invitation. 'So you slept with me to try and wreck my Dad's big business deal with Sergios. At least I know what a four letter word of a man you are now,' she breathed. 'You used my business to lure me into a trap, deliberately deceived me, took inexcusable advantage of my trust and stole my virginity—'

'Your *virginity*?' Vitale stressed with incredulous bite. 'You couldn't have been a—'

'I *was*. You were my first lover. I don't sleep around. Were you foolish enough to believe all the rubbish printed about me in newspapers?' Zara demanded fierily, standing up now, narrow shoulders thrown back as she voiced her feelings without embarrassment. 'Of course now I wish I hadn't slept with you but I'm even more relieved to find out firsthand what an unscrupulous bastard you are, so that I can ensure that I have nothing more to do with you—'

'Zara—'

'No, you listen to me for a change!' Zara told him, interrupting with raw driving determination. 'I didn't do anything to harm you or your sister. I didn't even know you existed until I met you. If you had a problem with my father you should have had the courage and decency to talk to him about it and left me out of it. You had no excuse whatsoever for dragging me into your vengeful attack on him.'

Vitale withstood that verbal onslaught in brooding silence. Perhaps, she thought wildly, he realised that she was entitled to her say.

'Are you getting into the car?' he enquired flatly.

'No, call me a taxi. I wouldn't take a lift off you if I was dying!' Zara flung back at him, stepping forward to reach into the car and yank out her case again with a strength born of pure anger.

Vitale made use of his cell phone. 'The taxi will be here in ten.' He lowered the phone again and studied her. 'Was I truly your first lover?'

Zara used two very rude words to tell him where to go and she shocked him with that succinct retort almost as much as she shocked herself, for she was not in the habit of using that kind of language. At the same time, though, she was not prepared to stand there exchanging further conversation with a man who had deliberately set out to ensnare and hurt her.

'You might as well sit down indoors to wait,' Vitale advised curtly.

Zara shot him a look of loathing and remained where she was. 'You ensured that the paps saw me here with you—that's why you kissed me!' she suddenly realized. Her eyes were full of bitter condemnation and contempt but she was ashamed as well because even though Sergios would not be marrying her now he would surely be embarrassed by that sort of publicity and he had done nothing to deserve that from her.

The truth, Vitale had pronounced, when he told her the story about his sister—was that what it was? She knew there could be many shades of the truth and she doubted his version. Had Monty Blake honestly stood by and let some young pregnant girl drown? It would surprise her if it was true. She didn't like her father and feared him when he was in a temper. He had adored her brother, Tom, the clever son he had longed to see follow in his narcissistic footsteps, but Zara had only ever been a disappointment to him. Her father was obsessed with money and social status. He had a mean amoral streak, a violent temper and a tendency to lash out physically, but he had never done anything, to her knowledge, that suggested he might be downright evil.

It dawned on her then that her father would kill her for getting involved with another man and offending Sergios. Even in the sunshine, a chill of genuine apprehension ran down Zara's taut spine and turned her skin clammy and cold. Only the brave crossed Monty Blake. Her mother would be outraged as well. And Zara would have to avoid Bee to ensure that her half-sister did not get involved in her troubles because her father would go spare if Bee supported her. In fact, Zara recognised painfully, she wasn't going to be anybody's flavour of the month after that photo of her kissing Vitale appeared in print. She might not have been engaged to Sergios, but even without an official announcement lots of people had guessed that a wedding was in the offing.

Vitale watched the taxi disappear down the wooded lane. It was over and, honour satisfied, he could return to his smooth, civilised existence, organising multimillion-euro deals and travelling between the apartments he owned round the world. He had done what he set out to do, smoothly and effectively. He should be pleased that after so many years the only kind of justice that a man of Monty Blake's greed would understand was finally about to be served to him. But impending victory had a strangely hollow and unsatisfying feel.

In his mind's eye the banker renowned for his cold calculation and emotional detachment could still see Zara Blake's pale heart-shaped face and the incredulity etched in her eyes. In a sudden movement he punched the wall with a clenched fist. It was a crazy thing to do and he was not a man who did crazy things and it hurt like the very devil. Blood from his bruised and scraped knuckles dripped on the tiled floor but that aberrant surge of violence did serve to vent a little of the raging sense of frustration Vitale was struggling to suppress. He had no idea why he felt this way.

Had Zara been a virgin? He saw no reason for her to lie on that score and he had only dismissed the suspicion because it had seemed so unlikely that a rich and beautiful party girl could still be that innocent at her age. He recalled her lack of assurance in the bedroom and his wide, shapely mouth twisted as he acknowledged that he *had* been guilty of believing what he had read in the media about her. Few party girls were virgins, but she had been and he had ignored his suspicion precisely because it had suited him to do so. Had he known the truth about Monty Blake's daughter would he still have used her as a weapon to strike at her father? He could not answer that question. He still wondered why there had been no man before him and then he shook his head, killing the thought as well as that dangerous seed of burning curiosity. It was done and there was no going back. Now he only had to wait for Demonides to ditch the buyout of the Royale hotel group at an inflated price and he would have achieved his final goal.

Even so, for the very first time Vitale was tentatively questioning the desire for revenge that had driven him since the age of thirteen. It was like probing a ragingly sensitive tooth. As a boy he had known it would be a foolish waste of time to stage a personal confrontation with his sister's former lover. Monty Blake would simply lie to him as he had lied at the inquest. He was a vain and devious man, not to be trusted with women. Vitale shut out the reflection that the end might not always justify the means. He had done what had needed to be done. The scornful condemnation in those amazing lavender eyes could not destroy the painful memories of his innocent and trusting sister or his powerful need to hit back on her behalf. Loredana hadn't been a 'someone'. She had had no powerful connections—at least, Vitale adjusted grimly, none who *cared* enough to question the judgement of accidental death made at that inquest.

In comparison, Zara Blake meant nothing to him, less than nothing, he affirmed with vigour. He was not an emotional man. In all likelihood he would never see her again. Unless she proved to be pregnant, he thought abruptly, and, after what he had done, wouldn't that be a disaster to end all disasters? He still could not credit that he could have taken that risk with her. Since when had sex been so overwhelming an event? He had always been proud of his self-control, not a trait that came naturally to those of his bloodline, he conceded grimly. So, how could passion have betrayed him to that extent? In truth it had been an extraordinary weekend—Zara had defied his expectations at every turn and precious little had gone according to plan.

But why was he questioning his behaviour? Why the hell had he smashed his fist into a wall? He was a goal-orientated man and, having achieved his objective, he ought to be celebrating. After all, Demonides was never going to go ahead and marry Zara Blake once he saw that photo of her in another man's arms in the newspapers. Vitale decided that the problem was that he had got too close to his quarry. He had found her intensely desirable and quite impossible to resist, and all that was wrong was that the shock of that was still ricocheting through a man who rated his strength of mind and self-discipline as exceptional.

'Ignore them, darling,' Jono advised Zara in a tone of crisp dismissal as he helped her stack another box in the van he had borrowed to help her move into her new home. Fluffy was peering out of her carrier, little round eyes full of anxiety. The rabbit hated change and travel of any kind.

A pair of enormous sunglasses anchored on her nose, Zara endeavoured to look indifferent to the pair of reporters shouting rude questions while taking photos to record her departure from her parents' elegant town house. If only she had moved out and embraced independence long ago, she reflected ruefully, she wouldn't be feeling quite so lost. On the other hand, every cloud had a silver lining. This was the first day of her new life, she reminded herself bracingly. Her parents might have thrown their troublesome daughter out and washed their hands of her, but at least she was now free to do as she liked and concentrate on Blooming Perfect.

Jono glanced at Zara's tense profile before he drove off and squeezed her hand in a comforting gesture. 'Things will get better once you can settle into your new flat.'

'They could hardly get worse.' Blond and blue-eyed, Jono, a successful PR consultant, was one of the few friends who had stuck by Zara when the proverbial had hit the fan ten days earlier.

As a well-known socialite and the rumoured future bride of one of the world's wealthiest men, Zara had been extremely popular. Stripped of her father's money and the luxury lifestyle that had accompanied it, she had learned that she was more of an acquired taste in the friendship stakes. She would no longer be able to afford the shopping expeditions, the trips abroad or the expensive pastimes that she had once taken for granted. Of course, given the chance Bee would have stood by her side, but Zara had been determined not to enrage her father even more by encouraging her half-sister to get involved in her problems.

After all, Zara accepted that she had made some very bad decisions and it was the way of the world that she should have to pay the price for her mistakes. That photo of her with Vitale after spending the weekend with him in what had been gruesomely described as a 'love nest in the Tuscan hills' had appeared in one of the murkier tabloids. Sergios had wasted little time in cutting her loose. Her former bridegroom's phone call, Zara recalled with a cringing sense of mortification, had been a masterpiece of icy restraint. Sergios had not reproached or condemned her, he had merely pointed out that it was obvious that they would not suit and that had been that. He had rung off while she was still stuck like a record in a groove trying to apologise for the sort of scandal and behaviour that no woman could adequately apologise for.

In comparison to Sergios' moderation, her parents' fury had known no bounds. Things had been hurled in vicious verbal onslaughts that had almost inevitably led to Monty Blake's raging demand that his daughter move out from below his roof. But, she acknowledged ruefully, at least her enraged father had confined himself to vocal abuse and retained some shred of control over his temper. Sadly that was not always the case.

She had done a search on the Net in an effort to dig up the story of her father and the yacht episode. The sparse facts available had left her none the wiser when it came to apportioning blame. An Asian earthquake and the resulting waves had caused the hired yacht to sink in the middle of the night. Apparently it had happened very quickly. One member of the crew and a passenger called Loredana, described as an Italian fashion model, had been listed missing, presumed drowned. When her father was already furious she had seen little point in mentioning an incident that would only madden him even more. Furthermore, if even an inquest had failed to extract any damaging admission of culpability from the older man she had little faith in the likelihood of her own persuasive powers doing a better job. And why wasn't she being more honest with herself? She had not brought up that business with the yacht because she was frightened of pushing her father's temper over the edge. No, she had been too much of a coward.

The studio apartment she had rented was a masterpiece of clever design in which the minimum possible space was stretched to cover the essentials but it covered nothing well, Zara conceded ruefully as she unpacked, aghast at the lack of storage space. If there was little room for the requirements of ordinary life, there was even less for Fluffy. A neighbour had already informed Zara that no pets were allowed in the building and had threatened to report her to the landlord. Just then that seemed to be the least of Zara's worries, though. By the time she had finished shopping for bed linen, food and kitchen necessities, the balance in her bank account had shrunk alarmingly. Bearing in mind that she had only the small salary she could draw from her late aunt's business, she would have to learn to do without things if she didn't want to run into debt. Now that she was in a position to work full-time it would have suited her to dispense with Rob's services as manager, but, owing to Zara's dyslexia and the restrictions it imposed, Rob had become an essential component in the successful running of the business.

She went to bed early on her first night in the apartment. The instant she closed her eyes in a silence disturbed only by the sounds of traffic the anguish she had fought off to the best of her ability all day flooded back: the intense sense of loss and betrayal, the conviction that she had to be the most stupid woman ever born, the swelling, wounding ache of deep hurt. And she walled up that giant mess of turmoil and self-loathing, shut it out and reminded herself that tomorrow was another day.

That same week in his Florence head office, Vitale's oft-admired powers of concentration let him down repeatedly in meetings when his mind would drift and his shrewd dark eyes would steadily lose their usual needle-sharp focus. The teasing image of a tiny blonde haunted his sleep and shadowed his working hours with unfamiliar introspection. By night he dreamt of Zara Blake in all sorts of erotic scenarios doing all sorts of highly arousing things to his insatiable body. Evidently with her in a starring role his imagination took flight.

Even a resolute procession of cold showers failed to chase the pain of his constant lingering arousal and, being innately practical, he immediately sought a more effective solution to his overactive libido. Since Zara had returned to the UK he had dined out with two different women, taken another to the opera and accompanied a fourth to a charity event. All were extremely attractive and entertaining. Any one of them would have slept with him without attaching strings to the occasion, but not one of those women had tempted him and for the first time he had found himself actively avoiding intimate situations. He had also discovered flaws in all four women and now asked himself when he had become so very hard to please. But while he loathed constant female chatter one of the women had proved too quiet, another had had a very irritating laugh, the third had talked incessantly about shopping and the fourth had constantly searched out her own reflection in mirrors.

Every day Vitale had all the key English newspapers delivered to his office and he skimmed through them mid-morning over his coffee without once admitting to himself what he was actually on the lookout for. Yet every day he contrived to take his coffee break just a little earlier. During the second week, however, he finally hit the jackpot when he saw the photo of Zara with another man. He frowned, at first wondering who the good-looking blond male by her side was. She looked tinier than ever pictured with a suitcase almost as big as she was. He read between the lines of the gossip column below. Her family was angry enough with her to throw her out of their home? What else was he supposed to think?

Vitale was very much shocked, mentally picturing a puppy being dumped at the side of a busy motorway, a puppy with no notion of how to avoid the car wheels racing past. Monty Blake's daughter, surely spoiled and indulged all her life to date, could have few survival skills to fall back on. Honed to a cutting edge by a very much tougher background and much more humble beginnings, Vitale was appalled on her behalf. He had not foreseen such a far-reaching consequence but he felt that he should have done. After all, the loss of Sergios Demonides as a son-in-law would have been a major disappointment and Monty Blake was not the type of man to deal gracefully with such a setback. Evidently he had taken his ire out on his only child.

Feeling disturbingly responsible for that development, Vitale lifted the phone and organised a flight to London in his private jet that evening. He only wanted to check that she was all right, that was all, nothing more complex, certainly nothing personal, although if she turned out to have conceived, he conceded broodingly, matters would swiftly become a great deal more personal. Vitale, after all, knew that he would be the last man alive to take a casual approach to an unplanned pregnancy. He knew too well the potential drawbacks of such a route. It took another couple of phone calls to establish where Zara was staying and the unwelcome gossip he received along with that information persuaded him that Monty Blake's daughter must be having a pretty tough time.

But why should that matter to him? Vitale frowned heavily, deeply ill-at-ease with his reactions. Why did he feel so accountable for what might happen to her? While Vitale was, at least, a free agent Zara had chosen to betray the trust of the man she had promised to marry. She was a faithless liar without a conscience, the spoilt daughter of a man he loathed. But he still could not shake the recollection that he had been Zara's one and only lover. The reflection that he had been wrong about her on that score made him wonder whether there could be other things he might have been wrong about as well. And for a man as self-assured as he was that was a ground-breaking shift in outlook.

The next day, Vitale called at Zara's apartment at

nine in the morning. Even before he entered the building he was asking himself why the hell he was making
a social call on the daughter of his enemy. He might
have got her pregnant, he reminded himself with fierce
reluctance, his handsome mouth down curving. If there
was a child he had a duty of care towards her and until
he knew one way or the other he could not turn his
back on her and ignore her predicament. Born into a
comfortable background, she had enjoyed a sheltered
upbringing, so how was she coping without that safety
net?

Vitale stepped out of the lift on Zara's floor and right
into a heated dispute. A burly older man was standing
at Zara's front door saying aggressively, 'This isn't open
to negotiation—either the rabbit goes or you move out!'

Zara gave him a stricken look. 'But that's—'

'No pets of any kind. You signed the rent agreement
and you're in breach of the conditions,' he pronounced
loudly. 'I want that animal out of here today or I'm giving you notice to quit.'

'I don't have anywhere else to take her,' Zara was
arguing heatedly.

'Not my problem,' the landlord told her, swinging on
his heel and striding into the lift that Vitale had only
just vacated.

Only as Vitale moved forward did Zara register his
presence and her eyes flew wide, her lips parting in furious surprise and dismay. 'What the hell are you doing
here?'

CHAPTER SIX

AT first glimpse of Vitale, shock shrouded Zara like a cocoon, so that external sounds seemed to come from a very long way away. The traffic noise, the doors opening and closing in the busy life of the building faded fast into the background. As her landlord stomped angrily away, offended by her combative stance, Vitale took his place. Even at a glance, Vitale looked fabulously, irretrievably Italian in a faultlessly cut grey business suit that had that unmistakeable edge of designer style. From his cropped black hair and staggeringly good bone structure to his tall, well-built body, he was a breathtakingly handsome man.

But it hurt to look at him, and as Zara felt the pain of his deception afresh her anger ignited like a roaring flame. Her eyes cloaked, hiding her vulnerability. He hadn't cared about her, hadn't even really wanted her for herself. He had simply used her as a weapon to strike at her father. 'What do you want?' she asked, her intonation sharp with anger. 'And how did you find out where I was living?'

'I have my sources,' Vitale fielded, his stunning dark deep-set eyes trained on her to track any changes.

Casually clad in cropped trousers and flip-flops, she seemed smaller and younger than he had recalled but, if anything, even more beautiful. Her creamy natural skin was flawless. The wealth of silvery waves falling round her narrow shoulders was bright as a beacon, providing the perfect frame for delicate features dominated by wide lavender eyes and an impossibly full and tempting pink mouth. And that fast Vitale wanted her again. The tightening heaviness at his groin was a response that unnerved him more than a little. He operated very much on cold, clever logic—he had no time and even less understanding of anything uncontrolled or foolish. He could not compute the sheer irrational absurdity of such an attraction when he had remained indifferent to so many more suitable women. In self-defence, he immediately sought out her flaws. She was *too* small, her hair was *too* bright, she talked like an express train rarely pausing for breath and much of it was totally superfluous stuff. But in defiance of popular report, he recalled abstractedly, she was anything but stupid. She had a quirky sense of humour and very quick wits.

While Vitale looked her up and down as though he had every right to do so, his face sardonic and uninformative, Zara's resentment merely took on a sharper edge. 'You still haven't told me what you're doing here.' Her heart-shaped face had tightened, irate colour stealing into her cheeks as she belatedly grasped the most likely reason for his reappearance, and she winced in discomfiture. 'Oh, of course, you want to know *if*—'

'May I come in?' Vitale incised, not being a fan of holding intimate conversations in public places.

'I don't want to let you in but I suppose I don't have much choice,' Zara countered ungraciously, reflecting that far from worrying about the possibility of an accidental pregnancy she had shelved the concern in Italy and had refused to think about it again when it seemed that she had so many more pressing things to worry about.

A thumping noise broke the tense silence. At Vitale's entrance, Fluffy thumped the floor with her hind feet in protest and let out a squeal of fright before hotfooting it for her hutch.

Vitale was even more taken aback by the display. 'You keep a…rabbit indoors?' he queried, his only prior experience of rabbits being the belief that people either shot them or ate them and sometimes both.

'Yes, Fluffy's my pet. She's nervous of men,' Zara remarked, wishing she had been as sensibly wary as Fluffy when she had first met him, for it might have protected her from harm.

Indeed in a rage of antipathy, she was looking fixedly at Vitale. Somehow she couldn't stop looking and all of a sudden and without the smallest warning she was recalling much more of that night in the love nest in the Tuscan hills than was necessary or decent. She remembered the early morning light gleaming over the black density of his tousled hair. She had run her fingers through that hair before she ran them over the corrugated flatness of his incredibly muscular torso and traced the silken length of his shaft, exploring him in a way she had never wanted or needed to explore any other man. Her heart was beating so fast in remembrance of those intimacies that she wanted to press a hand against it to slow it down before it banged so hard it burst loose from her chest.

'I don't know if I'm pregnant or not yet,' she admitted frankly, descending straight to the prosaic in the hope of bringing herself back down to planet earth again, safe from such dangerous mental wanderings. He might be gorgeous but he was her enemy and a callous con artist and she hated him for what he had done to her.

Still disconcerted by the presence of a bunny rabbit whose quivering nose was poking out of the elaborate hutch, Vitale frowned, uneasy with a situation he had never been in before. The sort of lovers he usually had took precautions and accidents didn't happen, or at least if they did they were kept quiet, he acknowledged cynically. 'I believe there are tests you can do.'

'I'll buy one and let you know the result when I've done it,' she muttered carelessly. 'But right now I've got more important things to worry about—'

Vitale raised a brow. 'Such as…what exactly?'

'Fluffy, my pet rabbit—what am I going to do with her? My neighbour has already lodged a complaint and you heard the landlord! He wouldn't budge an inch. He's going to chuck me out of here if I don't rehome Fluffy!' she exclaimed.

'Rules are rules,' Vitale pronounced, a little out of

his depth when it came to keeping pets because he had never had one of any kind. It was a challenge for him to understand the depth of her attachment to the animal, but her distraught expression did get the message across. Growing exasperation gripped him. 'Perhaps you could give the rabbit away.'

Zara dealt him a furious look of condemnation. 'I couldn't give Fluffy away!' she gasped. 'She's been with me since my sixteenth birthday and I love her. Thanks to you I've been put through an awful lot of grief over the last couple of weeks but I can cope with it because I'm strong.'

Vitale was still very much focused on what was most important to him and detached from the rabbit scenario. 'I'll buy you a pregnancy test and bring it back here—'

'Don't put yourself out!' Zara slung him a seething look of hatred that startled him, for he had not appreciated that those lavender eyes could telegraph that amount of aversion.

Vitale compressed his sensual mouth and heaved a sigh. 'I must. I'm equally involved in this situation and I can't relax until we have found out where we stand.'

'Well, if wondering about where you stand is all you're worrying about I can help you right now!' Zara fired back at him. 'I hate you. If I find out I'm pregnant, I'll hate you even more. What will I do? I'll trail you through every court in the land for financial support and I'll hope it embarrasses the hell out of you!'

Vitale dealt her a seething look of impatience. 'If you are pregnant you won't have to trail me through a court for financial support. I would pick up the bills without argument.'

Unimpressed by that declaration and cringing at the unhappy thought of being beholden to him, Zara stood so straight her spine ached and her eyes glowed like embers in a banked down fire. 'Then I'll fight *not* to accept your financial support!' she slung back.

Vitale was not slow on the uptake and he got the message that whatever it took she was currently out for his blood. As there was nothing that whet his appetite more than a challenge, a sardonic smile slashed his wonderfully well-shaped mouth. She didn't know who she was dealing with. 'I'll be back soon,' he warned her before he turned on his heel.

'You're not the Terminator,' she told his back acidly before the lift doors closed on him.

Vitale, her sleek sophisticated banker, had gone to buy her a pregnancy test, surely a humble task beneath his high-powered notice? He was not hers, she scolded herself angrily, marvelling that such a designation had even occurred to her. Why was she even speaking to him? Her period was already four days late, a fact she had kept pushed to the back of her mind because she already had more than she could handle on her plate. Usually, however, she was as regular as clockwork in that department, so her disrupted cycle was a source of concern. She stroked Fluffy, inwardly admitting that she really didn't want to do a test yet because she much preferred to keep her spirits up by concentrating on sunnier prospects. My goodness, she reflected with a creeping feeling of apprehension, becoming a single parent in her current circumstances would be a nightmare.

Within the hour, Vitale returned and handed her a carrier bag. Zara extracted, not one, but four different boxes containing pregnancy-testing kits.

'I had no idea which you would prefer,' Vitale declared without a shade of discomfiture. Zara dug into the biggest box and extracted the instructions. The print was so tiny she couldn't read it and the diagram just blurred. Her hand shook, a sense of intense humiliation threatening to eat her alive and turning her skin clammy with perspiration. 'Go home,' she told him shakily.

'Why? I might as well wait.' Vitale's impatience to know the result was etched on his face and hummed from his taut restive stance. He lifted one of the other boxes. 'Use that one. From what I read on the box I understand it can give an immediate result.'

Grateful for that information, Zara took it and unwrapped it, spreading out the instructions on the table with a careful hand, squinting down at it as calmly as she could in an unsuccessful attempt to focus on the minuscule print. All she could see was a blur of mismatched symbols. She thought it was most probably her mood and the awful awareness that she had an audience that was making her dyslexia even worse than it usually was. She needed to stay calm and focused but just at that instant her self-discipline was absent.

'What's wrong?' Vitale queried rather curtly.

Zara breathed in slow and deep. 'The print is so small I can't read it,' she complained.

Assuming that she had imperfect sight but was not

prepared to own up to the fact or indeed have anything done about it, Vitale suppressed a groan and lifted the sheet to read the relevant sentences. Zara would have much preferred to have read it herself. Her cheeks flared red and hot but, veiling her gaze, she made no comment. As she locked herself into the tiny shower room with the kit she thought that anything was better than him discovering the truth about her affliction.

Only when Zara reached sixth form had a concerned teacher asked her mother to allow an educational psychologist to test her daughter. Identified as severely dyslexic, Zara had finally been offered the assistance that she needed to catch up with her peers. Unfortunately by that stage her self-esteem had sunk to rock-bottom and she had been unable to believe that reasonable exam grades might be within her reach. Her father, after all, had immediately dismissed her dyslexia as a 'poor excuse for stupidity' and had refused to credit the existence of such a condition.

Although a speech-language therapist had been recommended to teach Zara how to handle the problem, her father had refused to consider that option, saying it would be a waste of time and money. Unsurprisingly Zara had never recovered from her father's shame and disgust at the news that his daughter suffered from something labelled 'a learning disability'. It was a subject never ever mentioned in her home but she often suspected it was the main reason why her parents continued to look on her as some sort of perpetual child, rather than the adult that she was.

Zara stood in the shower room with her attention on

the novelty wall clock left behind by a previous tenant, refusing to allow herself to simply stare at the test to see if it had changed colour. The waiting time up, she straightened her shoulders and finally directed her gaze to the tiny viewing window on the test wand and there was the line of confirmation that she had most feared to see. Her legs almost buckled beneath her and she broke out in a cold sweat of horror.

Wrenching open the door, Zara reeled out. 'It's bad news, I'm afraid,' she proclaimed jaggedly.

'Let me see.' Accustomed to trusting in only his own powers of observation, Vitale insisted on checking the test. He might have paled had his attention not been on Zara, who was displaying more than enough shock and consternation for both of them.

'You can leave now,' she told him woodenly.

But Vitale stayed where he was, his attention involuntarily fixing to her flat stomach. A baby, she was going to have *his* baby. He was going to have a child with Monty Blake's daughter. He was utterly appalled at the news. A selfish moment of inattention in the heat of passion was all it had taken to permanently change both their lives. Yet he more than anyone had known the potential cost of such negligence and had the least excuse for the oversight, he conceded with stormy self-loathing.

'I can't simply leave you like this,' Vitale declared with a harsh edge to his deep drawl.

'Why not?' Zara gave him a deadened look, still too traumatised to think beyond what she had just learned about her own body. 'Don't you think you've already done enough?'

In the face of that unnecessary reminder, Vitale stood his ground. It was a bad moment but in almost thirty years he had lived through an awful lot of bad moments and he would not allow himself to flinch from anything unpleasant. But for him the worst aspect was that this was an event outside his control and he liked that reality least of all. 'I'd like to deal with this before I leave.'

Zara folded her arms and lifted her chin, suspicious of that particular choice of wording. '*Deal* with it?' she questioned, astonished by the current of protectiveness towards her unborn child that sprang into being inside her and stiffened every defensive muscle. 'I should tell you now—I'm not prepared to have a termination—'

'I'm not asking you to consider that option,' Vitale countered, exasperated by her drama, craving a sensible solution even though he already knew there probably wasn't one. 'You don't trust me but I assure you that I will only act in my child's best interests.'

Zara was unimpressed. How could she trust anything he said? How did she know that getting her pregnant hadn't been part of his revenge? Hadn't he accused her father of getting his sister pregnant? How much faith could she put in Vitale's promises now?

'That's quite a sudden change of attitude you've had,' she remarked in a brittle voice.

His lips set in a firm line, his eyes flaring bright and forceful before he cloaked them. Even though she tried not to, she found herself staring because, regardless of her hatred and distrust, nothing could alter the reality that he was sleek and dark and beautiful as sin.

'Whether I like it or not the fact that you're going to have my child does change everything between us,' he responded darkly.

Zara released a tart laugh of disagreement. 'Even though you believe that my father is the equivalent of a murderer and hate me for being his daughter?'

Anger lent a feverish hint of colour to his exotic high cheekbones and gave Vitale's appearance such striking strength and magnetism. 'I do *not* hate you.'

Scorn crossed Zara's heart-shaped face. 'You're not being honest with yourself. You hate me for the blood that runs in my veins. How else could you think it was acceptable to treat me so badly?'

Vitale did not think in the emotive terms that came so naturally to her. He was in a stormy mood, naturally resentful of the predicament they were in, but still logical enough to accept that anger would do nothing to solve the problems they faced. He saw even less sense in harking back to the past. 'The day we learn that you are carrying my baby is not the time to discuss such issues,' he told flatly. 'We have more important matters to consider—'

'The fact that I hate and distrust you tends to overpower every other impression,' Zara shot back at him, furious at being targeted by that superior little speech and wishing that she knew exactly what he was thinking. Unfortunately that lean darkly handsome face was uniquely uninformative.

'At the very least I would ask you to see a doctor for a check-up as soon as possible,' Vitale advised.

'When I can find the time.' Zara glanced at her watch. 'You really do have to leave. I have an appointment with a client in an hour and I'm not even dressed yet! Oh, my goodness, I forgot, what am I going to do about Fluffy?'

Vitale's sculpted lips parted. 'I'll take her,' he said, startling himself with that announcement almost as much as he startled his companion.

'Are you serious?' Zara stared back at him in stunned disbelief.

'Why not?' Having made the offer, Vitale refused to back down from the challenge. She had quite sufficient thoughts to occupy her without stressing about her pet's impending homelessness. She needed peace of mind to concentrate on her own condition and if removing the wretched rabbit could deliver that he was willing to take care of the problem for her.

'You can't give her away to someone, you know,' she warned him doubtfully. 'Or have her put down or anything like that.'

Vitale dealt her a grimly comprehensive scrutiny, now fully acquainted with how low she feared he might sink even when it came to a dumb animal. 'In this instance you can be confident that your pet will enjoy the best of care.'

Zara frowned, glancing worriedly at the little animal. 'You're not planning to just dump her in a pet-care place, are you? They're always full of dogs and she's terrified of dogs.'

As that was exactly what Vitale had planned to do with Fluffy, it was a tribute to his ability to think fast that he didn't betray a shred of discomfiture. 'Of course not,' he insisted as though such a thought had not even occurred to him.

Vitale then learned a great deal more than he ever cared to know about bunny rabbits. Fluffy did not travel light either. Even with Zara helping it took two trips down to his car to transport all Fluffy's possessions.

'I'll look after her,' he asserted, challenged to retain his patience.

'I'll need your phone number,' Zara told him. 'I'll ring you later to see how you're getting on.'

If ever there was a moment when an unprecedented attack of benevolence on his part had paid off this was it, Vitale recognised with fearless self-honesty. Ironically the mother of his unborn child was more concerned about her pet than about herself, but an avenue of communication had at least opened again. He was going to be a father. The shock of that thought suddenly engulfed Vitale like an avalanche. A baby, he was thinking in a daze of lingering horror as he installed Fluffy in her three deck condo in the corner of his open plan lounge. The brightly coloured plastic rabbit version of a palace with all mod cons looked incongruous against his elegant décor.

On learning that the rabbit was there to stay for the foreseeable future, Vitale's part-time housekeeper told him thinly that she was allergic to animal fur, and when he failed to offer an immediate solution she handed in her notice on the spot. Zara phoned briefly just to tell

Vitale that Fluffy liked MTV for company, apparently being a bunny with a musical bent.

'Tough luck, Fluff,' Vitale breathed, switching on the business channel to catch the most recent stock figures. 'The guy with the remote calls all the shots.'

Fluffy sidled into view like a bunny with a very good idea of how welcome a house guest she was. She slunk along the skirting and then settled down happily to munch at the corner of a very expensive rug. As Vitale rose to intervene and Fluffy took fright at the movement and fled back to her condo it occurred to him that a young child would, at times, be equally trying to his reserves of patience.

That was, if Zara Blake *allowed* him anywhere near their child. His blood ran cold with apprehension as he pictured that possible scenario of parental powerlessness. He cursed the situation he was in. He had several good friends supporting children they rarely, if ever, saw. He knew that a child's mother generally controlled how much access a father might receive and he was well aware that some mothers preferred not to share. As an unmarried father he would have virtually no rights at all over his own flesh and blood. Vitale had been the son of an unstable mother and the defenceless victim of an abusive stepfather. That he might have little say in his own child's upbringing was a prospect that Vitale could not bear to contemplate. How would he ever be able to protect his child from the risk of abuse? His appetite for work suddenly abating, Vitale shut down his laptop. He fed Fluffy, who had the fine taste of a gourmand, and then he paced the floor to consider his options with a new driving urgency.

In the meantime, Zara was having a very busy day. She spent an hour chatting to a potential client before checking out the current job that Blooming Perfect was engaged in and finally returning to the firm's office to finish a plan.

'It really is quite something,' Rob remarked when he saw the plan she had completed for the villa in Italy.

Zara smiled as she rolled it up and slotted it into a protective cardboard tube. 'Well, we'll see.'

'When will the client get it?'

'This week. He's staying in London.'

'Convenient,' Rob commented, already engaged in closing up for the night.

Only as she drove back to her new apartment and struggled to find a parking spot was Zara at long last free to think of the tiny seed of life growing inside her. A baby, *her* baby. She could still hardly believe it was true and could not suppress a sense of wonderment over the conception that embarrassed her. After all, she could hardly celebrate falling pregnant by a man with whom she no longer had a relationship. That was very bad news for her child. Or was it? Thinking about her own father, Zara was not sure that she had ever enjoyed a single advantage from his presence in her life and he was a fearsome man in a temper. On the other hand she had friends who adored their fathers and found them very supportive and good at giving advice, she conceded fairly.

Her unplanned pregnancy would also give her parents yet another reason to criticise her, although they would have fewer grounds than most to complain, because Zara and her brother had been eight years old before their parents even moved in together. Certainly her father had been in no hurry to commit to the mother of his twins. Indeed even at that point Monty Blake must already have been involved with her sister Tawny's mother.

But Zara was not like either of her parents and she told herself that there was no reason why she shouldn't make a good single mother. As she had no trust fund to fall back on she was lucky to have Edith's business to help her survive on the financial front. She was strong and sensible. In a crisis she would bend, not break, and she was willing to make the best of things. So, she had been more than a little foolish over Vitale? She just had to learn to live with that as he was no doubt learning to live with Fluffy. The serious expression on Zara's face slid away and she almost smiled at that incongruous image. Now that offer of his to look after her pet had come as an enormous surprise. But then Vitale was deep, so deep and complex that she couldn't fathom him and she quite understood how she had been taken in by him. Vitale did not wear his true and tricky nature on the surface.

As she was wondering what to make for her evening meal her cell phone beeped with a text.

Join me for dinner? I'll cook. V

No, absolutely not, Zara thought in dismay and annoyance. What was he playing at? And then a more responsible inner voice reminded her that she was set to have a relationship with Vitale through her child that would stretch quite a few years into her future. Ignoring him, refusing to see him or speak to him might be tempting, but it would not be the sensible path to follow. Sadly, on one issue Vitale was correct. Her pregnancy did mean that everything had changed, although her feelings towards him hadn't changed in the slightest: she still hated him like poison. Bolstered by that conviction, Zara texted back her agreement. After all, meeting up with Vitale would also provide her with an easy way of delivering the plan for the grounds of the Italian villa.

CHAPTER SEVEN

FLUFFY was watching television on the leather sofa when Vitale returned to his apartment that evening. He wouldn't have believed it if he hadn't seen it with his own eyes: the wretched bunny was watching music videos while basking in the comfort of a well-upholstered seat! But no sooner did Zara's pet hear the noise of the front door closing than it raced like a furry streak for the safety of its home in the corner. And there, in spite of the food Vitale brought it, the rabbit stayed firmly out of sight.

But Fluffy had not spent an entirely lazy day, Vitale noted grimly, because the rug had been chewed and the wooden foot of a coffee table had been gnawed. It was a destructive bunny rabbit, utterly unsuited to civilised life in a luxury apartment. On the other hand, Zara had agreed to come to dinner, most probably because she wanted to see how her pet was doing.

The plan for the villa tucked below one arm, Zara arrived sporting an ice-blue dress teamed with incredibly high heels. The pale shade accentuated her eyes and her hair shimmered round her shoulders. For the first time ever Vitale admired a woman's legs and then, quite unnervingly for him, thought of her safety instead. What if she stumbled and fell and got hurt?

'Those shoes are like stilts,' he remarked before he could think better of the comment, only to watch in amazement as Fluffy bounded out into the hall to greet her mistress and gambol round her feet in a welcoming display.

Zara petted Fluffy and talked to her. Anything was better than focusing on Vitale, breathtakingly handsome even casually clad in jeans and an open-necked black shirt. She decided that she was horrendously overdressed and felt as though she had lost face in some secret contest of who could act the most laid-back. Her heart was doing that bang-bang-bang thing again but that was just the natural effect of Vitale's manifold attractions hitting her defences with all the subtlety of a ten-ton truck.

He served the meal immediately in the spacious dining annexe off the lounge. He had made steak and salad, nothing fancy, but she was impressed all the same, her one and only attempt to cook steak having resulted in a lump of tough and rubbery meat that nobody could eat. The silence stretching between them seemed to shout in her ears, reminding her with a painful pang of regret how easily they had once talked in Italy. That, of course, she recalled, had only been part and parcel of his deception.

'How do you feel?' Vitale asked her levelly.

'Like I'm stuck inside a soap bubble. The baby

doesn't really feel real yet, probably because it's such an unexpected development,' she admitted.

'I intend to give you all the support that I can.'

At that austere unemotional promise, a tight little smile formed on Zara's lips. 'Then give me space.'

Space was the very last thing Vitale could imagine offering her at that moment. In one of those infuriating shifts of awareness that infiltrated his formidable calm a surge of heat consumed him as he focused on her luscious mouth and recalled what she could do with it. Subjected to an instant erection, Vitale breathed in deep and slow, furiously willing his undisciplined body back under control and deeply resentful of the effect she could have on him. 'I don't think I can do that. I feel responsible for you now.'

Her eyes were cool and flat as glass. 'But that's not how I feel and not what I want.'

'Don't make our child pay the price for what I did in Italy,' he urged her forcefully, already concerned about a future in which he might not be in a position to ensure that his child received the very best of care.

'Maybe I'm thinking that after what you did to me you might be a bad influence to have in a child's life,' Zara told him honestly.

In receipt of that admission, his strong bone structure showed prominently below his bronzed skin and his jaw line clenched hard. In one sense he was outraged that Monty Blake's daughter could question his integrity when her father had none whatsoever. But he could hardly expect her to appreciate that when he had deceived her in Tuscany. He should be grateful, however, that she refused to see him as her only support in a hostile world just because she had fallen pregnant by him. After all, just how much was he prepared to sacrifice to ensure his child's welfare?

'I'm trying to forge a new and different relationship with you,' he delivered tautly.

She gazed into his stunning dark eyes and it was as if a thousand butterflies fluttered free in the pit of her stomach. Instantly she closed him out again, refusing to be entrapped by his raw physical appeal. 'I can't give you a fresh start with me. I don't forgive men who try to use me.'

His brows drew together as he picked up on the pained note she could not suppress. 'There was someone else? Who? What did he do?'

Zara dealt him a bleak look and then wondered what she had to hide. Maybe if she explained he'd understand that there was no way back into her good graces. 'I met Julian when I was eighteen. He was twenty five and he told me he loved me. After he had asked me to marry him he took me away for a weekend. The first night he got me drunk in our hotel room...' Her strained voice ran out of steam and power, her heart-shaped face drawn, her eyes haunted by unpleasant memories. 'I must've passed out. When I came round he had me handcuffed half naked to the headboard of the bed—'

'He had you...*what*?' Vitale repeated in thunderous disbelief.

'When I opened my eyes he had a camera trained on me. All he wanted was sleazy photos of me undressed, so that he could blackmail my father with them. He took my clothes off while I was unconscious. He hadn't even bothered to wait until after he had slept with me—but then he wasn't that interested.' A laugh that had a wounded edge fell from her lips. 'In fact he said I wasn't really his type, he preferred curvy brunettes—'

'Per amor di Dio!' Vitale had a disturbing image of her naked and bewildered, innocent and frightened. The newly protective instincts he had formed since he learnt of her pregnancy were inflamed by the idea of her being stripped of her dignity and at the mercy of a man who only saw her as a source of profit. Julian had badly betrayed her trust when she was still very young and naïve. Vitale refused to think about the damage he might have done pursuing revenge on his sister's account. Regretting the past was always, in his opinion, a waste of time.

'My father may be a womaniser but he's a complete dinosaur when it comes to the behaviour of the women in his family and very conscious of his public image. He paid up and the photos were destroyed although I still haven't heard the last of that disaster even now,' Zara confided painfully. 'I got Julian thrown in my face again last week and the week before. I was young and stupid and too easily impressed, but that's twice I've seriously embarrassed my family now.'

'But what Julian did was criminal. He assaulted you. You father should've reported him to the police.'

'Dad didn't want to risk the newspapers getting hold of the story. It's ancient history now.' Zara's tone was dismissive and she lifted her chin. 'And I thought I had learned my lesson with Julian, but then I met you.'

'What happened between us in Italy is over and done with—'

'Is it? It may be over but it's not forgotten,' Zara pointed out, her quiet voice harshening with the antipathy she was struggling to restrain. 'And I'm not going to give you the chance to cause me any more grief.'

Vitale realised that in the light she saw him now, only the ultimate sacrifice was likely to convince her of the strength of his intentions. With every fibre of his being he baulked at that option, for marriage was a hell of a price to pay for a contraceptive oversight. Yet how else could he make sure that he had a permanent place in his future child's life? How else could he acquire the legal rights with which he could always protect his child from any threat? And how could she possibly cope well as a single parent without adequate family support? Yet if he married her, he would lose the freedom he valued, the choices he luxuriated in and the privacy he had always cherished. Suppressing his reluctance and his resentment, Vitale recalled his own wretched childhood and accepted that no price was too high if it protected his unborn son or daughter from the risk of growing up in a similar hell.

Vitale studied Zara carefully. 'Will that answer still hold good even if I ask you to marry me?'

Zara jerked in astonishment, her brow furrowing, her eyes wide as she decided that that must be his idea of a joke after what she had told him about Julian using a marriage proposal to gain her trust. 'You can't be serious.'

'I am perfectly serious—I'm asking you to be my

wife,' Vitale countered with cool assurance. 'In the hope that we can raise our child together.'

'Not so long ago you told me that you avoided women with wedding rings in their eyes and that that's why you're still single,' she reminded him ruefully.

'But then you fell pregnant with my child and naturally my priorities altered,' Vitale pointed out drily. 'We can't turn the clock back. We have to look to the future.'

Her appetite having disappeared in tune with the tension rising in the atmosphere, Zara pushed aside the dessert and stood up, her eyes dark with strain. If an offer of marriage was his attempt at restitution he could forget it—she was not about to be taken in again. 'No, absolutely not. You don't need to worry. The baby and I will be fine on our own. Thankfully I'm not a helpless teenage girl with no idea how to manage—'

Vitale was not convinced by that argument. He sprang up to his full commanding height, the vital force and energy of his gaze welded to her. 'We have to talk this out. Don't leave.'

Zara veiled her eyes and fought to recapture the composure he had cracked with his astonishing proposal. 'I wasn't leaving yet. I've brought the villa plan with me. If you've finished eating we can look at it now.'

Desperate for a distraction, Zara removed the plan from the tube and spread it on the unused portion of the polished table. She explained the meaning of various symbols she had used and discussed possibilities. Vitale was impressed by the intricate detail of the design, not having appreciated that she would actually be drawing the plans with her own fair hand.

'Those borders—could some of them be left empty?'

Her brow furrowed. 'Yes, of course, but—'

'The lady whom I hope will be living there,' Vitale began with uncharacteristic hesitancy lacing his dark deep voice, 'may have an interest in the garden and if the planting is not quite complete that may encourage her to get more involved.'

'That's a good idea,' Zara remarked, insanely curious about the identity of the individual, for he had been careful to keep that information confidential when they had been together in Italy. His innate reserve would always seek to impose distance between them, she registered. He was not a man given to casual confidences and he kept his own counsel. Working out what made him tick would always be a challenge for her.

Zara laughed when Fluffy nudged her ankle with one of her toys and Vitale watched in surprise as Zara threw it and the rabbit played fetch. 'She loves games,' she told him, a natural smile chasing the tension from her lush mouth.

Vitale watched her stroke the rabbit's head with delicate fingers. She was so gentle with the little animal and it clearly adored her. 'I was serious about the proposal,' he asserted, exasperated that she could think otherwise.

'Being pregnant isn't a good enough reason to get married,' Zara replied doggedly, her senses awakened by the faint aromatic hint of his cologne assailing her nostrils because he was standing close to her. Even the scent of him was awesomely familiar. Her spine stiffened as tingling warmth pooled at the heart of her, her body instantly reacting to the proximity of his. He was pure temptation but she was too much on her guard to betray the weakness he could evoke.

His frustration increasing, Vitale stared down at her with brooding dark eyes. 'It is very important to me that I should be in a position to play a proper part in my child's life—'

'You don't have to marry me to play that part—'

Thinking of his destroyed childhood with his cruel stepfather, Vitale barely repressed a shudder of disagreement. 'If we're not married, if we stay separate, we will both end up with other partners and it will be much more difficult—'

'But other people manage it,' Zara sliced in flatly even as her heart clenched at the very thought of him with another woman.

It was going to happen, possibly had even happened already, she scolded herself angrily. Vitale was going to be with other women and she had to adapt to that idea. That the idea bothered her was just some weird jealous and possessive prompting, most probably because he had become her first lover. On the other hand, a scheming little voice murmured somewhere in the depths of her brain, if *you* married him, nobody else could have him. She stifled that inner voice, embarrassed by its foolishness.

The following morning Zara attended an appointment with her GP. He confirmed the test results and sent her off to see the practice nurse, who gave her a bunch of leaflets packed with pregnancy advice. They were still clutched in her hand when a man walking past her in the street knocked her shoulder, loosening her grip so that the sheets spun across the pavement in an arc. As the man sped on without noticing Zara stooped to pick up the leaflets.

'*Zara?*' a familiar voice queried and Zara straightened, recognising the elegant brunette. 'I wasn't expecting to see you round this neighbourhood. Didn't I hear that you'd moved to another part of town?'

Meeting Ella's big blue curious eyes, Zara reddened. 'Yes, I have—'

'Oh, my goodness, are those for you?' Ella exclaimed, flicking one of the leaflets, which clearly showed a pregnant woman, with a manicured fingernail and accompanying the question with a delighted squeal. 'Are you pregnant?'

'I'm meeting someone in ten minutes. Lovely seeing you again, Ella,' Zara fielded with a bright smile, stuffing the informative leaflets into her bag and walking on without further comment. Her cheeks were hot as she queried her bad luck at running into one of the biggest gossips she knew at the wrong moment.

Vitale was not having a good day either. He had offered to fall on his sword like a proper little soldier when he had asked her to marry him. The sacrifice had been necessary: she was carrying his baby and he had a deep need to be a genuine part of his child's life. But it would also entail sharing his life. When had he ever dreamt of sharing his life with another person?

When had he ever longed for a child of his own? He had never wanted those things and his entire life had been devoted to achieving emotional self-sufficiency. He told himself that he should be grateful that she had turned him down. He should walk away while he could, avoid getting personally involved. He should be content to ensure that his only responsibility towards her and the child was financial. Why could he not settle for that eminently practical option? Realistically what were the chances that Zara would some day bring a man into her life as brutal as Vitale's late stepfather?

Zara was at Blooming Perfect going through the accounts with Rob when Jono phoned her and drew her attention to a paragraph in a gossip column. Although she was grateful for the warning her heart sank and she went out to buy the paper and there it was, clearly the result of a tip-off from Ella or one of her pals, the loaded suggestion that party girl and socialite Zara Blake might be expecting a baby. Her phone rang again: it was her mother asking her to come home for a chat.

Zara knew what she was going to be asked and she definitely didn't want to go and face the music. Unfortunately being adult and independent demanded that she not avoid the inevitable, no matter how unpleasant it might prove to be. Monty and Ingrid Blake were going to be even more disappointed in her than they already were. An unmarried pregnant daughter was no consolation for one who mere weeks ago had been set to marry a Greek billionaire in the society wedding of the year.

'Is it true?' Ingrid Blake demanded the instant her daughter entered the sparsely furnished drawing room where elegance counted for more than comfort.

Her heart beating very fast, Zara glanced nervously at her father standing by the fireplace, his still-handsome face set hard as granite. 'Yes, I'm pregnant.'

'We'll organise a termination for you straight away,' her mother said without an ounce of hesitation.

Zara straightened her slight shoulders and eased them back. 'No. I want to have my baby.'

'Who's the father?' Monty Blake growled.

'I'm sorry but I don't want to discuss that.'

'I bet you don't, you brainless little—' the older man launched furiously at her, a red flush of rage staining his cheeks.

Her tension palpable, Zara's mother rested a soothing hand lightly on her husband's arm. 'Don't let her upset you, darling… She's not worth it—'

'You're telling me, she's not!' Monty Blake seethed, grinding his teeth as he strode forward, his face a mask of fury. 'It's out of the question for you to have this baby.'

Struggling not to back away from her enraged parent as she had so often seen her mother do without any happy result, Zara stood her ground.

'Listen to your father for once, Zara,' Ingrid ordered thinly. 'You simply *can't* have this baby! Be reasonable. Once you have a child in tow, your life will be ruined.'

'Did Tom and I ruin your life?' Zara asked painfully, deeply hurt that her mother could so immediately dismiss the prospect of her first grandchild being born.

'Don't you dare mention your brother's name, you stupid little cow!' Monty Blake spat at her, erupting into a white hot rage at that fatal reference and swinging up his hand to slap her hard across one cheekbone.

Eyes filling with fear and pain, Zara was almost unbalanced by the force of that blow and she had to step back to stay upright. Her hand crept up to press against her hot, stinging cheek. 'Don't you dare hit me,' she told her father angrily. 'I should call the police on you—'

'Don't be silly,' her mother interrupted in alarm at such a threat from her daughter. 'You asked for it.'

'The same way you always did?' Zara prompted shakily before turning scornful eyes on her father. 'I'll never set foot in this house again.'

'We'll live,' her father shot back at her with derision. 'You're no loss!'

Sick with shock in the aftermath of that traumatic confrontation, Zara returned to her apartment. When she climbed out of her car she could feel something trickling down her face and when she dashed it away saw blood on the side of her hand. In her compact mirror she saw the cut on her cheek where the stone in her father's signet ring must have broken the skin. She couldn't still the shaking in her body, but she was asking herself why she was so surprised by what had happened for, although it was the first time that her father had hit her since she had become an adult, it was far from being the first time that he had struck her.

It was a fact of Zara's childhood that Monty Blake had an unmanageable temper and that he lashed out with his fists whenever he lost control. Usually Ingrid had paid the price of her husband's need for violence to satisfy his rage or frustration. In fact as a terrified child of ten years old seeing her mother beaten up Zara had once called the police and the fallout from that unwelcome intervention had taught her an unforgettable lesson. Branded a wicked liar and winning even her twin's censure for 'letting down' the family, she had been sent away to boarding school. That night she had learned that anything that happened behind the doors of the Blakes' smart town house was strictly private and not for sharing, not even with Bee.

'It's between Mum and Dad—it's nothing to do with us. He hardly ever lifts the hand to either of us,' Tom used to point out when they were teenagers. 'It's only the odd slap or punch—I'm sure there's a lot worse goes on in other families.'

But dread of their father's sudden violent outbursts had created a horribly intimidating atmosphere in Zara's home while she was growing up. All of them had worked very hard at trying to please or soothe Monty Blake. Tom, the apple of his father's eye, had always been the most successful. The aggressive attacks on their mother, however, had continued in secret for occasionally Zara had noticed that her mother was moving slowly and stiffly as if she was in pain and had known that her father was usually too careful to plant a fist where a bruise might show.

By the time she reached her apartment stress had given Zara a nasty headache and her face was hurting her like mad. She was on the brink of taking painkillers before she remembered that she was pregnant and realised that without medical advice it would be safer to do without medication. She examined her swollen cheekbone in the mirror. It was hot and red and a livid scratch trailed across her skin while the darkening of her eye socket suggested that a bruise was forming. When the buzzer on her door sounded she snatched up her sunglasses and put them on.

It was Vitale, long and lean in a black business suit and impatiently about to stab on the buzzer a second time when she opened the door. His hand fell back from the wood and he stared down at her.

'Why are you wearing sunglasses indoors?' he questioned, strolling past her although she had not invited him in.

Just as Zara frowned Vitale flipped the specs off her nose and stilled when he saw her battered face. 'What the hell happened to you?' he growled angrily.

'I fell…tripped at the nursery,' she lied.

'Don't lie to me. I can spot a lie at sixty paces,' Vitale warned her, frowning as he traced the swelling with a gentle fingertip. 'This looks more like someone punched you.'

'Don't be ridiculous,' Zara said in a wobbly voice, her eyes welling up with tears. 'Why are you here?'

Vitale tossed down the newspaper he carried in a silent statement. It was the same edition that had implied that she might be pregnant.

'Oh, that…' she muttered abstractedly as he closed the door behind him. Although she had only read that gossip column this morning it already felt as if a hundred years had passed since then.

'I don't believe that you fell. I want to know who did that to your face. Who hit you?' Vitale breathed soft and low, but there was a fire in his penetrating gaze. 'I think you might have a black eye tomorrow.'

Nervousness made it difficult for Zara to swallow and her throat was tight. She was tired and upset and sore. 'It's not important.'

'You've been assaulted. How can that not be important?' Vitale demanded, cutting through her weary voice. 'Who are you trying to protect?'

Zara paled at that accurate stab in the dark, but the habit of secrecy where her family was concerned was too deeply engrained in her to be easily broken. 'I'm not protecting anyone.'

'You're pregnant. What sort of a person attacks a pregnant woman?' he demanded rawly. 'He could have hit your stomach rather than your face, causing you to miscarry—would you still be protecting him then?'

The hunted expression in Zara's strained eyes deepened as she dropped her head to avoid his searing gaze. 'I don't want to talk about this, Vitale.'

He closed a hand round hers and drew her closer. 'I'm not leaving until you tell me. When you were attacked our child was put at risk and I can't walk away from that.'

Reminded of her responsibility towards the baby she carried, Zara was engulfed by a dreadful tide of guilt. Her opposing loyalties made her feel torn in two and suddenly her resistance washed away in the tide of her distress. 'It was my father…okay?' she cried defiantly as she wrenched her hand free of Vitale's hold. 'But he didn't mean anything by it—he just loses his temper and lashes out—'

'Your...*father*?' His eyes flaring like golden fireworks, Vitale's angry voice actually shook, his accent thickening around the syllables as he yanked open the door again.

'Where are you going?' In consternation, Zara followed him and grabbed his arm to force him to stop in his tracks. 'What do you think you're going to do?'

Eyes veiled, Vitale rested his livid gaze on her anxious face. 'I'll make sure that this never happens again.'

'How can you do that? I don't want you fighting with my father... I don't want people to find out about this—it's private!' Zara gasped, clutching at the well-cut jacket of his business suit with frantic hands.

Vitale closed his fingers round her fragile wrists and gently detached her grip. His face was forbidding in its austerity, his eyes hard as iron. 'I'm not about to fight with your father. I am not planning to tell anyone else about this either—that is your choice to make. But I *am* going to make sure that he never ever dares to lay a finger on you again,' he spelt out in a wrathful undertone. 'I'll see you later.'

Left alone, Zara trembled from the force of all the emotions she was fighting to contain. She was shaking with stress. Her father would lose his head again when Vitale approached him and made his accusation. The older man would know that once again his daughter had talked. A headache hammered painfully behind her taut brow and she sank down on the edge of the bed and breathed in slow and deep in an attempt to calm down. She was appalled by Vitale's interference but even more shocked that she had surrendered and told him the truth. For so many years she had kept that family shame a deep, dark secret. Now all hell was about to break loose because she had just given a man who already hated her father another reason to despise and attack him.

For an instant though Zara was mentally swept back to the elegant drawing room where she had been rocked back on her heels by her father's blow. Whether she liked it or not she had to admit that Vitale had made a valid point. Had she fallen she might have injured her baby or even miscarried. There was no excuse for her father's violence; there never had been an excuse for his behaviour. But while she accepted that truth, intellectually dealing with something that had become so much a part of her family life was altogether something else. It had been her mother's refusal to condemn her husband's violence that had set the agenda of acceptance in Zara's home. Although it hurt to admit it, her brother Tom's insistence on ignoring the problem had also given strength to the idea that such violence had to be endured and concealed. Of course, her father had never struck Tom. Monty Blake had always aimed his violence at his womenfolk.

Feeling too sick to eat, Zara lay down on the bed and eventually fell asleep. Vitale's return wakened her and she answered the door barefoot, her hair a tousled silvery cloud round her face as she blinked up at him drowsily. She was startled to see her father standing by

Vitale's side. In the shadow of Vitale's greater height and raw energy, Monty Blake looked pale, wretched and diminished.

'Your father has something he wants to say to you,' Vitale proclaimed harshly.

'I'm sorry I hurt you—it will never happen again,' her father muttered with all the life of a battery-operated robot.

'I'm not having a termination,' she reiterated in a feverish whisper, wanting her father to know that that was not a price she was prepared to pay for family forgiveness.

In response to that revealing statement a murderous light flamed in Vitale's gaze. 'We're getting married as soon as it can be arranged,' he delivered.

Taken aback by the announcement, Zara shot him a confused glance. After all, he was already well aware of her thoughts on that subject. Dark eyes gleaming with purpose, Vitale stared back at her in blatant challenge. She parted her lips to argue and then decided to wait until her father was no longer present. She felt she owed Vitale that much after he had brought her father to her door to apologise to her. For the first time ever a man had tried to protect Zara rather than take advantage of her and she could only be impressed by that reality.

'You must do as you see fit,' Monty Blake responded flatly, turning back to Vitale to add, 'Are you satisfied?'

'For the moment, but watch your step around me and your daughter.'

Zara watched her father hurry back into the lift, keen to make his escape, and she slowly breathed in and out, the worst of her tension evaporating with his departure. 'How on earth did you persuade him to come here?'

'I didn't persuade him, I threatened him,' Vitale admitted without an ounce of regret. 'He's terrified of being forced to face the legal and social consequences of his behaviour. I'm surprised that you've never used that fear against him.'

Zara lowered her lashes, thinking of how she had been branded a troublemaking liar at the age of ten when she had tried to report her father's violence to the authorities. Nobody had backed up her story, not even her mother, and by the end of it all nobody had believed her either.

'He's hit you before, hasn't he?' Vitale prompted darkly.

'This was the first time since I grew up,' Zara admitted grudgingly. 'I don't think he can help himself. I think he needs professional help or anger-management classes but he wouldn't go to anything like that. He won't admit he has a problem.'

'Does he hit your mother?'

Zara glanced at his lean strong face and then looked away from the condemnation etched there to nod jerkily in reluctant confirmation. 'She won't do anything about it, won't even talk about it. I'm glad you didn't hit him though.'

'I would have enjoyed smashing his teeth down his throat,' Vitale admitted with a casual ease that shook her. 'But it wouldn't have helped anyone. Domestic violence is like an addiction for some men, but I believe that in your father's case the threat of public exposure might have forced him to seek treatment.'

'Did you confront him about your sister? About what happened the night that she drowned?' Zara pressed in a strained undertone.

There was a bitter light in his eyes and his sardonic mouth twisted. 'No, it wasn't the right moment for me to demand those answers. I was more concerned about you.'

Vitale swung away, his last words still echoing inside his head; even he questioned his own restraint. How could he have been more concerned about her? Granted she carried his child, but he had spent half a lifetime dreaming of a confrontation with Monty Blake. Only to discover that, in the flesh, Monty Blake was scarcely a challenging target. Loredana's former lover was a weak man, easily cowed by a more forceful personality and the threat of social humiliation.

Zara was frowning as well, marvelling that Vitale had had her father at such a disadvantage and yet had remained silent in spite of his fierce desire for revenge. 'Did he realise who you were? Didn't he recognise your name from your sister's?'

'Loredana and I had different surnames. Her name was Barigo.' His lean strong face had taken on a shuttered aspect that warned her she had touched on a sensitive subject. Vitale, she realised belatedly, had family secrets as well.

'Why on earth did you tell him that we were getting married?'

Vitale threw back his handsome dark head and settled his moody gaze on her. 'I'm convinced that when you consider your options you'll see that you have nothing to lose and everything to gain by becoming my wife—'

'How?' Zara interrupted baldly. 'I've already told you how I feel about you.'

'Take a risk on me.'

Her lips compressed. 'I don't take risks—'

'But I do. That's why I'm the CEO of a major investment bank,' Vitale told her with savage assurance. 'It makes sense for you to give marriage a chance for our child's sake. If it doesn't work out, we can get a divorce. But at least we'll know that we tried.'

Taken aback by his speech, Zara was momentarily silenced. *For our child's sake,* four little words that had immense impact on her impression of Vitale Roccanti, much as his earlier defence of her against her father had had. Slowly but surely Vitale was changing her opinion of him. Her father might not have added anything positive to her life but Vitale, she sensed, would be a far different prospect in the parenting stakes. Vitale was willing to put his money where his mouth was and put their baby's needs to the top of the pile. He was a handsome, wealthy and successful man yet he was still willing to give up his freedom to provide a more stable background for the child he had accidentally fathered. She could only admire him for that and admit that, given the choice, she would much prefer to raise her child with two parents.

'If we get married and it falls apart, it would be very upsetting for everyone concerned.'

'I would find watching you raise my child with another man infinitely *more* upsetting,' Vitale countered with blunt emphasis. 'All I'm asking you to do is give us the opportunity to see if we can make it work.'

'It's not that simple—'

Vitale released his breath in a driven hiss of impatience. 'You're the one making it complicated.'

Zara's tiny frame was rigid. Could she take a risk and give him another chance? But marriage wasn't an experiment. She could not marry him on a casual basis and walk away without concern if it failed. In her experience failure always bit deep and hurt. And just how far could she trust a man she couldn't read with any accuracy? 'I don't know enough about you. I can't forget that you plotted and planned against me.'

'I can put that past behind us if I have to, *angelina mia*. Our child's needs take precedence,' Vitale contended.

The silence buzzed. Her troubled gaze lingering on his wide, sensual mouth, she recalled the taste of him with a hot liquid surge low in her tummy that she struggled to quell. The tender flesh between her thighs dampened and a pink flush of awareness covered her face. Tensing, she looked hurriedly away from him.

'But I will be honest—I also want you,' Vitale conceded in a dark driven undertone, startling her with that additional admission. 'That's not what I chose, not what I foresaw and certainly not what I'm comfortable with. But it *is* how I feel right now. Ever since we were together in Italy I've wanted you back in my bed again.'

Although she flushed, Zara stood a little straighter,

strengthened by that raw-edged confession. It did her good to know that he was not quite as in control as he liked to pretend. Every time she looked at him she had to fight her natural response to his sleek dark magnetism. The idea that he had to fight the same attraction had considerable appeal. He bent his arrogant head, eyes narrowed to track her every change of expression with a lethal sensuality as integral to him as his aggressive take on life.

'All right, I'll give marrying you a trial for three months,' Zara declared, tilting her chin. 'If we can't make it work in that time we have to agree to split up without any recriminations on either side.'

'A sort of "try before you buy" option?' Vitale drawled silkily.

'Why not?' Feeling as though she was somewhat in control of events again, Zara settled her soft full lips into a wary smile. She could handle being attracted to him as long as he was attracted to her. If she kept a sensible grip on her emotions there was no reason why she should get hurt. Furthermore, after what he had done to her she would never make the mistake of viewing him through rose-coloured glasses again.

His hand curving to her narrow shoulder, Vitale lowered his head and claimed her mouth with his. As he pried her lips apart with the tip of his tongue an arrow of sizzling heat slivered through her with such piercing, drugging sweetness that she shivered violently in response. She dug her nails into her palms to stop herself from reaching out to him and she stood there stiff as a board while the greedy warmth and excitement of desire washed through her every skin cell, filling her with restless energy and longing.

He lifted his head again, dark golden eyes blazing with unconcealed hunger. 'I'll *make* it work for us,' he swore.

But the very fact that he acknowledged a need to work at their marriage was, to her way of thinking, the most likely reason why their efforts would fail. Natural inclinations often outgunned the best of good intentions, she reflected worriedly. Only when the going got tough would they discover how deep their commitment to a practical marriage could actually go.

CHAPTER EIGHT

Two weeks before the wedding, Vitale arranged to pick Zara up for lunch. Not having seen him at all in the preceding week owing to his demanding schedule, she was surprised by the invitation.

'I thought you were always too busy during the day for this sort of thing,' Zara reminded him of his own words on the phone several nights earlier as she climbed into his car.

'As a rule I am but this is rather different. We're going to see your father,' Vitale revealed grimly.

Her head swivelled, eyes bright with dismay and curiosity in her disconcerted face. 'Why the hell are we meeting up with Dad?'

'It's time I asked those questions about my sister's death,' Vitale volunteered tight-mouthed, his brooding tension palpable in the taut lines of his face. 'Now that we are getting married those questions have to finally be answered. He's your father. I can't leave you out of this.'

'I'm not sure I want to be there,' she confessed, disturbed by the prospect of being on the sidelines of such a sensitive confrontation. 'Although it hardly matters as relations currently stand between me and my parents, Dad won't forgive me for being present if you're planning to humiliate him.'

'I see no advantage to doing that,' Vitale admitted flatly fingers flexing and tightening round the steering wheel. 'I phoned your father first thing this morning and told him that I was Loredana's brother and that I need him to tell me the truth of what happened the night she drowned. He's had a few hours to think over his options.'

'And you think an upfront approach will work like some kind of magic charm with him?' Zara pressed doubtfully.

'Your father is not a stupid man. What does he have to lose? He knows I probably can't disprove anything he says. There were only two crew members on board that yacht. The stewardess, who was also the cook, died. Rod Baines, the sailor in charge of the boat, suffered head injuries and remembered very little about that night after he had recovered.'

Monty Blake was in his office on the first floor of the elegant flagship hotel of the Royale chain. He was standing by the window when they entered and he swung round, his mouth tightening with annoyance when he saw his daughter. 'Did you know about this connection when you got involved with the man you're planning to marry?' he demanded accusingly.

'That's not relevant. Why don't you just tell Vitale what happened that night?' Zara replied evenly.

'I told the full story at the inquest many years ago—'

'Yes, I believe you magically found yourself in the rescue dinghy and then fell conveniently unconscious while the yacht sank,' Vitale breathed witheringly. 'How long were you a part of my sister's life before that night?'

The older man grimaced. 'I wasn't a part of her life. I hardly knew her—'

'But she was pregnant—'

'Not by me, as I stated at the inquest,' Zara's father insisted quick as a flash. 'I was never intimate with her.'

Vitale frowned. 'Do I look like a fool?'

'I never got the chance. Check out the dates if you don't believe me. I met Loredana at your uncle's country house, dined with her the following week while I was at our hotel in Rome and invited her to go sailing with me at the weekend. She was a very beautiful young woman but it was a casual thing,' he declared, shooting a look of discomfiture at his daughter. 'I had quite enough complications in my life. Your mother and I were hardly speaking to each other at the time.'

Zara stiffened. 'Nothing you tell us will go beyond these walls,' she promised uneasily.

'Loredana was in a very emotional mood when she joined me that weekend,' Monty Blake revealed. 'Over our meal she admitted that she'd had a row with some boyfriend and that she was pregnant. It was hardly what I had signed up for when I invited her onto the yacht for a pleasure trip and we had a difference of opinion when I asked her why she had agreed to join me on board—'

'An argument?' Vitale queried darkly, his suspicions obvious.

'There was no big drama,' the older man replied wearily. 'Apparently Loredana only accepted my invite because she wanted to make her boyfriend jealous. She hoped he would try to stop her seeing me but he didn't and she was upset about that. When she started crying I suggested she retire to her cabin for the night—and I mean no disrespect when I say that I'd had quite enough of her histrionics by then.'

Vitale managed not to flinch but he did remember his sister as being a very emotional and vivid individual, easily roused to laughter, temper or tears. There had been no reference to an argument, no mention of Loredana's supposedly troubled state of mind during the inquest. But for all that there was a convincing ring of authenticity to the older man's story and he could imagine how irritated Monty Blake must have been when he realised why Loredana had accepted his invitation and that his seduction plans were unlikely to come to anything.

'Your sister made me feel like I was too old to be chasing girls her age,' Zara's father claimed with a curled lip. 'She depressed me. I didn't go to bed. I sat up getting very drunk that night and fell asleep in the saloon. Some time during the night, Rod, the chap in charge of the boat, woke me up, said there was a bad storm. He told me to go and fetch your sister and Pam, the stewardess, while he sorted the escape dinghy. He said the two women were together...' Monty shook his greying head heavily. 'I was drunk and the generator failed, so the lights went out…'

'And then what did you do?' Vitale growled.

'Your sister wasn't in her cabin and I didn't know my way round the crew quarters. The yacht was lurching in every direction. I couldn't see where I was going or keep my feet. I started shouting their names. Water was streaming down the gangway. It was terrifying. I fell and hurt myself. I rushed back up on deck to get Rod to help but Rod had been injured and he was bleeding heavily from a head wound.' Something of the desperation Monty Blake had felt that night had leaked into his fracturing voice and stamped his drawn face with the recollection of a nightmare. 'The boat was sinking and I panicked. Is that what you want me to admit?'

'All I want is the truth,' Vitale breathed tightly, almost as strained as Zara's father.

'Well, I'm sorry I wasn't a hero, but with the sea pouring in I was too scared to go below deck alone again,' he gritted in a shamed but also defiant undertone, as if that was a moment and a decision he had weighed many times over the years that had passed since that fateful night. 'I pulled on a life jacket and helped Rod into his, struggled with the dinghy while he tried to tell me what to do. I can't swim, you know…I never learned. The boat was going down, there was no time for a search, no time to do anything else—'

'You hardly knew her,' Vitale remarked with hollow finality. 'You saved yourself. I don't believe it would be fair to judge you for that. '

Zara never did get lunch. They left the hotel in silence. Neither of them had any appetite after that meeting. She knew Vitale's thoughts were still on his dead sister. She knew the truth had been hard for him to hear. Loredana had been very young and agreeing to go sailing with a virtual stranger had clearly been an impulsive act. Her father had been drunk and less than brave in an emergency, but only a special few were willing to risk their own life for another person's and it wouldn't be fair to blame him for falling short of a heroic ideal.

'No, there's not even a hint of a little bump!' Bee declared two weeks later on Zara's wedding day, as she scrutinised her half-sister's stomach from every angle. Bee reckoned that only a woman who had never had a weight problem would have fallen pregnant and then chosen a figure-hugging wedding gown calculated to reveal the smallest bulge. Luckily for Zara, she had no surplus flesh to spoil the perfect symmetry of her flowing lace dress.

Zara studied her reflection, grateful that her pregnancy did not yet show. True, her breasts were a little fuller, but that was the sole change in her shape that she had noticed. Her gown was slender and elegant, maximising her diminutive height. 'I hope Vitale doesn't think I'm overdressed.'

'How can you be overdressed at your own wedding?' Bee demanded.

'When it's a quiet do with only a couple of witnesses attending,' Zara pointed out, wincing at that reality.

'Does that bother you?' Bee asked worriedly. 'I know

this can't be the sort of wedding you ever expected to have.'

'It's what I want. I was never into all the fuss and frills of the wedding arrangements Mum insisted on when I was supposed to be marrying Sergios,' Zara admitted, a look of discomfiture crossing her delicate features, 'and this wedding is still only a formality—'

'I think it's a little more than a formality when the man you're about to marry is the father of your baby,' Bee cut in with some amusement.

'I'm very grateful that Vitale's willing to share that responsibility.'

Bee pulled an unimpressed face. 'Which is exactly why you picked a gorgeous dress and got all dollied up in your fanciest make-up and shoes for Vitale's benefit?' she teased. '*Please*, do I look that stupid?'

Zara said nothing, for it was true that she had gone to no end of trouble to look her very best for the occasion. She had not required a church full of guests as an excuse to push the glamour boat out. But it had taken an ironic ton of make-up and every scrap of artistry she possessed to achieve the natural effect she had sought. The natural effect she knew he admired. Her shoes, sparkling with diamanté, were the very cute equivalent of Cinderella's slippers. To satisfy the something-old rhyme she had her late brother's school badge tucked into her bra and her thigh sported a blue garter. If the wedding was only a formality why had she bothered with all those trappings?

The circumstances being what they were, she had only invited her half-sisters to share the brief ceremony

with her. Bee was accompanying her to the church and
Tawny had promised to meet them there. Afterwards
she and Vitale were flying straight out to Italy. She had
packed up her apartment, surrendered it and had spent
the previous night with Bee. She was retaining Rob to
manage Blooming Perfect in London. She was hoping
that there would be sufficient demand for her services
in Tuscany for her to open another small branch of the
business. Fluffy had already flown out to her future
new home. Zara, however, was as apprehensive as a
climber hanging onto a frayed rope: she was terrified
that she was doing the wrong thing. In one life there
was only room for so many mistakes and on this occasion she was very conscious that she had a child's welfare to consider.

The car Vitale had sent to collect her drew up outside the church. She got out with Bee's assistance and
her younger sister, Tawny, hurried towards her.

'Zara!' she exclaimed, pushing a long curl of fiery
copper hair out of her eyes. 'You look amazing! Who
is this Italian? And why didn't I get the chance to meet
him before this?'

'I'm pregnant and we're in a hurry,' Zara confided,
watching her sibling's bright blue eyes shoot wide in
surprise and drop almost inevitably to her stomach.

'Oh…' Tawny grimaced. 'And you're marrying him?
I hope you know what you're doing—'

'When does Zara ever know what she's doing?' Bee
chimed in ruefully. 'She never takes the long view.'

'My sisters are supposed to be universally supportive on my wedding day,' Zara cut in with a warning frown. 'Get supporting.'

And nothing more was said. Her siblings escorted her up the church steps and smoothed out the hem of her gown in the porch. The organ began to play and the doors opened for Zara to walk down the aisle. Marriage, she was thinking on the edge of panic, marriage was such a big complex step. Was she even cut out to be a wife? There was so much she didn't know about Vitale, so much they hadn't discussed. He was waiting at the altar, his head held high, and she needn't have worried about being overdressed because he and the man by his side were kitted out in fancy grey morning suits.

At the exact moment that Vitale turned his handsome head to look at her, his gaze every bit as edgy as her own, her apprehension evaporated because he smiled. A wolfish smile that took him from being a very good-looking guy to an absolutely gorgeous one. There was admiration in his gaze and she basked in it.

'*Like* the dress,' he breathed in a discreet aside before the vicar began to speak. 'You look wonderful.'

The last knot of tension in her stomach dissolved into a feeling of warmth and acceptance. The ceremony progressed and her hand stayed steady as he slid a wedding ring on her finger. And then almost dizzyingly fast the service was over, the organ music was swelling and Vitale was escorting her back down the aisle, a light hand resting on hers. In the porch he met her siblings and she learned that his companion was his lawyer and also a friend from his university days.

They drove straight to the airport.

'Did you mind that your parents weren't part of the ceremony?' Vitale asked her as soon as they were alone.

'Not at all. It wouldn't have been fancy enough for my mother and somehow my father would have found a way of ruining the day by calling me stupid.' Her soft mouth compressed and she shrugged a forlorn shoulder, conscious of his bewildered appraisal and saying nothing more.

'Why would he have done that?'

'I should have told you by now—I suffer from dyslexia. *Badly*,' Zara stressed, her hands tightly curled together on her lap because it took courage to confess a weakness that had been regarded with such disgust by her family. 'Regardless of what my father thinks, though, I'm not slow-witted. I have some difficulty reading, writing and spelling but I manage most things fine with the help of a computer.'

Vitale frowned because he was recalling her blank appraisal of the instructions on the pregnancy test and suddenly he was rethinking that scene with a tight feeling inside his chest. The anxiety, the fear of rejection, in her gaze screamed at him. He realised that, regardless of her attempt to refer casually to the condition, what she had just admitted was a very big deal for her. 'I went to school with a couple of dyslexics. I know you're not slow-witted and fortunately dyslexics can get a lot of help these days.'

Zara grimaced. 'My father doesn't believe dyslexia exists. He just thinks I'm stupid and he wouldn't allow me to have speech-language therapy.'

'That's ridiculous. Didn't you get help at school?'

'I was sixteen before I was diagnosed and I left a few months later. Although I dropped out of my A-level studies, I do manage,' she said again, clearly keen to drop the subject.

He remembered how pale and tense she had been while she struggled with those instructions, clearly terrified of him realising that she had a problem, and his rage with Monty Blake roared up through him like volcanic lava. Instead of being taught how to cope with the disorder, she had been taught to be ashamed of it and left to struggle alone. He wondered why that image bothered him, why he should feel so angry on her behalf. When had he ever felt protective about a woman? Only once before and even then his intelligence warning him to keep his distance had warred with more natural instincts.

'It's never too late to learn. Some sessions with a professional would help you handle the condition now,' Vitale remarked evenly. 'And lift your confidence.'

Zara went pink. She bit back the tart comment that she was sure he hadn't expected to take a wife still in need of lessons, because she was well aware that when she put herself down she was revealing low self-esteem. Furthermore she recognised that he had seen shrewdly right to the heart of her problem. Her family's attitude to her dyslexia had imposed secrecy on her and her subsequent fear of exposure had only made the problem worse.

'I thought you'd be embarrassed that I'm a dyslexic.'

'It would take a great deal more to embarrass me, *gioia mia*. Your parents overreacted. Albert Einstein and some very famous people were also dyslexic,' Vitale fielded casually.

They boarded a private jet and as Zara settled into a cream leather seat in the cabin she was thinking once again about how very little she knew about the man she had married. 'I had no idea that you owned your own plane,' she confided.

'I travel a lot. It speeds up my schedule and ensures that I can move quickly in a crisis—'

'Where are we heading?' she prompted.

'It's a surprise, hopefully one which will please you.'

Lunch was served. After several sleepless nights spent worrying about the unknowns in her future, Zara was too exhausted to do more than pick at the food on her plate. Finally she pushed the plate away and closed her heavy eyes to rest them. That was the last thing she registered until the jet landed and Vitale shook her shoulder to rouse her from a deep sleep.

She was torn between pain and pleasure while he drove her through the Tuscan hills, for although she loved the Italian landscape she could not forget how much he had hurt her on her last visit.

'Isn't this the road we took to the Palazzo Barigo?' she pressed at one point.

'*Sì.*' His classic profile was taut, his response clipped.

When the car actually turned beneath the arched entrance to the palazzo, Zara turned with a frown to exclaim, 'What are we doing here?'

'You'll see.' Vitale parked at the front of the palazzo and, filled with curiosity, Zara scrambled out. Was he planning to introduce her to his uncle? Smoothing her dress down while wishing he had given her some warning of his intentions, she mounted the shallow flight of steps to the front door, which was already opening. She came to a sudden halt when she saw the domestic staff assembled in the marble hall, clearly waiting to greet them.

Joining her, Vitale curved a hand to her elbow and introductions were made. There was no sign of any member of the family and she was confused when a middle-aged manservant called Edmondo showed them into a spacious reception room where once again she expected to meet Vitale's relatives, only nobody awaited them there either.

'What on earth are we doing here?' she demanded of Vitale in a perplexed whisper. 'Is this where we're going to stay?'

'I own the palazzo,' Vitale told her flatly, breaking the news with the minimum possible fanfare.

CHAPTER NINE

VITALE'S blunt confession hit Zara like a brick thrown at a glass window, shattering her composure. She recalled the tour of the gardens that he had said he had arranged. She remembered the gardener waving at him that same day and she turned pale before a flush of mortified pink mantled her cheekbones.

'Oh, my goodness, what an idiot I am!' she gasped, her temper rising hot and fast because she felt exceedingly foolish. 'But you told me this place belonged to your uncle—'

'No, I didn't. I only told you that I was staying here with my uncle and his family when your aunt worked on the garden—'

'Semantics—you *lied*!' Zara shot the furious accusation back at him. 'You're so tricky I'll never be able to trust a word you say!'

Vitale stood very still, reining back the aggression that her condemnation threatened to unleash. 'I bought the palazzo two years ago when my uncle decided to sell up but, while I have instigated repairs and maintained the property, I have not attempted to make personal use of the house until now,' he admitted without any expression at all.

He watched her, the daylight flooding through the tall windows burnishing her eye-catching hair and illuminating the fine lacework on her dress while enhancing the slender, striking elegance of her figure. He wondered when her pregnancy would start showing and experienced a glimmer of excitement at the prospect that shook him. But the awareness that her body would soon swell with visible proof of *his* baby turned him on hard and fast, no matter how fiercely he fought to repress the primitive reaction. Once again in her presence he was at the mercy of feelings and thoughts that were foreign to him and he hated it, craving the cool distance and self-discipline that were more familiar to him.

Zara settled furious lavender eyes on her bridegroom. 'Why not? If you bought the palazzo why haven't you used it?'

'I didn't feel comfortable here. When I was a teenager I stayed in this house during my term breaks and I have no good memories of those visits,' he admitted with a hard twist of his eloquent mouth.

'So what are we doing here?' Zara demanded baldly, still all at sea.

'You love the garden—I assumed that you might also like the house. It is a fine one.'

Zara was more confused than ever. An ancestral home was right off the grid of her scale of experience. To talk of it in terms of liking or disliking seemed positively cheeky. Yes, she had friends who inhabited such properties and she had occasionally stayed in them for the weekend but it had never occurred to her that she might one day actually live in one. 'Why did you buy a place this size if you don't even like it?'

'The palazzo has belonged to the Barigo family for centuries. I felt it was my duty to buy it and conserve it for the next generation.'

'But your name isn't Barigo…' Zara was still hopelessly at a loss.

'I have chosen not to claim the name but I am a Barigo.'

The penny of comprehension dropped noisily in Zara's head and she was embarrassed that it had taken her so long to make that leap in understanding. That was why he and his sister had had different surnames. They must have had different fathers. Evidently he was an illegitimate Barigo, born outside marriage and never properly acknowledged by the rest of the family. Yet he seemed so very much at ease against the grandeur of the great house, she mused. He had the education, the sophistication, the inborn classy assurance to look at home against such a splendid backdrop. He also had a level of worldly success and wealth that the most recent of the palazzo's owners had evidently lacked. Yet in spite of all that, deep down inside himself, Vitale had still not felt good enough to stay in the palazzo he owned and relax there and that disturbing truth twisted inside Zara's heart like a knifepoint turning.

'If you buy a house, you should use it,' Zara told him squarely. 'You seem to have a lot of staff employed here and you maintain it. My aunt used to say that a house that isn't lived in loses its heart.'

'I'm not sure that the Palazzo Barigo ever had a heart,' Vitale contended wryly. 'My sister grew up here. It was different for her. This was her home until her father died and my uncle inherited.'

'Why didn't your sister inherit?'

'The palazzo only goes to the men in the family. Loredana got the money instead,' he explained.

'So, why did you have to buy it to get it?' Zara pressed curiously. 'Because you're illegitimate?'

'I'm *not* illegitimate…it's too complicated to get into now,' Vitale countered with a dismissive shrug of a broad shoulder.

He didn't want to talk about his background and the shutters came back down. He was shutting her out because he didn't want to tell her any more. But these surroundings, his evidently troubled early life and what had happened to him since then were the key to Vitale's complex personality. Just then she recalled the strange scarring on his back and wondered once again what had caused it. At the same time, Zara was mystified by the depth of her longing to understand what drove Vitale Roccanti. Once she had thought he was a cold, callous guy focused purely on revenge, but the tiny seed of life inside her womb had steamrollered over that conviction and triumphed. As had her own personal safety, she conceded, recalling how he had brought her father to her door.

'Let's take a look at the house,' she responded lightly,

eager to distract him from the bad memories that he had mentioned.

'You're hardly dressed for a grand tour—'

'I can change.'

'I was rather looking forward to taking that dress off for you, *cara mia*,' Vitale admitted with a charismatic smile playing attractively at the corners of his beautifully shaped mouth.

'Well, you're going to have to help me get out of it. Getting into it was a two-person job,' Zara confided, thinking of the complex lacing that ran down her spine. 'I would never have managed without Bee's help this morning.'

As they reached the imposing marble staircase Edmondo appeared to show them the way and set off ahead of them at a stately pace that very nearly gave Zara a bout of irreverent giggles. Her dancing eyes meeting Vitale's in shared amusement, she had to swallow hard. The massive bedroom Edmondo displayed for their benefit was full of such extravagantly gilded furniture, embroidered, tasselled and fringed drapes and grandeur that Zara thought it would have been better suited to a reigning monarch. But there was no mistake because their luggage awaited them beside a pair of monumentally vast mirrored wardrobes.

'Wow…' she framed in a fading voice once they were alone again, unable to even imagine sleeping in that huge bed festooned in crimson drapes falling from a giant ceiling-mounted golden crown.

'What do you really think?' Vitale prompted as she bent to open her case and extract a change of clothing.

'It's hideous but I'm sure the antiques are worth a fortune and very historic,' she added in a rush, recognising that she might just have been tactless in the extreme.

'We could put them in storage and refurnish. It's not my style either,' Vitale admitted, stepping behind her to unknot the satin lacing closing the back of her dress. 'But Edmondo is a stickler for tradition and this is where the owner of the palazzo has always slept.'

'My goodness, your predecessors must've enjoyed their pomp and ceremony.' Zara shivered a little as cooler air brushed her bare shoulder blades and the fitted bodice of her gown loosened and fell forward. 'While you're a dab hand at unlacing.'

Vitale bent his head and pressed his lips to the tender side of her throat where a tiny pulse was going crazy. Lingering to enjoy her smooth, delicately perfumed skin, he used his mouth to nuzzle the soft skin there. His attention to that particular spot was unbearably arousing and a helpless gasp was wrenched from her as streamers of fire shot to every erotic zone she possessed. Stretching back against him for support, she caught her reflection in one of the wardrobe mirrors. She looked wanton, possessed, her hair shimmering round her shoulders, her face turned up eagerly to his, her breasts swelling and straining over the slightly too small cups of her lace strapless bra.

'I look like a shameless hussy,' she cried in embarrassment, her hands reaching down to pull up her dress again.

'Shameless works a treat for me, *angelina mia*,'

Vitale told her, his hands releasing her hold from the fabric so that her gown slid off her hips and down to her ankles. He lifted her out of the entangling folds and brought her down on the bed where he studied her scantily clad body with smouldering appreciation. 'You look gorgeous, Signora Roccanti.'

Self-conscious heat seemed to flood Zara from her head to her toes. She felt as though she were burning up inside her skin while her nipples tingled into straining buds and the tender flesh at the heart of her tingled with awareness. Dispensing with his tie, his waistcoat and his jacket and shoes, he lay down beside her, eyes full of anticipation. Zara propped herself up on her elbows, secure in his admiration, satisfied that she was both wanted and desired. He captured her lips with devastatingly erotic urgency so that even before he eased a small breast free of the bra her breath was parting her lips in rapid, uneven gasps. He rubbed the stiff rosy peak between thumb and forefinger and then dropped his mouth there to tease the throbbing tip with his lips and his tongue. As he simultaneously stroked the band of taut silk fabric stretched between her legs and felt the dampness there he groaned out loud. 'I've been fantasising about this moment for weeks,' he confided in a roughened undertone.

Only as he undid her bra to remove it did he spot the small blue badge she had attached to it. 'What's this?' he questioned.

'The something blue from the wedding luck rhyme and to remind me of my brother. He got it at school for playing rugby or something,' she muttered vaguely.

'I didn't even know you had a brother.'

'Tom was my twin. But he died in a car crash two years ago.' Flinching from her poignant recollections, she let her fingers delve into his tousled black hair to draw his mouth back to hers again and when he took her invitation to stop talking and kiss her it was so exhilarating that all sad memories left her head.

Her bra melted away, quickly followed by her panties. Vitale reared back on his knees to shed his remaining garments with a great deal more haste than cool. She revelled in his impatience, his eagerness to make love to her.

'I wanted this to be slow and perfect, unlike the last time,' Vitale admitted in a tone of frustration.

'Human beings don't do perfect,' she quipped, lifting a slender hand to run her fingertips gently down his cheek. 'And I don't expect it.'

'But you should,' Vitale informed her, eyes welded to her like padlocks.

With a gentle laugh of disagreement she arched her back below the hands curving to the pert swell of her sensitised breasts.

'Is it my imagination or is there more of you than there was a few weeks ago?' he teased.

'Falling pregnant does have some advantages,' she told him seductively. 'Alcohol may not be a good idea but I'm getting very bosomy indeed.'

Vitale laughed and kissed her breathless. She quivered as he found her clitoris with the ball of his thumb and pleasured her, gently delving and stroking until she moaned in helpless response to his stimulation. She was twisting and turning, her hips rising long before he rose over her and eased into her honeyed depths in a long deep thrust that sent a wave of excitement currenting through her.

'Don't stop,' she told him at an ecstatic peak of pleasure when it was a challenge to even find her voice.

She couldn't lie still as his fluid movements grew more insistent, more passionate and the intolerable tightness and tension within her gathered with every heartbeat and then exploded into an earthshaking climax. She hit that high with a startled cry of delight that she muffled by burying her mouth in a strong brown shoulder. She was as weak as a kitten once the tingling ripples of rapture had slowly coursed away from her again.

'I don't want to stroke your ego but that...*that* was perfect,' Zara whispered shakily, her hands sliding down from his shoulders to his back and instinctively massaging the roughened skin there with a gentle touch. 'What happened to you?' she asked him abruptly.

His muscles jerked taut below her fingers, and he stared down at her with bleak eyes. 'I was beaten, tortured as a child by my stepfather. He went to prison for it.'

A surge of horror swiftly followed by tears of sympathy flooded Zara's eyes. She lowered her lashes before he could see and when he tried to pull away from her, she held on tight to him. 'I thought I'd bottomed out in the parenting stakes,' she remarked tightly. 'But obviously you did a lot worse.'

Vitale realised that it would be more dignified to

stop fighting the comforting hug being forced on him.
There was a ghastly moment when he just didn't know
how to respond and he froze in her arms. She was always petting the rabbit, he reminded himself grimly;
affectionate gestures were second nature to the woman
he had married. He would have to learn how to handle them. He dropped a brief and awkward kiss on her
brow, watching in dismay as a single tear inched down
her flushed cheek on his behalf. 'We may not have done
well in the parent lottery but that won't stop us being
amazing parents,' he stated with powerful conviction.
'I'm sure we both know what *not* to do with our child.'

Zara thought of the mess that had been made of his
back, the pain he must have endured and the despair
he must have felt until he was removed from that cruelly abusive environment and she wanted to weep, but
she had to confine herself to a subtle sniff or two and
a comparatively modest hug. He saw hope in the future
and refused to dwell on past suffering, she recognised
with respect. Their marriage truly did have all the potential it needed to survive.

'My mother, Paola, married a wealthy businessman
when she was eighteen. His name was Carlo Barigo
and he was twenty years older,' Vitale said in a charged
undertone, finally caving in and telling Zara the story
that she had longed to hear since the day of her arrival
as a bride at the palazzo.

Unfortunately prising that tale out of a male as reserved as Vitale was had taken determination and spot-
on timing even from a wife of almost eight weeks'

standing. At that instant, Vitale was at his most relaxed in a post-sex sprawl in the tangled sheets of their
bed and her fingers were gently engaged in smoothing
through his black hair.

'Go on,' she encouraged, quick to react to a hint of
hesitation.

'Loredana was born within the first year of the marriage and within five years Paola was taking advantage
of the fact that her husband was often away on business.
She made friends with the wrong people, got into drink
and drugs and started an affair. The marriage broke
down. Carlo threw her out and her parents turned their
back on her. She had never worked in her life and she
was pregnant so she moved in with her lover—'

'The guy who beat you?' Zara cut in with a frown.

'*Sì*…he was a drug dealer to the rich. He married her
because he assumed the divorce settlement would be
huge—it was not. He also assumed that the child she
was expecting was his.'

'That was you,' she guessed.

'I was Carlo Barigo's legitimate son but Paola lied
and said I wasn't because my father had already deprived her of her daughter and she didn't want to lose
me as well,' Vitale explained curtly. 'That was also my
stepfather's excuse for beating me—that I wasn't his
kid—but the truth was he got off on brutality.'

'Didn't your mother try to stop him?'

'By that stage all she cared about was her next fix.'

'There must have been someone who cared,' Zara
said painfully.

'Not until Loredana decided that she wanted to meet

her mother after Carlo Barigo died. But when my sister visited us Paola was out of her head on drugs and Loredana got to know me instead. When she saw my bruises she notified the authorities of her suspicions. I went into the foster system and my stepfather eventually went to prison. I owe my life to Loredana's intervention,' he breathed heavily. 'I was eleven when she became my guardian. I went to boarding school while she worked as a model.'

For the first time she understood the foundation of his deep attachment to his late sister and her memory. Although his mother had failed him Loredana had saved him from a life of abuse.

Zara gazed down at his strong profile, so beautiful, so strong and yet so damaged, she conceded painfully. 'So how did you manage to visit this house as a teenager?'

'Loredana was an heiress, *gioia mia*. My uncle encouraged her to continue treating the palazzo like her home because he hoped that she would marry one of his sons and bring her money back into the family. That's why she was allowed to bring me here. It was that or leave me at school all the year round,' he proffered with a rueful sigh. 'My sister accepted me just as I was and I *was* rough round the edges. It never occurred to her that her snobbish cousins would be outraged to have a drug dealer and a junkie's son forced on them as a guest.'

Her brow furrowed. 'But that's not who you were.'

'It's what they believed. My cousins used to drag me out of bed in the middle of the night and thump and kick me and, thanks to their desire to ensure that I didn't get too big for my boots, I learned that my mother was selling her body to survive.'

Zara was pale. 'I bet you didn't even tell your sister what was happening.'

'Of course I didn't. I idolised her. She thought I was being treated to a slice of the family life she couldn't give me.' His mouth quirked. 'She was very trusting that way, always thought the best of everyone—'

'What age were you when she died?'

'Thirteen.'

'And how did you find out who your father really was?'

Vitale grimaced. 'The DNA testing that had to be done to identify Loredana's body revealed that we were full siblings. I chose to keep that news to myself. She hadn't changed her will to include me but a portion of her estate was set aside by the courts to cover my educational and living costs. My uncle got the rest and, being conscious of what people might think, he insisted that I continue to spend my term breaks at the palazzo.'

'Your sister was part of your life for such a short time.' Zara could only imagine how painful that loss must have been for a boy who had never known love and caring from any other source. It was even sadder that their true relationship had only been discovered after his sister had drowned.

'She first met your father here at the palazzo,' Vitale volunteered abruptly, his tone harsh. 'The grounds were being used for a fashion shoot and your aunt, Edith, was still working on her design. Loredana was modelling and your father flew in to see your aunt and he was invited to stay to dinner.'

'Oh,' Zara pronounced, it being her turn to pull a face, for she did not wish to tackle that controversial issue again at that moment for she was too well aware that, had her father been a braver man, Loredana might have survived the sinking of the yacht. 'Let's not discuss that now. Give me one positive thought about the palazzo, Vitale.'

'That is *so* childish, *cara mia*,' he groaned, looking at her in reproach.

'It's not...you can be very prone to taking a negative stance.'

A rueful smile chased the tension from his well-shaped mouth and he threw his untidy dark head back on the pillow. As dark, bronzed and glossy as a tiger at rest, he looked incredibly handsome. 'I commissioned the temple above the lake as a tribute to Loredana. The top of that hill was her favourite place—'

'That was a cheat thought...a sort of positive and negative together,' Zara censured.

'I won't need to commission anything to remember you,' Vitale teased with sudden amusement. 'Everywhere I look you've made your mark on this household.'

The huge pieces of gilded furniture had already gone into storage in favour of contemporary pieces in oak, which looked surprisingly well against the silk-panelled walls. Welcoming seating had arrived along with cushions, throws, unusual pieces of pottery and flower arrangements to illuminate dark corners and add comfort and character. Edmondo, who thoroughly approved of such nest-building instincts, had cheerfully described the new mistress of the palazzo to her husband as a 'force of nature'.

'You don't need to remember me,' Zara countered. 'I'm not going anywhere.'

His attention suddenly fell on the little jewelled enamel clock by her side of the bed and he stiffened and sat up in an abrupt movement. 'I didn't realise it was almost six!'

Within ten seconds of that exclamation, Vitale had vacated the bed and the shower was running in the adjoining bathroom. Zara lay on in the bed as stiff as a wooden plank while her mind whirled off on a wheel of frantic resentful activity. Sadly, she knew exactly why Vitale was in such a hurry. Well, at least she knew and she didn't know…

Once again, after all, it was a Friday night and every Friday night for the past five weeks Vitale had religiously gone out alone and not returned home until around two in the morning. He would only say that he visited a longstanding female 'friend', who lived near Florence, for dinner and if Zara tried to extract any more details from him he became irritable and broodingly silent. She suspected and had asked if that female friend was living in the villa for which she had done the garden plan but, rather tellingly, he had ignored the question.

'You must learn to trust me. You may be my wife but that doesn't mean I have to tell you *everything*!' he had argued without hesitation the previous week.

But Zara thought marriage should mean exactly that even though she had backed off from the looming threat of a row for the sake of peace. When Vitale returned to the palazzo tomorrow, however, she already knew that he would be grim and distant and that it would probably be at least forty-eight hours before he so much as touched her again. His Friday nights away from her, it seemed, did not put him in a good mood.

Was he spending that time placating another woman who mattered to him? A woman he had reluctantly set aside so that he could marry Zara because she had fallen pregnant? It was Zara's worst fear but what else could explain his tense, troubled attitude in the aftermath of those evenings? Vitale was betraying every sign of a man being torn between opposing loyalties.

It had to be admitted, though, that his mysterious Friday outings were the one and only storm cloud in Zara's blue sky and at first she had not been at all concerned when he left her to her own company one evening during the week. Her concern had grown only in proportion to his reticence. She did not like secrets and did not feel she could sit back and quietly allow him to maintain his secrecy.

Yet at the same time she had lived in Tuscany with Vitale for eight long weeks and had during that period discovered a happiness and a sense of security that was wonderfully new and precious to her. He had devoted the first three weeks of their marriage entirely to her, but after that point had had to return to the bank and his travels abroad. While he was away she had flown back to London on several occasions to catch up with business at Blooming Perfect and see clients.

Round her neck she wore a teardrop diamond pendant on a chain that Vitale hated her to take off. He had said the flash of the diamond in sunlight reminded him of her hair and her luminous smile. He had said loads and loads of romantic flattering stuff like that, words that she cherished, compliments that she took out and analysed whenever she was on her own or worried about the depth of his commitment to her and their marriage. He was very generous, had bought her innumerable gifts, everything from jewellery to flowers and artworks to pieces of furniture he thought she might like. Even more impressive he had also quietly engaged a speech-language specialist to visit weekly and help Zara overcome the problems caused by her dyslexia. She was already able to read more easily. Even Fluffy had benefited from Zara's move to Italy, having acquired more toys than even the most spoilt bunny could play with.

Vitale had become Zara's whole world without her even noticing it until she began to panic on Friday nights, worry about where he was and who he was with, and it made her realise her heart was more vulnerable than she had ever really appreciated. She was hopelessly in love with the guy she had married and to whom she had foolishly suggested a three-month-long trial marriage. Three months? Seriously, what sort of a stupid idea had that been? She already knew that she would not willingly give Vitale up after even a thousand months. What would she say at the end of the trial period if he was the one who turned round and jumped through that escape hatch she had handily provided to ask for *his* freedom back? It was a prospect that made her blood run cold.

She didn't know when she had fallen for Vitale or when she had first overcome that bad beginning when he had set her up for the paparazzi. But she was crazy about him and she really did understand that she had landed herself an extremely passionate, 'all or nothing' guy, who had switched his original allegiance to his sister's memory to their child instead. At heart she really did grasp what motivated Vitale more strongly than any other factor.

And what did inspire him was his movingly strong concept of what a man owed to his family. Her pregnancy had shot her right up the pecking order in his mind and brought her out at the top of the pile. She was carrying his baby, she was his wife and he really did treat her as though she was something incredibly precious. It touched her to the heart that even after the horrific experiences he had endured as a child he could still set such a very high value on the importance of family.

His cell phone rang and he emerged from the bathroom, a towel anchored precariously round his lean hips, to answer it. He frowned, thrust long impatient fingers through his damp black hair, spiking it up, and spoke in fluid Italian for several minutes, clearly issuing instructions. Setting the phone down again, he glanced at her. 'I'm afraid I have to fly to Bahrain this

evening to meet a major investor. I won't be home until
late tomorrow.'

As he broke the news Zara found herself smiling. If
he had to be in Bahrain he couldn't also be dining somewhere near Florence with his unknown female friend.
But if he didn't make it there this week he would presumably make it there at a later date. He walked over
to the window and made another call, his attractive accented drawl apologetic, gentle in tone. Zara knew in
her bones that he was talking to another woman and it
wounded her, plunging her straight back into her uneasy thoughts.

Exactly what did Vitale get up to on Friday nights?
He was risking their relationship by maintaining such
secrecy. Didn't that bother him? Did he think this
woman was worth that risk? Was he keeping a mistress in that luxury villa? A mistress he needed more
than he needed his pregnant wife? She had to know.
Who was he protecting her from? Or was it that he was
protecting another woman from her?

Suddenly, Zara was determined to satisfy some of
the questions that Vitale had refused to answer. Once
he had left for the airport, she would drive over to the
villa, make the excuse that she had come to check on
the garden and discover who lived there. She had to
know, she *needed* to know, and tough if he didn't like
it when he found out that she'd gone behind his back
to satisfy her curiosity…

CHAPTER TEN

THE local landscaping firm hired by Vitale to bring Zara's plan for the villa grounds to fruition had done an excellent job. A wide terrace girded by graceful trees and elegant shrubs had removed the old-fashioned formal aspect from the original frontage. Her heart beating very fast, Zara parked the car and approached the front door.

Whatever she discovered she would deal with it quietly and calmly, she reminded herself bracingly. She was ready to handle any eventuality. There would be no distasteful scene, no tears, certainly no recriminations. Hadn't she promised Vitale that before she married him? She was engaged in a trial marriage, which either one of them could walk away from without a guilt trip. If he *was* keeping another woman at the villa, if he *was* maintaining an extra-marital relationship, she had to set him free and get on with her life. Those far-reaching reflections were all very well, she reasoned in sudden dismay, as long as she didn't acknowledge that the very thought of having to live without Vitale, or raise her child without him, was terrifying.

It was a shock, therefore, while she hovered apprehensively on the doorstep, when without her even knocking to announce her presence the front door suddenly shot open and framed Giuseppina. Zara frowned when she recognised the housekeeper, who had looked after her and Vitale at the farmhouse where she had stayed several months earlier.

'Buona sera, Signora Roccanti,' Giuseppina greeted her with a welcoming smile and a further flood of Italian, which Zara did not understand.

With a display of enthusiasm that suggested that it was very unlikely that Vitale could be engaged in an improper extra-marital relationship with the villa occupant, Giuseppina ushered Zara into the hall. Quick light steps echoed across a tiled floor somewhere nearby and a woman appeared in the doorway.

She was an older woman, trim and not particularly tall with short silvery grey hair, anxious dark eyes and a heavily lined face. When she saw Zara she came to a sudden halt while Zara continued to stare, ensnared by a fleeting physical resemblance that took her very much by surprise.

'You must be Zara,' the woman breathed in accented English, her discomfiture unhidden. 'Did Vitale tell you about me? I made him promise that he would keep me a secret but I knew it would be difficult for him—'

'He didn't break his promise,' Zara admitted tautly, suddenly wishing she had stayed home, suddenly wishing she did not still suffer from that impulsive streak that invariably got her into trouble. 'I must apologise for dropping in without an invitation. I'm afraid I couldn't rest until I knew who was living here, who Vitale was seeing every Friday night...'

In the face of that explanation, the anxious expression on the other woman's face eased somewhat. '*Naturalmente*...of course. Come in—Giuseppina will make us English tea.' She spoke to the housekeeper in her own language before extending a hesitant hand. 'I am Paola Roccanti.'

'I thought you might be,' Zara almost whispered, shock still winging through her in embarrassing waves as she lightly touched that uncertain hand. 'Vitale has your eyes.'

Smiling as though that comment was a compliment, Paola took her into the lounge, smartly furnished now in contemporary style. 'I should have allowed Vitale to tell you I was here. I can see now that I put him in a difficult position. That was not my intention. I simply didn't want to embarrass you or him. I didn't want you to feel that you had to acknowledge me—'

'How could you embarrass me?' Zara asked in bewilderment. 'Why wouldn't I acknowledge you?'

Paola sighed. 'You're married to my son. You must know how badly I let him down as a child. Many people despise me for the life I have led and I understand how they feel. I've taken drugs, lived on the streets, I've been in prison for stealing to feed my addiction—'

'If Vitale wants to see you that is enough for me,' Zara broke in quietly, feeling that such revelations were none of her business.

'Since I came out of rehabilitation my son and I have been trying to get to know each other. It is not easy for either of us,' his mother confessed with a regret that she couldn't hide. 'It is hard for Vitale not to judge me and sometimes I remember things that make it almost impossible for me to face him.'

'I think it's good that both of you are trying, though,' Zara responded with tact as Giuseppina entered with a tray of tea.

Paola compressed her lips. 'Coming to terms with my past and facing up to the mistakes I made is part of my recovery process. I attend Narcotics Anonymous meetings regularly,' she explained. 'I have a good sponsor and Vitale has been very supportive as well.'

'That's good.' Still feeling awkward, Zara watched her companion pour the tea with a slightly trembling hand, her tension obvious.

'On Fridays we usually go for a meal and we talk, sometimes about difficult things…like my daughter, Loredana,' Paola continued quietly. 'I have no memory of her beyond the age of six or seven when I left my first husband, Carlo. She visited twice when she was grown up but I was in no condition to speak to her and I can't remember her—'

'Vitale told me…'

'You must know some of the bad things at least.' Paola's eyes were moist, her mouth tight with anxiety. 'He could have died when he was a child. I think he often wished he had when he was younger. I deprived him of his true father and his inheritance and yet he puts me in a house like this and takes me out to dine in fancy restaurants as if I was still the respectable young woman who married his father…the woman I was before I became an addict. He says I can be whoever I want to be now.'

'He's right. You can be,' Zara said gently, soothingly. It was impossible not to recognise how fragile Paola was and how weighed down she was with shame for her past mistakes. She found herself praying that the older woman did make it successfully through the recovery process and managed to stay off drugs.

Paola asked her about the garden and then offered to show it to her. Zara began to relax as they discussed the design and Vitale's mother asked for advice on what to plant in the empty borders behind the villa. Paola had already visited a garden centre nearby. Zara was quick to suggest that they should go back there together the following week and she agreed a date and time while hoping that Vitale would approve and not think her guilty of interference.

It was late afternoon the next day before Vitale returned to the palazzo. Dressed in a simple white sundress, Zara was arranging an armful of lavender in a fat crystal vase in the hall. He strode through the door and came to a halt, brilliant dark eyes locking to her tiny figure, picking up straight away on the troubled look she shot at him. Her pregnancy was becoming obvious now, a firm swell that made her dress sit out like a bell above her slender shapely legs.

'You can shout if you want,' Zara told him ruefully.

An ebony brow rose. 'Why would I shout?'

'I went to see your mother. I assumed you'd already know.'

'I did. Paola rang me as soon as you left the villa,'

Vitale confided with a wry smile. 'She likes you very much and thinks I did very well for myself, which I already knew—'

'But I went behind your back quite deliberately,' Zara pointed out guiltily, keen to ensure that he had grasped exactly what she had done. 'I just had to know where you went on Friday nights and who you were spending time with—'

'It was hell not telling you but I didn't want to spook Paola by forcing the issue. It took a lot of persuasion to get her to move into the villa. She's afraid of encroaching on our lives and of embarrassing us—'

'Are we that easily embarrassed?'

'I'm not, if you're not.' His sardonic mouth hardened. 'She lost thirty years of her life to drug abuse and she's made a huge effort to overcome her problems. I think she deserves a fresh start.'

'But you've found seeing her…difficult,' she selected the word uneasily.

'I didn't like the secrecy and it does feel strange being with her. I never knew her when I was a child and from the age of eleven until this year I had no contact with her, nor did I want any. We have a lot of ground to catch up but I've learned stuff from her that I'm grateful to have found out,' he admitted levelly, accompanying her up the marble staircase. 'Do you mind if I go for a shower? I feel like I've been travelling all day.'

'Not at all. What did you learn from Paola?' she probed curiously as he thrust wide the door of their bedroom.

'That my father kept a mistress throughout the whole

of their marriage.' Vitale raised a brow with expressive scorn. 'He only married my mother to have children and he didn't treat her well. It's not surprising that the marriage broke down or that she was suffering from such low self-esteem that she went off the rails.'

'But it was a tragedy for both you and her...and your sister as well,' Zara completed. 'How did your mother come back into your life again?'

'I was first approached on her behalf by a social worker several years ago but at the time I refused to have anything to do with her,' Vitale confided as he shrugged free of his jacket. 'Then I met you and I began to realise that human beings are more complicated than I used to appreciate.'

'What have I got to do with it?' Zara prompted with a frown.

'I used to be very black and white about situations. People, though, are rarely all good or all evil but often a mixture of both and we all make mistakes. After all, I made a big mistake targeting you to get at your father,' Vitale volunteered grimly. 'That was wrong.'

'I never thought I'd hear you admit that.' Zara curled up on the bed and looked at him expectantly. 'When did you reach that conclusion?'

Vitale dealt her a sardonically amused appraisal. 'There were quite a lot of helpful pointers after I met you, *angelina mia*. How about my discovery that you could get under my skin in the space of one weekend when I had already wrecked my chances with you? How about when you learned that you were pregnant and told me at the same time that you hated and distrusted me? Or even how about your need to impose a ridiculous three-month trial on our marriage so that you could get out of the commitment again if you had to? Do you think I'm so slow that I couldn't learn from those experiences?'

'It has never once crossed my mind that you might be slow—'

'But I was when it came to recognising and understanding my emotions,' Vitale interrupted, trailing his tie loose and tossing it aside. 'When I was a kid, it was safer to squash my feelings and get by without them because anything I felt only made me more vulnerable.'

'I can understand that,' Zara conceded, picking up the tie he had dropped on the floor and frowning at him.

'So I'm untidy,' he conceded with a flourish of one dismissive hand, well into his stride now with his explanation. 'As an adult I didn't recognise emotions for what they were, the same way as I didn't recognise what I felt for my mother until it was almost too late for me to get the chance to know her. By the time a priest who worked with Paola in rehab came to see me this year you were in my life and I was more willing to credit that I might not know everything there was to know and to listen to what he had to tell me.'

'I don't get my connection,' she admitted freely, draping the tie over the back of a chair in a manner that she hoped he would learn to copy.

'Well, once I fell in love with you it opened the floodgates to the whole shebang!' he pointed out mockingly. 'I mean, I've even learned to be reasonably fond of Fluffy now. Going from loving you to trying to understand my mother's need to make amends and be forgiven wasn't that difficult…'

Zara blinked and stared at him in disbelief, lavender eyes huge. 'You fell in love with me…*when*?'

A wicked grin flashed across his beautifully shaped mouth as he realised he had taken her by surprise. 'Oh, I think it probably happened that first weekend when I was playing at being the evil seducer and setting you up with the paparazzi. In fact, as I later appreciated, I was setting myself up for a fall. I didn't know I was in love back then, I just felt like you had taken over my brain because I couldn't get you out of my head, nor could I stay away from you.'

'So when did you decide it was love?'

'Slowly, *painfully*…' Vitale stressed ruefully, his face serious. 'When I'm with you I'm happy and secure. When I've been away from you and I'm coming home I'm downright ecstatic. Everything has more meaning when you're with me. Loving you has taught me how to relax, except when I'm worrying about you.'

'What have you got to worry about me for?'

'It's that naturally negative bent my thoughts suffer from,' Vitale confided ruefully, shedding his shirt. 'The more you mean to me, the more scared I am of losing you, and sometimes when I look at you I am terrified of what I feel—like when I came through the front door and saw you standing there with those purple things—'

'The lavender,' she slotted in.

'Whatever, *angelina mia*.' With a fluid shift of one hand he dismissed an irrelevant detail. 'You were standing there looking so beautiful and pleased to see me and yet worried and I had this moment of panic that something had happened, that something was wrong—'

'I was just worried that you would be annoyed at my having gone behind your back to see who was living in the villa.'

'No, I was touched by your compassion. You spent time with Paola. You didn't make her feel bad. You even invited her out—'

'She needs company,' Zara pointed out. 'It's no big deal.'

'It would be a very big deal to some women. There will be gossip, even scandal if Paola becomes a part of our lives. Some people will approve, others will not.'

'That doesn't matter to me. Let's see how things go,' Zara suggested, knowing that the older woman still had a long way to go as part of her recovery process and that the continuing success of her rehabilitation could not be taken for granted.

'She needs us to have faith in her—she's got nobody else.' Naked but for his boxer shorts, Vitale ran a knuckle gently down the side of Zara's face. 'But I've been hell to live with while this was going on, haven't I?'

'You were a little moody after seeing her.'

'And you don't like moody guys,' he reminded her with a grimace. 'It was tough at first. But although seeing Paola roused bad memories it also made me view my past in a more even light.'

'I really like the fact that you're making that effort for your mother,' Zara confided softly, her tender heart touched. 'It would have been easier for you to turn your back on her.'

'I think it's actually harder to hang onto the prejudices, as I did over Loredana.' Vitale compressed his handsome mouth. 'I will never like your father—he is not a pleasant man and he hurt you. But speaking to him about the night my sister drowned did show me that I was still thinking of that incident with the vengeful attitude of a teenager distraught over his sister's death.'

'Yes,' Zara agreed feelingly.

'Someone else isn't always to blame for the bad things that happen,' he acknowledged heavily. 'Although your father, in fact *both* your parents are very much to blame for your unhappy childhood. To have stood by and allowed you to be branded a liar at the age of ten to conceal your father's violence towards your mother and you was unforgivable. That was a huge betrayal of your trust.'

'I got over it.'

'And I don't think I will ever understand why you were still willing to marry Sergios Demonides just to cement a business deal and win your parents' approval.'

'It was very foolish but I had spent so many years craving their approval without ever getting it. I didn't have enough self-respect,' she admitted wryly. 'I had to come to Tuscany to realise that to marry a man I didn't love or care about was a very bad idea.'

'I had an identical moment of truth when I met you. You changed my outlook, *gioia mia*,' Vitale confided in a tone of immense appreciation. 'I didn't like emotions, didn't trust them, preferred not to get involved with anything or anybody that made me feel too much. But you taught me how much of a difference love could make to my life and then you taught me to want your love…'

Heaving a delighted sigh at that assurance, Zara rested a small hand on his shoulder. 'You know that three-month trial marriage I mentioned?'

'Don't I just?'

'I won't keep you in suspense,' Zara told him teasingly. 'I've decided to keep you for the long haul.'

The beginnings of a smile started to tug at the corners of Vitale's mouth. 'Finally she lets me off the hook.'

'I'm not convinced it did you any harm to be on that hook in the first place.' Zara mock-punched his shoulder. 'Sometimes you're far too sure of yourself. But I do love you,' she whispered, suddenly full of heartfelt emotion. 'I love you very much indeed.'

Vitale did not make it into the shower until much later that evening. In fact he didn't even make it out of the bedroom, for Edmondo was instructed to bring dinner to his employers upstairs. Having declared their love and revelled in the wonder of sharing the same feelings and opinions, Vitale and Zara made passionate love. Afterwards they lay on in bed for ages talking about the why and the how and the when of those first seeds of love until even Zara was satisfied that they had talked the topic to death.

It was definitely not hard for her to listen, however, to how enraged Vitale had felt on her behalf when he appreciated how little her parents valued her in comparison to the twin brother whom they assumed would have been perfect had he lived beyond his twentieth year. In turn, Vitale was hugely amused by the news that his kindness to Fluffy had alerted Zara to the idea that he might have a softer centre than his initial behaviour towards her might have suggested.

'So, I'm not on probation any longer,' Vitale commented with a hint of complacency.

'And how do you work that out?' Zara enquired, surveying him questioningly.

'You said you wanted me for the long haul.'

'Depends on your definition of long haul,' she teased.

'For ever and ever just like the fairy tales,' Vitale hastened to declare, spreading a large hand across the swell of her stomach and laughing in satisfaction as he felt the faint kick of the baby she carried. 'You and the baby both, *angelina mia*.'

'That's an ambition I'm happy to encourage,' Zara told him happily.

EPILOGUE

THREE years later, Zara watched her daughter, Donata, play in the bath in their London town house before scooping her out into a fleecy towel and dressing her little squirming body in her pjs. Her dark eyes were so like Vitale's that the little girl was very talented at wheedling things out of her mother.

'Daddy?' Donata demanded, first in Italian and then in English, demonstrating her bilingual language skill with aplomb.

'Later,' Zara promised, tucking the lively toddler into bed and reflecting that it would be the next morning before Donata saw the father she adored.

Vitale had spent the whole week in New York and, although Zara and occasionally their daughter sometimes travelled with him, she had taken advantage of his absence to catch up with plans needed for Blooming Perfect clients in both London and Tuscany. Business was booming in both countries to the extent that Zara had been forced to turn down work. Media interest and an award won for a garden she had designed for the Chelsea Flower Show had given her an even higher profile and resulted in a steady influx of clients. Rob had become a permanent employee and Zara had hired a junior designer to work under her in London.

Vitale's mother, Paola, had made it safely through her rehabilitation and as time went on had gained in confidence. Having undertaken training as a counsellor, Paola had recently found her feet in her new life by volunteering to work with other addicts. Vitale had also agreed to sponsor a charity for former addicts and their families. The older woman was now very much a part of Vitale and Zara's life and was a very fond grandparent—a fact that Zara was grateful for when her own parents had little to do with their lives.

While Vitale had managed to come to terms with his mother's malign influence on his childhood and had since established a more relaxed adult relationship with the older woman, little had occurred to improve Zara's relations with her parents in a similar way. Her father could not accept the fact that Vitale knew about the domestic violence that had cast such a shadow over Zara and her mother's life. In turn, Zara's mother, Ingrid, was too loyal to her husband to challenge his hostile attitude to their daughter and son-in-law.

Although Zara occasionally accompanied Vitale to social events in London that her parents also attended, and the two couples were always careful to speak for the sake of appearances, there was no true relationship beneath the social banter. Sometimes that hurt Zara a great deal more than she was willing to admit to Vitale. At the same time she did have reason to cherish some hope of a future improvement in relations because her mother made a point of phoning and asking her daughter when she would next be in London so that she could see Donata. Ingrid would then visit her daughter's home and play with her grandchild, but it was tacitly understood that those visits took place without Monty Blake's knowledge.

On the other hand Vitale had taught Zara that life by its very nature was imperfect and that nothing was to be gained from fighting the fact. Her sadness over her poor relationship with her parents was more than compensated for by the deep and happy bond of intimacy she had forged with her husband and child. Her confidence in his love made her smile when she wakened and smile again when she often fell asleep in the safe circle of his arms.

Their closeness had grown by leaps and bounds in the wake of Donata's birth. Vitale travelled less so that he could spend more time with his family. He was also very much a hands-on father, who enjoyed playing with his daughter and reading her stories. Zara could see that he was striving to give Donata the safe, loving childhood that fate had denied both of them and it touched her heart. On this particular evening, though, Zara gave her daughter less time to settle into bed than she usually did because it was the couple's third wedding anniversary and she and Vitale were going out to celebrate.

Zara donned an elegant blue designer dress that skimmed her slight curves and made the most of her height. As she did her make-up she was thinking of the announcement she had to make and smiling to herself, thinking of how different it would be this time from the last time when everything relating to her pregnancy had seemed so uncertain and scary.

Vitale strode through the door with all the impatience of a man who was always eager to see his wife after being away from her.

Zara appeared in the bathroom doorway. 'Vitale...' she murmured, skimming over him with helpless admiration, for she still marvelled over the fact that this gorgeous man was her husband and the father of her child.

'You look fantastic,' he breathed, his dark gaze running over the chic dress and lingering on that luminous smile echoed by the superb diamond pendant she always wore. 'Do we really have to go out?'

Her sultry mouth quirked. When Vitale was away from her for any appreciable length of time it took determination to get him out of the bedroom.

'I didn't go to all this trouble dressing up just to stay home—'

Vitale groaned, amusement and frustration etched in his lean dark face. 'I just want to grab you and unwrap you like a gift but I know this is a special occasion.'

'Our third anniversary,' Zara reminded him very seriously.

Her husband dug into his pocket and handed her a little box. 'A small mark of my appreciation and love...'

It was an eternity ring, composed of a hoop of beautiful diamonds that slotted onto her finger next to her wedding ring as though it had been made for that spot, which, as Vitale was very good at detail, it probably had been. 'It's gorgeous,' she carolled, pink with pleasure that he had made the effort to celebrate the occasion with such a present.

'I'm sorry, I'm going to have to wreck your make-up, *angelina mia*. I'm in the control of forces stronger than I am,' Vitale teased, closing his arms round her and claiming a passionate kiss.

And he did a lot more than wreck her make-up, for the passion that never failed them burst into being on contact with a strength that could not be denied and they happily gave way to pleasing each other in the oldest way of all. Afterwards, the dress was a little creased and the dinner reservation had to be moved to a later time.

They ate at their favourite Florentine restaurant by candlelight and somewhere between the first course and the final one Zara made her announcement and Vitale did not dare tell her that because she had refused the wine he had already guessed. Instead he gripped her hand and told her that the news she was carrying their second child was amazing, before adding quite truthfully that their three years together had been the happiest years of his life.

Meeting those dark golden eyes resting on her with adoration, Zara's gaze misted over. 'And mine…I love you so much.'

'And with every year that you are with me, I love you more, *angelina mia*.'

* * * * *

A DEAL AT
THE ALTAR

CHAPTER ONE

'WHAT do I want to do about the Royale hotel group?' The speaker, a very tall and well-built Greek male with blue-black hair, raised an ebony brow and gave a sardonic laugh. 'Let's allow Blake to sweat for the moment…'

'Yes, sir.' Thomas Morrow, the British executive who had asked the question at the behest of his colleagues, was conscious of the nervous perspiration on his brow. One-on-one encounters with his powerhouse employer, one of the richest men in the world, were rare and he was keen not to say anything that might be deemed stupid or naive.

Everybody knew that Sergios Demonides did not suffer fools gladly. Unfortunately, priding himself on being a maverick, the Greek billionaire did not feel the need to explain the objectives behind his business decisions either, which could make life challenging for his executive team. Not so long ago the acquisition of the Royale hotel group at any price had seemed to be the goal and there was even a strong rumour that Sergios might be planning to marry the exquisite Zara Blake, the daughter of the man who owned the hotel chain. But after Zara had been pictured in the media in the arms of an Italian banker that rumour had died and Sergios's curious staff had not noticed their boss exhibiting the smallest sign of annoyance over the development.

'I took the original offer to Blake off the table. The price will come down now,' Sergios pointed out lazily, brilliant black eyes glittering at that prospect for more than anything else in life he liked to drive a hard bargain.

Purchasing the Royale group at an inflated price would have gone very much against the grain with him, but a couple of months ago Sergios had been prepared to do it and jump through virtually any hoop just to make that deal. *Why?* His beloved grandfather, Nectarios, who had started his legendary business empire at the helm of the very first Royale hotel in London, had been seriously ill at the time. But, mercifully, Nectarios was a tough old buzzard, Sergios thought fondly, and pioneering heart surgery in the USA had powered his recovery. Sergios now thought that the hotel chain would make a timely little surprise for his grandfather's eightieth birthday, but he no longer had any intention of paying over the odds for the gift.

As for the wife he had almost acquired as part of the deal, Sergios was relieved that fate had prevented him from making that mistake. Zara Blake, after all, had shown herself up as a beautiful little tart with neither honour nor decency. On the other hand her maternal instincts would have come in very useful where his children were concerned, he conceded grudgingly. Had it not been for the fact that his cousin's premature death had left Sergios responsible for his three young children, Sergios would not even have considered taking a second wife.

His handsome face hardened. One catastrophe in that department had been quite sufficient for Sergios. For the sake of those children, however, he had been prepared to bite the bullet and remarry. It would have been a marriage of convenience though, a public sham to gain a mother for the children and assuage his conscience. He knew nothing about kids and had never wanted any of his own but he knew his cousin's children were unhappy and that piqued his pride and his sense of honour.

'So, we're waiting for Blake to make the next move,' Thomas guessed, breaking the silence.

'And it won't be long. He's over-extended and underfunded with very few options left,' Sergios commented with growling satisfaction.

'You're a primary school teacher and good with young kids,' Monty Blake pointed out, seemingly impervious to his eldest daughter's expression of frank astonishment as she stood in his wood-panelled office. 'You'd make the perfect wife for Demonides—'

'No, stop right there!' Bee lifted a hand to physically emphasise that demand, her green eyes bright with disbelief as she used her other hand to push the heavy fall of chestnut-brown hair off her damp brow. Now she knew that her surprise and disquiet that her father should have asked her to come and see him were not unfounded. 'This is me, not Zara, you're talking to and I have no desire to marry an oversexed billionaire who needs some little woman at home to look after his kids—'

'Those kids are not his,' the older man broke in to remind her, as though that should make a difference to her. 'His cousin's death made him their guardian. By all accounts he didn't either want or welcome the responsibility—'

At that information, Bee's delicately rounded face only tightened with increased annoyance. She had plenty of experience with men who could not be bothered with children, not least with the man standing in front of her making sexist pronouncements. He might have persuaded her naive younger sister, Zara, to consider a marriage of convenience with the Greek shipping magnate, but Bee was far less impressionable and considerably more suspicious.

She had never sought her father's approval, which was just as well because as she was a mere daughter it had never been on offer to her. She was not afraid to admit that she didn't like or respect the older man, who had taken no interest in her as she grew up. He had also badly damaged her self-esteem at sixteen when he advised her that she needed to go on a diet and dye her hair a lighter colour. Monty Blake's image of female perfection was unashamedly blonde and skinny, while Bee was brunette and resolutely curvy. She focused on the desk photograph of her stepmother, Ingrid, a glamorous former Swedish model, blonde and thin as a rail.

'I'm sorry, I'm not interested, Dad,' Bee told him squarely, belatedly noticing that he wore an undeniable look of tiredness and strain. Perhaps he had come up with that outrageous suggestion that she marry Sergios Demonides because he was stressed out with business worries, she reasoned uncertainly.

'Well, you'd better get interested,' Monty Blake retorted sharply. 'Your mother and you lead a nice life. If the Royale hotel group crashes so that Demonides can pick it up for a song, the fallout won't only affect me and your stepmother but *all* my dependants...'

Bee tensed at that doom-laden forecast. 'What are you saying?'

'You know very well what I'm saying,' he countered impatiently. 'You're not as stupid as your sister—'

'Zara is *not*—'

'I'll come straight to the point. I've always been very generous to you and your mother...'

Uncomfortable with that subject though she was, Bee also liked to be fair. 'Yes, you have been,' she was willing to acknowledge.

It was not the moment to say that she had always thought his generosity towards her mother might be better described as 'conscience' money. Emilia, Bee's Spanish mother, had been Monty's first wife. In the wake of a serious car accident, Emilia had emerged from hospital as a paraplegic in a wheelchair. Bee had been four years old at the time and her mother had quickly realised that her young, ambitious husband was repulsed by her handicap. With quiet dignity, Emilia had accepted the inevitable and agreed to a separation. In gratitude for the fact that she had returned his freedom without a fuss, Monty had bought Emilia and her daughter a detached house in a modern estate, which he had then had specially adapted to her mother's needs. He had also always paid for the services of a carer to ensure that Bee was not burdened with round-the-clock responsibility for her mother. While the need to help out at home had necessarily restricted Bee's social life from a young age, she was painfully aware that only her father's financial support had made it possible for her to attend university, train as a teacher and actually take up the career that she loved.

'I'm afraid that unless you do what I'm asking you to do the gravy train of my benevolence stops here and now,' Monty Blake declared harshly. 'I own your mother's house. It's in my name and I can sell it any time I choose.'

Bee turned pale at that frank warning, shock winging through her because this was not a side of her father that she had ever come up against before. 'Why would you do something so dreadful to Mum?'

'Why should I care now?' Monty demanded curtly. 'I married your mother over twenty years ago and I've looked after her ever since. Most people would agree that I've more than paid my dues to a woman I was only married to for five years.'

'You know how much Mum and I appreciate everything that you have done for her,' Bee responded, her pride stung by the need to show that humility in the face of his obnoxious threatening behaviour.

'If you want my generosity to continue it will *cost* you,' the older man spelt out bluntly. 'I need Sergios Demonides to buy my hotels at the right price. And he was willing to do that until Zara blew him off and married that Italian instead—'

'Zara's deliriously happy with Vitale Roccanti,' Bee murmured tautly in her half-sister's defence. 'I don't see how I could possibly persuade a big tough businessman like Demonides to buy your hotels at a preferential price.'

'Well, let's face it, you don't have Zara's looks,' her father conceded witheringly. 'But as I understand it all Demonides wants is a mother for those kids he's been landed with and you'd make a damned sight better mother for them than Zara ever would have done—your sister can barely read! I bet he didn't know that when he agreed to marry her.'

Stiff with distaste at the cruelty of his comments about her sister, who suffered from dyslexia, Bee studied him coolly. 'I'm sure a man as rich and powerful as Sergios Demonides could find any number of women willing to marry him and play mummy to those kids. As you've correctly pointed out I'm not the ornamental type so I can't understand why you imagine he might be interested in me.'

Monty Blake released a scornful laugh. 'Because I know what he wants—Zara told me. He wants a woman who knows her place—'

'Well, then, he definitely doesn't want me,' Bee slotted in drily, her eyes flaring at that outdated expression that assumed female inferiority. 'And Zara's feistier than you seem to appreciate. I think he would have had problems with her too.'

'But you're the clever one who could give him exactly what he wants. You're much more practical than Zara ever was because you've never had it too easy—'

'Dad...?' Bee cut in, spreading her hands in a silencing motion. 'Why are we even having this insane conversation? I've only met Sergios Demonides once in my life and he barely looked at me.'

She swallowed back the unnecessary comment that the only part of her the Greek tycoon had noticed had appeared to be her chest.

'I want you to go to him and offer him a deal—the same deal he made with Zara. A marriage where he gets to do as he likes and buys my hotels at the agreed figure—'

'*Me*...go to *him* with a proposal of marriage?' Bee echoed in ringing disbelief. 'I've never heard anything so ridiculous in my life! The man would think I was a lunatic!'

Monty Blake surveyed her steadily. 'I believe you're clever enough to be convincing. If you can persuade him that you could be a perfect wife and mother for those little orphans you're that something extra that could put this deal back on the table for me. I need this sale and I need it now or everything I've worked for all my life is going to tumble down like a pack of cards. And with it will go your mother's security—'

'Don't threaten Mum like that.'

'But it's not an empty threat.' Monty shot his daughter an embittered look. 'The bank's threatening to pull the plug on my loans. My hotel chain is on the edge of disaster and right now that devil, Demonides, is playing a waiting game. I can't afford to wait. If I go down you and your mother will lose everything too,' he reminded her doggedly. 'Think about it and imagine it—no specially adapted house, day-to-day responsibility for Emilia, no life of your own any more...'

'Don't!' Bee exclaimed, disgusted by his coercive methods. 'I think you have to be off your head to think that Sergios Demonides would even consider marrying someone like me.'

'Perhaps I am but we're not going to know until you make the approach, are we?'

'You're crazy!' his daughter protested vehemently, aghast at what he was demanding of her.

Her father stabbed a finger in the air. 'I'll have a For Sale sign erected outside your mother's house this week if you don't at least go and see him.'

'I couldn't...I just *couldn't*!' Bee gasped, appalled by his persistence. 'Please don't do this to Mum.'

'I've made a reasonable request, Bee. I'm in a very tight corner. Why, after enjoying all my years of expensive support and education, shouldn't you try to help?'

'Oh, puh-lease,' Bee responded with helpless scorn at that smooth and inaccurate résumé of his behaviour as a parent. 'Demanding that I approach a Greek billionaire and ask him to marry me is a *reasonable* request? On what planet and in what culture would that be reasonable?'

'Tell him you'll take those kids off his hands and allow him to continue enjoying his freedom and I think you're in with a good chance,' the older man replied stubbornly.

'And what happens when I humiliate myself and he turns me down?'

'You'll have to pray that he says yes,' Monty Blake answered, refusing to give an inch in his desperation. 'After all, it is the *only* way that your mother's life is likely to continue as comfortably as it has done for years.'

'Newsflash, Dad. Life in a wheelchair is not comfortable,' his daughter flung at him bitterly.

'And life without my financial security blanket is likely to be even less comfortable,' he sliced back, determined to have the last word.

Minutes later, having failed to change her father's mind in any way, Bee left the hotel and caught the bus home to the house she still shared with her mother. She was cooking supper when her mother's care assistant, Beryl, brought Emilia back from a trip to the library. Wheeling into the kitchen, Emilia beamed at her daughter. 'I found a Catherine Cookson I haven't read!'

'I won't be able to get you off to sleep tonight now.' Looking down into her mother's worn face, aged and lined beyond her years by illness and suffering, Bee could have wept at the older woman's continuing determination to celebrate the smallest things in life. Emilia had lost so much in that accident but she never ever complained.

When she had settled her mother for the night, Bee sat down to mark homework books for her class of seven-year-olds. Her mind, however, refused to stay on the task. She could not stop thinking about what her father had told her. He had threatened her but he had also told her a truth that had ripped away her sense of security. After all, she had naively taken her father's continuing financial success for granted and assumed that he would always be in a position to ensure that her mother had no money worries.

Being Bee, she had to consider the worst-case scenario. If her mother lost her house and garden it would undoubtedly break her heart. The house had been modified for a disabled occupant so that Emilia could move easily within its walls. Zara had even designed raised flower beds for the back garden, which her mother could work at on good days. If the house was sold Bee had a salary and would naturally be able to rent an apartment *but* as she would not be able to afford a full-time carer for her mother any more she would have to give up work to look after her and would thus lose that salary. Monty Blake might cover the bills but there had never been a surplus or indeed a legal agreement that he provide financial support and Emilia had no savings. Without his assistance the two women would have to live on welfare benefits and all the little extras and outings that lightened and lifted her mother's difficult life would no longer be affordable. It was a gloomy outlook that appalled Bee, who had always been very protective of the older woman.

Indeed when she thought about Emilia losing even the little things that she cherished the prospect of proposing marriage to a very intimidating Greek tycoon became almost acceptable. So what if she made a fool of herself? Well, there was no 'if' about it, she would make a colossal fool of herself and he might well dine out on the story for years! He had seemed to her as exactly the sort of guy likely to enjoy other people's misfortunes.

Not that he hadn't enjoyed misfortunes of his own, Bee was willing to grudgingly concede. When her sister had planned to marry Sergios, Bee had researched him on the Internet and she had disliked most of what she had discovered. Sergios had only become a Demonides when he was a teenager with a string of petty crimes to his name. He had grown up fighting for survival in one of the roughest areas of Athens. At twenty-one he had married a beautiful Greek heiress and barely three years later he had buried her when she died carrying their unborn child. Yes, Sergios Demonides might be filthy rich and successful, but his personal life was generally a disaster zone.

Those facts aside, however, he also had a name for being an out-and-out seven-letter-word in business and with women. Popular report said that he was extremely intelligent and astute but that he was also famously arrogant, ruthless and cold, the sort of guy who, as a husband, would have given her sensitive sister Zara and her cute pet rabbit, Fluffy, nightmares. Fortunately Bee did not consider herself sensitive. Growing up without a father and forced to become an adult long before her time as she learned to cope with her mother's disability and dependence, Bee had forged a tougher shell.

At the age of twenty-four, Bee already knew that men were rarely attracted to that protective shell or the unadorned conservative wrapping that surrounded it. She wasn't pretty or feminine and the boys she had dated as she grew up had, with only one exception, been friends rather than lovers. She had never learned to flirt or play girlie games and thought that perhaps she was just too sensible. She had, however, for a blissful few months been deeply in love and desperately hurt when the relationship fell apart over the extent of her responsibility for her disabled mother. And while she couldn't have cared less about her appearance, she *was* clever and passing so many exams with distinction and continually winning prizes did, she had learned to her cost, scare off the opposite sex.

The men she met also tended to be put off when Bee spoke her mind even if it meant treading on toes. She hated injustice or cruelty in any form. She didn't do that fragile-little-woman thing her stepmother, Ingrid, was for ever flattering her father with. It was hardly surprising that even Zara, the sister she loved, had grown up with a healthy dose of that same fatal man-pleasing gene. Only her youngest sister, Tawny, born of her father's affair with his secretary, resembled Bee in that line. Bee had never known what it was to feel helpless until she found herself actually making an appointment to see Sergios Demonides…such a crazy idea, such a very pointless exercise.

Forty-eight hours after Bee won the tussle with her pride and made the appointment, Sergios's PA asked him if he was willing to see Monty Blake's daughter, Beatriz. Unexpectedly Sergios had instant recall of the brunette's furious grass-green eyes and magnificent breasts. A dinner in tiresome company had been rendered almost bearable by his enticing view of that gravity-defying bosom, although she had not appreciated the attention. But why the hell would Blake's elder daughter want to speak to him? Did she work with her father? Was she hoping to act as the older man's negotiator? He snapped his long brown fingers to bring an aide to his side and requested an immediate background report on Beatriz before granting her an appointment the next day.

The following afternoon, dressed in a grey trouser suit, which she usually reserved for interviews but which she was convinced gave her much-needed dignity, Bee waited in the reception area of the elegant stainless-steel and glass building that housed the London headquarters of SD Shipping. That Sergios had used his own initials to stamp his vast business empire with his powerful personality didn't surprise Bee at all. Her heart rate increased at the prospect that loomed ahead of her.

'Mr Demonides will see you now, Miss Blake,' the attractive receptionist informed her with a practised smile that Bee could not match.

Without warning Bee was feeling sick with nerves. She was too intelligent not to contemplate the embarrassment awaiting her without inwardly cringing. She was quick to remind herself that the Greek billionaire was just a big hulking brute with too much money and an inability to ignore a low neck on a woman's dress. She reddened, recalling the evening gown with the plunge neckline that she had borrowed from a friend for that stupid meal. While his appraisal had made Bee blush like a furnace and had reminded her why she usually covered up those particular attributes, she had been stunned by his apparent indifference to her beautiful sister, Zara.

When Beatriz Blake came through the door of Sergios's office with a firm step in her sensible shoes, he instantly recognised that he was not about to be treated to any form of charm offensive. Her boxy colourless trouser suit did nothing for her womanly curves. Her rich brown hair was dragged back from her face and she wore not a scrap of make-up. To a man accustomed to highly groomed women her lackadaisical attitude towards making a good impression struck him as almost rude.

'I'm a very busy man, Beatriz. I don't know what you're doing here but I expect you to keep it brief,' he told her impatiently.

For a split second Sergios Demonides towered over Bee like a giant building casting a long tall shadow and she took a harried step back, feeling crowded by his sheer size and proximity. She had forgotten how big and commanding he was, from his great height to his broad shoulders and long powerful legs. He was also, much though it irritated her to admit it, a staggeringly handsome man with luxuriant blue-black hair and sculpted sun-darkened features. The sleek unmistakeable assurance of great wealth oozed from the discreet gleam of his thin gold watch and cufflinks to the spotless white of his shirt and the classy tailoring of his dark business suit.

She collided with eyes the colour of burnished bronze that had the impact of a sledgehammer and cut off her breathing at its source. It was as if nerves were squeezing her throat tight and her heart started hammering again.

'My father asked me to see you on his behalf,' she began, annoyed by the breathlessness making her voice sound low and weak.

'You're a primary school teacher. What could you possibly have to say that I would want to hear?' Sergios asked with brutal frankness.

'I think you'll be surprised…' Bee compressed her lips, her voice gathering strength as reluctant amusement briefly struck her. 'Well, I *know* you'll be surprised.'

Surprises were rare and even less welcome in Sergios's life. He was a control freak and knew it and had not the smallest urge to change.

'A little while back you were planning to marry my sister, Zara.'

'It wouldn't have worked,' Sergios responded flatly.

Bee breathed in deep and slow while her white-knuckled hands gripped the handles of her bag. 'Zara told me exactly what you wanted out of marriage.'

While wondering where the strange dialogue could possibly be leading, Sergios tried not to grit his teeth visibly. 'That was most indiscreet of her.'

Discomfiture sent colour flaming into Bee's cheeks, accentuating the deep green of her eyes. 'I'm just going to put my cards on the table and get to the point.'

Sergios rested back against the edge of his polished contemporary desk and surveyed her in a manner that was uniquely discouraging, 'I'm waiting,' he said when she hesitated.

His impatient silence hummed like bubbling water ready to boil over.

Beneath her jacket, Bee breathed in so deep her bosom swelled and almost popped the buttons on her fitted blouse and for a split second Sergios dropped his narrowed gaze there as the fabric pulled taut over that full swell, whose bounty he still vividly recalled.

'My father utilised a certain amount of pressure to persuade me to come and see you,' she admitted uncomfortably. 'I told him it was crazy but here I am.'

'Yes, here…you…are,' Sergios framed in a tone of yawning boredom. 'Still struggling to come to the point.'

'Dad wanted me to offer myself in Zara's place.' Bee squeezed out that admission and watched raw incredulity laced with astonished hauteur flare in his face while hot pink embarrassment surged into hers. 'I know, I told you it was crazy but he wants that hotel deal and he thinks that a suitable wife added into the mix could make a difference.'

'Suitable? You're certainly not in the usual run of women who aspire to marry me.' Sergios delivered that opinion bluntly.

And it was true. Beatriz Blake was downright plain in comparison to the gorgeous women who pursued him wherever he went, desperate to attract his attention and get their greedy hands on, if not the ultimate prize of a wedding ring, some token of his wealth. But somewhere deep in his mind at that instant a memory was stirring.

'Homely women make the best wives,' his grandfather had once contended. 'Your grandmother was unselfish, loyal and caring. I couldn't have asked for a better wife. My home was kept like a palace, my children were loved, and my word was law. She never gave me a second of concern. Think well before you marry a beauty, who demands more and gives a lot less.'

Having paled at that unnecessary reminder of her limitations, Bee made a fast recovery and lifted her chin. 'Obviously I'm not blonde and beautiful but I'm convinced that I would be a more appropriate choice than Zara ever was for the position.'

A kind of involuntary fascination at the level of her nerve was holding Sergios taut. His straight black brows drew together in a frown. 'You speak as though the role of being my wife would be a job.'

'Isn't it?' Bee came back at him boldly with that challenge. 'From what I understand you only want to marry to have a mother for your late cousin's children and I could devote myself to their care full-time, something Zara would never have been willing to do. I also—'

'Be silent for a moment,' Sergios interrupted, studying her with frowning attention. 'What kind of pressure did your father put on you to get you to come here and spout this nonsense?'

Bee went rigid before she tossed her head back in sudden defiance, wondering why she should keep her father's coercion a secret. Her pride demanded that she be honest. 'I have a severely disabled mother and if the sale of the Royale hotel chain falls through my father has threatened to sell our home and stop paying for Mum's care assistant. I'm not dependent on him but Mum is and I don't want to see her suffer. Her life is challenging enough.'

'I'm sure it is.' Sergios was unwillingly impressed by her motivation. Evidently Monty Blake was crueller within his family circle than Sergios would ever have guessed. Even Nectarios, his grandfather and one of the most ruthless men Sergios had ever met, would have drawn the line at menacing a disabled ex-wife. As for Beatriz, he could respect her honesty and her family loyalty, traits that said a lot about the kind of woman she was. She wasn't here for his enviable lifestyle or his money, she was here because she didn't have a choice. That was not a flattering truth but Sergios loathed flattery, having long since recognised that few people saw past his immense wealth and power to the man behind it all.

'So, tell me why you believe that you would make a better wife than your sister?' Sergios urged, determined to satisfy his curiosity and intrigued by her attitude towards marriage. A wife as an employee? It was a new take on the traditional role that appealed to him. A businessman to the core, he was quick to see the advantages of such an arrangement. A paid wife would be more likely to respect his boundaries while still making the effort to please him, he reasoned thoughtfully. There could be little room for messy human emotion and misunderstanding in such a practical agreement.

'I would be less demanding. I'm self-sufficient, sensible. I probably wouldn't cost you very much either as I'm not very interested in my appearance,' Bee pointed out, her full pink mouth folding as if vanity could be considered a vice. 'I'm also very good with kids.'

'What would you do with a six-year-old boy painting pictures on the walls?'

Bee frowned. 'Talk to him.'

'But he doesn't talk back. His little brother keeps on trying to cling to me and the toddler just stares into space,' Sergios told her in a driven undertone, his concern and incomprehension of such behaviour patent. 'Why am I telling you that?'

Surprised by his candour, Bee reckoned it was a sign that the children's problems were very much on his mind 'You thought I might have an answer for you?'

With a warning knock the door opened and someone addressed him in what she assumed to be Greek. He gave a brief answer and returned his attention to Bee. Something about that assessing look made her stiffen. 'I'll think over your proposition,' he drawled softly, startling her. 'But be warned, I'm not easy to please.'

'I knew that the first time I looked at you,' Bee countered, taking in the sardonic glitter of his eyes, the hard, uncompromising bone structure and that stubborn sensual mouth. It was very much the face of a tough guy, resistant to any counsel but his own.

'Next you'll be telling me you can read my fortune from my palm,' Sergios retorted with mocking cool.

Bee walked out of his office in a daze. He had said he would consider her proposition. Had that only been a polite lie? Somehow she didn't think he would have given her empty words. But if he was seriously considering her as a wife, where did that leave her? Fathoms deep in shock? For since Bee had automatically assumed that Sergios Demonides would turn her down she had not, at any stage, actually considered the possibility of becoming his wife...

CHAPTER TWO

Four days later, Bee emerged from the gates of the primary school where she worked and noticed a big black limousine parked just round the corner.

'Miss Blake?' A man in a suit with the build of a bouncer approached her. 'Mr Demonides would like to offer you a lift home.'

Bee blinked and stared at the long glossy limo with its tinted windows. How had he found out where she worked? While wondering what on earth Sergios Demonides was playing at, she saw no option other than to accept. Why queue for a bus when a limo was on offer? she reflected ruefully. Had he come in person to deliver his negative answer? Why would he take the trouble to do that? A man of his exalted status rarely put himself out for others. As a crowd of colleagues and parents parted to give Bee and her bulky companion a clear passage to the opulent vehicle self-conscious pink warmed her cheeks because people were staring.

'Beatriz,' Sergios acknowledged with a grave nod, glancing up from his laptop.

As Bee slid into the luxury vehicle she was disturbingly conscious of the sheer animal charisma that he exuded from every pore. He was all male in the most primal sense of the word. Smell the testosterone, one of her university friends would have quipped. The faint tang of some expensive masculine cologne flared her nostrils, increasing her awareness. She felt her nipples pinch tight beneath her bra and she went rigid, deeply disconcerted by her pronounced awareness of the sexual charge he put out. Her shielded gaze fell on his lean masculine profile, noting the dark shadow of stubble outlining his angular jaw. He was badly in need of a shave. It was the only sign in his otherwise immaculate appearance that he was nearing the end of his working day rather than embarking on its beginning. Aware that her hair was tossed by the breeze and her raincoat, skirt and knee-high boots were more comfortable than smart, she was stiff and awkward and questioning why because as a rule her sole concern about her appearance was that she be clean and tidy.

As the limousine pulled away from the pavement Sergios flipped shut his laptop and turned his arrogant head to look at her. His frown was immediate. She was a mess in her unfashionable, slightly shabby clothing. Yet she had flawless skin, lovely eyes and thick glossy hair, advantages that most women would have made the effort to enhance. For the first time he wondered why she didn't bother.

'To what do I owe the honour?' Bee enquired, watching him push the laptop away. He had beautiful shapely hands, she registered, and then tensed at that surprising thought.

'I'm leaving for New York this evening and I would like you to meet my children before I go.'

'Why?' Green eyes suddenly wide with confusion, Bee stared back at him. 'Why do you want me to meet them?'

A very faint smile curled the corners of his wide sensual mouth. 'Obviously because I'm considering you for the job.'

'But you *can't* be!' Bee told him in disbelief.

'I am. Your father played a winning hand sending you to see me,' Sergios fielded, amused by her astonishment, which was laced with a dismay that almost made him laugh out loud. She was a refreshing woman.

Her well-defined brows pleated and she frowned. 'I just don't understand...you could marry anybody!'

'Don't underestimate yourself,' Sergios responded, his thoughts on the enquiries and references he had gathered on her behalf since their last meeting. He had vetted her a good deal more thoroughly than he had vetted her flighty sister, Zara. 'According to my sources you're a loyal, devoted daughter and a gifted and committed teacher. I believe that you could offer those children exactly what they need—'

'Where did you get that information from?' Bee asked angrily.

'There are private investigation firms which can offer such details within hours for the right price,' Sergios fielded with colossal calm. 'Naturally I checked you out and I was impressed with what I learned about you.'

But I wasn't *seriously* offering to marry you, she almost snapped back at him before she thought better of that revealing admission and hastily swallowed it back. After all her father's threat still hung over her and his financial security was integral to her mother's support system. Take away that security and life as her mother knew it would be at an end. Suddenly Bee was looking down a long, dark, intimidating tunnel at a future she could no longer predict and accepting that if Sergios Demonides decided that he did want to marry her, she would be in no position to refuse him.

'If your cousin's children are disturbed, I have no experience with that sort of problem,' Bee warned him quietly. 'I have no experience of raising children either and I'm not a miracle worker.'

'I don't believe in miracles, so I'm not expecting one,' Sergios said very drily, resting sardonic golden eyes on her strained face. 'There would also be conditions which you would have to fulfil to meet my requirements.'

Bee said nothing. Still reeling in shock at the concept of marrying him, she did not trust herself to speak. As for his expectations, she was convinced they would be high and that he would have a very long list of them. Unhappily for her, Sergios Demonides was unaccustomed to settling for anything less than perfection and the very best in any field. She dug out her phone and rang her mother to warn her that she would be late home. By the time she finished the call the limousine was already filtering down a driveway adorned with silver birch trees just coming into leaf. They drew up outside a detached house large and grand enough to be described as a mansion.

'My London base.' Sergios shot her a rapier-eyed

glance from level dark eyes. 'One of your duties as my wife would be taking charge of my various homes and ensuring that the households run smoothly.'

The word 'wife', allied to that other word, 'duties', sounded horribly nineteenth century to Bee's ears. 'Are you a domestic tyrant?' she enquired.

Sergios sent her a frowning appraisal. 'Is that a joke?'

'No, but there is something very Victorian about mentioning the word wife in the same sentence as duties.'

His handsome mouth quirked. 'You first referred to the role as a job and I prefer to regard it in the same light.'

But Bee very much liked the job she already had and registered in some consternation that she was literally being asked to put her money where her mouth was. She had done what her father had asked her to do without thinking through the likely consequences of success. Now those consequences had well and truly come home to roost with her. As she accompanied Sergios into a sizeable foyer, he issued instructions to the manservant greeting him and escorted Bee into a massive drawing room.

'Unlike your sister, you're very quiet,' he remarked.

'You've taken me by surprise,' Bee admitted ruefully.

'You look bewildered. Why?' Sergios breathed, his bronzed eyes impatient. 'I have no desire for the usual kind of wife. I don't want the emotional ties, the demands or the restrictions, but on a practical basis a woman to fulfil that role would be a very useful addition to my life.'

'Perhaps I just don't see what's in it for me—apart from you buying my father's hotels which would hopefully ensure my mother's security for the foreseeable future,' Bee volunteered frankly.

'If I married you, *I* would ensure your mother's security for the rest of her life,' Sergios extended with quiet carrying emphasis, his dark deep drawl vibrating in the big room. 'Even if we were to part at a later date you would never have to worry about her care again, nor would she have to look to your father for support. I will personally ensure that your mother has everything she requires, including the very best of medical treatment available to someone with her condition.'

His words engulfed her like a crashing burst of thunder heralding a brighter dawn. Instantly Bee thought of the expensive extras that could improve Emilia Blake's quality of life. In place of Bee's home-made efforts, regular professional physiotherapy sessions might be able to strengthen Emilia's wasted limbs and something might be found to ease the breathing difficulties that sometimes afflicted her. Sergios, Bee appreciated suddenly, was rich enough to make a huge difference to her mother's life.

A young woman in a nanny uniform entered the room with a baby about eighteen months old in her arms and two small children trailing unenthusiastically in their wake.

'Thank you. Leave the children with us,' Sergios instructed.

Set down on the carpet the youngest child instantly began to howl, tears streaming down her little screwed-up face, a toddler of about three years old grabbed hold of Sergios's trousered leg while the older boy came to a suspicious halt several feet away.

'It's all right, pet.' Bee scooped up the baby and the little girl stopped mid-howl, settling anxious blue eyes on her. 'What's her name?'

'Eleni…and this is Milo,' Sergios told her, detaching the clinging toddler from his leg with difficulty and giving him a little helpful prod in Bee's direction as if he was hoping that the child would embrace her instead.

'And you have to be Paris,' Bee said to the older boy as she crouched down to greet Milo. 'My sister Zara told me that you got a new bike for your birthday.'

Paris didn't smile but he moved closer as Bee sank down on the sofa with the baby girl in her arms. Milo, clearly desperate for attention, clambered up beside her and tried to get on her lap with his sister but there wasn't enough room. 'Hello, Milo.'

'Paris, remember your manners,' Sergios interposed sternly.

With a scared look, Paris extended a skinny arm to shake hands formally, his eyes slewing evasively away from hers. Bee invited him to sit down beside her and told him that she was a teacher. When she asked him about the school he attended he shot her a frightened look and hurriedly glanced away. It did not take a genius to guess that Paris could be having problems at school. Of the three children, Milo was the most normal, a bundle of toddler energy in need of attention and entertainment. Paris, however, was tense and troubled while the little girl was very quiet and worryingly unresponsive.

After half an hour Sergios had seen enough to convince him that Beatriz Blake was the woman he needed to smooth out the rough and troublesome places in his life. Her warmth and energy drew the children and she was completely relaxed with them where her sister had been nervous and, while friendly, over-anxious to please. Bee, on the other hand, emanated a calm authority that ensured respect. He called the nanny back to remove the children again.

'You mentioned conditions…' Bee reminded him, returning to their earlier conversation and striving to stick to necessary facts. Yet when she tried to accept that she was actually considering marrying the Greek billionaire the idea seemed so remote and unreal and impossible that her thoughts swam in a sea of bemusement.

'Yes.' Poised by the window with fading light gleaming over his luxuriant black hair and accenting the hard angles and hollows of his handsome features, Sergios commanded her full attention without even trying. His next words, however, took her very much by surprise.

'I have a mistress. Melita is not negotiable,' Sergios informed her coolly. 'Occasionally I have other interests as well. I am discreet. I do not envisage any headlines about that aspect of my life.'

The level of such candour when she had become accustomed to his cool reserve left Bee reeling in shock. He had a mistress called Melita? Was that a Greek name? Whatever, he was not faithful to his mistress and clearly not a one-woman man. Bee could feel her cheeks inflame as her imagination filled with the kind of colourful images she did not want to have in his vicinity. She lowered her lashes in embarrassment, her rebellious brain still engaged in serving up a creative picture of that lean bronzed body of his entangled with that of a sinuous sexy blonde.

'I do not expect intimacy with you,' Sergios spelt out. 'On the other hand if you decide that you want a child of your own it would be selfish of me to deny you that option—'

'Well, then, there's always IVF,' Bee broke in hurriedly.

'From what I've heard it's not that reliable.'

Bee was now studying her feet with fixed attention. He had a mistress. He didn't expect to share a bed with her. But where did that leave her? A wife who wasn't a wife except in name.

'What sort of a life am I supposed to lead?' Bee asked him abruptly, looking up, green eyes glinting like fresh leaves in rain.

'Meaning?' Sergios prompted, pleased that she had demonstrated neither annoyance nor interest on the subject of his mistress. But then why should she care what he did? That was exactly the attitude he wanted her to take.

'Are you expecting me to take lovers as well… discreetly?' Bee queried, studying him while her colour rose and burned like scalding hot irons on her cheeks and she fought her embarrassment with all her might. It was a fair question, a sensible question and she refused to let prudishness prevent her from asking it.

His dark eyes glittered gold with anger. 'Of course not.'

Bee was frowning. 'I'm trying to understand how you expect such a marriage to work. You surely can't be suggesting that a woman of my age should accept a future in which any form of physical intimacy is against the rules?' she quantified very stiffly, fighting her mortification every step of the way.

Put like that her objection sounded reasonable but Sergios could no more have accepted the prospect of an unfaithful wife than he could have cut off his right arm. Features taut and grim, his big powerful length rigid, he breathed with the clarity of strong feeling, 'I could not agree to you taking lovers.'

'That old hypocritical double standard,' Bee murmured, strangely amused by his appalled reaction and not even grasping why she should feel that way. So what was good for the goose was not, in this case, good for the gander? Yet she could barely believe that she was even having such a discussion with him. After all, she was a twenty-four-year-old virgin, a piece of information that would no doubt shock him almost as much as the idea of a wife with an independent sexual appetite.

In response to that scornful comment, Sergios shot her a seething appraisal, his dark eyes flaming like hot coals. 'Don't speak to me in that tone...'

Lesson one, Bee noted, he has a very volatile temper. She breathed in deep, quelling her wicked stab of amusement at his incredulous reaction to the idea of an adulterous wife. 'I asked you a reasonable question and you did not give me a reasonable answer. How long do you expect this marriage to last?'

'At least until the children grow up.'

'My youth,' Bee remarked without any emotion, but it was true. By the time the children acquired independence her years of youth would be long gone.

Sergios was studying her, recalling those lush violin curves in the evening gown she had worn at their first meeting. Full pouting breasts, generous womanly hips. He was startled when that mental picture provoked the heavy tightness of arousal at his groin.

'Then we make it a real marriage,' Sergios fielded with sardonic bite, blanking out his physical response with male impatience. 'That is the only other possible option on the table. If you want a man in your bed you will have me, no other.'

The flush in Bee's cheeks swept up to her brow and her dismayed eyes skimmed away from the intrusion of his. 'I don't really wish to continue this discussion but I should say that while you have other women in your life I would not be willing to enter an intimate relationship with you.'

'We're wasting time with this nonsense and we're adults. We will deal with such problems as and when they arise,' Sergios delivered curtly. 'There will be a pre-nuptial contract for you to sign—'

'You mentioned your homes and your, er…mistress. What other conditions are you planning to impose?'

'Nothing that I think need concern you. Our lawyers can deal with the contracts. If you choose to argue about terms you may do so through them,' Sergios completed in a crushing tone of finality. 'Now, if you will excuse me, I will have you driven home. I have business to take care of before I leave for New York.'

Bee, who had had a vague idea that he might invite her to stay to dinner, learned her mistake. She smoothed down her raincoat and rose slowly upright. 'I have a condition as well. You would have to agree to be polite, respectful and considerate of my happiness at all times.'

As that unanticipated demand hit him Sergios froze halfway to the door, wondering if she was criticising his manners. Since he had reached eighteen years of age before appreciating that certain courtesies even existed, he was unusually sensitive to the suggestion. He turned back, brooding black eyes glittering below the lush fan of his lashes. 'That would be a tall order. I'm selfish, quick-tempered and often curt. I expect my staff to adapt to my ways.'

'If I marry you I won't be a member of your staff. I'll be somewhere between a wife and an employee. You will have to make allowances and changes.' Bee studied him expectantly, for it would be disastrous if she allowed him to assume that he could have everything his way. She had no illusions about the fact that she was dealing with a very powerful personality, who would ride roughshod over her needs and wishes and ignore them altogether if it suited him to do so.

Sergios was taken aback at her nerve in challenging him, viewing him with those cool assessing green eyes as though he were an intellectual puzzle to be solved. His stubborn jaw line squared. 'I may make some allowances but I will call the shots. If we're going ahead with this arrangement, I want the wedding to take place soon so that you can move in here to be with the children.'

Consternation filled Bee's face. 'But I can't leave my mother—'

'You're a teacher, good at talking but not at listening,' Sergios chided with a curled lip. '*Listen* to what I tell you. Your mother will be taken care of in every possible way.'

'In every possible way that facilitates what *you* want!' Bee slammed back at him with angry emphasis.

He raised a brow, sardonic amusement in his intent dark gaze. 'Would you really expect anything different from me?'

CHAPTER THREE

LIFE as Bee knew it began to change very soon after that thought-provoking parting from Sergios.

Indeed Bee came home from school the very next day to find her mother troubled by the fact that her father had made an angry phone call to her that same afternoon.

'Monty told me that you're getting married,' Emilia Blake recounted with a look of frank disbelief. 'But I told him that you weren't even seeing anyone.'

Bee went pink. 'I didn't tell you but—'

Her mother stared at her with wide, startled eyes. 'My goodness, there is someone! But you only go out twice a week to your exercise classes—'

Bee grimaced and reached for her mother's frail hands. Not for anything would she have told the older woman any truth that might upset her. Indeed when it came to her mother's peace of mind, Bee was more than ready to lie. 'I'm sorry I wasn't more honest with you. I do want you to be happy for me.'

'So, obviously you weren't at classes all those evenings,' Emilia assumed in some amusement while she studied her blushing daughter with fond pride in her shadowed eyes. 'I'm so pleased. Your father and I haven't set you a very good example and I know you haven't had the same choices as other girls your age—'

'You still haven't told me what my father was angry about,' Bee cut in anxiously.

'Some business deal he's involved in with your future husband hasn't gone the way he hoped,' Emilia responded in a dismissive tone. 'What on earth does he expect you to do about it? Take my advice, don't get involved.'

Dismayed by her explanation, Bee had tensed. 'Exactly what did Dad say?'

'You know how moody he can be when things don't go his way. Tell me about Sergios—isn't he the man you met at that dinner your father invited you to a couple of months ago?'

'Yes.' So, although the marriage was going ahead, it seemed that her father was not to profit as richly as he had expected from the deal. Clearly that was why the older man was angry, but Bee thought there was a rare justice to the news that her sacrifice was unlikely to enrich her father: threats did not deserve a reward.

'My word, you've been having a genuine whirlwind romance,' Emilia gathered with a blossoming smile of approval. 'Are you sure that this Sergios is the man for you, Bee?'

Bee recalled Sergios Demonides's assurance that she would never again have to look to her father to support her mother. She remembered the fearless impact of those shrewd dark eyes and although she was apprehensive about the future she had signed up for she did believe that Sergios would stand by his word. 'Yes, Mum. Yes, I'm sure.'

Sergios phoned that evening to tell her that a member of his personal staff would be liaising with her over the wedding arrangements. He suggested that she hand in her notice immediately. His impatience came as a surprise when he had seemingly been content to wait several months before taking her sister Zara to the altar. He then followed that bombshell up with the news that he expected her to move to Greece after the wedding.

'But you have a house here,' Bee protested.

'I will visit London regularly but Greece is my home.'

'When you were planning to marry Zara—'

'Stop there—you and I will reach our own arrangements,' Sergios cut in deflatingly.

'I don't want to leave my mother alone in London.'

'Your mother will accompany us to Greece—but only after we have enjoyed a suitable newly married period of togetherness. I have already issued instructions to have appropriate accommodation organised for her. Have you heard from your father yet?'

In shock at the news that he was already making plans for her mother to accompany them to Greece, Bee was in a complete daze, her every expectation blown apart. On every issue he seemed to be one step ahead of her. 'I believe he was annoyed about something when he was talking to my mother today,' she admitted reluctantly.

'Your father did not get the deal he wanted,' Sergios

informed her bluntly. 'But that is nothing to do with you and so I told him on your behalf.'

'Did you indeed?' Bee questioned with a frown, her hackles rising at the increasingly authoritarian note in his explanations. Acting as chief spokesperson for the women in his life evidently came very naturally to Sergios. If she wasn't careful to keep his controlling streak within bounds, Bee thought darkly, he would soon have her behaving with all the self-will of a glove puppet.

'You are the woman I'm going to marry. It is not appropriate for your father to speak of either you or your mother with disrespect and I have warned him in that regard.'

Bee's blood ran cold in her veins, for she could picture the scene and the warning with Monty Blake raging recklessly and Sergios cold as ice and equally precise in his razor-sharp cutting edge. Her father was outspoken in temper but Sergios was altogether a more guarded and astute individual.

'How soon can you move into my London house?' Sergios pressed. 'It would please me if you could make that move this week.'

'*This* week?' Bee exclaimed in dismay.

'The wedding will be soon. I'm out of the country and the domestic staff are in charge of the children right now. If possible I would prefer you to be in the house while I'm away. If you're concerned about your mother being alone, you need not be—I've already requested a live-in companion for her from a vetted source.'

Bee came off the phone feeling unusually harassed

as she accepted that regardless of how she felt about it, her life was about to be turned upside down. Although she could not fault Sergios for his wish that she become involved with the children as soon as possible, she felt very much like an employee having her extensive duties listed and held over her head. As she had already told her mother about the three orphaned kids in Sergios's life, Emilia Blake was quick to understand her daughter's position.

'You really *must* put Sergios and those children first, Bee,' the older woman instructed worriedly. 'You mustn't make me more of a burden than I already am. I'll manage, I always have.'

Bee gently squeezed her parent's shoulder. 'You've never been a burden to me.'

'Sergios expects to come first and that's normal for a man who wants to marry you,' Emilia told her daughter. 'Don't let me become a bone of contention between you.'

Having drawn up innumerable lists and tendered her letter of resignation, for it was the last day of the spring term, Bee attended her evening pole exercise class and worked up a sweat while she tried not to fret about the many things that she still had to do. The list grew even longer after a visit from Annabel, the glossily efficient PA Sergios had put in charge of the wedding.

'I'm to have a consultation with a personal stylist and shopper?' Bee repeated weakly, staring down at the heavy schedule of appointments already set up for her over the Easter break that began that weekend. As well as a consultation with an upmarket legal firm concerning the pre-nuptial agreement, there was a day-long booking at a famous beauty salon. 'That's ridiculous. That's got nothing to do with the wedding.'

'Mr Demonides gave me my instructions,' Annabel told her in a steely tone.

Bee swallowed hard and compressed her lips. She would argue her case directly with Sergios. Possibly he thought a makeover was every woman's dream but Bee felt deeply insulted by the proposition. Her mother's new live-in companion/carer arrived that same evening and Bee chatted to her and helped her to settle in before she packed her own case ready for her move into Sergios's house the next morning.

When she arrived there she was shown upstairs into a palatial bedroom suite furnished with every possible necessity and luxury, right down to headed notepaper on a dainty feminine desk. The household seemed to operate just like an exclusive hotel. A maid came to the door to offer to unpack for her. Overcoming her discomfort at the prospect of being waited on by the staff, Bee smiled in determined agreement and went off to find the children instead.

Only Eleni, the youngest, however, was at home. Paris was at school and Milo was at a play group, the nanny explained. A rota of three nannies looked after the children round the clock. Bee found out what she needed to know about the children's basic routine and got down on her knees on the nursery carpet to play with Eleni. Initially when she was close by and utilised eye contact the little girl was more responsive but her attention was hard to hold. When the wind caught the door and it slammed shut Bee flinched from the loud noise but noted in surprise that Eleni did not react at all.

'Has her hearing been checked?' Bee asked with a frown.

The newly qualified nanny, who had replaced some-one else and only recently, had no idea. During the preceding months the children had suffered several changes in that line and had enjoyed little continuity of care. Having tracked down the children's health record booklets and drawn another blank, Bee finally phoned the medical practice to enquire. She discovered that Eleni had missed out on a standard hearing check-up a couple of months earlier and she made a fresh appoint-ment for the child. When she returned to the nursery the nanny was engaged in conducting her own basic tests and even to the untrained eye it did seem as though the little girl might have a problem with her hearing.

Milo, who was indiscriminately affectionate with al-most everybody, greeted her as though they were long-lost friends. She was reading a picture book to the little boy as he dropped off for a nap when Paris appeared in the nursery doorway and frowned at the sight of her with his little brother.

'Are you looking after us now?' Paris asked thinly.

'For some of the time. You won't need so many nan-nies because I'll be living here from now on. Sergios and I will be getting married in a few weeks.' Bee ex-plained, striving to sound much calmer than she actu-ally felt about that event.

Paris shot her a resentful glance and walked past

into his own room, carefully shutting the door behind him to underline his desire for privacy. Resolving to respect his wishes until she had visited his school and met his teacher, Bee suppressed a rueful sigh. She was a stranger. What more could she expect? Establishing a relationship with children who had lost their parents, their home and everything familiar only months before would take time and a good deal of trust on their part and she had to hope that Sergios was prepared for the reality that only time would improve the situation.

Forty-eight hours later, it was a novelty for Sergios to return to a house with a woman in residence and not worry about what awaited him. He could still vividly remember when he had never known what might be in store for him when he entered his own home. That experience had left him with an unshakable need to conserve his own space. Bee didn't count, he told himself irritably, she was here for the kids, not for him personally and she would soon learn to respect his privacy. He was taken aback, however, when his housekeeper informed him that Bee had gone out. He was even less impressed when he rang her cell phone and she admitted that she was travelling back on public transport.

'I wasn't expecting you back this soon…I was visiting my mother,' she told him defensively.

When Bee finally walked back into the mansion, she was flushed and breathless from walking very fast from the bus stop and thoroughly resentful of the censorious tone Sergios had used with her on the phone. Didn't he think she had a right to go out? Was she supposed to ask for permission first? Was her life to be entirely consumed by his? Heavy dark brown hair flopping untidily round her face, she stepped into the echoing hall.

Sergios appeared in a doorway and she lost her breath at that first glimpse, his impact thrumming through her like a sudden collision with a brick wall. He was still dressed in a black business suit and striped shirt, his only hint of informality the loosening of his tie. He looked like an angry dark angel, lean strong features taut, stubborn jaw line squared and once again he needed a shave. Stubble suited him though, sending his raw masculine sex appeal right off the charts, she conceded numbly, reeling in shock from the sudden loud thump of her heartbeat in her ears and the dryness of her mouth.

Sergios subjected his flustered bride-to-be to a hard scrutiny. From her chaotic hair to her ill-fitting jeans she was a mess. He realised that he was eager for the makeover to commence. 'I gave orders that if you went out you were to use a car and driver,' he reminded her flatly.

Bee reacted with a pained look. 'A bit much for a girl used to travelling by bus and tube.'

'But you are no longer that girl. You are the woman who is to become my wife,' Sergios retorted crisply. 'And I expect you to adapt accordingly. I am a wealthy man and you could be targeted by a mugger or even a kidnapper. Personal security must now become an integral part of your lifestyle.'

The reference to kidnapping cooled the heated words on Bee's ready tongue and, although she had stiffened, she nodded her head. 'I'll remember that in future.'

Satisfied, Sergios spread wide the door behind him. 'I want to talk to you.'

'Yes, we do need to talk,' Bee allowed, although in truth she wanted to run upstairs to her bedroom and stay there until her adolescent hormonal reaction to him died a natural death and stopped embarrassing her. Her face felt hot as a fire. It had been such a long time since a man had had that effect on her. When it had happened in his office she had assumed it was simply the effect of nerves and mortification but this time around she was less naive and ready to be honest with herself. As a physical specimen, Sergios Demonides was without parallel. He was absolutely gorgeous and few women would be impervious to his powerful attraction. That was all it was, she told herself urgently as she walked past him, her head held high, into a room furnished like an upmarket office. He had buckets of lethal sex appeal and all her body was telling her was that she had a healthy set of hormones. It was that simple, that basic, nothing to fret about. It certainly did not mean that she was genuinely attracted to him.

Sergios asked Bee about the children and she relaxed a little, telling him that Eleni had performed very poorly at her hearing test and the doctor suspected that she was suffering from glue ear. The toddler was to be examined by a consultant with a view to receiving treatment. Bee went on to talk about the picture that Paris had drawn on his bedroom wall. She considered his depiction of his once-happy family complete with parents and home to be self-explanatory. He had no photos of his late parents and Bee asked Sergios if there was a reason for that.

'I thought it would be less upsetting that way—he has to move on.'

'I think Paris needs the time to grieve and that family photos would help,' Bee pronounced with care.

'I put his parents' personal effects into storage. I'll have them checked for photo albums,' Sergios proffered, surprising her by accepting her opinion.

'I think that all that is wrong is that the children have endured too many changes in a short space of time. They need a settled home life.'

Sergios expelled his breath with a slight hiss, his expression grim. 'I've done my best but clearly it wasn't good enough. I know nothing about children. I don't even know how to talk to them.'

'The same way you talk to anyone else—with interest and kindness.'

A grudging smile played at the corners of his sardonic mouth. 'Not my style. I'm more into barking orders, Beatriz.'

'Call me Bee...everyone does.'

'No, Bee makes you sound like a maiden aunt. Beatriz is pretty.'

Bee almost winced at that opinion. 'But I'm not.'

'Give the beauty professionals a chance,' Sergios advised without hesitation.

At that advice, Bee took an offended stance, her spine very straight, her chin lifting. 'Actually that's what I wanted to discuss with you.'

With veiled attention, Sergios watched the buttons pull on her shirt, struggling to contain the full globes of her breasts. He wanted to rip open the shirt and release that luscious flesh from captivity into his hands. More than a comfortable handful, he reckoned hungrily, his body hardening. Startled by the imagery, he decided that he had to be in dire need of sexual fulfilment. Clearly he had waited too long to release his desire. He did not want to look on his future wife in that light.

Lost in her own thoughts, Bee breathed in deep and spoke with the abruptness of discomfiture. 'I don't want a makeover. I'm happy as I am. Take me or leave me.'

Sergios was not amused by that invitation. His clever dark eyes rested on her uneasy face. 'You must appreciate that when it comes to your appearance a certain amount of effort is required. Right now, you're making no effort at all.'

Incensed by that critical and wounding statement, Bee threw her slim shoulders back. 'I'm not going to change myself to conform to some outdated sexist code.'

Sergios released an impatient groan. 'Leave the feminism out of it. What's the matter with you? Why don't you care about your appearance?'

'There's nothing the matter with me,' Bee answered with spirit. 'I'm just comfortable with myself as I am.'

'But I'm not. I expect you to smarten up as part of the job.'

'That's too personal a request…beyond your remit,' Bee spelt out in case he hadn't yet got the message. 'I have already given up my home, my job…surely how I choose to look is my business.'

His brilliant dark eyes flamed gold, dense black

lashes lowering over them to enhance the flash-fire effect. 'Not if you want to marry me, it's not.'

Bee flung her head back, glossy chestnut strands trailing across her shoulders, an angry flush across her cheekbones. 'That's ridiculous.'

'Is it? I find you unreasonable. It's normal for a woman to take pride in her appearance. What happened to you that made you lose all interest?' Sergios demanded starkly.

The silence hummed like a buzz saw against Bee's suddenly exposed nerves. She very nearly flinched, for that incisive question had cut deep and hit home hard. There had been a time when Bee had taken great interest in her personal appearance and had chosen her clothes with equal care. But it was not a period she cared to recall. 'I don't want to talk about this. It's absolutely none of your business.'

'The makeover is not negotiable. There will be public occasions when I expect you to appear by my side. There is no longer any excuse for you to go around in unflattering clothes with your hair in a mess,' Sergios asserted with derisive cool.

Rage surged up through Bee like lava seeking a vent. 'How dare you speak to me like that?'

'I'm being honest with you. Come over here,' Sergios urged, a firm hand at her elbow guiding her across to the mirror on the wall. 'And tell me what you see...'

Forced to acknowledge a reflection that displayed windblown hair, an old shirt and baggy jeans, Bee just wanted to slap him. Her teeth gritted. 'It doesn't matter what you say or what you want. I'm not having a makeover and that's that!'

'No makeover, no marriage,' Sergios traded without a second of hesitation. 'It's part of the job and I will not compromise on my expectations.'

Trembling though she was with the force of her emotions, Bee slung him a look of loathing and lifted and dropped her hands in a gesture of finality. 'Then there'll be no marriage because we need to get one thing straight right now, Sergios—'

Sergios lifted a sardonic black brow. 'Do we?'

'You are not going to rule over me like this! You are *not* going to tell me what I do with my hair or what I should wear,' Bee launched back furiously at him, green eyes pure and bright as emeralds in sunshine. 'You're a domineering guy but I won't stand for that.'

Her magnificent bosom was heaving. Was he, at heart, a breast man? he suddenly wondered, questioning his preoccupation with those swelling mounds and seeking an excuse for his strange behaviour. Her eyes were astonishingly vivid in colour. Indeed she looked more attractive in the grip of temper than he had ever seen her but he would not tolerate defiance. 'It is your choice, Beatriz,' Sergios intoned coldly. 'It has always been your choice. At this moment I am having second thoughts about marrying you because you are acting irrationally.'

Assailed by that charge, Bee quivered with sheer fury. '*I'm* being irrational?' she raked back at him incredulously. 'Explain that to me.'

His face set in forbidding lines, Sergios opened the door for her exit instead. 'This discussion is at an end.'

Bee stalked up the stairs in a tempestuous rage. She had never stalked before and she had definitely never been so mad with anger but Sergios Demonides had made her see red. Rot the man, rot him to hell, she thought wildly. How dared he criticise her like that? How dared he ask what had happened to make her lose interest in her appearance? How dared he have that much insight into her actions?

For something traumatic *had* happened to Bee way back when she was madly in love with a man who had ultimately dumped her. That man had replaced her with a little ditsy blonde whose looks and shallow personality had mocked what Bee had once foolishly believed was a good solid relationship. After that devastating wake-up call, the fussing with hair, nails and make-up, not to mention the continual agonising over which outfits were most becoming, had begun to seem utterly superficial, pathetic and a total waste of time. After all, given a free choice Jon had gone for a woman as physically and mentally different from Bee as he could find. For months afterwards, Bee had despised herself for having slavishly followed the girlie code that insisted that a woman's looks were of paramount importance to a man. That code had let her down badly for in spite of all her efforts she had still lost Jon and ever since then she had refused to fuss over her appearance and compete with the true beauties of the world.

And why should she turn herself inside out for Sergios Demonides? He was just like every other man she had met from her father to Jon. Sergios might have briefly flattered her by telling her that she was a loyal daughter and a gifted teacher, but regardless of those qualities he was still judging her by her looks and ready to dump her for failing to meet his standards of feminine beauty. Well, that didn't matter to her, did it?

No, *but* it would certainly matter to her mother, a little voice chimed up quellingly at the back of Bee's brain and she froze in consternation, recalled to reality with a vengeance by that acknowledgement. If Bee backed out of the marriage, Emilia Blake would most probably lose her home, for Bee was convinced that her angry father would try to punish Bee for his failure to get the price he wanted for the Royale hotel group. Monty Blake was that sort of a man. He always needed someone else to blame for his mistakes and losses and Bee and her mother would provide easy targets for his ire.

And if Bee didn't marry Sergios, Paris, Milo and Eleni would suffer yet another adult betrayal. Bee had encouraged the children to bond with her, had announced that she was marrying Sergios and had promised to stay with them. Paris had looked unimpressed but Bee had guessed that he wanted her to prove herself before he took the risk of trusting her. Her sister Zara had already let those children down by winning their acceptance and then vanishing from their lives when she realised that she couldn't go through with marrying their guardian because she had fallen for another man. Was Bee willing to behave in an equally self-centred fashion?

All over the prospect of a visit to a beauty salon and some shopping trips? Wasn't walking out on Sergios because of such trivial activities a case of overkill? He had too much insight though, she acknowledged unhappily. When he had asked her what had happened to her to make her so uninterested in her appearance he had unnerved her and hurt her pride. That was why she had lost her head. He had mortified her when he marched her over to that mirror and forced her to see herself through his eyes. And unhappily Bee had not liked what she saw either. She had seen that her hair needed a decent cut and her wardrobe required an urgent overhaul and that she was being thoroughly unreasonable when she expected a man of his sophistication and faultless grooming to accept her in her current au naturel state.

Bee tidied her hair before descending the stairs at a much more decorous pace than she had raced up them. A mutinous expression tensing her oval face, she lifted a hand as if she was about to knock on the door and then she thought better of the gesture and simply walked back unannounced into his home office.

Sergios was at his desk working on his laptop. His head lifted and glittering dark eyes lit on her, his expression hard and unwelcoming.

It took near physical force for Bee to rise above her hurt pride and part her lips to say, 'All right, I'll do it… the makeover thing.'

'What changed your mind?' Sergios pressed impassively, his expression not softening in the slightest at her capitulation.

'My mother's needs…the children's,' she admitted

truthfully. 'I can't walk out on my responsibilities like that.'

His hard cynical mouth twisted. 'People do it every day.'

Bee stood a little straighter. 'But I don't.'

Sergios pushed away his laptop and rose fluidly upright, astonishingly graceful for a man of his height and powerful build. 'Don't fight me,' he told her huskily. 'I don't like it.'

'But you don't always know best.'

'There are more subtle approaches.' He offered her a drink and she accepted, hovering awkwardly by his desk while she cradled a glass of wine that she didn't really want.

'I'm not sure I do subtle,' Bee confided.

He was suddenly as remote as the Andes. 'You'll learn. I won't be easy to live with.'

And for the first time as she tipped the glass to her lips and tasted an expensive wine as smooth and silky as satin, Bee wondered about Melita. Was he different with his mistress? Was she blonde or brunette? How long had she been in his life? Where did she live? How often did he see her? The torrent of questions blazing a mortifying trail through her head made her redden as she attempted to suppress that flood of unwelcome curiosity. It was none of her business and she didn't care what he did, she told herself squarely. She was to be his wife in name only, nothing more.

'We will drink to our wedding,' Sergios murmured lazily.

'And a better understanding?' Bee completed.

Sergios dealt her a dark appraisal. 'We don't need to understand each other. We won't need to spend that much time together. After a while we won't even have to occupy the same house at the same time...'

Chilled to the marrow by that prediction, Bee drank her wine and set the glass down on the desk. 'Goodnight, then,' she told him prosaically.

And as she climbed the stairs she wondered why she should feel lonelier than she had ever felt in her life before. After all, had she expected Sergios to offer her his company and support? Was he not even prepared to share parenting responsibilities with her? It seemed that in his head the parameters of their relationship were already set in stone: he didn't love her, didn't desire her and, in short, didn't need her except as a mother to the children. Being his wife really would be a job more than anything else...

CHAPTER FOUR

Bᴇᴇ stepped out of the spacious changing cubicle and up onto the dais to get the best possible view of her wedding dress in the mirrored walls of the showroom.

Although it galled her to admit it, Sergios had done astonishingly well. She had had a sharp exchange of words with him when he had startled her with the news that he had actually selected a gown for her.

'What on earth were you thinking of?' Bee had demanded on the phone. 'A woman looks forward to choosing her wedding dress.'

'I was at a fashion show in Milan and the model came down the catwalk in it and I knew immediately that it was *your* dress,' Sergios had drawled with immense assurance.

She had wanted to ask him whom he had accompanied to the fashion show, for she did not believe that he had attended one alone, but she had swallowed back the nosy question. Ignorance, she had decided, was safer than too much information in that department. What she didn't know couldn't hurt her, she told herself staunchly, and not that she was in any danger of being hurt. She could not afford to develop silly notions or possessive feelings towards a man who would not even share a bed with her. Although he had *offered*, she reminded herself darkly, preferring to sacrifice himself if she decided that she could not live without sex rather than allow her to engage in an extra-marital affair.

Now she posed in the wedding gown Sergios had chosen for her, noting how the style showcased her voluptuous cleavage while emphasising her small waist. The neckline was lower than she liked but the fitted bodice definitely flattered her fuller figure. Apparently, Sergios hadn't earned his notorious reputation with women without picking up some useful fashion tips along the way. Bee would have been the first to admit that her appearance had already undergone a major transformation. Her chestnut hair now curved in a sleek layered shoulder-length cut that framed her face, all the heaviness gone. Cosmetics had helped her rediscover her cheekbones and accentuate her best features while every inch of her from her manicured nails to her smooth skin had been waxed, polished and moisturised to as close to perfection as a mortal woman was capable of getting. The irony was that, far from feeling exploited or belittled by the beauty makeover, she was enjoying the energising feel of knowing she looked her very best.

In thirty-six hours it would be her wedding day, Bee acknowledged, breathing in deep and slow to steady her nerves. That afternoon she had a final appointment to sign the pre-nuptial agreement, which had already been explained to her in fine detail during her first visit to the upmarket legal firm employed by Sergios to protect her interests. Her mother's long-term care was comprehensively covered, but she had had to request the right of regular access to the children in the event of their marriage breaking down. Bee was more concerned that Sergios might refuse that demand than she was by the fact that divorce would leave her a wealthy woman. The more time she spent with Paris, Milo and Eleni the more they felt like *her* children.

As Bee left the showroom, elegant in a grey striped dress and light jacket, a bodyguard was by her side and within the space of a minute a limousine was purring up to the kerb to pick her up. She was getting used to being spoilt, she registered guiltily, as she emerged again directly outside the lawyer's plush offices. After only three weeks she was already forgetting what it was like to walk in the rain or queue for a bus.

She was seated in the reception area when she saw a familiar face and she was so shaken by the resulting jolt of recognition that she simply stared, her heartbeat thumping very loudly. It was her ex-boyfriend, Jon Townsend, and more than three years had passed since their last meeting. Now, without the smallest warning, there he was only ten feet away, smartly clad in a business suit and tie. He was slim, dark-haired and attractive, not particularly tall but still taller than she was. As she struggled to overcome her shock she wondered if perhaps he worked for the firm because he had just qualified in law when she first met him.

Jon turned his head and recognised her at almost the same moment as the receptionist invited her to go into Mr Smyth's office. Blue eyes full of surprise, Jon crossed the foyer with a frown. 'Bee?' he queried as though he couldn't quite believe that she was physically there in front of him.

'Jon…sorry, I have an appointment,' Bee responded, rising to her feet.

'You look terrific,' Jon told her warmly.

'Thanks.' Her smile was a mere stretch of her tense lips, for she had not forgotten the pain he had caused her and all her concentration was focused on retaining her dignity. 'Do you work here?'

'Yes, since last year. I'll see you after your appointment and we'll chat,' Jon declared.

Her fake smile dimmed at that disconcerting prospect and she hastened into Halston Smyth's office with a peculiar sense of both relief and anticipation. What could Jon possibly want to chat to her about? It might have happened three long years ago but he *had* ditched her, for goodness' sake. Did they even have any old times to catch up on? Having lost contact with mutual friends after they broke up, she did not think so. He was married now—or at least so she had heard—might even have children, although when she had known him he had not been sure he wanted any. Of course he had been equally unsure he was the marrying kind until he had met Jenna, Bee's little blonde bubbly replacement, the daughter of a high-court judge. A most useful connection for an ambitious young legal whiz-kid, her more cynical self had thought back then.

Mr Smyth ran through the pre-nup again while a more junior member of staff hovered attentively. On her first visit, Bee had realised that as the future wife of a billionaire she was considered big business and they were eager to please. As soon as she realised that her desire to retain contact with the children in the event of a divorce had been incorporated in the agreement, she relaxed. In spite of all the warnings to carefully consider what she was doing she signed on the dotted line while wondering how soon she could book physiotherapy sessions for her mother.

Mr Smyth escorted her all the way to the lift and at the last possible minute before the doors could close Jon stepped in to join her and her bodyguard.

'There's a wine bar round the corner,' Jon informed her casually.

Her brow furrowed. 'I'm not sure we have much to talk about.'

'Well, I can't physically persuade you to join me with a security man in tow,' he quipped with a familiar grin.

'Do you know this gentleman, Miss Blake?' her bodyguard, Tom, asked, treating Jon to an openly suspicious appraisal.

Meeting Jon's amused look, Bee almost giggled. 'Yes. Yes, I do,' she confirmed. 'I can't stay long, though.'

Curiosity had to be behind his request, Bee decided. After all, three years ago when Jon had been with her she had been a final-year student teacher from a fairly ordinary background. While her father might be wealthy, Bee had never enjoyed a personal allowance or, aside of the occasional family invite, an entrée into Monty Blake's exclusive world. Jon was most probably aware that she was on the brink of marrying one of the richest men in Europe and wondering how that had come about. She suppressed a rueful smile over the awareness that few people would believe the truth behind that particular development.

In the bar her bodyguard chose a seat nearby and talked on his phone. Jon ordered drinks and made light conversation. She remembered when his smile had made her tummy tighten and her heart beat a little faster and crushed the recollection.

'Jenna and I got a divorce a couple of months ago,' Jon volunteered wryly.

'I'm sorry to hear that,' Bee said uncomfortably.

'It was an infatuation.' Jon pulled a rueful face. 'I lived to regret leaving you.'

'Never mind about that now. I don't hold grudges,' Bee interposed, feeling a shade awkward beneath the earnest onslaught of his blue eyes.

'That's pretty decent of you. Now let me get to the point of my invite and you are, of course, welcome to tell me that I'm a calculating so-and-so!' Jon teased, extracting a leaflet from his pocket and passing it across the table to her. 'I would be very grateful if you would consider becoming a patron for this charity. It does a lot of good work and could do with the support.'

Bee was taken aback, for the Jon she recalled had been too intent on climbing the career ladder to spend time raising money for good causes. Maturity, it seemed, had made him a more well-rounded person and she was impressed. He was a trustee for a charity for disabled children, similar to one she had volunteered with when she was a student. 'I doubt that I could do much on a personal basis because I'll be based in Greece after the wedding.'

'As the wife of Sergios Demonides, your name alone would be sufficient to generate a higher profile for the organisation,' Jon assured her with enthusiasm. 'And if you were to decide to get more involved the occasional appearance at public events would be very welcome.'

Bee was relieved then that it appeared Jon's desire to see her was professional rather than personal. She very much appreciated the fact that he studiously avoided asking her anything about Sergios. They parted fifteen minutes later but before she could turn away, Jon reached for her hand.

'I meant what I said earlier,' he stressed in an undertone. 'I made a colossal mistake. I've always regretted losing you, Bee.'

Green eyes turning cool, Bee was quick to retrieve her hand. 'It's a little late in the day to tell me that, Jon.'

'I hope you'll be happy with Demonides.' But the look on his face told her that he didn't think she would be.

Unsettled by that exchange, Bee travelled back to Sergios's house to have tea with the children. Sergios had been jetting round the world on business for over two weeks and their only contact had been by phone. After their meal Bee supervised Paris's homework assignment and bathed Milo and Eleni before tucking them into bed. In a month's time, Eleni was scheduled for surgery to have grommets inserted in both ears to resolve her hearing problems. Having consulted Paris's teacher, Bee had learned that the boy was struggling to make friends at school and she had tried to improve the situation by inviting some of his classmates over to play after school. Paris was beginning to find his feet and as he did so he had become more receptive to Bee and less suspicious of her.

Just before Bee went to bed, Sergios called from Tokyo. 'Who was the man you accompanied to the wine bar?' he demanded.

Bee stiffened defensively. 'So, Tom's a spy, is he?'

'Beatriz…' Sergios growled impatiently, forceful as a lion roaring a warning to an unwary prey.

'He was just an old friend I hadn't seen since university.' Bee hesitated but decided to say nothing more, feeling she didn't owe Sergios any more of an explanation.

'You'll find that plenty of old friends will come scurrying out of the woodwork now that you're marrying me,' Sergios replied cynically.

'I find that offensive. This particular friend is asking me to get involved with a children's charity. You can scarcely find fault with that.'

'Is that why he was holding hands with you?'

Bee flushed scarlet. 'He grasped my hand—big deal!'

'In public places I expect you to be discreet.'

Her anger rose. 'You always have to have the last word, don't you?'

'And I'm always right, *latria mou*,' Sergios agreed equably, not one whit disturbed by the accusation.

That night Bee lay in her big luxurious bed and played the game of 'what if' with Jon in a starring role.

Well, she was only human and naturally she could not help wondering what might have happened had she met her charming ex when she was not on the brink of getting married to another man. Probably nothing would have happened, she decided ruefully, for had it not been for the pressure Sergios had put on her she would have looked like a real Plain Jane and Jon would have been less than impressed. In any case, Sergios was much better looking and had a great deal more personality...

Now where on earth had that thought come from? Bee wondered in confusion. There was no denying that Sergios was a very, very handsome guy but he was not *her* guy in the way Jon had once seemed to be and he never would be. Bee decided that she was far too sensible to indulge in 'what if' dreams. Besides she had long since worked out that if Jon had truly loved her he would never have dumped her because she had a mother who would always need her support. Jon's rejection had shattered the dream of family, which Bee valued most.

'That's a very romantic dress,' Tawny commented, studying her half-sister with frankly curious eyes, for the fitted lace gown with the flowing skirt was exceedingly feminine and not in Bee's usual conservative style. 'And a very thoughtful choice for a guy entering a very practical marriage of convenience.'

Bee went pink, wishing her other sister, Zara, had not been quite so frank with their youngest sister, who thoroughly disapproved of what Bee was doing in marrying a man she didn't love. She also wished Zara had not chosen to avoid what might have been an uncomfortable occasion for her by pleading her reluctance to travel while pregnant. 'Sergios isn't romantic and neither am I.'

'Granted the kids are cute,' Tawny conceded, her coppery head held at a considering angle, blue eyes troubled. 'And Sergios, on the outside he's sex on a stick, but only for an adventurous woman and you're as conventional as they come.'

'You never know,' Bee quipped, lifting her bouquet.

'If I was the suspicious type I would suspect that you're doing this for your mother's benefit,' Tawny commented with a frown, revealing a glimpse of wits that were sharp as a knife. 'You'd do anything for her and she's a lovely woman.'

'Yes, isn't she? My mother is also very happy for me today,' Bee slotted in with a pointed glance. 'Please don't spoil that for her by giving her the wrong idea about my marriage...'

'Or even the *right* idea,' Tawny muttered half under her breath, not being that easy to silence. 'Just promise me that if he's awful to live with you'll divorce him.'

Bee nodded instant agreement to soothe her half-sibling's concerns and descended the stairs with care in her high heels. She was in her mother's house for she had spent the last night of her single life there at the older woman's request. Tawny was not acting as a bridesmaid because Bee had drawn the line at taking the masquerade of her wedding that far.

'But I know you, you won't do it if it means leaving those cute kids behind.' Tawny sighed. 'You'll be like faithful Penelope, stuck with him for ever, and I bet he plays on it when he realises what a softy you are.'

Bee had no intention of being a pushover, convinced as she was that Sergios would happily tread a softy right into the ground and walk on without a backward glance. He was tough, so she had to be even tougher. She reminded herself of that fact when her scowling father extended his arm to her at the mouth of the church aisle and fixed a social smile to his face. Monty Blake had recently been trodden on by Sergios and his ego and his pockets were still stinging from the encounter. She thought it said even more about Sergios's intimidating influence that her father was still willing, however, to play his part at their wedding.

Full of impatience, Sergios wheeled round at the altar to watch his bride approach. His face unreadable, he studied her and started to frown. She had had her long hair cut back to her shoulders. Whose very stupid idea had that been? But aside from that, Beatriz looked… luscious, he finally selected after a long mental pause while he ran his brooding dark gaze from the sultry peach-tinted fullness of her mouth down to the generous curves he never failed to admire. He wondered absently if men developed a taste for larger breasts when they reached a certain age. He was thirty-two, not fifty-two though. But as he saw the burgeoning swell of those plump creamy mounds so beautifully displayed in that neckline there was no denying that he was spellbound. The model on the catwalk in Milan had had nothing to show off but an expanse of flat bony chest. In her place, however, Beatriz would have been a show-stopper. He frowned at that thought.

Determined not to be cowed by the fact her bride-groom was glowering at her, Bee lifted her chin. Even the most critical woman would have had to admit that Sergios did look spectacularly handsome in a beauti-fully cut morning suit. Encountering those hard eyes trained on her, she felt briefly dizzy and breathless. The minister of her church was inclined to ramble a little, but he soon controlled the tendency after Sergios urged him in an impatient undertone to 'speed it up'. Affronted by her bridegroom's intervention, Bee red-dened to the roots of her hair. Had Sergios no idea how to behave in church? Well, it was never too late for a man to learn, although she suspected he would fight learning anything from her every step of the way. He thrust the wedding ring onto her finger with scant cer-emony. She rubbed her hand as though he had hurt her, although he had not.

'You were rude to the minister,' she said on the way down the aisle again.

A brow lifted. 'I beg your pardon?'

'You heard me. There are some occasions when you just have to be patient for the sake of good manners and a wedding service is one of those occasions.'

In the thunderous silence that now enfolded the bridal couple, Milo wriggled like an eel off his nanny's lap and rushed to Bee's side to clutch her skirt. She pat-ted his curly head to quieten him and took his hand in hers.

'He was repeating himself,' Sergios breathed harshly,

but, watching the toddler beam his big trusting smile up at Bee, he restrained the outrage her impertinence had sent hurtling through him. After little more than two weeks abroad he had returned to his London home and noticed a distinct change for the better in his cousin Timon's children. All the kids had calmed down. Milo had become less frantic in his need for attention, the little girl was smiling and even Paris was occasionally venturing into shy speech.

Sergios had never had a best friend but had he done so Timon would have come the closest, although on the surface serious, steady and quiet Timon would have appeared to have had little in common with Sergios's altogether more aggressive extrovert nature. But the bond had been there all the same and it was a matter of honour to Sergios to see Timon's children thrive in his care. Beatriz, it seemed, had the magic touch in that department.

A line of cameras greeted their emergence from the church. As Bee's eyes widened and she froze with the dismay of someone unaccustomed to media attention Sergios took immediate advantage of the moment. He swung her round into the circle of his arms and, with one hand braced to the shallow indentation of her spine to draw her close, he bent his head and kissed her, instinctively righting the status quo in the only way available to him.

Shock crashed through Bee and made her knees shake at that first breath-taking instant of physical contact. She had never been less prepared for anything and impressions hit her in a flood of overwhelming sensuality: the exotic tang of his designer cologne, the uncompromising strength and power of that lean, muscular body crushing her softer curves, the hard, demanding pressure of his erotic mouth on hers. And while at the back of her mind a voice was shrieking no and urging her to pull back her body was singing entirely another song. There was a wildly addictive fire to the taste of him. She wanted more, she wanted *so* much more she trembled with the astonishing force of that wanting. His raw masculine passion sliced through her every defence and roused a surge of naked hunger within her. The plunge of his tongue into the sensitive interior of her mouth made her body tremble, while heat pooled between her thighs and her breasts swelled, pushing against the lace of her bra so that it felt too tight for comfort.

'You're not supposed to taste that good, *yineka mou*,' Sergios breathed in a roughened undertone, drawing back, his brilliant dark eyes cloaked and cool, his face taut.

Dragging her clinging hands from his broad shoulders, Bee was aghast and she turned blindly to pose for the cameras, her head swimming, her treacherous body torn by silent anguish as she struggled to suppress that monstrous hunger he had awakened. She had never felt like that in her life before, not even with Jon. It was as if Sergios had called up something she hadn't known existed within her and that treacherous loss of control had embarrassed the hell out of her. My goodness, she had *clung* to him, pushed her breasts into his chest like a wanton hussy and kissed him back with far too much gusto. She could not bring herself to look at him again and inside she was dying of mortification. Obviously he had planned to give her a social kiss for the benefit of the cameras but she had flung herself into it as though she were sex-starved.

Teeth gritted behind his determined smile, Sergios willed his arousal into subjugation and reminded himself forcefully that sleeping with his wife would curtail his freedom and deprive him of the choices that any intelligent man would value. One woman was much like another; all cats were grey in the dark. He repeated that oft-considered mantra to himself with rigorous determination: he had no plans to bed his bride, no need to do so either. To think otherwise was to invite chaos into his head and home. Breaking the rules of his marriage would cost him and why take that risk? Unless he was very much mistaken, and when the subject was women Sergios was rarely mistaken, his mistress would push out every sexual stop to impress him on his next visit. Satisfaction could be had without complications and wasn't that all that really mattered?

The reception was staged at an exclusive hotel where security staff vetted every arriving guest.

'Zara was such a fool,' Bee's stepmother, Ingrid Blake, remarked in her brittle voice. 'It could have been her standing here in your place today.'

Features austere, Sergios settled an arm to his bride's rigid spine. 'There can be no comparison. Beatriz is... special,' he murmured huskily.

Bee went pink at the unexpected compliment, although the apparent slur on Zara embarrassed her and as the older woman moved out of earshot Bee muttered, 'Ingrid has a wasp's tongue but I could have managed her on my own.'

'I will never stand in silence while my wife is being insulted,' Sergios asserted. 'But only the most foolish would risk incurring my wrath.'

'Ingrid is a sourpuss but she's my father's wife and a member of the family,' Bee reminded him gently.

Noting the anxious light in her gaze, Sergios laughed out loud. 'You can't protect everyone from me.'

His vital laugh, so full of his essential energy, ironically chilled her, reminding her how much ruthless power and influence he had in the world and how much he took it for granted. She thought of her father walking her down the aisle even though it would have been more in character for the older man to express his resentment by refusing to take part in the wedding. Monty Blake's submission to her husband's wishes had shaken Bee and shown her the meaning of true supremacy. She had no doubt that if she ever dared to cross Sergios he would become her most bitter enemy.

'I understood that your grandfather was planning to come today,' Bee admitted.

'He has bronchitis and his doctor advised him to stay at home. You'll meet him tomorrow when we arrive in Greece. I didn't want him to take the risk of travelling.'

It was not a particularly large wedding: Sergios equated small with the privacy and discretion with which he liked to separate his private life from his public one. Although there were only fifty guests everybody on Sergios's list was a *somebody* in the business world. He seemed to have very few actual relatives, explaining that his grandfather had had only two children, both of whom had died relatively young.

'Was he looking for an heir when he discovered you?'

'No. In those days he had Timon. Social services discovered my connection to Nectarios and informed him about me. He didn't know I even existed before that. He came to see me when I was seventeen. I needed a decent education, he offered the opportunity,' Sergios admitted tautly.

She wanted to ask him more about his parentage but his reluctance to discuss his background was obvious and it seemed neither the time nor the place to probe further. Tense at being so much the centre of attention, she ate a light meal. A celebrity group entertained them. Bee noticed a beautiful female guest casting lascivious eyes in Sergios's direction and felt her fingers flex like claws ready to scratch. She didn't like other women looking at him in that speculative sexual way as if trying to imagine what he would be like in bed. It was that wretched kiss, it had changed everything, even the way she thought about him, Bee conceded unhappily.

She had not known that a mere kiss could make her feel hot and hungry and frantic for another. In fact she had always believed that she wasn't that sexual, and even when she was in love with Jon keeping him at arm's length had not proved much of a challenge for her. She had longed for some sign of commitment from him before she slept with him, had wanted sexual intimacy to mean something beyond the physical. With hindsight she suspected that she had always sensed that

Jon was holding back as well and reluctant to get in too deep with her.

'This day seems endless,' Sergios breathed tersely as he checked his phone for the hundredth time, fingers tapping a restive tattoo on the table.

'It'll be over soon,' Bee said calmly, for she had guessed at the church that he found almost every aspect of their wedding day a demanding challenge. It made her wonder what his first wedding and his first wife had been like. Was he reliving disturbing memories? Had his first wedding been a day of love and joy for him? How could she not wonder? Yet Sergios didn't strike her as the kind of guy likely to have buried his heart with his dead wife and unborn child in the grave eight years earlier. He was too pragmatic and abrasive and far too fond of female company.

'Let's get the dancing over with,' Sergios breathed abruptly, springing upright and extending a hand to her.

'I love your enthusiasm,' Bee riposted, smiling brightly as her mother beamed at her. Emilia Blake was a happy woman and Sergios had not only visited her before the wedding but had also made the effort to sit down and talk that afternoon to her, which Bee appreciated. Emilia believed that her son-in-law was the sun, the moon and the stars and not for worlds would Bee have done or said anything to detract from that positive impression.

This marriage *had* to work, she reflected anxiously. If her mother came out to live in Greece their relationship would be on constant display, so she had to ensure from the start that the marriage worked for both of them. She would have to be practical, even-tempered and tolerant…for he was neither of the last two things. Sergios shifted his lean powerful length against her as he danced with a fine sense of rhythm and all those rational uplifting thoughts left her head in one bound for suddenly all she was conscious of were the tightening prominence of her nipples and the smouldering dark gold of his eyes as he gazed moodily down at her. Heat and butterflies rose and fluttered in the pit of her tummy. Desire, she recognised as the twisty sensation stirring up hunger in her pelvis, was digging talon claws of need into her.

'*Theos*…you move well,' Sergios husked, whirling her round and admiring both her energy and the pert stirring curve of her derriere as she wriggled it in time to the music.

'After years of dance classes, I ought to.'

From there the day seemed to speed up. Moving from table to table, group to group, they spoke to all their guests. Bee was impressed that Sergios put on such a good show. He did not strike her as a touchy-feely guy, but the whole time he was by her side he maintained physical contact with either an arm or a hand placed on her. The children got tired and the nannies took them back to the house. Within an hour of their departure Sergios decided they could leave as well and they climbed into a waiting limousine and were carried off. From below her feathery lashes, Bee glanced covertly at her new husband, recognising his relief that the occasion was over.

'Is it all weddings you don't like or just your own?'

'All of them,' he admitted, his handsome mouth hardening. 'I can't stand the starry eyes and the unrealistic expectations. It's not real life.'

'No, it's hope and there's nothing wrong with the fact that people long for a happy ending.'

Sergios shrugged a big broad shoulder in what struck her as the diplomatic silence of disagreement. He sprawled back into the corner of the leather seat, long powerful thighs splayed in relaxation. 'Do you long for a happy ending, Beatriz?'

'Why not?' Bee fielded lightly.

'It won't be with me,' he promised her grimly. 'I don't believe in them.'

Well, that was certainly telling her, she thought ruefully as the limo drew up outside the London house that had become her new home. They mounted the splendid staircase together and were traversing the landing to head off in different directions when Sergios turned to Bee, his face impassive. 'I'm getting changed and going out. I'll see you at the airport tomorrow.'

And with that concluding assurance delivered with the minimum of drama he strode down the corridor where his bedroom suite lay and vanished from view. A door thudded shut. Bee had fallen still and she was very pale. She felt as if he had punched her in the stomach, winding her so that she couldn't catch her breath. It was the first day of their marriage, their wedding night, and he was going out, leaving her at home on her own.

And why should he not? This was not a normal marriage, she reminded herself doggedly. It was not his duty to keep her company, was it? But was he going to see another woman? Why should that idea bite as if an arrow tipped with acid had been fired into her flesh? She didn't know why, she only knew it hurt and she felt horribly rejected. It felt humiliating to ask one of the maids for her assistance in getting out of her wedding finery. Yet, she knew that had he even been available she would not have approached Sergios for the same help. Still feeling gutted and furious with herself for a reaction she could not understand, Bee went for a shower to remove the last remnants of bridal sparkle from her body. Sergios wasn't her husband, not really her husband, so what was the matter with her?

Did Melita live in London or was she here visiting for a prearranged meeting? Or could it be that Sergios was rendezvousing with some other woman? Presumably he would be having sex with someone else tonight. Her tummy muscles tightened as if in self-defence and perspiration dampened her brow, leaving her skin clammy. There was no point being prudish or naive about the emptiness of her marriage, she told herself in exasperation. Right from the start Sergios had demanded the freedom to get naked and intimate with other women on a regular basis. According to the media and those ladies who, when he was younger, were anything but discreet about his habits in the bedroom, he was very highly sexed.

And what exactly did she have to complain about? Sergios was doing only what he had said he would do and by loathing what he was doing *she* was the one breaking the rules by getting too personally involved! It was time she was more honest with herself, she reasoned irritably. In the normal way a man of Sergios's dazzling good looks and wealth would never be attracted to a woman as ordinary as she was. She should not forget that his first wife, Krista, had been gorgeous, similar to Zara with her fragile blonde loveliness. Bee had won Sergios as a husband solely by agreeing to allow him to retain his freedom within the marriage and be a mother to his cousin's children. That was how it was and that was the reality that she had to learn to live with.

A knock sounded on the door and she called out. Paris, clad in his superhero pyjamas and slippers, peered in, a photo album tucked snugly beneath one arm. 'I saw Uncle Sergios going out. Do you want to see my photos?'

'Why not?' Bee said with resolute good cheer, for a regular appraisal of photos of his parents and his baby years had become quite a feature of the little boy's life in recent days. He would show Bee the pictures and explain who the people were and where and when he thought they were taken and she would *ooh* and *aah* with appreciation and ask questions while he worked through his sadness for a period of his life that was now gone.

'Would you like a hot drink to help you sleep?' she prompted, deciding that this was a wedding night that she would never forget.

And if Bee blinked back tears while she sat on the side of her bed with an arm anchored comfortingly round Paris's skinny little body and a mug of cocoa in her other hand, her companion was too intent on sharing his photo album to notice.

CHAPTER FIVE

Two nannies, Janey and Karen, were accompanying Bee and the children to Greece. Shown around Sergios's incredibly large and opulent private jet by an attentive stewardess late the next morning, Bee saw the entire party settled in the rear cabin, which was separate from the main saloon. Armed with enough toys, magazines and films to while away a much longer flight, the young women were thrilled by their deluxe surroundings.

In a lighter mood, Bee would have found it equally difficult not to be seduced by her newly luxurious mode of travel, but she had too much on her mind. She had slept badly and had been forced to out-act a Hollywood film star with her good cheer over the breakfast table, for she had been keen to soothe the boys' nervous tension. After all, Paris and Milo were apprehensive about making yet another move for they had already had to adjust to so much change in their short lives. Paris, however, was quick to address the steward in Greek and Milo's head tipped to one side and his brow furrowed as though he too was recalling the language of his very first words. Although they would not be returning to their former home in Athens, they were heading back to the country of their birth and they might well find Sergios's home on the island of Orestos familiar, for they had often visited it with their parents.

Having ensured that everyone was comfortable, Bee returned to the main saloon and took a seat to leaf through a magazine that she couldn't have cared less about. Having teamed a green silk top and cardigan with white linen trousers, she felt both smart and comfortable. Her hand shook a little when she heard voices outside and her fingers clenched tightly into the publication in her hand, her body tensing, her heartbeat literally racing as she heard steps on the metal stairs. Sergios was tearing her in two, she suddenly thought in frustration. One half of her could barely wait to lay eyes on him while the other half would have preferred to never see him again.

'*Kalimera*…good morning, Beatriz,' Sergios intoned, as tall, dark and gloriously handsome as an angel come to earth, perfect in form but exceedingly complex in nature.

And with her breath convulsing in her dry throat, she both looked at him and blanked him at one and the same time so that their eyes did not quite meet, a polite smile of acknowledgement on her lips combined with an almost inaudible greeting. Why was she embarrassed? Why the hell was she embarrassed? Enraged by her ridiculous oversensitivity, Bee glanced up at him unwarily and collided with golden eyes full of energy and wariness. She *knew* it, he was no fool, and indeed he was just waiting for her to say or do something she shouldn't, to react in some inappropriate way to his departure the night before. Keeping her smile firmly in place, Bee was determined to deny him that satisfaction and she dropped her attention resolutely back to her magazine.

And there her attention stayed…throughout take-off, a visit to the children, lunch and the remainder of the flight. Sergios shot her composed profile a suspicious appraisal. She had said not one word out of place, not one word. He could not understand why he was not pleased by the fact, why indeed he felt almost affronted by her comprehensive show of disinterest and detachment. He did not like and had even less experience of being ignored by a woman. But Beatriz was very much a lady and he appreciated that trait. The acknowledgement sparked a recollection and he dug into his pocket to remove a jewel box.

'For you,' he murmured carelessly, tossing the little box down on the table between them.

Her teeth gritted. She lifted the box almost as though she were afraid it might soil her in some way, flipped up the lid, stared down at the fabulous diamond solitaire ring, closed the lid and set it aside again. 'Thank you,' she pronounced woodenly with anything but gratitude in her low-pitched voice.

Too clever not to work out that the denial of attention was some form of challenge and punishment, Sergios was becoming tenser because his brand-new bride was already revealing murky depths he had not known she possessed. Frustration filled him. Why did women *do* that? Why did they pretend to be straightforward and then welch on the deal with a vengeance? He knew she was strong-willed, stubborn and rather set in her conventional ways but he had not foreseen any greater problem and had by his own yardstick done what he could to cement their relationship.

'Aren't you going to put it on?' Sergios prompted flatly.

Bee opened the box again, removed the ring and rammed it roughly down over the third finger of her right hand with a lack of ceremony or appreciation that was even more challenging than her previous behaviour. She then returned to perusing her magazine with renewed concentration. She was so furious with him she could neither trust herself to speak to or look at him. If she did look, she would only end up picturing him cavorting in a messy tangle of bed sheets with some sinuous, sexy lover to whom she could never compare in looks or appeal. Yet until that very day looks or sex appeal had never seemed that important to Bee, who had been happier to put a higher value on her health and peace of mind. Unfortunately marrying Sergios appeared to have destroyed her peace of mind.

After a long moment of disbelief, for no woman had ever accepted a gift from him with such incivility before, dark temper stirred in Sergios. Simmering, he studied her, catching the jewelled glint of defiance in her green eyes as she sneaked a glance at him from below her curling lashes and bent her head. Shining chestnut hair fell against the flawless creamy skin of her cheek and her voluptuous pink mouth compressed. That fast he went taut and hard, sexual heat leaving him swallowing back a curse under his breath as he imagined what she might do with those full pouting lips if he got her in the right mood, and Sergios had never once doubted his ability to get a woman in the right mood.

'Excuse me,' Bee said without expression, breaking the tense silence. She was on her feet before he was even aware she was about to move. Seconds later she disappeared into the rear cabin and he heard Milo yell out her name in welcome.

Almost light-headed with relief at escaping the fraught atmosphere in the saloon, Bee sat down to amuse the children. The younger nanny, Janey, caught her hand and gasped at the huge diamond on her finger. 'That ring is out of this world, Mrs Demonides!' she exclaimed, impressed to death.

No, that ring is the price of lust, Bee could have told her. Bee was deeply insulted. He had had sex with another woman and it had meant so little to him that he had betrayed not a shred of discomfiture in Bee's presence. He was, as always, beautifully dressed and immaculate without even a hint of another woman's lipstick or perfume on him. That he was as cool as ice as well offended her sense of decency. She had wanted to throw that ring back at him and tell him to keep it. She had had to leave the saloon before she did or said something that she would live to regret.

Why couldn't she start thinking of him as a brother or a friend? Why was she burdened with this awful sense of possessiveness where Sergios was concerned? Why did she have to be so hatefully attracted to him? It was an appalling admission to make but she already knew that she couldn't bear the idea of Sergios with another woman in an intimate situation. Had she developed some kind of silly immature crush on him? She cringed at the suspicion but what else could be causing all these distressingly unsuitable feelings?

She had to reprogramme her brain to view him in the light of a brother, an asexual being, she instructed herself firmly. That was the only way forward in their relationship. That was the only way their marriage of convenience could possibly work for all of them. She had her mother's happiness to think about as well as that of Paris, Milo and Eleni. This marriage was not all about *her* and her very personal reactions to Sergios were a dangerous trap that she could not afford to fall into.

After all, Sergios was not all bad. He was tough, ruthless, arrogant and selfish, but while he might have the morals of an alley cat he had been remarkably kind to her mother. Without even being asked to do so, he had behaved as though theirs was a normal marriage for Emilia Blake's benefit. Although he appeared to have little interest in his cousin's kids or kids in general, he had still retained guardianship of the troubled trio and had married Bee on their behalf. Yet he could more easily have shirked the responsibility and retained his freedom by paying someone else to do the job of raising them for him.

The jet landed in Athens and the entire party transferred to a large helicopter to travel to the island of Orestos. Conscious of the cool gleam in Sergios's appraisal, Bee went pink and pretended not to notice while peering out of the windows to get a clear view of the island that was to be her future home. Orestos was craggy and green with a hilly interior. Pine forests backed white sand beaches that ran down to a violet blue shining sea and a sizeable small town surrounded the harbour.

'Gorgeous, just like a postcard!' one of the nannies commented admiringly.

'Has the island been in your family for long?' Bee asked Sergios.

'My great-grandfather accepted it in lieu of a bad debt in the nineteen twenties.'

'It looks like a wonderfully safe place for children to run about,' the other nanny remarked approvingly to her companion.

Bee thought of the far from safe and tough inner city streets where Sergios had grown up. Perhaps it was not that surprising that he was so hard and uncompromising in his attitude to the world and the people in it, she conceded reluctantly. The helicopter landed on a pad within yards of a big white house adorned with a tall round tower. Surrounded by the pine forest, it could not be seen except from the air. Sergios jumped out and spun round to help her leave the craft. Laughing uproariously in excitement, Milo jumped out too and would have run off had Sergios not clamped a restraining hand into the collar of his sweatshirt.

'There are dangers here with such easy access to the sea and the rocks,' he informed the hovering nannies. 'Don't let the boys leave the house alone.'

The warning killed the bubbly holiday atmosphere that had been brewing, Bee noted. Janey and Karen looked intimidated.

'The children are going to love it here but they'll have to learn new rules to keep them safe,' Bee forecast, stepping into the uneasy silence.

The housekeeper, Androula, a plump, good-natured woman with a beaming smile, came out to welcome them with a stream of Greek. Sergios came to a sudden halt as if something she had said had greatly surprised him.

'Nectarios is here,' he said in a sudden aside, his ebony brows drawing together in a frown.

'I assumed that your grandfather lived with you.'

'No, he has his own house across the bay. Androula tells me that his home suffered a flood during a rain storm, rendering it uninhabitable,' he said with the suggestion of gritted teeth. 'This changes everything.'

Bee had no idea what he was talking about. Androula swept them indoors and a tall, broad-shouldered and eagle-eyed elderly man came out to meet them. Paris rushed eagerly straight to his white-haired great-grandfather's side, Milo trailing trustingly in his brother's wake. Keen dark eyes set below beetling brows rested on Bee and she flushed, feeling hugely self-conscious.

'Introduce me to your bride, Sergios,' the old man encouraged. 'I'm sorry to invade your privacy at such a time.'

'You're family. You will always be a welcome guest here,' Bee declared warmly, some of the strain etched in her face dissipating. 'Look how pleased the boys are to see you.'

'Beauty and charm,' Nectarios remarked softly to his grandson. 'You've done well, Sergios.'

Bee did not think she was beautiful, but she thought it was very kind of the old man to pretend otherwise. At that very moment her make-up had worn off and she was wearing creased linen trousers stained by Milo's handprints. Eleni was whinging and stretching out her arms to her and she took the child and rested her against her shoulder, smoothing her little dark head to soothe her. The children were getting tired and cross and she took advantage of the fact to leave the men and follow Androula to the nursery. While the boys enthused over toys familiar from previous visits, Bee asked Androula to show her to her room. Her accommodation was in the tower and her eyes opened very wide when she entered the huge circular bedroom with full-height French windows opening out onto a stone balcony with the most fabulous view of the bay. It was a spectacular and comparatively new addition to the house and her eyes only opened wider when she was taken through the communicating door to inspect a luxurious en suite and matching dressing rooms. Purpose-built accommodation for two and her cheeks warmed. Naturally the household would be expecting Sergios and his bride to share this amazing suite of rooms.

Assured that she had time before dinner, Bee scooped up the wrap she glimpsed in one of her open cases and left the maids to unpack while she went for a bath. She was just in the mood to soak away her stress. Leaving her clothes in an unusually untidy heap and anchoring her hair to the top of her head to keep it dry, she tossed scented bath crystals into the water and climbed in, sinking down into the relaxing warmth with a sigh of appreciation.

A knock sounded on the door and she frowned, recalling that she had not locked it. She was in the act of sitting up when the door opened without further warning to frame Sergios.

Bee whipped her arms over her breasts and roared, 'Get out of here!'

'No, I will not,' Sergios responded with thunderous bite.

CHAPTER SIX

THE smouldering gold of anger in Sergios's stunning eyes dimmed solely because he was enjoying the view.

There Beatriz was, all pink and wet and bare among the bubbles. Her fair skin was all slippery and his hands tingled with the need to touch. Those breasts he had correctly calculated at more than a handful were topped by buds with the size and lushness of ripe cherries. Erect at that tempting vision within seconds, Sergios was deciding that the need to share facilities might not be quite the serious problem and invasion of privacy that he had gloomily envisaged. In fact it might well pay unexpected dividends of a physical nature.

Outraged green eyes seethed at him. 'Go!' Bee yelled at him.

Instead, Sergios stepped into the bathroom and closed the door to lean back against the wood with infuriating cool. 'Don't raise your voice to me. The maids are unpacking next door and we're supposed to be on our honeymoon,' he reminded her huskily. 'For someone so hung up on good manners you can be very rude. I knocked on the door—you chose not to answer!'

'You didn't give me the chance.' Bee said resentfully

before she reached for a towel, fed up with huddling like some cowed Victorian maiden in the water and all too well aware that her hands didn't cover a large enough expanse of flesh to conceal the more sensitive areas. As she got up on her knees she deftly used the towel as cover and slowly stood up, keen not to expose anything more.

Fully appreciating the rolling violin curve visible between her waist and hip, Sergios treated her to a wolfish grin of amusement. 'You need a bigger towel, Beatriz.'

And just like that Beatriz became instantly aware of the fact she was large and clumsy rather than little and dainty. Equally fast she was recalling her size zero sister, Zara, whom Sergios had initially planned to marry, not to mention his equally tiny first wife. That was the shape of woman that was the norm for her Greek husband. On his terms she *was* a big girl.

'Or you could just drop the towel altogether, *yineka mou*,' Sergios continued huskily, his dark deep drawl roughening round the edges at that prospect.

'If I wasn't so busy trying to knot this stupid towel I would slap you!' Beatriz countered, assuming that he was teasing her, for by no stretch of the imagination could she even picture circumstances in which she might deliberately stand naked in front of a man, even if he was the one whom she had married.

Sergios tossed her a much larger towel from the shelf on the wall and she wrapped it round her awkwardly. 'We have to share this suite,' he spelt out, suddenly serious.

Her brow indented. 'What are you talking about?'

'My grandfather is staying and I want him to believe that this is a normal marriage. He won't believe that if we occupy separate rooms and behave like brother and sister,' he said with a sardonic curl to his wide sensual mouth. 'We don't have a choice. We'll just have to tough it out and hope our acting skills are up to the challenge.'

'You're expecting me to share that bedroom with you...even *the bed*?' Bee gasped. 'I won't do it.'

'I didn't offer you a choice. We have an arrangement and it includes providing cover for each other.' Eyes dramatised by black spiky lashes raked her truculent face in an unashamed challenge. 'We do what we have to do. I don't want to upset Nectarios just as you didn't want to worry your mother. He needs to believe that this is a real marriage.'

'But I am not willing to agree to share a bed with you,' Bee repeated with clarity. 'And that's all I've got to say on the subject apart from the fact that if you sleep out there, I'll have to sleep somewhere else.'

His eyes glittered as bright as stars in the night sky. 'Not under my roof—'

Bee felt somewhat foolish and at a disadvantage swaddled in her unflattering towel for if she looked large without it how much larger must she look engulfed within its capacious folds? And had a towel the size of a blanket been a deliberate choice on his part or a coincidence?

'I'll get dressed for dinner,' Bee announced, waiting for him to step aside and let her out of the bathroom. *Not under my roof?* He could be as threatening as a sabre-toothed tiger but she was not about to change her mind: she was entitled to her own bed.

Eyes narrowed with brooding intensity, Sergios lounged back against the door frame like the lean, powerful predator that he was and the atmosphere was explosive. As she moved past he rested a hand on the bare curve of her shoulder and she came to a halt.

'I want you,' Sergios declared, using his other hand to ease her back against him and run his fingers lightly up from her waist to her ribcage.

In the space of a moment Bee froze and stopped breathing, panic gripping her. *I want you?* Since when?

'That's not part of our agreement,' she said prosaically, standing as still as a statue as if movement of any kind might encourage him.

Above her head, Sergios laughed, the sound full of vitality and amusement. 'Our agreement is between adults and whatever we choose to make of it—'

'Trust me,' Bee urged. 'We don't want to muddy the water with sex.'

'This is the real world. Desire is an energy, not something you can plan or pin down on paper,' he intoned, and his hands simply shifted position to cover her towel-clad breasts.

Even beneath that light pressure, her heartbeat went crazy. Boom-boom-boom it went in her ears as he boldly pushed the fabric down out of his path and closed his hands caressingly round the firm globes, teasing the stiffly prominent nipples between his fingers. A startled gasp escaped from Bee. She looked down at those long fingers stroking the swollen pink peaks, flushed crimson and then shut her eyes tight again, her legs trembling beneath her. She should push him away, she should push him away, tell him to stop, *insist* that he stop.

Sergios swept her up off her feet while she was still struggling to reclaim her poise and strode into the bedroom to lay her down on the big wide bed. He hit a button above the headboard and she heard the door lock and she sat up, wrenching the towel back up over her exposed flesh.

'You're not going anywhere...' Sergios husked with raw masculine assurance, coming down to the bed on his knees and reaching for her.

'This is not a good idea,' Bee protested in a voice that without the slightest warning emerged as downright squeaky.

'You sound like a frightened virgin!' Sergios quipped, using one hand to tip up her chin and kiss her with hard, hungry fervour, his teeth nipping at her full lower lip, his tongue plunging in an erotic raid on her tender mouth. With his other hand he stroked the straining sensitive buds on her breasts and it was as if he had jerked a leash to pull her in, for instead of pushing back from him she discovered that she only wanted to go one way and that was closer.

'Sergios...' she cried against the demanding onslaught of his sensual mouth.

'*Filise me*...kiss me,' he urged, his strong hands roaming. 'I love your breasts.'

As sweet tempting sensation executed its sway over her treacherous body, Bee felt her lack of fight travelling through her like a debilitating disease. In a sudden move of desperation she flung herself sideways off the bed. She fell with a crash that bruised her hip and jolted every bone in her body and Sergios sat up to regard her with a look of bewilderment. He reached down to help her up again. 'How did you do that?' he questioned. 'Are you hurt?'

'No, but I had to stop what we were doing,' Bee volunteered jerkily, hauling at the towel again and feeling remarkably foolish.

'Why?' Sergios countered in frank astonishment.

Bee veiled her eyes and shut her mouth like a steel trap. 'Because I don't want to have sex with you.'

'That's a lie.' Smouldering eyes came to a screeching halt on her. 'I can tell when a woman wants me.'

Sitting on the wooden floor on a rug that did not make the floor any more comfortable, Bee marvelled that she did not simply scream and launch herself at him like a Valkyrie. He was like a dog with a bone; he wasn't going to give it up without a fight. 'I forgot myself for a moment…a weak moment. It won't happen again. You said you didn't want intimacy—'

'I've changed my mind,' Sergios admitted without skipping a beat.

Bee very nearly did scream then in frustration. 'But I haven't—changed my mind, that is.'

An utterly unexpected grin slanted his beautiful shapely mouth, lending a dazzling charisma to his already handsome features that no woman could have remained impervious to. He lounged fluidly back on the bed and shifted a graceful hand. 'So, then we deal, *yineka mou*—'

'*Deal?*' Bee parroted in a tone of disbelief.

'You're so uptight, Beatriz. You need a man like me to loosen you up.'

Tousled chestnut hair tumbling round her wildly flushed oval face, Bee stood up still clutching the towel. 'I don't want to loosen up. I'm quite happy as I am.'

Sergios released his breath in an impatient hiss. 'You can get pregnant if you want,' he proffered with a wry roll of his stunning dark eyes as if he were inviting her to take two pints of his blood. 'We're already saddled with three kids—how much difference could another one make?'

Her eyes wide with consternation at that shockingly unemotional appraisal, Bee backed away several feet. 'I think you're crazy.'

Sergios shook his arrogant dark head. 'Think outside the box, Beatriz. I'm trying to make a deal with you. As you're not in business, I'll explain—I give you what you want so that you give me what I want. It's that simple.'

'Except when it's my body on the table,' Bee replied in a tone of gentle irony. 'My body is not going to figure as any part of a deal with you or anybody else. We agreed that there would be no sex and I want to stick to that.'

'That is not the message your body is giving me, *latria mou*,' Sergios drawled softly.

'You're reading the signals wrong—maybe it's your healthy ego misleading you,' Bee suggested thinly as she hit the button he had used to lock the door to un-lock it again.

As Bee leant across him Sergios hooked his fin-gers into the edge of the towel above her breasts. Immobilised, she looked up at him and collided with his dazzling eyes enhanced by ridiculously long lush lashes. Her heart seemed to jump into her throat.

'It's *not* my ego that's talking,' Sergios purred like a prowling big cat of the jungle variety.

'Yes, it is. Even though you don't really want me and I'm not your type.'

'I don't go for a particular type.'

'Zara? Your first wife? Let me remind you—*slim, glamorous*?' Bee stabbed without hesitation, watching his face tauten and pale as though she had struck him. The hand threatening the closure of the towel fell back and Bee was quick to take advantage of his unchar-acteristic retreat. 'That's your type. I'm not and never could be.'

Sergios dealt her a steely-eyed appraisal. 'You don't know what turns me on'

'Don't I? Something you've been told you can't have. A challenge—that's all it takes to turn you on!' Bee hissed at him, fighting to hide the depth of her outrage. 'And I accidentally made myself seem like a challenge this evening. You're so perverse. If I was throwing my-self at you, you would hate it.'

'Not right at this moment, I wouldn't,' Sergios purred in silken contradiction, running a hand down over the extended stretch of one long powerful thigh and by doing so drawing her attention to the tented effect of his tailored trousers over his groin. 'As you can see, I'm not in any condition to say no to a reasonable offer.'

As he directed her gaze to the evidence of his arousal Bee could feel a tide of mortified heat rush up from her throat to her hairline and she did not know where to look even as a kernel of secret heat curled in her pelvis. 'You're disgusting,' she said curtly and knew even as she said it that she didn't mean it. The knowledge that lust for her had put him in that state was strangely stimulating and there was something even more satisfying in that unsought but graphic affirmation of her femininity.

'Over dinner, think about what you want most,' Sergios advised lazily. 'And remember that there's nothing I can't give you.'

Consternation in her eyes, Bee stepped back from the bed, her oval face stiff with angry condemnation. 'Are you offering me money to sleep with you?'

Sergios winced. 'You're so literal, so blunt—'

'You just can't accept the word no, can you?' Bee launched at him in a furious flood. 'You even sank low enough to try and use a baby as a bargaining chip!'

'Of course you want a baby—I've watched you with my cousin's kids. Nobody could be that way with them if they didn't want one of their own,' Sergios opined with assurance. 'I've had enough experience with women to know that at some point in our marriage you will decide that you want a child of your own.'

'Right at this very moment,' Bee told him shakily, 'I'm wondering how I can possibly stay married to such a conniving and unscrupulous man!'

'Your mother, the kids, the fact that you don't like to fail at anything? You're not a quitter, Beatriz. I admire that in a woman.' Straightening his tie and finger-combing his black hair back off his brow, Sergios sprang off the bed, his big powerful body suddenly towering over her. 'But I do have one small word of warning for you,' he murmured in a tone as cool as ice. 'I don't talk about my first wife, Krista...*ever*, so leave her out of our...discussions.'

Shell-shocked from that spirited encounter and that final chilling warning, Bee got back into her cooling bath and sat there blinking in a daze. When he had touched her, a tide of such longing had gripped her that she had almost surrendered. But she wasn't stupid, and even though she had never been so strongly affected before by a man she had always accepted that sex and the cravings it awakened could be very powerful and seductive. Why else did the lure of sex persuade so many people to succumb to temptation and get into trouble over it? It might be a sobering discovery but she had only learned that she was as weak as any other human being.

After Krista's death—she who must not be mentioned—Sergios had become a notorious playboy. He had to be a very experienced lover and he knew exactly how to pull her strings and extract ladies who ought to have known better from towels, she allowed in growing chagrin. Well, he hadn't got the towel the whole way off, she told herself soothingly. With a male as ferociously determined and untamed as Sergios even the smallest victory ought to be celebrated.

It was silly how it actually hurt her pride that Sergios didn't *really* desire her. He was annoyed that his grandfather's presence in his home would force them to live a lie to conceal the reality that their marriage was a fake. His ego was challenged by the prospect of having to share a bed with a woman he had agreed not to touch, so he was trying to tear up the terms of their agreement by whatever means were within his power. Even so, she reckoned it had to be a very rare event for a man to try to seduce a woman by offering to get her pregnant.

Sergios could certainly think on his feet. Indeed he was utterly shameless and callous in pursuit of anything he wanted. But he was also, Bee thought painfully, extremely clever and far too shrewd for comfort. He had sensed the softy hiding below her practical surface and made an educated guess that the prospect of having her own child would have more pulling power with her than the offer of money or diamonds. And he had guessed right, *so* right in fact that she wanted to scream in frustration and embarrassment.

How could he see inside her heart like that? How could he have worked out already what she had only recently learned about herself? Only since she had been in daily contact with Paris, Milo and Eleni had Bee appreciated just how much she enjoyed being a mother. Out on a shopping trip she had bought baby clothes for Eleni and found herself drawn to examining the even tinier garments and the prams, newly afflicted by a broodiness that she had heard friends discuss but until then had never experienced on her own behalf.

But common sense warned her that right now she had

to stand her ground with Sergios. If she allowed him to walk over her so early in their marriage she would be the equivalent of a cipher within a few years, enslaved by her master's voice. He had to respect the boundaries they had set together. After all, he had Melita and other women in his life and she had no wish to join that specific party. The reflection tightened her muscles and made her head begin to ache as she appreciated that she truly was caught between a rock and a hard place with a man who attracted her but whom she could not have. She stretched back against the padded headrest, desperate to shed her tension and troubled thoughts. Sergios was an absolute menace to her peace of mind. He kept on moving the goalposts to suit himself. He was like a pirate on the high seas, always in pursuit of an advantage or a profit. But when it came to fencing with Bee he was just as likely to run aground on the rocks hidden beneath her deceptively calm surface.

When Sergios strolled into the bedroom, Bee was putting the finishing touches to her appearance. Her full-length blue evening dress fitted her like a glove without showing a surplus inch of flesh. His brilliant eyes narrowing, she watched in the mirror as Sergios subjected her to a considering appraisal.

'Sexy,' he pronounced approvingly.

Bee stiffened defensively. 'It's high at the neck and it doesn't even show my legs,' she argued.

Her immediate protest at his comment made amusement curl the corners of his handsome mouth. He scanned the lush swell of breast and derriere so clearly defined by the clinging fabric and said nothing at all.

No skin might be on show but the dress hugged her every curve and those she had in abundance.

He touched the end of a straying strand of her dark hair where it lay on her shoulder. 'Grow your hair again. I liked it longer.'

'Are you used to women doing what *you* like with their appearance?' Bee prompted a tad sourly.

'Yes,' Sergios proclaimed without a shred of discomfiture.

'Any other orders, boss?' Bee could not resist the crack.

'Smile and relax,' he urged. 'Nectarios is already very taken with you. He sees a big improvement in his great-grandsons—'

'My goodness, it's not down to my influence. I've only been with the children a few weeks—'

'But they didn't see that much of their own mother, so your attention means a great deal to them.'

'Why didn't they see much of their mother?'

'She was a popular TV presenter and rarely at home. Timon adored her.'

Suddenly she wanted to know if Sergios had adored Krista but she found that she couldn't imagine him in thrall to a woman, eager to impress and please. There was a bone-deep toughness and a reserve to Sergios that suggested that nothing less than pole position in a relationship would satisfy him. Yet he had only been twenty-one when he wed Krista and to marry so young he must have been a good deal less cynical about the institution of marriage. Comparing that to his attitude at their wedding the day before, Bee could only assume that he had got badly burned by Krista in some way. Of course there was the alternative view that losing Krista and their unborn child had hurt him so much that he had resolved never to fall in love or marry again.

Suddenly irritated by her curiosity, she asked herself why she should care. He had married her purely for the sake of Timon's children and she needed to remember that. This afternoon he had wanted to bed her and the motivation for that staggering turnaround was not that hard to work out, Bee reflected ruefully. How many other sexual options could this little Greek island offer Sergios? He was supposed to be on his honeymoon and if he wanted his grandfather to believe that it was a normal marriage he could scarcely ditch his bride and rush off to seek satisfaction in some other woman's bed. So, for the present, Sergios was trapped in a masquerade and Bee had become miraculously desirable through a complete absence of competition. Right now she was the only option her sensual Greek husband had. It was an acknowledgement that would certainly ensure she didn't develop a swollen head about the precise nature of her attractions.

Dinner was served on a terrace outside the formal dining room. The sun was going down over the sea in fiery splendour and the food was delicious. Bee ate with relish while Nectarios entertained her with stories about the history of the island and family ownership. As the two men finally succumbed to catching up on business, it amused her to recognise how alike Sergios and his grandfather were in looks and mannerisms and she told them she would not be offended if they switched to talking in Greek. She would have to learn the language and quickly, she recognised, grateful that learning languages came relatively easily to her, for it was essential that she be able to communicate effectively with the staff and the children. She did not want to be shut out of half of the conversations going on around her.

She contemplated Sergios over her fresh fruit dessert. The low lights gleamed over his cropped black hair and cast shadows on his strong bronzed profile. He was extraordinarily handsome and even the way he moved was sensual, she thought abstractedly, her eyes following the elegant arc inscribed by an eloquent hand as he spoke. When she glanced up and realised that Nectarios was watching her watch Sergios she went pink. A few minutes later she said it was time she looked in on the children and she left the table.

Having checked on the kids and agreed to take Paris down to the beach in the morning, Bee walked past the door of the main bedroom and on up the final flight of stairs to the bedroom at the top of the tower. Earlier that evening she had found the room and had decided that it would do her nicely as a bolthole. Hadn't she read somewhere recently that it was fashionable for couples with sufficient space in their homes to pursue a better night's sleep by occupying different bedrooms? Separate beds need not mean that anyone's relationship was on the rocks and that was what she would tell Sergios if he tried to object.

She slid on a light cotton nightdress that was far from glamorous, for she had disdained the silk and satin lingerie the personal shopper had directed her towards in London. She climbed into her big comfortable bed and lay with her cooling limbs splayed in a starfish shape to let all her tension drain away. In time this house and the new life she was leading would feel familiar and comfortable, she told herself soothingly.

The door opened and she jerked in surprise, lifting her head several inches off the pillow to peer across the room. The light from the stairwell fell on Sergios's lean strong features and glimmered over his bare, hair-roughened chest and the towel that appeared to be all he was wearing. Bee's short-lived relaxation dive-bombed and her limbs scissored back together again as she sat up and switched on the light.

'What are you doing in here?'

'As you've deserted the marital bed so must I. Wherever we sleep, we stay together,' Sergios spelt out with hard dark eyes and an unyielding angle to his jaw line.

Bee was intimidated by the amount of naked masculine flesh on view. He was tall and broad and, stripped, his big strong shoulders, powerful torso and tight flat stomach were distinctly imposing. 'Don't you dare take off that towel!' she warned him thinly.

'Don't be such a prude,' Sergios told her impatiently. 'I sleep naked. I always have.'

'I can't treat you like a brother if I've seen you naked!' Bee snapped back in embarrassment.

Sergios, engaged in wondering why she would want to treat him like a brother when his own intentions had roamed so far from the platonic plane, threw up both hands in a sudden gesture of exasperation. 'You must've seen loads of guys naked!'

'Oh, is that a fact?' Bee hissed, insulted by that assumption. 'You think I've slept with a lot of men?'

'I've had quite a few women. I'm not a hypocrite,' Sergios said drily.

Bee was seething. 'FYI some of us are a little more particular.'

'Did they all wear pyjamas?' Sergios asked, unable to resist that crack as his wondering gaze took in the full horror of the nightdress she wore: a baggy cotton monstrosity edged with fussy lace.

Bee cringed inwardly. 'There hasn't actually been anyone yet,' she admitted, hoping dismay at her inexperience would persuade him that she really did need her privacy.

Sergios came to an abrupt halt about ten feet from the foot of the bed. A frown had drawn his brows together. 'You can't mean that you've never had a lover...'

Bee reddened but she lifted and dropped both shoulders in a dismissive shrug as though the subject did not bother her at all. 'I haven't.'

Momentarily, Sergios was transfixed by the concept. He had believed virgins had died out around the same time as efficient contraception was developed. He had certainly never expected to find one in his bed. He swung on his heel and strode back out of the room without another word. Released from stasis, Bee breathed in slow and deep and switched out the light. Well, that news had certainly cooled his jets, she conceded. She had fallen out of the challenge category into the sort of unknown territory he evidently had no desire to explore.

But in that conviction Bee was wrong for the bedroom door opened again, startling her, and she raised herself on her elbows with a frown. Sergios was back, minus the towel and clad in a pair of black boxers, which did spectacularly little to conceal the muscular strength and bronzed beauty of his powerfully masculine body.

Sergios got into the far side of the bed in silence. A *virgin*, he was thinking with unholy fascination, a novelty calculated to appeal to even the most jaded palate.

Bee's toes encountered a masculine leg and she pulled hurriedly away as if she had been burned by the contact. His persistence in doing exactly what he wanted to do, regardless of her objections, was beginning to wear down even her nerves of steel.

'I've never gone to bed with a virgin before...' Sergios informed her in his deep drawl. 'In today's world you're as rare as a dinosaur.'

And at that astonishing assurance a bubble of unquenchable mirth formed and swelled in Bee's chest and then floated up into her throat to almost choke her before she finally gave vent to her laughter.

Sergios snaked out an arm and hauled her close. 'I wasn't trying to be funny.'

'Try to picture yourself as a d-dinosaur!' Bee advised, shaking with a hilarity she could not restrain. 'I just hope you weren't thinking of a T-Rex.'

Her laughter was even more of a surprise to a man who took life very seriously and sex more seriously still. He held her while wave after wave of uncontrollable amusement rippled through her curvy body and rendered her helpless. Her breasts rubbed his chest, her thighs shifted against his and he breathed in the soapy scent of her, picturing her equally helpless from passion in his arms. Desire roared through him afresh with a savagery that took even him aback.

Knotting one hand into the fall of her hair to hold her steady, Sergios dipped his tongue between her parted lips with erotic heat. All lingering amusement left her in the space of a moment as he plundered her ready response, nibbling and suckling at her full lower lip, skating an exploration over the sensitive roof of her mouth until her toes were curling and she was stretching up to him helpless in the grip of her need for more.

'Sergios...' she framed in vague protest when he let her breathe again.

'You'll still be a virgin in the morning,' Sergios murmured. 'I promise, *yineka mou*.'

CHAPTER SEVEN

BEE was trembling, insanely conscious of every erog-
enous zone on her body, but that saying that curiosity
had killed the cat was playing in the back of her mind
as well. Sergios was playing a game with her and she
didn't know the rules, was convinced that she would
live to regret letting down her defences. But there was
a tightening sense of pressure at the heart of her that
pulled tighter with every insidious flick of his tongue
against hers and she could not resist its sway.

He inched the nightdress down over her slim shoulders, trapping her arms at the same time as he exposed
her generous breasts. In the moonlight pouring through
the filmy drapes those high round swells were the most
tempting he had ever seen. He kneaded them with firm
hands, closed his mouth hungrily to a rigid pink nipple
and teased with his lips and his teeth while her back
arched and she whimpered beneath his attentions. He
switched his focus to her other breast, treating her to
one tantalising caress after another, steadily utilising
more pressure and urgency on her increasingly sensitised flesh.

It was like being taken apart and put together again

in a different sequence, Bee acknowledged in an agony of uncertainty that did nothing to stop the raging hunger that controlled her. She might never be the same again yet she still could not summon the will power to pull back or insist that he stop touching her. Her clenching fingers delved into his luxuriant hair while he stroked deliciously at her pointed nipples and kissed and licked his passage across the creamy slopes of her breasts before possessing her mouth again, drinking deep from her. She was wildly, seethingly aware of the brimming heat and moisture between her thighs and the ache of longing that had her hips digging into the bed beneath her. Her hands shifted back and forth across his satin-smooth shoulders as the knot of tension at the heart of her built and built. She pushed up to him desperate for more powerful sensation and she couldn't stay still then, couldn't find her voice, couldn't stop the gasps emanating from her throat either. And then suddenly it was all coalescing into one explosive response and she was arching and jerking and crying out in ecstasy as her body took her soaring onto another plane and there was nothing she could do to control any of it.

Afterwards, Bee wanted to leap out of the bed and run but there was nowhere to run to. The thought of cowering behind the bathroom door was not appealing. Still in his arms, she lay like a stone that had been dropped from a height, insanely conscious of her ragged breathing and racing heartbeat, not to mention the feel of his potent arousal against her hip. Dear heaven, what had she done?

'That was interesting,' Sergios purred with dark amusement. 'Definitely an ice breaker.'

'Er…you…?' Bee mumbled unevenly, conscious that events had been distinctly one-sided.

'I'll have a cold shower,' Sergios said piously.

Her face burning, Bee was relieved by the get-out clause. She knew it was selfish to be relieved but she was out of her depth and feeling it. She hadn't known, hadn't even guessed that she could reach a climax that way and she was not pleased that he had put her on that path of sexual discovery.

'You're a very passionate woman, *moli mou*,' Sergios intoned as he vaulted out of bed. 'Obviously Townsend wasn't the right guy for you.'

Bee went rigid. 'What do you know about Jon?'

Sergios paused in the doorway of the bathroom and swung back. 'More than you were prepared to tell me,' he admitted unrepentantly. 'I had him checked out.'

'You did…what?' Bee was righting her nightdress and trying to get out of bed at one and the same time, the simultaneous actions resulting in a clumsy manoeuvre that only infuriated her more. 'Why on earth did you do that? I *told* you he was a friend of mine—'

'But he wasn't—he was your ex, which made the little get-together in the bar rather less innocent, *moli mou*,' Sergios intoned, studying her furious face with level dark eyes. 'But, as I see it, since you never slept with him he doesn't really count.'

'If you ever touch me again I'll scream.'

'No complaints on that score. I love the way you

scream in my arms,' Sergios traded with silky sardonic bite and shut the bathroom door.

Bee knotted her hands into furious fists and contemplated throwing something at that closed door. It would be childish and she was *not* childish. But she had let herself down a bucketful by succumbing to his sexual magnetism. A tide of irritation swept through her then. No wonder he had called her a prude. She might feel mortified but they had hardly done anything in terms of sex. She was taking it all far too seriously and it would be much cooler to behave as though nothing worthy of note had happened.

But, without a doubt, Sergios was lethal between the sheets. The minute he got in she should have got out because compared with him she was a total novice and certain to come off worse from any encounter. And why had he checked Jon Townsend out after her single trivial meeting with her former boyfriend? Didn't Sergios trust anybody? Obviously not. How often had he been betrayed to become that suspicious of other human beings? It was a sobering thought and, although he had not been in love with her sister, Zara had agreed to marry him and then let him down. Perhaps had Bee chosen to be more honest with him he might have had more faith in her.

Around that point of self-examination, Bee must have drifted off to sleep because she wakened when Sergios stowed her into a cold bed. 'Er….what… where…*Sergios*?'

'Go back to sleep, Beatriz,' he intoned.

Her eyes fluttered briefly open on a view of the circular main bedroom in the moonlight and she simply turned over and closed her eyes again, too exhausted to protest. She woke alone in the morning, only the indent on the pillow across from hers telling her that she had had company. After a quick shower she put on Bermuda shorts and a sapphire-blue tee for the trip to the beach she had promised the boys. Nectarios was reading a newspaper out on the terrace where Androula brought Beatriz tea and toast.

'Sergios is in the office working,' his grandfather told her helpfully, folding his paper and setting it aside. 'What are you planning to do today?'

'Take the boys to the beach,' Bee confided.

'Beatriz…this is your honeymoon,' the elderly Greek remarked thoughtfully. 'Let the children take a back seat for a while and drag my grandson out of his office.'

Her imagination baulked at the image of getting Sergios to do anything against his will, but she could see that Nectarios was already picking up flaws in their behaviour as a newly married couple. He asked her about her mother and said he was looking forward to meeting her. Having eaten, Bee went off to find Sergios, although after their intimate encounter the night before she would have preferred to avoid him.

Sergios was working on a laptop in a sunlit room while simultaneously talking on the phone. Her troubled gaze locked to his bold bronzed profile. No matter how angry he made her she could never deny that he was drop-dead beautiful to look at any time of day. Finishing the call, he turned his sleek dark head, brilliant eyes welding to her, and her colour fluctuated wildly while her mouth ran dry at the impact of his gaze. 'Beatriz...'

'I'm taking the children to the beach. You should come with us. Nectarios is surprised that you've already gone back to work.'

'I don't do kids and beaches,' Sergios replied with a suggestive wince at the prospect of such a family outing.

Bee threw back her slim shoulders and spoke her mind, 'Then it's time you learned. Those kids need you...they *need* a father as well as a mother.'

'I don't know how to be a father. I never had one of my own—'

'That doesn't mean you can't do better for your cousin's children,' Bee cut in, immediately dismissing his argument in a manner that made his stubborn jaw line clench. 'Even an occasional father is better than no father at all. My father wasn't interested in me and I've felt that lack all my life.'

Under attack for his views, Sergios had sprung upright. He shrugged a broad shoulder and raked an impatient hand through his hair. His wide sensual mouth had taken on a sardonic curve. 'Beatriz—'

'No, don't you dare try to shut me up because I'm saying things you don't want to hear!' Beatriz shot back at him in annoyance. 'Even if you can only bring yourself to give the kids an hour once a week it would be better than no time at all. One *hour*, Sergios, that's all I'm asking for and then you can forget about them again.'

Sergios studied her grimly. 'I've told you how I feel. I married you so that you could take care of them.'

'Was that our "deal"?' Bee queried in a tone of scorn.
'I was just wondering. As you've already changed the
terms on my side of the fence, why do you have to be
so inflexible when it comes to your own?'

Sergios raised a brow. 'If I come to the beach will
you share a room without further argument?'

Bee sighed in frustration. 'Relationships don't work
like deals.'

'Don't they? Are you saying that you don't believe
in give and take?'

'Of course, I do but I don't want to give or take sex
like it's some sort of service or currency,' Bee told him
with vehement distaste.

'Sex and money make the world go round,' Sergios
jibed.

'I'm better than that—I'm worth more than that and
so should you be. We're not animals or sex workers.'

Her love of frankness was peppered with an unexpected penchant for drama that amused him and he
marvelled that he could ever have considered her plain
or willing to please. With those vivid green eyes, that
perfect skin and ripe pink mouth she was the very striking image of natural beauty. He could still barely believe that she was the only woman he had ever met to
have refused him. While rejection might gall him her
unattainability was a huge turn-on for him as well and
when she had admitted she was a virgin he had understood her reluctance a great deal better and valued her
all the more.

Recognising the tension in the atmosphere, Bee stiffened. He gave a look, just a look from his smouldering

dark golden eyes and her nipples tightened, her tummy flipped and moist heat surged between her thighs. Colouring, she hastily fixed her eyes elsewhere, outraged that she could have so little control over her own body.

'All right,' she said abruptly, spinning back to deal him a withering look that almost made him laugh. 'If you do the hour a week with the children without complaining, I won't argue about sharing a room any more. Over breakfast I realised that your grandfather doesn't miss a trick and he is suspicious.'

'I said a long time ago that I would never marry again and he knows me well. Naturally he's sceptical about our marriage.'

'See you down at the beach,' Bee responded a touch sourly, for she was not pleased that she had had to give way on the bedroom issue. Unfortunately her previous attempts to persuade Sergio to get involved with his cousin's children had proved fruitless and if there was anything she could do to improve that situation she felt she had to make the most of the opportunity.

Karen was on duty and the children were already dressed in their swimming togs while a beach bag packed with toys and drinks awaited her. Paris led the way down through the shady belt of pine forest to the crisp white sand. They were peering into a rock pool when Sergios arrived. Wearing denim cut-offs with an unbuttoned shirt and displaying a flat and corrugated muscular six-pack that took Bee's breath away, Sergios strode across the sand to join them. The boys made a beeline for him, touchingly eager for his attention. Paris

chattered about boy things like dead crabs, sharks and
fishing while Bee held Milo and Eleni's hands to prevent them from crowding Sergios. She paddled with the
toddlers in the whispering surf to amuse them. When
Paris began building a sandcastle, Milo and Eleni ran
back to join their brother.

Sergios walked across to Bee.

'Thirty-two minutes and counting,' she warned him
in case he was thinking of cutting his agreed hour short.

An appreciative grin slashed his handsome mouth.
'I haven't got a stopwatch on the time.'

'What happened to your father?' she asked in a rush
before she could lose her nerve.

As he looked out to sea his eyes narrowed. 'He died
at the age of twenty-two trying to qualify as a racing
driver.'

'You never knew him?'

'No, but even if Petros had lived he wouldn't have
taken anything to do with me.' Sergios volunteered that
opinion with telling derision. 'My mother, Ariana, was
a teenage receptionist he knocked up on one of the rare
days that he showed up to work for Nectarios.'

'Did your mother ever tell him about you?' Bee
prompted.

'He refused her calls and got her sacked when she
tried to see him. She didn't know she had any rights and
she had no family to back her up. Petros had no interest
in being a father.'

'It must have been very tough for so young a girl to
get by as a single parent.'

'She developed diabetes while she was pregnant. Her

health was never good after my birth. I stole to keep us,' he admitted succinctly. 'By the age of fourteen I was a veteran car thief.'

'From that to...*this*...' Her spread hands encompassed the big opulent house beyond the forest and the island owned by his grandfather. 'Must have been a huge step for you.'

'Nectarios was very patient. It must've been even harder for him. I was poorly educated, bitter about my mother's death and as feral as an animal when he first employed me. But he never gave up on me.'

'You were probably a more worthwhile investment of his time than the father you never met,' Bee offered.

Sergios surveyed her steadily, his stunning gaze reflecting the sunlight as he slowly shook his arrogant head in apparent wonderment at that view. 'Only you would think the best of me after what I've just told you about my juvenile crime record, *yineka mou*.'

Bee coloured, noticed that Milo was approaching the sea with a bucket and sped off to watch over the little boy. But it was Sergios who stepped from behind her and scooped up Milo as he teetered uncertainly ankle deep in the surging water, swinging the child up in the air so that he laughed uproariously before depositing him and, thanks to Bee's efforts, a filled bucket of water back beside the sandcastle.

Eleni her silent companion, Bee spread the rug and Sergios threw himself down beside her. As she knelt he closed a hand into her chestnut hair and lifted her head, searching her oval face with brooding eyes. She gazed back at him with a bemused frown. 'What do you want from me?' she questioned in frustration.

'Right now?' Sergios released a roughened laugh that danced along her taut spine like trailing fingertips. 'Anything you'll give me. Haven't you worked that out yet?'

He crushed her mouth under his, tasting her with an earthy eroticism that fired up every skin cell in her quivering body. Hunger rampaged through her like a fire burning out of control and the strength of that hunger scared her so much that she thrust him back from her, her attention shooting past him to check that the children were still all right. Paris had been watching them kiss and he turned away, embarrassed by the display but no more so than Bee was. Sergio rested back on an elbow, one raised thigh doing little to conceal the bold outline of his arousal below the denim. Suddenly as hot as though she were roasting in the fires of hell, Bee dragged her gaze from him and watched the children instead.

'You're trying to use me because I'm the only woman available to you right now,' she condemned half under her breath.

Sergios ran a fingertip down her arm and she turned her head reluctantly to collide with his glittering dark eyes. 'Do I really strike you as that desperate?'

Her full mouth compressed. 'I didn't say *desperate*.'

'I can leave the island any time I like to scratch an itch.'

'Not if you want to convince your grandfather that you're a happily married man.'

'I could easily manufacture a business crisis that demanded my presence,' Sergios countered lazily. 'You have a remarkably low opinion of your own attraction.'

'Merely a realistic one. Men have never beaten a path to my door,' Bee admitted without concern. 'Jon was special for a while but once he realised that my mother and I were a package he backed off.'

'And married a wealthy judge's daughter. He's ambitious, not a guy with a bleeding heart,' Sergios commented, letting her know how much he knew and making her body tense with resentment over the professional snooping that had delivered such facts. 'Doesn't it strike you as odd that he should now be approaching you as the representative of a children's charity?'

Bee ignored the hint that Jon was an opportunist because she did not intend to adopt Sergios's cynicism as her yardstick when it came to judging people's motives. 'No. As your wife I could be of real use to the charity.'

'And as my ex-wife you could be of even more use to Jon,' Sergios completed with sardonic bite. 'Be careful. You could be his passport to another world.'

'I'm not stupid.'

'Not stupid, but you are naive and trusting.' He studied her with amusement. 'After all, you ignored all the warnings and married me.'

'If you treat me with respect I will treat you the same,' Bee swore. 'I don't lie or cheat and I don't like being manipulated.'

Sergios laughed out loud. 'And I'm a very manipulative guy.'

'I know,' Bee said gravely. 'But now you've got me in the same bed that's as far as it goes.'

His curling black lashes semi-concealed his stunning eyes. 'That would be such a waste, Beatriz. We have the opportunity, the chemistry.'

'With all due respect, Sergios,' Beatriz murmured sweetly, cutting in, 'that's baloney. You only want to bed me because you believe it'll make us seem more intimate and therefore more of a couple for your grandfather's benefit. And while I think he's a lovely old man, I don't want to go that far to please.'

'I can make you want me,' Sergios reminded her smooth as silk but it was the tough guy talking, his dark eyes hard as ebony, his strong bone structure taut with controlled aggression.

'But only in the line of temporary insanity. It doesn't last,' Bee traded, longing for the smile and the laughter that had been there only minutes earlier and suddenly recognising another danger.

It would be so easy to fall for this man she had married, she grasped with a sudden stab of apprehension. He wasn't just gorgeous to look at, he was an intensely charismatic man. Unfortunately he had very few scruples. If she let him, he would use her and discard her again without thought or regret. Where would she be then? Hopelessly in love with a guy who didn't love her back and who betrayed her with other women? She suppressed a shudder at that daunting image, and her heart, which he had made beat a little faster, steadied again.

A ball suddenly thumped into her side and the breath

she was holding in escaped in a startled huff. Instantly Sergios was vaulting upright and telling Paris off, but Bee was relieved by the interruption and quick to intervene. She threw the ball back to the boys, retrieved Eleni from the shells she was collecting and joined in their game.

Unappreciative of the fact that she was using the children as a convenient shield, Sergios was equally challenged by the idea that she could so easily discard the idea of becoming a proper wife. He thought of the countless women who had gone to extraordinary lengths to get him to the altar and failed and then he looked at Beatriz, distinctly unimpressed by what he had to offer in bed or out of it. He was out of his element with a woman who put a value on things without a price. He didn't do feelings, fidelity or…virgins. Basically he operated on the belief that women were all the same, money greased the wheels of his affairs and he had few preferences. That ideology had carried him along a safe smooth path after his first marriage right up to the present day. But nothing in that credo fitted Beatriz Blake. In her own quiet way she was a total maverick.

A manservant came down to the beach to tell Sergios about an important call. He departed and Bee tried not to care that he had gone, leaving behind a space that absolutely nothing else could fill. It was impossible to be unaware of a personality and a temperament as larger than life as Sergios Demonides. When Bee trekked up from the beach late afternoon with two tired little boys and an equally tired and cross little girl, she was damp and sandy and pink from the sun in spite of her high factor sun cream.

Having fed Eleni and spent some time cuddling the little girl while chatting with the nannies about the child's upcoming surgery that would hopefully improve her hearing, Bee left the nursery and went for a shower before changing for dinner. In the bedroom she found several boxes of exclusive designer nightwear on the bed in her size, items fashioned to show off the female body for a man's benefit and not at all the sort of thing that Bee wore for comfort and cosiness. She could barely believe Sergios's nerve in ordering such items for her but it was certainly beginning to sink in on her that he was a very determined man. When she returned to the bedroom, clad in her own light robe, Sergios was there and she stiffened, unaccustomed to the lack of privacy entailed in sharing a bedroom. Engaged in tying the sash on the robe to prevent it from falling open, she hovered uncomfortably.

'Did you order those nightgowns for me?' she pressed.

'Yes. Why not?'

'They're not the sort of thing I would wear.'

Sergios shrugged off the assurance. 'My grandfather has decided to return to his home.'

'I thought it was uninhabitable.'

'Two rooms are but it's a substantial property. I think that was an excuse to allow him to check us out,' Sergios confided wryly. 'He's taking the children and their nannies back with him.'

Her head flew up, green eyes wide with surprise and

bewilderment 'Why on earth would he take the kids with him?'

'Because it's a rare newly married couple who want three children around on their honeymoon,' Sergios drawled, his face impassive. 'Don't make a fuss about this. It's a well-meant offer and he is their grandfather—'

'Yes, I know he is *but*—'

'Objecting isn't an option,' Sergios sliced in with sudden impatience. 'It's a done deal and it would look strange if we turned him down.'

Bee could not hide her consternation at the arrangement that had been agreed behind her back. He had married her to act as a mother to those children but it seemed that she was not entitled to the rights or feelings of a mother if they conflicted with his wishes. 'Yes, but the children are just getting used to me. It's unsettling for them to be passed around like that.'

'You can go over and see them every day if you like.' His beautiful wilful mouth took on a sardonic slant. 'First and foremost you are my wife, Beatriz. Start acting like one.'

Bee reddened as though she had been disciplined for wrongdoing, her temper flaring inside her. 'Is that an order, sir?'

'*Ne*…yes, it is,' Sergios confirmed without hesitation or any hint of amusement. 'Let's keep it simple. I tell you what I want, you do it.'

Those candid words still echoing in her ears, Bee vanished back into her bathroom to do her make-up. Being ordered around when she was naked below a wrap didn't feel right or comfortable. But then she never had liked being told what to do. In addition she was very angry with him. He had encouraged her to act like a mother, only to snatch the privilege back again when it no longer suited him. *Act like a wife?* If she did that he wouldn't like it at all…for a wife would make demands.

CHAPTER EIGHT

CLEARLY in no mood to make the effort required to convince the staff that he was an attentive new husband, Sergios did not join Bee at the dinner table until she was halfway through her meal and the silence while they ate together screamed in her ears like chalk scraping down a blackboard.

'I didn't think you'd be the type to sulk.'

'Am I allowed to shout at you, sir?'

'Enough already with the sir,' Sergios advised impatiently.

Her appetite dying, Bee pushed her plate away.

'I'll take you out sailing tomorrow morning,' he announced with the air of a man expecting a round of applause for his thoughtfulness.

'Lucky me,' Bee droned in a long-suffering voice.

'Later this week, I'll take you over to Corfu to shop.'

'I hate shopping—do we have to?'

The silence moved in again.

'When I married you I believed you were a reasonable, rational woman,' Sergios volunteered curtly over the dessert course.

'I believed you when you said you wanted a platonic

marriage,' Bee confided. 'Just goes to show how wrong you can be about someone.'

'Do you think your own mother will be fooled by the way we're behaving into believing that this is a happy marriage?'

Hit on her weakest flank by that question, Bee paled.

'Don't wait up for me,' Sergios told her as he too pushed away his plate, the food barely touched. 'Last month I took over my grandfather's seat on the island council and it meets tonight. I'll stay for a drink afterwards.'

Frustrated by his departure when nothing between them had been resolved, Bee phoned her mother and lied through her teeth about how very happy she was. She then tried very hard to settle down with a book but her nerves continued to zing about like jumping beans and at well after ten that evening she decided that, as she wasn't the slightest bit tired, vigorous exercise might at least dispel her tension. At her request a pole had been fitted in the house gym and she had politely ignored Sergios's mocking enquiry as to what she intended to do with it. Like all too many people Sergios evidently assumed that pole dancing was a lewd activity best reserved for exotic dancers in sleazy clubs. Clad in stretchy shorts and a crop top, Bee did her warm-up exercises to loosen up before putting on her music.

Sergios was resolutely counting his blessings as he drove back along the single-track road to his home. Unhappily a couple of drinks and all the jokes with his colleagues on the island council that had recognised his status as a newly married man hadn't taken the edge off his mood. In fact he was engaged in reminding himself that being married was by its very nature tough. Learning how to live with another person was difficult. Nobody knew that better than him, which was why he had cherished his freedom for so long. Indeed the lesson of having once lost his freedom was engraved on his soul in scorching letters, for Sergios never forgot or forgave his own mistakes. He knew he should be grateful that Beatriz was so very attached to children who were not her own. She was a good woman with a warm heart and strong moral values. He knew he should be appreciative of the fact that if he came home unexpectedly he was highly unlikely to walk into a wild party...

When he walked into the lounge, however, he was vaguely irritated to find that Beatriz had not waited up for him, thereby demonstrating her concern for his state of mind and their marriage. He was hugely taken aback to recognise that he actually *wanted* her to do wifely things of that nature. That she had just taken herself off to bed was definitely not a compliment. It was hardly surprising, he acknowledged in sudden exasperation, that Beatriz should be confused about what he wanted from her when he no longer knew himself.

The bedroom, though, was also empty and Androula, plump and disapproving in her dressing gown, answered his call and informed him that Beatriz was in the gym. Having dispensed with his tie and his jacket, Sergios followed the sound of the music but what he saw when he glanced through the glass doors of the gymnasium brought him to a sudden stunned halt.

Beatriz was hanging upside down on a pole. By the

time he got through the door she was doing a hand-stand and swirling round the pole, legs splaying in a distinctly graphic movement that he would not have liked her to do in public. He was astonished by how fit she was as she went through an acrobatic series of moves. That stirring display was so unexpected from such a quiet conservative woman that it made it seem all the more exciting and illicit. He watched her kick, toes pointed, slender muscles flexing in a shapely leg and in a rounded, deliciously plump derriere. Around that point he decided simply to enjoy the show. As she undulated sexily against the pole, full breasts thrust out, hips shifting as though on wires, he was hard as a rock and her sinuous roll on the floor at the foot of the pole was frankly overkill.

'Beatriz?' Sergios husked.

In consternation at the sound of his voice, Bee flipped straight back upright, wondering anxiously for how long she had had an audience. Brilliant dark eyes welded to her, Sergios was by the door, tall, darkly handsome and overwhelmingly masculine. Lifting her towel to dry the perspiration from her face, she paused only to switch off the music.

'When did you get back?'

'Ten minutes ago. How long have you been doing that for?'

'About three years,' she answered a little breathlessly, drawing level with him. 'It was more fun than the other exercise classes.'

His gaze smouldering, he bent his dark head and crushed her parted lips hotly beneath his, ravishing her mouth with the staggering impact of a long, drugging kiss. A shiver of sensual shock ran through her as his arms came round her and she felt the hard urgency of his erection against her stomach.

'*Se thelo*…I want you,' he breathed raggedly. 'Let's make this a real marriage.'

Taken aback by that proposition, Bee tried to step back but Sergios had a strong arm braced to her spine as he walked her down the corridor. 'We need to think about this,' she reasoned, struggling to emerge from that potent kiss, which had made her head swim.

'No, I believe in gut instinct. We've been thinking far too much about things,' Sergios fired back with strong masculine conviction. 'You're not supposed to agonise over everything you do in life and look for all the pitfalls, Beatriz. Some things just happen naturally.'

He thrust open their bedroom door, whirled her round and devoured her mouth hungrily beneath his again, his tongue darting into the tender interior of her mouth, setting up a chain reaction of high voltage response inside her. This, she registered, was the sort of thing he believed should happen naturally, but from Bee's point of view there was nothing natural about the fact that she was trembling and unable to think straight. The force of his passion knocked her off balance while a raging fire leapt up inside her to answer it. Locked together, they stumbled across the room and down on the bed, his hands smoothing over her Lycra-clad curves with an appreciative sound deep in his throat.

'I don't want anyone else seeing you dance like that,' Sergios spelt out. 'It's too sexy—'

'But that's how I keep fit—it's only exercise.'

'It's incredibly erotic,' Sergios contradicted, wrenching off the shorts with impatient hands.

'We really ought to be discussing this,' she told him anxiously.

A heart-breaking smile slashed his beautiful mouth. 'I don't want to talk about it…we've talked it to death.'

That smile made her stretch up to kiss him again, her fingertips smoothing over a hard cheekbone and delving into his silky black hair with a licence she had never allowed herself before. If they made love he would be hers as no other man had ever been and she wanted that with every fibre of her being and a strength of longing she had not known she was capable of feeling. Unbuttoning his shirt, she pulled it off his shoulders and he cast it off, laughing at her impatience. Standing up, he dispensed with the rest of his clothing at efficient speed and a tingling hum of arousal thrummed through her as she looked at his powerfully aroused body. He was ready for her.

Sergios pulled her up and peeled her free of the crop top and the sports bra she wore beneath. With a groan of sensual satisfaction he cupped the creamy swell of her breasts and licked and stroked the swollen pink tips until she shivered. 'Perfect,' he husked.

Liquid heat pooled between her legs as he located the damp stretch of fabric between her legs and eased a finger beneath it to trace her delicate centre. She twisted beneath his touch and lifted her hips as he took off her knickers. He kissed a trail down over her writhing length until he found the most truly sensitive spot of all. As he lingered there to subject her to the erotic torment of his skilled mouth and hand, she had to fight her innate shyness with all her might.

Had she been in control it would have been wrenched from her by the power of her response. As it was, she was free to abandon herself to sensation and she did, her head moving restively back and forth on the pillow, shallow gasps escaping her throat as her hips rose and fell on the bed. She was at the very height of excitement before he came over her and entered her in one effortless stroke. Even so there was still a stark moment of pain and she cried out as he completed his possession, driving home to the very core of her. The discomfort swiftly ebbed even as his invasive hard male heat awakened and stimulated her need again.

'Sorry,' he sighed with intense male pleasure. 'I was as gentle as I could be.'

'You're forgiven,' she murmured, very much preoccupied as she arched her spine and lifted her hips to accept more of him, desire driving her to obey her own needs.

'You're so tight,' he breathed with earthy satisfaction, rising up on his elbows and withdrawing only to thrust back deeper into her receptive body in a movement that was almost unbearably exhilarating.

Her breath catching in her throat, her heart thundering with growing fervour she shut her eyes, revelling in the feel of him inside her. She writhed beneath him as he drove deeper with every compelling thrust and his fluid rhythm increased, plunging her into an intoxicating world of erotic and timeless delight. The excitement took over until all she was aware of was him and the hot, sweet pleasure gathering stormily at the heart of her. She reached an explosive climax and plunged over the edge into ecstasy, gasping and writhing in voluptuous abandon.

Shuddering over her, Sergios cried out with uninhibited fulfilment gripped by the longest, hottest climax of his life. As her arms came round him to hold him he pulled back, however, releasing her from his weight. He threw himself back against the pillows next to her, enforcing a separation she was not prepared for at that most intimate of moments.

'That was unbelievably good, *yineka mou*,' Sergios savoured, breathing in a lungful of much-needed air. 'Thank you.'

Thank you? Bee blinked in bewilderment at that polite salutation and reached for his hand, closing her fingers round his and turning over to snuggle into his big powerful body, spreading her fingers across a stretch of his warm muscular torso. He stiffened at the contact.

'I don't do the cuddling thing, *glikia mou*.'

'You're not too old to learn,' Bee told him dreamily, dazed by what they had just shared but also happy at the greater closeness she sensed between them. 'You just persuaded me to do something spontaneous and that's not usually my style.'

Recognising the truth that Beatriz almost always had a smart answer for everything, Sergios made no comment. Instead he settled curious dark golden eyes on her flushed face. 'I hurt you. Are you sore?'

Bee gave a little experimental shift of her hips and winced. 'A little.'

'Shame,' he pronounced with regret, a sensual curve to his firm mouth. 'Right now, I would love to do it all over again but I'll wait until tomorrow.'

'You didn't use a condom,' Bee remarked, her surprise at that oversight patent.

'I'm clean. I have regular health checks. Hopefully we'll get away with it this once on the contraception front. I don't keep condoms here,' he admitted bluntly. 'I don't bring women to my home. I never have done.'

There were so many questions brimming on her lips but she wouldn't let herself ask them. She liked the fact that the room and bed had not been used by other women. But she did want to know about his first wife—there was not even a photo of Krista on display in the house. Then there was his mistress, and where Bee and Sergios were to go from here, but that thorny question would be a case of too much too soon for a guy who had fought so hard to retain his freedom and keep his secrets. He wasn't going to change overnight, she told herself ruefully.

Let's make this a real marriage, he had said in the gym. Had he truly meant it? Or had a desire for sex momentarily clouded his judgement when her dancing awakened his libido? Could he simply have told her what he thought she wanted to hear? Uneasy at that suspicion, Bee tensed but refused to lower herself to the level of asking him if he was genuinely committed to their marriage. Expressing doubt, after all, might just as easily encourage what she most feared to come about.

'We'll put a pole up in the bedroom so that you can exercise in here where nobody else can see you,' Sergios informed her lazily.

Bee could not believe her ears. His persistence on that subject was a revelation. He had not been joking in the gym when he said he didn't want anyone else to see her dancing. 'I didn't think you would be such a prude.'

'You're my wife,' Sergios reminded her, but his face was taut, as if giving her that label pained him.

Looking up into those darkly handsome features, Bee could already see the wheels of intellect turning as he questioned their new intimacy. How did he really feel about that? She lowered her lashes, refusing to agonise over something she had no control over. Living with Sergios would be a roller-coaster ride and as he did not suffer anything in silence she had no doubt that she would soon know exactly how he felt.

'I'll be late back tonight,' Sergios told her, sinking down on the side of the bed. He hesitated for a split second before he grasped the hand that she had instinctively extended to stop him leaving the room.

Still half asleep, for it was very early, Bee studied him drowsily, noting the brooding tension etched into his face while loving the warmth of his hand in hers and the golden intensity of his gaze. 'Why?'

'It's the anniversary of Krista's death today. I usually attend a memorial service with her parents and dine with them afterwards,' Sergios explained, his intonation cool and unemotional.

Taken aback, for although they had been married for

six weeks he still never ever mentioned his first wife, Bee nodded and belatedly noticed the sombre black suit that he wore.

'It's an annual event,' he said with an uneasy shrug. 'Not something I look forward to.'

She bit back the comment that some people regarded a memorial service as an opportunity to celebrate the life of the departed. 'Would you like me to go with you?' she asked uncertainly.

'That's a generous offer but I don't think Krista's parents would appreciate it. She was their only child. I get the impression that they don't want to be reminded that my life has moved on,' Sergios commented, compressing his handsome mouth with the stubborn self-discipline that was so much a part of his character.

Her ignorance of what he was feeling troubled Bee for the rest of the day. But then she was madly, hopelessly in love with Sergios and prone to worrying about what was on his mind. Although the sexual chemistry they shared was indisputably fantastic, that wasn't what had awakened more tender feelings in her heart. It was while Bee was busily working out what made Sergios tick that she had fallen head over heels in love with him.

When he was away on business she felt as though she were only half alive. Deprived of his powerful and often unsettling charismatic presence, she would watch her phone like a lovesick adolescent desperate for his call, count the hours until he came home and then lavish attention on him in bed until he purred like a big jungle cat. He was in her heart as though he had always been there, strong and stubborn and infuriatingly unpredictable.

In learning to love him she had also recognised his vulnerabilities. He was unsure how to behave with the children because his mother's ill health had deprived him of a carefree childhood. Although Bee had come from a similar background the burden of caring had been lightened in her case by her mother's deep affection. Sergios's mother, however, had been very young and immature and might possibly have resented the adverse impact of a child on her life and health. For whatever reasons, Sergios had not received the love and support he had needed to thrive during his formative years.

Within days of being removed to their grandfather's home on the other side of the bay Paris, Milo and Eleni had made it clear how much they were missing Bee and Sergios had swiftly accepted the inevitable and agreed to their return. With Bee's support since then Sergios had gradually spent more time with his cousin's kids, getting to know them so that he no longer froze when Milo hurled himself at him or looked uneasily away when Eleni opened her arms to him. Bridges were being built. Paris turned to Sergios for advice, Milo brought his ball and Eleni smiled at him when he risked getting close. Sergios was slowly learning how to accept affection and how to respond to it.

Bee had been relieved when she received the proof that their unprotected lovemaking on the first night they had spent together had not led to her conceiving a child. In her opinion an unplanned pregnancy would have been a disaster for their marriage. Sergios was very much a man who needed to make the decision that he wanted to be a father for himself. Yet when she had told him that he need not worry on that score, he had shrugged.

'I wasn't worrying about that,' he had insisted. 'If you had conceived we would have coped.'

But Bee would not have been happy while he merely 'coped'. She only wanted to have a baby with a man who was actively *keen* for her to have his baby. She did not want Sergios to make the best of an accidental conception or to offer her the option of a pregnancy because she was broody: she wanted him to make a choice that he wanted a child with her, a child of his own.

The weeks they had shared on the island had not been only about the children. Bee had stopped fretting about the future and had lived for the moment and Sergios had made many of those moments surprisingly special. He had proudly given her a tour of the wheelchair-friendly cottage in the grounds where her mother was to live. A carer whom Emilia would choose for herself from a list that had already been drawn up would come in every day to help her cope. Bee could hardly wait to see the older woman's face when she enjoyed her first cup of tea on the sunny terrace with its beautiful view of the bay.

Sergios had also flown Bee to Corfu for a week. The busy streets lined with elegant Italianate buildings, sophisticated shops and art studios had delighted her and one afternoon when Sergios had briefly lost her in the crowds he had anchored his hand to hers and kept it there for the rest of the day. He had bought her a beautiful silver icon she admired and they had had drinks on The Liston, an arcaded building modelled on the Rue de Rivoli in Paris. By the time they had returned to their designer hotel she was giggly and tipsy and he had made passionate love to her until dawn when she fell asleep in his arms. Opening her eyes again on his handsome features in profile as he worked at his laptop, getting some work out of the way before the day began, she had seen into her own heart and had known in the magic of that moment that she loved him. Loved him the way she had never thought she would ever love any man, with tenderness and appreciation of both his flaws and his strengths.

They had enjoyed numerous trips out and about on Orestos. He had shown her all over the island, had taken her swimming and sailing and snorkelling, letting the children join in whenever possible. He had enjoyed the fact that she was energetic enough to share the more physical pursuits with him. She also now knew that he was very competitive when it came to building sandcastles or fishing and that he was crazy about ice cream. He also loved it when she and the children were there to greet him when he came home from a trip. There was an abyss of loneliness deep inside Sergios that she longed to assuage.

With such uneasy thoughts dominating her mind about Krista's memorial service and what those memories might mean to her husband, Bee could not settle that afternoon. She received another text from Jon Townsend, who had stayed in surprisingly regular contact with her since her arrival in Greece, and suppressed a sigh. Her ex-boyfriend had sent her reams of information about the charity he was involved with and was keen to set up a meeting with her during her approaching visit to the UK.

On such a beautiful day it had seemed a good idea to collect Milo from his playgroup in town on foot rather than drive there as she usually did. The summer heat, however, was intense and by the time she picked up Milo Bee was questioning the wisdom of having trudged all the way along the coast road, particularly when she had no alternative other than to walk back again. Milo, in comparison, hopped, jumped and skipped along by her side with the unvarnished energy that was his trademark.

She was walking through the town square with Eleni dozing below a parasol in her pushchair when Nectarios waved at them from a table outside the taverna. He wore his faded peaked cap, and only a local would have recognised him as the powerful business tycoon that he still was even in semi-retirement. She guessed by his clothing that he had been out sailing in the small yacht he kept at the harbour and she crossed to that side of the street.

'What are you doing here on foot?' he asked with a frown, spinning out a chair for her and snapping his fingers for the proprietor's attention.

'Milo was at his playgroup. It didn't seem quite so warm when I left the house.'

'My lift will be here in ten minutes. You can all ride back with me.' The old man ordered drinks for Bee and the children while calmly allowing Milo to clamber onto his lap and steal his cap to try it on and then treat it like a frisbee.

While they sat there enjoying the welcome shade of the plane tree beside the terrace various passers-by came over to chat to Nectarios. Bee was daily picking up more Greek words and she understood odd snatches of the conversations about fishing trips, weddings and christenings. Tomorrow she was returning to London, where Eleni would have surgery on her ears, and when they came back to the island her mother would be travelling with her. She was helping Eleni with her feeding cup when she became aware of a flutter of whispers around her. Glancing up, Bee noticed the statuesque blonde walking through the square. She wore a simple figure-hugging white dress and she had that swaying walk and brash confidence that men almost always seemed to find irresistible. Certainly every man in the vicinity was staring in admiration.

'Who's that?' she asked the man beside her, who had faltered into a sudden silence. 'Is she a tourist?'

The woman looked directly at them with big brown eyes and a sultry smile on her red-tinted lips, her attention lingering with perceptible curiosity on Bee.

Nectarios gave the blonde a faint nod of acknowledgement. 'That's Melita Thiarkis.'

That familiar first name struck Bee like a slap but she would have thought nothing of it if Nectarios had not looked distinctly ill at ease.

'And she's...*who*?' she pressed, hating herself for her persistence in the face of his discomfiture.

'A fashion designer in Athens, but she was born on the island and maintains a property here.'

That fast Bee's stomach threatened to heave and she struggled to control her nausea with perspiration beading her brow and her skin turning unpleasantly clammy. The blonde *had* to be Sergios's mistress, Melita. There could not be such a coincidence. Indeed Nectarios's embarrassment at her appearance had confirmed the fact. But Bee was in shock at the news that Melita was actually staying on the island. That possibility had not even occurred to her and she had naively assumed that Orestos offered Sergios no opportunity to stray. But how many evenings had he left her alone for several hours while he attended island council meetings? Or to visit his grandfather's home? Lately there had been several such occasions and she had thought nothing of them at the time. Had she been ridiculously naive?

'May I offer you some advice?' Nectarios enquired as the four-wheel drive that had picked them up raised a trail of dust on the winding, little-used road back to the big white house with the tower on the headland.

Bee shot him a glance from troubled eyes. 'Of course.'

'Don't put pressure on my grandson. Give him the time to recognise what you have together. His first marriage was very unhappy and it left deep scars.'

The old man was the product of another generation in which men and women were not equal and women expected and even excused male infidelity. Bee had no such guiding principle to fall back on and she could not excuse what she could not live with. And she knew that she would never be able to live in silence with the suspicion that Sergios might have laid lustful hands on another woman while he was sharing a bed with Bee.

Oh, how the mighty had fallen, Bee conceded wretchedly. Now she had to face up to the reality that she had allowed Sergios to run their marriage *his* way rather than hers. They had not renegotiated the terms of their original marriage plan. There had been no earnest discussions, no agreements and no promises made on either side. For almost two months they had coasted along without the rules and boundaries that she had feared might make Sergios feel trapped. Take things slowly, Bee had thought in her innocence, eager to pin her husband down, but too sensible not to foresee the probable risks of demanding too much from him upfront.

Now she was paying the price of not frankly telling him that he could not have her *and* a mistress. Strange how she had no doubt that he would angle for that option if he thought he could get away with it. Bee was well aware of how ruthless Sergios could be. In any confrontation he was hardwired to seek the best outcome that he could. Sometimes he manoeuvred people into doing what he wanted purely as a means of amusement. She had stood on the sidelines of his life watching him, learning how he operated and monitoring her own behaviour accordingly. Although she loved him she didn't tell him that and she certainly didn't cling to him or cuddle him or flatter him or do or say any of the things that would have given her true feelings away. She had decided that she was happy to give him time to come to terms with their new relationship…as long as he was faithful.

The thought that he might not have been, that he might already have betrayed her trust in another woman's arms, threatened to tear Bee apart. In the circumstances he might even try to persuade her that he had assumed that their original agreement that he could have other women still held good. After all, Sergios thought fast on his feet and was, she reckoned ruefully, liable to fight dirty if she pushed him hard enough.

But Melita Thiarkis was a different kettle of fish. She was an islander, a local born and bred on Orestos, so Sergios had probably known her for a very long time. A fashion designer as well—no wonder he was so hung up on even his wife being stylish. There would be ties between Melita and Sergios stronger than Bee had ever wanted to consider. Melita was strikingly attractive rather than beautiful but very much the hot, sexy type likely to appeal to Sergios's high-voltage libido. The blonde was also confident of her place in Sergios's life, Bee recognised worriedly, recalling the way the other woman had looked her over without a shade of discomfort or concern. Melita, Bee reflected wretchedly, did not seem the slightest bit threatened by the fact that Sergios had recently got married. And what did that highly visible confidence signify? Had Sergios slept with his mistress since he had become Bee's husband?

As for the confirmation from Nectarios that Sergios's first marriage had been unhappy, Bee had long since worked that out for herself. The fact that there were no photos of Krista and her name was never mentioned had always suggested that that had been anything but a happy marriage. But Sergios, even though given every opportunity to do so, had still not chosen to confide that truth in Bee.

On the other hand, Bee reminded herself doggedly, she *had* been really happy and contented until she laid eyes on Melita Thiarkis and realised that temptation lived less than a mile from their door. Sergios, after all, had been remarkably attentive since they had first made love, but how could Bee possibly know what he got from his relationship with Melita? That he had insisted Melita was a non-negotiable feature of his life even *before* their marriage suggested the blonde had very good reason to be confident.

He did have a thing for blondes even though he wouldn't admit it, Bee thought bitterly as she peered at her dark brown locks in the bedroom mirror and tried to imagine herself transformed into a blonde. It would be sad to dye her hair just for his benefit, wouldn't it? Just at that moment of pain and stark fear she discovered that she didn't care if it was sad or not and she decided that she might well return from London with a mane of pretty blonde hair.

CHAPTER NINE

'I THOUGHT you would be in bed,' Sergio admitted when he landed in a helicopter after eleven that evening and strolled into the house. His tie was loosened and he was unshaven, his stunning eyes shadowed with tiredness. His sense of relief at being home again was intense and it startled him. 'It's been a long day and we have an early flight to London tomorrow morning.'

Bee glanced at him in surprise. 'You're coming with us?'

'Eleni's having surgery,' he reminded her with a frown. 'Of course I'm coming. Didn't you realise that?'

'No, I didn't.'

Delighted by his readiness to be supportive, Bee resisted the urge to immediately dredge up Melita's presence on the island. After all, if the blonde had a home and relatives on Orestos, she had a perfect right to visit and it might have nothing to do with Sergios. Was that simply wishful thinking? Bee asked herself as she put together a light supper in the big professional kitchen. She saw no need to disturb the staff so late when she was perfectly capable of feeding Sergios with her own fair hands.

He came out of his bathroom with a towel wrapped round his hips and sat down at the small table she had set up for his use. With his black hair flopping damply above his face and clean shaven, he looked less weary.

'Was it a difficult day?' Bee prompted uncertainly.

'It's always difficult.' Sergios grimaced and suddenly shrugged, acknowledging that it no longer felt reasonable to continue to keep Beatriz in the dark when it came to the touchy subject of his first marriage. 'Krista's parents remember a young woman I never knew, or maybe the young woman they talk about is the imaginary daughter they would have *liked* to have had—she certainly bears no resemblance to the woman I was married to for three years.'

Bee was confused. 'I don't understand...'

'Krista was a manic depressive and she loathed taking medication, didn't like what the prescribed tablets did to her. I didn't know about that when I married her. To be fair I hardly knew her when I asked her to marry me,' Sergios confided with a harsh edge to his dark deep drawl. 'I was young and stupid.'

'Oh.' Bee was so shattered about what his silence on the subject of his first wife had concealed that she could think of nothing else to say. A manic depressive? That was a serious condition but treatable with the right medical attention and support.

'I fell in love and rushed Krista to the altar, barely able to believe that the girl of my dreams was mine. Unfortunately the dream turned sour for us both,' he volunteered grittily, his face grim. 'As she refused medication there was no treatment that made an appreciable difference to her moods. For most of our marriage she was out of control. She took drugs and threw wild parties before crashing drunk at the wheel of one of my cars. She died instantly.'

'I am so sorry, Sergios,' Bee whispered with rich sympathy, her heart truly hurting for him. 'So very sorry you had to go through that and lose your child into the bargain.'

'The baby wasn't mine. I don't know who fathered the baby she was carrying at the time of her death.' His handsome mouth twisted. 'By then we hadn't shared a bed for a long time.'

'I wish you'd shared this with me sooner.' Bee was still struggling to accept his wounding admission of how much he had loved Krista, for she had convinced herself that Sergios didn't know *how* to love a woman. Now she was finding out different and it hurt her pride.

'I've always felt guilty that Krista died. I should've been able to do more to help her.'

'How could you when she wouldn't accept that her condition needed treatment?' Bee prompted quietly as she got into bed and rested back against the pillows. 'Didn't her parents have any influence over her?'

'She was an adored only child. They were incapable of telling her no and they refused to recognise the gravity of her problems. Ultimately they blamed me for her unhappiness.'

Striding restively about the room, his stunning eyes bleak with distressing memories and his strong jaw line clenched, he finally told her what his life had been like with Krista. When he came home to the apartment he

had shared with his late wife in Athens back then he
had never known what would greet him there. Violent
disputes and upsetting scenes were a daily occurrence,
as were his wife's periods of deep depression. Krista
had done everything from shopping to partying to ex-
cess. On various occasions he had found her in bed with
other men and high as a kite on the illegal drugs that
she was convinced relieved her condition better than
the proper medication. Staff walked out, friends were
offended, the apartment was trashed and valuable ob-
jects were stolen. For three long years as he struggled
to care for his deeply troubled wife Sergios had lived
a life totally out of his own control and the love he had
started out with had died. Bee finally understood why
he had been so determined to have a businesslike marriage, which demanded nothing from him but financial input. He had put everything he had into his first
marriage and it had still failed miserably. Krista had
betrayed him and hurt him and taught him to avoid getting too deeply attached to anyone.

'Now you know why I never mention her,' Sergios
murmured ruefully, sliding into bed beside her. 'I let
her down so badly.'

'Krista was ill. You should forgive her and yourself
for everything that went wrong,' Bee reasoned. 'You
did your best and that's the most that anyone can do.'

Eyes level, Sergios lifted a hand and traced the full
curve of her lower lip with a considering fingertip. 'You
always say the right thing to make people feel better.'

Insanely conscious of his touch as she was, her heart

was galloping and her mouth had run dry. 'Do I?' she asked gruffly.

'When Paris asked you if his mother was in heaven you said yes even though you know she was an atheist, *moli mou.*'

'She still could have made it there in the end,' Bee reasoned without hesitation. 'Paris was worrying about it. I wanted him to have peace of mind.'

'I should've told you about Krista a long time ago but I hate talking about her—it feels wrong.'

'I understand why now and naturally you want to be loyal to her memory.' Melita's name was on the tip of her tongue but she could not bring herself to destroy that moment of closeness with suspicion and potential conflict. That conversation about Krista was quite enough for one evening.

'So sweet, so tactful…' Sergios leant closer, his breath fanning her cheek, and pried her lips apart with the tip of his tongue. With one kiss he could make her ache unbearably for the heat and hardness of his body.

'Someone round here has to be,' she teased, her breath rasping in her throat.

His tongue explored her tender mouth in an erotic foray and her nipples tingled into prominence. Desire slivered through her then, sharp as a blade. He freed her of the silk nightdress, cupping her breasts with firm hands, stroking the prominent pink crests with ravishing skill. She gasped beneath his mouth as he found the heated core of her and he made a sound of deep masculine satisfaction when he discovered how ready she was.

He turned her round and rearranged her, firm hands

cupping her hips as he plunged into her velvety depths with irresistible force and potency. He growled with pleasure above her head and pulled her back hard against him as he slowly rotated his hips to engulf her in an exquisite wash of sensation. While he pumped in and out of her he teased her clitoris with expert fingers. A soul-shattering climax gripped Bee as the tightening knot of heat inside her expanded and then exploded like a blazing star. Shaking and sobbing with pleasure, she fell back against him, weak as a kitten and drained of every thought and feeling.

'Go to sleep,' Sergios urged then, both arms still wrapped round her damp, trembling body. 'You'll exhaust yourself fretting about Eleni tomorrow.'

That he should know her so well almost made her laugh but she was too tired to find amusement in anything. Worry about Melita and Eleni and the passion had exhausted her and she fell heavily asleep.

Her first night back in London, Bee spent with her mother, who was both excited and apprehensive about her approaching move to Greece. Eleni was admitted to hospital the next morning. Both a nurse and the surgeon had talked Bee through every step of the entire procedure, which was likely to take less than an hour to complete, but Bee remained as nervous as a cat on hot bricks on Eleni's behalf, particularly because the little girl was too young to be prepared for the discomfort that might follow the surgery.

'We've already discussed all this,' Sergios reminded Bee firmly, very much a rock in the storm of her concern and anxiety. 'There is very little risk attached to this procedure and she will recover quickly from it. It may not improve her hearing but she is falling so far behind with her speech that it is worth a try.'

Cradling Eleni's solid little body in her lap with protective arms, Bee blinked back tears that embarrassed her for she had long since decided that surgery was currently the best treatment available. 'She's just so little and trusting.'

'Like you were when you married me,' Sergios quipped with a rueful grin, startling her with that light-hearted sally. 'You really didn't have a clue what you were signing up for but it hasn't turned out too bad for you, has it?'

'Ask me that in a year's time,' Bee advised, in no mood to stroke his ego.

'What a very begrudging response when I'm trying so hard to be the perfect husband!' he mocked.

Bee looked up at his handsome face and felt her heart leap like a dizzy teenager's. The perfect husband? Since when? And why? She had made no complaints, so it could not be her he was trying to influence. Most probably he was trying to please his grandfather, who was openly keen to see his only surviving grandson settling down with a family. But she didn't want Sergios putting on an act purely to impress Nectarios. Anything of that nature was almost certain to make Sergios feel deprived of free choice and she did not want their marriage to feel like an albatross hanging round his neck.

Bee accompanied Eleni to the very doors of the operating theatre and then waited outside with Sergios. He had taken the whole day off, which really surprised her. It was true that he stepped out several times to make and receive phone calls and that a PA brought documents for his signature, but it was so unusual for him to put work second that she was very appreciative of his continuing support.

The surgery was completed quickly and successfully and Bee took a seat by Eleni's bed. By that stage the little girl was already regaining consciousness. While she was groggy she was not, it seemed, in pain and, reassured by Bee's presence at her bedside, she soon drifted off to sleep. One of the nannies arrived to sit with the child while Sergios took Bee out for a meal and a much-needed break.

'You're exhausted. Why do I employ a team of nannies only to find you in this state? Come home with me,' Sergios urged when Bee's head began to nod towards the latter stages of their meal.

Her eyes widened and she studied him ruefully. 'I should be there if Eleni wakes up again and there is a bed in the room for me to use,' she reminded him. 'I won't have an entirely sleepless night.'

'Sometimes you should put yourself first,' Sergios reasoned levelly.

Bee tensed at that declaration and lost colour. Would he tell himself that when he felt the need for something a little more exotic than the marital bed could offer him? Would boredom or lust be his excuse? Would he even need an excuse or was sex with Melita already so familiar that it would not feel like a betrayal of his marital vows? She studied his features: the level line of his brows, the stunning dark golden eyes above those blade-straight cheekbones and the wide carnal mouth that could transport her to paradise. Her cheeks burned as she tore her attention from him. She should challenge him about Melita. Why wasn't she doing that? When would there ever be a *right* moment for such a distressing confrontation?

When Eleni was lying in a hospital bed was definitely not the right time, she decided unhappily. That conversation was not something she wanted to plunge blindly into either. She needed to know exactly what she planned to say and right at that instant it felt like too emotive a subject for her to maintain a level head. She didn't want to shout or cry. She was determined to retain her dignity. After all she was in love with him and at the end of the day dignity might be all she had left to embrace, along with the empty shell of her marriage as they both retired behind their respective barriers. Would they ever share a bed again after that conversation?

'What's wrong?' Sergios demanded abruptly. 'You look haunted. Eleni's going to be fine. Stop doing this to yourself. It was a straightforward procedure and it went perfectly.'

'I know…I'm sorry. I think I'm just tired,' Bee muttered evasively, embarrassed that he could read her well enough to know that she was currently existing in a sort of mental hell. Melita was a sexy stunner; there was no getting round that hard fact. Every man in the taverna between fifteen and eighty-odd years had been staring appreciatively at the racy blonde. Just at that instant Bee could not forget, humiliatingly, that she had had to get half naked and swing provocatively round a pole to tempt her highly sexed and sophisticated husband into making their marriage a real one.

'You worry far too much about stuff.' Sergios shook his handsome dark head in emphasis. 'It's like you're always on the lookout for trouble.'

Bee was back by Eleni's bed when her cell phone vibrated silently in receipt of a text and she took it out of her jacket pocket, wondering wearily if it would be Jon Townsend again. Once he knew she would be over in London he had asked her to lunch with key charity personnel. Too concerned about Eleni's needs to spare the time for such an occasion, Bee had hedged. But it was not Jon texting her this time…

I'm in London. I would like to meet you in private. *Melita.*

Aghast at the idea while noting that the word private was emphasised, Bee looked at her phone as though it had jumped up and bitten her. Her husband's mistress was actually texting her? Was it for real? But for what possible reason would anyone try to set Bee up with a fake text purporting to be from Melita? Assuming the text was genuine, how on earth had Melita Thiarkis got Bee's phone number? Had she taken it from Sergios's phone? It was the most likely explanation and as such hit Bee's spirits hard because it was not long since she had got a new number and if Melita was in possession of it, it suggested very recent contact between Sergios and the other woman.

Bee got little sleep that night although Eleni slept like a little snoring log. Sergios put in an appearance on his way into his London office. Bee was in the corridor and noticed the ripple of interest that her extraordinarily good-looking husband excited among the nursing staff. With his tall, wide-shouldered, long-legged frame encased in a charcoal-grey designer suit, Sergios looked spectacular. Eleni was equally impressed and whooped with glee when he came through the door and held out her arms.

An odd little smile softened the hard line of Sergios's mouth as he set down the package in his hand. Bending down, he scooped the little girl gently out of her bed, addressing her in Greek as he did so.

And for the very first time Eleni answered, looking up at him with big dark eyes. The words were indistinct and the sentence structure non-existent, but it was a response she would not have attempted before the surgery.

'I noticed she was more attentive to what I was saying from the minute she woke up this morning,' Bee told him with forced brightness. 'She's definitely able to hear more. Her eyes don't wander the same way when you're speaking to her either.'

Bee helped Eleni unwrap the wooden puzzle that Sergios had brought and pulled up the bed table for the little girl's use. A ward maid popped her head round the door and offered them a cup of coffee.

'Not for me, thanks,' Sergios responded. 'I have an early meeting.'

'If her consultant thinks everything is in order, Eleni will be released later this afternoon,' Bee revealed.

'Good. The boys missed you last night,' Sergios told her.

If he had told her that *he* had missed her she would have thrown herself into his arms like a homing pigeon, but no such encouraging declaration passed his lips. Nor would it, Bee reflected wretchedly. Sergios didn't say sentimental stuff like that or make emotional statements. She loved a guy who would never ever tell her he loved her back. And why would he settle solely for Bee's charms when he already had a woman like Melita and countless other discreet lovers eternally on offer to him? He was an immensely wealthy tycoon and, when it came to women and sex, spoilt for choice and it would always be that way. Somehow, she didn't know yet *how*, she would have to come to terms with the reality of their marriage. Possibly meeting Melita Thiarkis in the flesh would be a sensible first step in that much-needed process.

That decision made, Sergios had barely left the building before Bee texted the other woman to set up the requested meeting. After all, what did she have to lose? Sergios wouldn't like the idea of them meeting at all but why should that bother her? He would never find out, would he? Had he chosen to be more frank about the relationship, however, Bee would probably have ignored the text from his mistress. Melita replied immediately and asked Bee to meet her in the bar of her Chelsea hotel mid-morning. Wary of staging such a delicate encounter in a public place, Bee suggested she come to her room instead.

Bee would very much have liked her entire designer wardrobe on hand to choose from before she met up with Melita. But, travelling direct from the hospital, that was not possible and Bee, not only had very little choice about what to wear, but despised the vain streak of insecurity that had prompted such a superficial thought. She could hardly hope to top a fashion designer in the style stakes, she told herself wryly as she freshened up her make-up and left Eleni with her nanny for company. Pausing only to tell her security team of two that she did not require them, she walked out of the hospital.

The receptionist sent her straight up to Melita's room on the first floor. She knocked only once on the door before it opened to frame the strikingly attractive woman, who even at that point impressed Bee as being vastly overdressed for morning coffee in her low-cut glittering jacket, narrow skirt and very high heels.

'Beatriz…' Melita murmured smoothly. 'I'm so grateful that you agreed to come, but let's not tell Sergios about this. Men hate it when we go behind their backs.'

CHAPTER TEN

BEE took due note of the fact that her husband's mistress, Melita, was more scared of consequences than she was. As Bee had no intention of keeping their meeting a secret unless it suited her to do so, she did not reply.

Melita already had a pot of coffee waiting in her opulent hotel room with its black and white designer chic decor. She sat down opposite Bee, a process that took a good deal of cautious lowering and wriggling in six-inch heels and a black skirt so tight it would split if put under too much pressure. Melita walked a thin line between sexy and tarty.

'I didn't think that Sergios would ever marry again,' the Greek woman said plaintively. 'But we're adults. There's no reason why we can't be, er...distant friends.'

Only one, Bee completed inwardly. *If you sleep with my husband I might try to murder you.*

'Sergios and I have been very close for a great many years,' Melita informed her with a self-satisfied smile.

Not a muscle moving on her taut face, Bee compressed her lips and pretended to sip at the too-hot coffee that Melita had poured for her. 'I guessed that.'

'I have no intention of poaching on your territory,'

Melita declared importantly. 'I've never wanted to be a wife or a mother, so I don't covet what you have.'

'But you do covet Sergios,' Bee heard herself say helplessly.

'*Any* woman would covet him,' the other woman fielded, her sultry eyes widening in amused emphasis. 'But there's no reason why we can't share him.'

'Just one,' Bee murmured flatly. 'I *don't* share.'

Melita's pencilled brows drew together in surprise at that bold statement. 'Is that a declaration of war?'

'It's whatever you choose to make of it. Why did you invite me here?' Bee enquired drily.

'I wanted to reassure you that I have no desire to damage your marriage. Sergios really does need a wife to do wifely things like looking after his houses and his children. Naturally I'm aware that it is a marriage of… shall we say…' Melita looked unconvincingly coy for a moment '…mutual convenience?'

'Oh, dear…is that what Sergios told you?' Bee asked, wincing with an acting ability she had not known she possessed, for she refused to cringe at the apparent level of Melita's knowledge about Sergios's reasons for marrying her. 'Men can be so reluctant to break bad news. I'm afraid our marriage is rather more than one of convenience.'

'If by that you mean that Sergios shares your bed, I expected that. After all you're there when I can't be and he's a man, very much a man,' Melita purred with glinting eyes of sensual recollection.

For a split second Bee felt so sick that she almost ran into the en suite and lost her sparse hospital breakfast.

She could not bear to think of Melita naked and intimately wound round Sergios. That *hurt*, that hurt like a punch in the stomach. Nor could she bear to consider herself a sexual substitute, a sort of cheap and available fast-food option instead of the grand banquet of thrilling sensuality that she imagined Melita might offer.

'You do realise, I hope, that your husband is still shagging me every chance he gets!' Dropping the civilised front with a resounding crash, Melita surveyed Bee with angry, resentful dark eyes. 'He was with me on your wedding night and I have no intention of giving him up.'

'Whatever,' Bee framed woodenly, setting down the cup with precise care and rising to her feet again with all the dignity she could muster. 'I think we've shared a little too much for comfort. If you contact me again I'll tell Sergios.'

'Don't you dare threaten me!' Melita ranted furiously.

Bee walked out and she didn't look back or breathe until she was safe inside the lift again. Sergios was still sleeping with his mistress and had been from the first night of their marriage. Why was she so shocked? What else had she expected? That a man with a notoriously active libido would suddenly turn over a new leaf on entering a platonic marriage? That had never been a possibility. Before their marriage she had agreed to him maintaining his relationship with Melita. He had said upfront that Melita was not a negotiable facet of his life. Having received that warning, she had chosen to ignore it by allowing their marriage to become much more real than either of them had ever envisaged.

Leaving the hotel, Bee was blank-eyed, her mind in chaos and emotions raging through her in horribly distressing waves. She didn't know where she was going but she knew she couldn't return to the hospital in such a state, nor would she involve her mother when she was so upset. Her cell phone was ringing and she checked it. It was Jon Townsend. Heaving a sigh, but in a strange way grateful for the distraction, Bee answered his call. He invited her to join him at his apartment for lunch with the charity's PR woman. It was somewhere to go, something to do in a world rocking on its foundations, and she agreed and boarded a bus, too wrapped in her own unhappy thoughts to notice that she was being followed.

Sergios had already cancelled appointments and left his office, planning to meet with Beatriz at the hospital. The news that she had met up with Melita had hit him like a torpedo and almost blown him out of the water. Where had that come from? How had that happened? What had he done to deserve that outcome? Nourishing a strong sense of injustice along with the suspicion that he was being royally stitched up, Sergios was in no mood to receive the bodyguard's second piece of news: Beatriz had entered an apartment owned by Jon Townsend?

'Beatriz…' From the minute Bee stepped through the door, she began regretting having agreed to lunch. Jon was alone, the PR lady apparently having been held up in traffic. Unfortunately her host's effusive welcome made Bee feel even more awkward.

Bee toyed with the salad on her plate and for the third time attempted to steer their conversation back to the subject of the charity and away from the past times that Jon seemed much more eager to discuss.

'We were so close back then.' Jon sighed fondly.

'Not as close as I thought at the time. We *were* still very young,' Bee pointed out lightly.

'I didn't realise how much you meant to me until it was too late and I'd lost you,' Jon said baldly.

'It happens.' Her attempted smile of acknowledgement was a mere twist of her lips, for she was in no frame of mind to deal tactfully with Jon's evident determination to resurrect their shared past. 'If you had been happy with me you wouldn't have strayed.'

Jon brought a hand down on top of hers and she was so irritated with him that she very nearly lifted her other hand to stab him with the fork. 'Jenna—'

Bee lifted a hand to silence him. 'Stop right there. I really don't want to hear about your marriage, Jon. It's none of my business.'

'Perhaps I want to make it your business.'

'More probably you're barking up the wrong tree— I'm in love with my husband,' Bee responded impatiently. 'And now I think it's time I went. I want to get back to the hospital.'

As she got up Jon leapt up as well and the doorbell went in one long shrill shriek as if the caller's finger had accidentally got stuck to the button.

'A shame your PR lady is arriving so late,' Bee remarked.

'That was just a ruse, Bee,' Jon snapped, his fair features twisting with bad temper and momentarily giving him the aspect of a disgruntled little boy.

'Evidently, Sergios was right to tell me that I'm too trusting,' Bee was saying as Jon angrily yanked open the front door, annoyed by the timely interruption.

Bee was totally shattered to see Sergios poised on the doorstep. 'What are you doing here?' she asked in astonishment. 'How did you find out where I was?'

His eyes had a smouldering glitter and were welded to Jon's discomfited face. 'Why did my wife say that I was right to call her too trusting?'

Bee really couldn't be bothered with Jon at that moment. The whole silly lunch set-up had thoroughly irritated her, but she didn't want Sergios to thump him. And that, she sensed, very much aware of the powerfully angry aggression Sergios exuded, was quite likely if she didn't act to defuse the tension.

'I was just joking. We were discussing a charity dinner—'

Sergios closed a hand round her wrist and drew her out of the apartment as if he couldn't wait to remove her from a source of dangerous contagion. His face hard as iron, he studied Jon, who was pale and taut. 'Leave my wife alone,' he instructed with chilling bite. 'What's mine stays mine. Try not to forget that.'

What's mine stays mine. Bee could have been very sarcastic about that assurance had she not been outraged by Sergios's intervention and sexist turn of phrase.

'Sometimes you're very dramatic,' she commented lamely, recognising that quality in him for the first time and surprised by the discovery.

'What were you doing in Townsend's apartment alone with him?' Sergios shot at her, visibly unrepentant.

'None of your business.'

As the lift doors opened on the ground floor Sergios shot Bee an arrested look. 'Explain yourself.'

'Are we going to pick up Eleni?' Bee enquired coldly instead, picturing Melita with her smug cat-got-the-cream smile. Nausea pooled in her tummy again and turned her skin clammy.

'Eleni was released an hour ago. Karen phoned me and I told her to take Eleni home.'

'Oh.' Bee made no further comment, stabbed by guilt that she had forgotten the little girl was due to leave hospital that afternoon. She felt drained by the emotional storm of the past couple of hours. The man she loved had a mistress whom he regularly slept with and would not give up. Where did she go from there? Did she really want to lower herself to the level of arguing about Melita? Did she want to run the risk of exposing how deep her own feelings went for him?

Or did she do the sensible thing? Take it on the chin and move on? Obviously no more sharing of marital beds. That kind of intimacy was out of the question with Melita in the picture. But she had signed up to a long-term relationship for the sake of her mother and for the children. Every fibre of her being might be urging her to make some sort of grand gesture like walking out on her marriage, but too many innocent people would be hurt and damaged by her doing that. Even Sergios had said that she wasn't a quitter and he had been right on that score. She gave her word and, my goodness, she stuck to it through thick and thin.

Even through Melita? Could she still stick to her word in such circumstances? Pain slivered through Bee and cut deep like a knife. They had roamed so far from their original agreement. Far too many tender feelings had got involved. Stepping back from that intimacy, learning to be detached again would be a huge challenge, she acknowledged wretchedly. Had she really once believed that she could treat Sergios like a rather demanding employer? Looking at Sergios's beloved face now, she was no longer sure that she had the strength to stand by her promise and survive the sacrifices that that would demand.

How could she bear to turn her back on what she had believed they had and know that Melita was replacing her in every way that mattered? From now on it would be Melita he kissed awake in the morning, Melita he took to dine in cosy little restaurants where nobody recognised him, Melita he bought whopping big diamonds for. How could Bee live with knowing that he had only made love to her because she was there when more tempting sexual prospects were not? What had meant so much to her had evidently meant very little to him. A cry of anguish was building up inside Bee. She felt as though she were being ripped apart.

The limo came to a halt. White-faced, she got out without even looking to see where she was going and came to a sudden bemused halt once she realised that they had not alighted at the mansion that was their London home but outside an apartment building she had never seen before. 'Where are we?'

'I own an apartment here.'

'Oh...do you?' she queried drily, wondering if this was where he had come on their wedding night to make love with his Greek blonde. She was ready to bet that he had not had to nudge Melita towards the sexy lingerie. Gut instinct warned her that Melita already had that kind of angle covered, or uncovered, as regarded his preference, she thought bitterly. Had she seriously considered dying her hair blonde? Had she really been that pathetic? Where had her pride and her independence gone?

Love had decimated those traits, she decided painfully, standing, lost and sick to the soul, in the lift on the way up to the apartment she had not known he possessed. Love had made her hollow and weak inside. Love had made her want to cling and dye her hair and wear the fancy lingerie if that was what it took to hold him. But her brain told her that that was nonsense and that those were only superficial frills, not up to the challenge of keeping a doomed relationship afloat. And a relationship between plain, ordinary, sensible Bee Blake and rich and gorgeous Sergios Demonides had always been doomed, hadn't it? A union between two such different people was unlikely to be a marriage that ran and ran against all the odds...unless you believed in miracles and wild dreams coming true. And

Bee had so *badly* wanted to believe that she could have the miracle, the dream.

Virtually blind to her surroundings while that ferocity of emotion remained in control of her, Bee preceded Sergios into a spacious lounge that had that slightly bare, unlived in quality of a property not in daily use. 'So this is where you and Melita—'

Sergios froze in front of her as though she had said a very bad word, his face clenching hard, sensual mouth compressing. 'No, not here. My grandfather uses this place when he visits London—he likes his independence. It's a company property.'

Bee nodded and her spine relaxed just a jot. She had conceived a loathing for Melita Thiarkis, everywhere the other woman had ever been with Sergios and everything to do with her that was excessive to say the least.

'She's never been here—she has her own apartment,' Sergios breathed abruptly as if he were attuned to Bee's every thought.

Never having had quite so many mean, malicious thoughts all at once, Bee seriously hoped that he was not that attuned. Her disconcerted face was hot, her complexion flushed to the hairline with embarrassment and the distress she was fighting to conceal. Suddenly unable to bear looking at him, she spun away and faked an interest in the view.

'Whatever it takes I want to keep you,' Sergios breathed with startling harshness. 'I hope you appreciate the fact that I didn't knock Townsend's teeth down his throat the way I would've liked to have done.'

'You can be such a caveman.' In a twisty way that

appealed to the dark side of her temperament, she was painfully amused that despite his own extra-marital interests he could still be so possessive of *her*. The logic of his attitude escaped her. But, of course, he wanted to keep her as a wife: he needed her for the children. They loved her and she loved them. Now there had to be a compromise found that she and Sergios could both live with. Some magical solution that would provide a path through the messy swell of emotion currently blurring her view of the world.

'Look at me…' Sergios urged.

'I don't want to,' Bee said truthfully, but she turned round all the same.

She wondered why it was that she could now see that Jon sulked and pouted like a spoilt little boy when he didn't get his own way, but that in spite of what she had learned about Sergios she still could not see a visible flaw in him. He remained defiantly gorgeous from his stunning dark golden eyes to his slightly stubbled and shadowed chin.

'That's better,' he murmured, scrutinising her with an intensity that made her uncomfortable.

'Why did you bring me here?'

'If we're going to argue, if there's going to be dissension between us, I didn't want the children as an audience,' Sergios admitted flatly, features grave.

'My word, you think of everything!' Bee was all too wretchedly aware that she would not have considered that danger until it was too late.

'They deserve better from us—'

'Is that you reminding me of my duty?' Bee prompted tightly, her throat suddenly thickening with tears.

'Whatever it takes I want to hold onto you.'

'You already said that.'

'It's more than I've ever said to a woman,' Sergios breathed roughly, challenge in the stance of his big powerful body. He stood tall with broad shoulders thrown back and strong legs braced as though he were expecting a blow.

He wanted everything, he wanted too much, she reflected unhappily. He wanted his mistress and he wanted his wife, a combination he evidently believed necessary to his comfort and happiness. Emotion didn't come into it for him. If only it didn't come into it for her either! Her eyes prickled hotly and she kept them very wide, terrified that the tears threatening her would spill over in front of him.

'If we're staying here I could do with lying down for a while,' she said abruptly, desperate for some privacy.

'Of course.' He crossed the room and pressed open a door that led into a corridor. He showed her into the bedroom and startled her by yanking the bedspread off the bed and pulling back the duvet for her. He looked across at her, a dark uncertainty in his eyes that she had never seen before, and for the first time it occurred to her that he was upset as well.

'Thanks,' she said dully, taking off her jacket and kicking off her shoes.

'Would you like a drink?' he enquired without warning.

'A brandy,' she responded, dimly recalling that

being recommended for shock in a book she had read. Probably not at all the right remedy for shock in today's world, she thought ruefully. In fact, couldn't alcohol act as a depressant? In the mood she was in, she didn't need that, did she?

Seemingly glad, however, of something to do, Sergios strode out of the room and she sat down on the bed. Time seemed to move on without her noticing, for he reappeared very quickly and handed her a tumbler half full of brandy. 'Are you trying to get me drunk?' she asked in disbelief.

'You look like a ghost, all white and drawn. Drink up,' Sergios urged.

'I can't live like this with you…' she framed, the admission leaping off her tongue before she could stop it.

Sergios came down on his knees at her feet and pushed the tumbler towards her mouth. 'Drink,' he urged again.

'It might make me sick.'

'I don't think so.'

All of a sudden she noticed that the hand he had on the glass was trembling almost infinitesimally. He was behaving as though the drink might be a lifesaver, rather than a pick-me-up. She sipped, shuddering as the alcohol ran like a flame down her throat, making her cough and splutter. She collided with strained dark eyes.

'What the heck is the matter with you?' Bee demanded in sudden frustration. 'You're behaving very oddly.'

Sergios vaulted upright. 'What do you expect? You go and see my former mistress—then you run straight off to stage a private meeting with your ex, who's clearly desperate to get you back!' he exclaimed wrathfully. 'I mean, it's not exactly been my dream day and I still don't know what the hell is going on!'

Former mistress? Her ears were practically out on stalks. Was he planning to try and lie his way out of the tight corner he was in? Pretend that his relationship with Melita was over? While pondering that salient point, Bee drank deep of the brandy, grateful for the heat spreading and somehow soothing her cold, empty tummy.

'Why did you go and see Melita?' he demanded heavily. 'What the hell made you do such a thing?'

Her brow indented. 'She asked me to come and see her.'

His lean powerful face set granite hard at that claim. '*She* asked…*you*?'

Bee lifted her chin. 'Yes and I was curious. Of course I was. I saw her on the island last week.'

His gaze narrowed. 'Nectarios mentioned it but I hoped you didn't realise who she was.'

Bee rolled her eyes. 'I'm not stupid, Sergios.'

'Not obviously so,' he conceded. 'But if you believed I've been with her since we got married, you are being stupid.'

'According to Melita you've been shagging her every chance you got—that's a direct quote from her,' Bee told him.

Sergios looked astonished. 'I thought better of her. We parted—as I thought—on good terms.'

'When did you last see her?'

'About six weeks ago in Athens. We did not have sex,' Sergios added sardonically. 'I have not slept with her since we got married.'

Bee vented a scornful laugh. 'How am I supposed to believe that about the woman you insisted you had to keep in your life in spite of our marriage?'

'It's the truth. Melita was part of my routine.'

'Routine?' Bee repeated with distaste.

'It wasn't a romantic relationship. I financed her fashion house, she shared my bed. She travelled all round the world to meet up with me. It was easier keeping her as a mistress than having to adapt to different women,' Sergios admitted, his discomfort with the topic obvious. 'I've known her for a long time. I backed her first fashion collection because she was an islander. We ended up in bed after Krista died and I found Melita's casual approach to sex attractive at a time when I didn't want anything heavy.'

'If it was over why did she lie?'

'Presumably because she thought that if she could cause trouble between us I might come back to her,' Sergios suggested grimly. 'I'm furious that she approached you and lied to you. I made a generous settlement on her at the end of our affair and she should've been satisfied with that.'

'She said you were with her on our wedding night.'

Sergios swore only half below his breath, anger burning in his keen gaze. 'I was supposed to see her but I cancelled.'

'You went out.'

'I went to a casino, played the tables and drank.

Going to her didn't feel right. I know our marriage was supposed to be a fake but making a point of being with her that particular night...' Sergios shrugged uncomfortably. 'It would've felt disrespectful, so I didn't do it.'

'Disrespectful,' Bee echoed weakly, her attention nailed to his face, recognising the combination of discomfiture and sincerity she saw there.

'I swear I have not been with Melita,' Sergios growled, his patience taxed almost beyond its limits. 'And if I have to drag her here and make her admit that to your face, I will not shrink from the challenge.'

'She wouldn't come.'

'She would if I threatened to withdraw the settlement I made on her. She signed a legal agreement, promising to be discreet about our past relationship and approaching my wife and lying to her is not, by any stretch of the imagination, discreet!' he bit out thunderously, his anger at what he had learned unconcealed.

Bee recalled how very keen Melita had been to ensure that Sergios did not know about their meeting, hardly surprising if the money he had given her was dependent on her remaining tactfully silent about their affair. Was it possible that she had simply wanted to cause trouble? Naturally she would blame Bee for Sergios having broken off their relationship.

'I'm starting to believe you,' Bee confided with a frown, worried that she was being ridiculously credulous while at the same time recalling that she had yet to find out that Sergios had ever lied to her about anything. He was much more given to lethal candour than dishonesty.

'Thank God,' he breathed in Greek.

'But I still don't get why you were so determined to retain Melita that you even told me about her before the wedding…only to get rid of her a few weeks later.'

Sergios groaned like a man in torment. 'Obviously because I had you and didn't need her any longer.'

'Oh…' was all Bee could think to say to that. Was it really that simple for him? Instead of sex with Melita he had discovered sex with his wife and found it a perfectly adequate substitute? Seemingly it *was* that simple on his terms. It was a huge relief to appreciate that he had not betrayed her with Melita. Her head was swimming a little and she thought that perhaps she had had a little too much brandy.

'You're fantastic in bed, *yineka mou.*'

'Am I?' Bee settled big green eyes on him, wide with wonderment at that assurance.

'I haven't even looked at another woman since I married you,' Sergios spelt out forcefully. 'Nor will I in the future. That's a promise. Will you come home with me now?'

A huge smile was tugging the last of the stress from round her ripe mouth. 'You still haven't explained how you knew where I was this afternoon.'

'Your security team know not to listen to you if you try to go anywhere without them in tow. They followed you. What did Townsend want?'

'Me apparently, but after all this time I'm really not interested. I told him that I…er…' Bee hesitated at what she had almost revealed. 'I told Jon that I had become quite attached to you.'

'Attached? Is that a fact?' Sergios prompted softly, sitting down on the bed beside her and tucking her hair back behind one small ear with a gentle hand. 'I'm quite attached to you as well.'

'Sexually speaking,' Bee qualified, a glutton for accuracy.

'Well, I have to admit that you have the most fabulous breasts and I'm ashamed to admit that they are the first thing I noticed about you the night we met,' Sergios confessed with the beginnings of a wicked grin. 'But you've contrived to build whole layers on that initial impression. You're a great listener, marvellous company, very loyal, intelligent and affectionate. When I'm angry or stressed you make me feel calm. When I'm unkind you make me see another viewpoint. I'm not even mentioning how wonderful you are with the children because that's not what you and I are about any more—'

Bee went from hanging on his every flattering word to cutting in with a quick question. 'It's...*not*?'

'Of course, it's not. We started out with a practical marriage.'

'You told Melita that too, didn't you?' Bee recalled unhappily, her brow indenting with a remembered sense of humiliation.

His forefinger smoothed away the tension that had tightened her mouth. 'I'm afraid it slipped out but I really did believe we were going to have a marriage that was like a business deal.'

'And how do you feel now?' she whispered.

'Like I made the killing of a lifetime when I got you to the altar,' Sergios declared, his eyes warmer than she had ever seen them as he studied her intently. 'You've got to know how crazy I am about you. You taught me to love again. You taught me how to trust and you transformed my life.'

Bee stared at him wide-eyed. 'You're crazy about me?'

'I'm hopelessly in love with you.'

Bee wrapped both arms round him as though he were a very large teddy bear and dragged him down to her. 'I was trying to save face when I said I was attached to you.'

'I rather hoped that that was what you were doing, *agape mou*.'

'I love you too but I still don't know why.'

'Don't question it too closely in case you change your mind,' Sergios warned.

'It's just you weren't the most loveable guy around when we got married.'

'But I'm really working at it now,' he pointed out. 'And I won't stop.'

Bee studied him with bemused green eyes. 'You promise?'

'I promise. I love you. All I want is to make you happy.'

The sincerity in his liquid dark gaze went straight to her impressionable heart and tears stung the backs of her eyes. Finally, she believed him. Their marriage was safe. Even better, he was hers in exactly the way she had dreamed. He loved her and love was, she sensed, the only chain that would hold him.

'I should've known I was in trouble when I bought that wedding dress,' Sergios confided with a rueful laugh.

'What were you doing at a fashion show?' As he winced she guessed the answer. 'You were there because of Melita and yet you picked a dress for me?' she prompted in amazement.

'I saw the dress and I couldn't help picturing you wearing it and I know it was high-handed of me but I was determined that you should have it,' Sergios revealed.

She was touched by the admission that even before their wedding he had been attracted to her to that extent. 'Yet we both thought that I was going to be more of an employee than a real wife.'

'Even I can be stupid.'

Bee grinned with appreciation. 'Hold on while I get a microphone and record that statement.'

'Well, I was stupid about you. I was fighting what I felt for you right from the start.'

'Your marriage to Krista hurt you a great deal,' Bee commented softly, understanding that and willing to forgive the time it had taken for him to recognise his feelings for her.

'I thought I would be happier living without a serious relationship in my life. You rewrote everything I thought I knew about myself. I wanted you. I wanted you in my bed, my home, involved in every aspect of my day.' Sergios circled her mouth slowly, gently, with his. 'I know I didn't tell you that I'd finished with Melita but I didn't see the need.'

'I thought that maybe you thought you could still have both of us.'

Unexpectedly, Sergios laughed. 'No, I was never that stupid. I knew that wasn't an option but possibly I felt a little foolish about changing my mind so quickly and wanting the kind of marriage I said I definitely didn't want.'

Bee brushed a high cheekbone with gentle fingertips, loving the new confidence powering her. 'That aspect never occurred to me.'

'It should've done. I thought I had our marriage all worked out and it blew up in my face because I couldn't keep my hands off you.'

'When I saw Melita I decided you only liked blondes…and for just a little while I actually considered getting my hair dyed. It was my lowest moment,' Bee confided with a wince of shame.

Sergios groaned out loud, his long fingers feathering through her glossy dark hair. 'I'm very grateful you didn't do it. I love your hair the way it is—'

'I might grow it longer for you,' Bee proffered, feeling unusually generous.

Sergios pressed her back against the pillows and extracted a kiss that was full of hungry urgency. 'Now that we're here, we might as well take advantage.'

'Oh, yes,' Bee agreed, full pink lips swollen, eyes wide with desire as the tug of arousal pinched low in her tummy.

And the kissing shifted into a fairly wild bout of lovemaking. Afterwards, Bee lay in her husband's arms, feeling loved and secure and boundlessly happy and grateful for what she had.

On the drive back to their London home that evening, Sergios dealt her a slightly embarrassed appraisal and said abruptly, 'I thought that possibly in a few months' time we might consider having a baby.'

'On the grounds that we've got so many children we might as well have another?' Bee prompted very drily.

Sergios grimaced. 'I suppose I deserve that reminder but I've changed. I would like to have a child with you some day in the future.'

'I can agree to that now you've got the right attitude,' Bee told him chirpily and she flung herself into his arms with abandon and snuggled close. 'And now I know that you love me, you had better get used to me doing stuff like this.'

His strong arms enfolded her and dark golden eyes rested on her animated face with tender appreciation. 'And maybe I've even learned to like it, *yineka mou*.'

Bee relaxed and knew she could hug him to her heart's content. From here on in there would be no more boundaries she feared to cross.

EPILOGUE

'How do you feel?' Sergios asked, his anxiety obvious.

'Absolutely fine!' Bee exclaimed, widening her bright eyes in reproach. 'Stop fussing!'

But Bee was less than pleased with her reflection in the mirror. It was Nectarios's eighty-third birthday and they were throwing a big party for the older man at their home on the island. She was wearing a beautiful evening gown in one of her favourite colours but, it had to be said, nothing, not even the fabulous diamonds glittering in her ears and at her throat, could make her elegant in her own eyes while she was heavily pregnant. At almost eight months pregnant with their first child, she felt like a ship in full sail.

Sergios drew her back against him, his hands splaying gently across her swollen abdomen, his fascination palpable as he felt the slight ripple of movement as their daughter kicked. A little girl, that was what they were having according to the most recent sonogram. Eleni was four years old and she was very excited about the baby sister who would soon be born. Bee had enjoyed furnishing a nursery and had frittered away many a happy hour choosing baby equipment and clothing.

Bee, however, could hardly believe that she and Sergios had been married for going on for three years. They had waited a little longer than they had originally planned to try for a baby but she had conceived quickly. There was not a single cloud in Bee's sky. The previous year, Melita Thiarkis had sold her island property and set up permanent home in Milan with an Italian millionaire. Bee had never got involved with the charity Jon Townsend had worked with because he made her uncomfortable, but she had picked another charity, one that concentrated on disabled adults like her mother. When she was not running round after the children or travelling with Sergios, for they did not like to be kept apart for more than a couple of nights, she put in sterling work seeking out sponsors for the organisation and raising funds.

Bee's mother, Emilia was firmly settled now in her cottage on Orestos. Happier and healthier than she had been for several years, the older woman was fully integrated into island life and a good deal less lonely and bored. She loved living close to her daughter and took great pleasure in Paris, Milo and Eleni running in and out of her house and treating her as an honorary grandmother. Nectarios was a regular visitor to his grandson's home and a very welcome one. He was thrilled that his fourth great-grandchild was on the way.

'You've made so many arrangements for this party. I don't want you to tire yourself out,' Sergios admitted.

The house was full of guests and there was a distant hum, which probably signified the approach of another helicopter ready to drop off more guests.

'I'll be fine.' Bee was wryly amused by the level of his concern, for she had enjoyed a healthy pregnancy that had impinged very little on her usual routine. He was so supportive though, having rigorously attended every medical appointment with her.

Sergios studied the woman he loved and once again worked to suppress his secret fear of the idea of anything ever happening to her. The more he loved her, the more central she became to his world, and the more he worried but the bottom line, the payoff, he had learned, was a level of love and contentment he had never known until she entered his life.

'I love you, *agape mou*,' he murmured gently at the top of the sweeping staircase.

Bee met his stunning dark golden eyes and felt the leap of every sense with happy acceptance. The world they had made together was a safe cocoon for both them and the children. 'I love you more than I could ever say.'

* * * * *

A VOW OF
OBLIGATION

CHAPTER ONE

'WERE you seen coming up to my suite?' Navarre Cazier prompted in the Italian that came as naturally to him as the French of his homeland.

Tia pouted her famously sultry lips and in spite of her sophistication contrived to look remarkably young and naive as befitted one of the world's most acclaimed film stars. 'I slipped in through the side entrance—'

Navarre ditched his frown and smiled, for when she looked at him like that with her big blue eyes telegraphing embarrassed vulnerability he couldn't help it. 'It's you I'm concerned about. The paparazzi follow you everywhere—'

'Not here...' Tia Castelli declared, tossing her head so that a silken skein of honey-blonde hair rippled across her slim shoulders, her flawless face full of regret. 'We haven't got long though. Luke will be back at our hotel by three and I have to be there.'

At that reference to her notoriously volatile rock star husband, Navarre's lean, darkly handsome features hardened and his emerald-green eyes darkened.

Tia ran a manicured fingertip reprovingly below the implacable line of his shapely masculine mouth. 'Don't be like that, *caro mio*. This is my life, take me or leave me... and I couldn't bear it if you chose the second option!' she warned him in a sudden rush, her confident drawl splintering to betray the insecurity she hid from the world. 'I'm sorry, so sorry that it has to be like this between us!'

'It's OK,' Navarre told her soothingly although he was lying through his even white teeth as he said it. He loathed being a dirty little secret in her life but the alternative was to end their relationship and although he was remarkably strong-willed and stubborn, he had found himself quite unable to do that.

'And you're still bringing a partner with you for the awards ceremony, aren't you?' Tia checked anxiously. 'Luke is so incredibly suspicious of you.'

'Angelique Simonet, currently the toast of the Paris catwalk,' Navarre answered wryly.

'And she doesn't know about us?' the movie actress pressed worriedly.

'Of course not.'

'I know, I know…I'm sorry, I just have so much at stake!' Tia gasped strickenly. 'I couldn't stand to lose Luke!'

'You can trust me.' Navarre closed his arms round her slim body to comfort her. Her blue eyes glistened with the tears that came so easily to her and she was trembling with nerves. Navarre tried not to wonder what Luke Convery had been doing or saying to get her into such a state. Time and experience had taught him that it was better not to go there, better neither to know nor to enquire. He did not interfere in her marriage any more than she questioned his choice of lovers.

'I hate going so long without seeing you. It feels wrong,' she muttered heavily. 'But I've told so many lies I don't think that I could ever tell the truth.'

'It's not important,' Navarre told her with a gentleness

that would have astounded some of the women he had
had in his life.

Navarre Cazier, the legendary French industrialist and
billionaire, had the reputation of being a generous but distant lover to the beautiful women who passed through his
bed. Yet even though he made no secret of his love of the
single life, women remained infuriatingly keen to tell him
that they loved him and to cling. Tia, however, occupied
a category all of her own and he played by different rules
with her. Accustomed as he was to independence from an
early age, he was tough, self-reliant and unapologetically
selfish but he always restrained that side of his nature with
Tia and at least tried to accommodate her needs.

Later that afternoon when she had gone, Navarre was
heading for the shower when his mobile buzzed beside the
bed. Tia's distinctive perfume still hung in the air like a
shamefaced marker of her recent presence. He would see
her again soon but their next encounter would be in public
and they would have to be circumspect for Luke Convery
was a hothead, all too well aware of his gorgeous wife's
chequered history of previous marriages and clandestine
affairs. Tia's husband was always on the watch for signs
that his wife's attention might be straying.

The call was from Angelique and Navarre's mood dive-
bombed when he learned that his current lover was not,
after all, coming to London to join him. Angelique had
just been offered a television campaign by a famous cosmetics company and even Navarre could not fault her desire to make the most of such an opportunity.

Even so, it seemed to Navarre that life was cruelly con-
spiring to frustrate him. He *needed* Angelique this week
and not only as a screen to protect Tia from the malicious
rumours that had linked his name with hers on past occasions. He also had a difficult deal to close with the hus-

band of a former lover, who had recently attempted to reanimate their affair. A woman on his arm and a supposedly serious relationship had been a non-negotiable necessity for Tia's peace of mind as well as good business practice in a difficult situation. *Merde alors,* what the hell was he going to do without a partner at this late stage in the game? Who could he possibly trust to play the game of a fake engagement and not attempt to take it further?

'Urgent—need 2 talk 2 you,' ran the text message that beeped on Tawny's mobile phone and she hurried downstairs to take her break, wondering what on earth was going on with her friend, Julie.

Julie worked as a receptionist in the same exclusive London hotel and, although the two young women had not known each other long, she had already proved herself to be a staunch and supportive friend. Her approachability had eased Tawny's first awkward days as a new employee when she had quickly discovered that as a chambermaid she was regarded as the lowest of the low by most of the other staff. She was grateful for Julie's company when their breaks coincided, but their friendship had gone well beyond that level, Tawny acknowledged with an appreciative smile. When, at short notice, Tawny had had to move out of her mother's home, Julie had helped her to find an affordable bedsit and had even offered her car to facilitate the move.

'I'm in trouble,' Julie, a very pretty brown-eyed blonde, said with a strong air of drama as Tawny joined her at a table in the corner of the dingy, almost empty staff room.

'What sort of trouble?'

Julie leant forwards to whisper conspiratorially, 'I slept with one of the guests.'

'But you'll be sacked if you've been caught out!' Tawny

exclaimed in dismay, brushing back the Titian red spiral curls clinging to her damp brow. Changing several beds in swift succession was tiring work and even though she was already halfway through a glass of cooling water she still felt overheated.

Julie rolled her eyes, unimpressed by the reminder. 'I haven't been caught out.'

Her porcelain-pale skin reddening, Tawny wished she had been more tactful, for she did not want Julie to think that she was judging her for her behaviour.

'Who was the guy?' she asked then, riven with curiosity for the blonde had not mentioned anyone, which could only mean that the relationship had been of sudden or short duration.

'It was Navarre Cazier.' Wearing a coy look of expectancy, Julie let the name hang there.

'Navarre Cazier?' Tawny was shocked by that familiar name.

She knew exactly who Julie was talking about because it was Tawny's responsibility to keep the penthouse suites on the top floor of the hotel in pristine order. The fabulously wealthy French industrialist stayed there at least twice a month and he always left her a massive tip. He didn't make unreasonable demands or leave his rooms in a mess either, which placed him head and shoulders above the other rich and invariably spoilt occupants of the most select accommodation offered by the hotel. She had only seen him once in the flesh, though, and at a distance, the giving of invisible service being one of the demands of her job. But after Julie had mentioned him several times in glowing terms Tawny had become curious enough to make the effort to catch a glimpse of him and had immediately understood why her friend was captivated. Navarre

Cazier was very tall, black-haired and even to her critical gaze, quite shockingly good-looking.

He also walked, talked and behaved like a god who ruled the world, Tawny recalled abstractedly. He had emerged from the lift at the head of a phalanx of awe-inspired minions clutching phones and struggling to follow reams of instructions hurled at them in two different languages. His sheer power of personality, volcanic energy and presence had had the brilliance of a searchlight in darkness. He had outshone everyone around him while administering a stinging rebuke to a cringing unfortunate who didn't react fast enough to an order. She had got the impression of a ferociously demanding male with a mind that functioned at the speed of a computer, a male, moreover, whose intrinsically high expectations were rarely satisfied by reality.

'As you know I've had my eye on Navarre for a while. He's absolutely gorgeous.' Julie sighed.

Navarre and Julie...*lovers?* A little pang of distaste assailed Tawny as she pulled free of her memories and returned to the present. It struck her as an incongruous pairing between two people who could have nothing in common, but Julie was extremely pretty and Tawny had seen enough of life to know that that was quite sufficient inducement for most men. Evidently the sophisticated French billionaire was not averse to the temptation of casual sex.

'So what's the problem?' Tawny asked in the strained silence that now stretched, resisting a tasteless urge to ask how the encounter had come about. 'Have you fallen pregnant or something?'

'Oh, don't be daft!' Julie fielded as if the very suggestion was a bad joke. 'But I did do something very stupid with him...'

Tawny was frowning. *'What?'* she pressed, unaccustomed to the other young woman being hesitant to talk about anything.

'I got so carried away I let him take a load of pictures of me posing in the nude. They're on his laptop!'

Tawny was aghast at the revelation and embarrassment sent hot colour winging into her cheeks. So, the French businessman liked to take photographs in the bedroom, Tawny thought with a helpless shudder of distaste. Navarre Cazier instantly sank below floor level in Tawny's fanciability stakes. *Ew!*

'What on earth made you agree to such a thing?' she questioned.

Julie clamped a tissue to her nose and Tawny was surprised to see tears swimming in her brown eyes, for Julie had always struck her as being rather a tough cookie. 'Julie?' she prompted more gently.

Julie grimaced in evident embarrassment, clearly fighting her distress. 'Surely you can guess why I agreed?' she countered in a voice choked with tears. 'I didn't want to seem like a prude…I wanted to please him. I hoped that if I was exciting enough he'd want to see me again. Rich guys get bored easily: you have to be willing to experiment to keep their interest. But I never heard from him again and now I feel sick at the idea of him still having those photos of me.'

Even though such reasoning made Tawny's heart sink she understood it perfectly. Once upon a time her mother, Susan, had been equally keen to impress a rich man. In Susan's case the man had been her boss and their subsequent secret affair had continued on and off for years before finally running aground over the pregnancy that produced Tawny and her mother's lowering discovery that she was far from being her lover's only extra-marital interest.

'Ask him to delete the photographs,' Tawny suggested stiffly, feeling more than a little out of her depth with the subject but naturally sympathetic towards her friend's disillusionment. She knew how deeply hurt her mother had been to ultimately discover that her long-term lover didn't consider her worthy of a more permanent or public relationship. But after only one night of intimacy, she felt that Julie would recover rather more easily from the betrayal than Tawny's mother had.

'I asked him to delete them soon after he arrived yesterday. He flatly refused.'

Tawny was stumped by that frank admission. 'Well er...'

'But all I would need is five minutes with his laptop to take care of it for myself,' Julie told her in an urgent undertone.

Tawny was unsurprised by the claim for she had heard that Julie was skilled in IT and often the first port of call when the office staff got into a snit with a computer. 'He's hardly going to give you access to his laptop,' she pointed out wryly.

'No, but if I could get hold of his laptop, what harm would it do for me to deal with the problem right there and then?'

Tawny studied the other woman fixedly. 'Are you seriously planning to try and steal the guy's laptop?'

'I just want to borrow it for five minutes and, as I don't have access to his suite and you *do,* I was hoping that you would do it for me.'

Tawny fell back in her seat, pale blue eyes wide with disbelief as she stared back at the other woman in dismay. 'You've got to be joking...'

'There would be no risk. I'd tell you when he was out, you could go in and I could rush upstairs and wait next door in the storage room for you to bring the laptop out to me. Five minutes, that's all it would take for me to delete those photos. You'll replace it in his room and he'll never know what happened to them!' Julie argued forcefully. *'Please,* Tawny…it would mean so much to me. Haven't you ever done something you regret?'

'I'd like to help you but I can't do something illegal,' Tawny protested, pulling a face in the tense silence. 'That laptop is his personal property and interfering with it would be a criminal offence—'

'He's never going to know that anyone's even touched it! That possibility won't even occur to him,' Julie argued vehemently. 'Please, Tawny. You're the only person who can help me.'

'I couldn't— There's just no way I could do something like that,' Tawny muttered uneasily. 'I'm sorry.'

Julie touched her hand to regain her attention. 'We haven't got much time—he'll be checking out again the day after tomorrow. I'll talk to you again at lunch time before you finish your shift.'

'I won't change my mind,' Tawny warned, compressing her soft full mouth in discomfiture.

'Think it over—it's a foolproof plan,' Julie insisted as she stood up, lowering her voice even more to add huskily, 'And if it would make a difference, I'm willing to pay you to take that risk for me—'

'Pay me?' Tawny was very much taken aback by that offer.

'What else can I do? You're my only hope in this situation,' Julie reasoned plaintively. 'If a bit of money would make you feel better about doing this, of course I'm going to suggest it. I know how desperate you are to help your grandmother out.'

'Look, money's got nothing to do with the way I feel. Just leave it out of this,' Tawny urged in considerable embarrassment. 'If I was in a position to help out, it wouldn't cost you a penny.'

Tawny returned to work with her thoughts in turmoil. Navarre Cazier, handsome, rich and privileged though he was, had cruelly used and abused Julie's trust. Another rich four-letter word of a man was grinding an ordinary woman down. But that unfortunately was life, wasn't it? The rich lived by different rules and enjoyed enormous power and influence. Hadn't her own father taught her that? He had dumped her mother when she refused to have a termination and had paid her a legal pittance to raise his unwanted child to adulthood. There had been no extras in Tawny's childhood and not much love on offer either from a mother who had bitterly regretted her decision to have her baby and a father who did not even pretend an interest in his illegitimate daughter. To be fair, her mother *had* paid a high price for choosing to bring her child into the world. Not only had her lover ditched her, but she had also found it impossible to continue her career.

Tawny suppressed those unproductive reflections and thought worriedly about Julie instead. She felt really bad about having refused to help her friend. Julie had been very good to her and had never asked her for anything in return. But why the heck had Julie offered her a financial bribe to get hold of that laptop? She was deeply embarrassed that Julie should be so aware of her financial constraints and regretted her honesty on that topic.

In truth, Tawny only worked at the hotel to earn enough money to ensure that her grandmother could continue to pay the rent on her tiny apartment in a private retirement village. Celestine, devastated by the combined death of her beloved husband and, with him, the loss of her marital home, had, against all the odds, contrived to make a happy new life and friends in the village, and there was little that Tawny would not do to safeguard the old lady's tenure there. Unfortunately rising costs had quickly outstripped her grandmother's ability to pay her bills. Tawny, having taken charge of Celestine's financial affairs, had chosen to quietly supplement her grandmother's income without her knowledge, which was why she was currently working as a chambermaid. Prior to the crisis in the old lady's finances, Tawny had made her living by illustrating children's books and designing greeting cards, but sadly there was insufficient work in that field during an economic crisis to stretch to shoring up Celestine's income as well as covering Tawny's own living costs. Now Tawny's artistic projects took up evenings and weekends instead.

But, regardless of that situation, wasn't it rather insulting that a friend should offer to *pay* you to do something for them? Tawny reasoned uneasily. On the other hand, wasn't that inappropriate suggestion merely proof of Julie's desperate need for her assistance?

Would it be so very bad of her to do what she could to help Julie delete those distasteful photos? While Tawny could not even imagine trusting a man enough to take pictures of her naked body, she could understand Julie's cringing reluctance to continue featuring in some sort of X-rated scalp gallery on the guy's laptop. That was a downright demeaning and extremely offensive prospect to have to live with. Would he let other men access those pictures? Tawny grimaced in disgust, incensed that a guy she had believed was attractive could turn out to be such a creep.

'All right, I'll have a go at getting hold of it for you,' she told Julie at lunchtime.

Her friend's face lit up immediately and a wide smile of satisfaction formed on her lips. 'I'll make sure you don't regret it!'

Tawny was unconvinced by that assurance but concealed her fear of the consequences, feeling that she ought to be more courageous. She wore colourful vintage clothing, held strong opinions and her ultimate ambition was to become a cartoonist with a strip of her own in a magazine or newspaper. In short she liked to think of herself as an individual rather than a follower. But sometimes, she suspected that deep down inside she was more of a conventional person than she liked to admit because she longed for a supportive family and had never broken the law by even the smallest margin.

'We'll do it this afternoon. As soon as his room is empty, if there's no sign of him having the laptop with him I'll ring up and you can go straight in and get it. Just leave it in the storage room. I'll be there within two minutes,' Julie told her eagerly.

'You're absolutely sure that you want to do this?' Tawny pressed worriedly. 'Perhaps you should speak to him again. If we get caught—'

'We're not going to get caught!' Julie declared with cutting conviction. 'Stop making such a fuss.'

Tawny went pink, assumed that Julie's outburst was the result of nervous tension and fell silent, but that tart response had set her own fiery temper on edge.

'Just go back to work and act normally,' Julie advised, shooting Tawny an apologetic look. 'I'll call you.'

Tawny returned with relief to changing beds, vacuuming and scrubbing bathrooms. She kept so busy she didn't allow herself to think about that call coming and yet on some level she was on hyper alert for when she heard the faint ping of the lift doors opening down the corridor she jumped almost a foot in the air. Julie's call telling her that his assistant had just left and the room was empty came barely a minute after that. Her heart beating very fast, Tawny sped down the passage with her trolley. Arming herself with a change of bedding as an excuse she used her pass key to let herself into Navarre Cazier's spacious suite. She set the fresh sheets down on the arm of a sofa as her eyes did a frantic sweep of the reception room and zoomed in on the laptop sitting conveniently on the table by the window. Although it was the work of a moment to cross the room, unplug the computer from its charger and tuck it below her arm, her skin dampened with perspiration and her stomach churned. Turning on her heel, she literally raced back to the exit door, eager to hand over the laptop to Julie and refusing to even think about having to sneak back in again to return it.

Without the slightest warning, however, there was a click and the door of the suite snapped open. Eyes huge with fright, Tawny clutched the laptop and froze into stillness. Navarre Cazier appeared and it was not a good time for her to realise that he was much bigger than he had seemed at a distance. He towered over her five and a half feet by well over six inches, his shoulders wide as axe handles in his formal dark suit. He was much more of an athlete in build than the average businessman. She clashed in dismay with frowning chartreuse-green eyes, startlingly bright and unexpected in that olive-skinned face. Close up he was quite breathtakingly handsome.

'Is that my laptop?' he asked immediately, his attention flying beyond her to the empty table. 'Has there been an accident? What are you doing with it?'

'I…I er…' Her heart was beating so fast it felt as if it

were thumping at the foot of her throat and her mind was a punishing blank.

There was a burst of French from behind him and he moved deeper into the room to make way for the body-guards that accompanied him virtually everywhere he went.

'I will call the police, Navarre,' his security chief, Jacques, a well-built older man, said decisively in French.

'No, no…no need to bring the police in!' Tawny exclaimed, now ready to kick herself for not having grabbed at the excuse that she had accidentally knocked the laptop off the table while cleaning.

'You speak French?' Navarre studied her with growing disquiet, taking in the uniform of blue tunic and trousers she wore with flat heels. Evidently she worked for the hotel in a menial capacity: there was an unattended cleaning trolley parked directly outside the suite. Of medium height and slender build, she had a delicate pointed face dominated by pale blue eyes the colour of an Alpine glacier set in porcelain-perfect skin, the combination enlivened by a mop of vivid auburn curls escaping from a ponytail. Navarre had always liked redheads and her hair was as bright as a tropical sunset.

'My grandmother is French,' Tawny muttered, deciding that honesty might now be her only hope of escaping a criminal charge.

If she spoke fluent French the potential for damage was even greater, Navarre reckoned furiously. How long had she had his laptop for? He had been out for an hour. Unfortunately it would only take minutes for her to copy the hard drive, gaining access not only to highly confidential business negotiations but also to even more personal and theoretically damaging emails. How many indiscreet emails of Tia's might she have seen? He was appalled by the breach in his security. 'What are you doing with my laptop?'

Tawny lifted her chin. 'I'm willing to explain but I don't think you'll want an audience while we have that conversation,' she dared.

His strong jawline clenched at that impertinent challenge as he read the name on her badge. Tawny Baxter, an apt label for a woman with such spectacular hair. 'There is no reason why you should not speak in front of my security staff,' he replied impatiently.

'Julie—the receptionist you spent the night with on your last visit,' Tawny specified curtly, surrendering the laptop as one of his security team put out his hands to reclaim the item. 'Julie just wants the photos you took of her posing wiped from your laptop.'

His ebony brows drawing together, Navarre subjected her to an incredulous scrutiny while absently noting the full pouting curve of her pink lips. She was in possession of what had to be the most temptingly sultry mouth he had ever seen on a woman. Exasperated by that abstracted thought, he straightened his broad shoulders and declared, 'I have never spent the night with a receptionist in this hotel. What kind of a scam are you trying to pull?'

'Don't waste your breath on this dialogue, Navarre. Let me contact the police,' the older man urged impatiently.

'Her name is Julie Chivers, she works on reception and right now she's waiting in the storage room next door for the laptop,' Tawny extended in a feverish rush. 'All she wants is to delete the photos you took of her!'

With an almost imperceptible movement of his arrogant dark head, Navarre directed Jacques to check out that location and the older man ducked back out of the room. Tawny sucked in a lungful of air and tilted her chin. 'Why wouldn't you wipe the photos when Julie asked you to?'

'I have no idea what you're talking about,' he countered with a chilly gravity that sank like an icicle deep into her tender flesh. 'There was no night with a receptionist, no photos. Ditch the silly story. What have you done with my laptop?'

'Absolutely nothing. I'd only just lifted it when you appeared,' Tawny replied tightly, wondering why he was still lying and eagerly watching the door for Julie's appearance. She was sure that once he recognised her friend as a former lover there would be no more talk of calling the police. But didn't he even recognise Julie's name? It occurred to her that she never wanted to become intimate with a man who didn't care enough even to take note of her name.

'It's unfortunate for you that I came back unexpectedly,' Navarre shot back at her, wholly unconvinced by her plea.

Of course she would try to tell him that she had not had enough time to do any real damage. But he was too conscious that she could have copied his hard drive within minutes and might even be concealing a flash drive beneath her clothing. He was in the act of doubting that the police would agree to have her strip-searched for the sake of his security and peace of mind so his attention quite naturally rested on her slender coltish shape.

She had a gloriously tiny waist. He could not help wondering if the skin of her body was as pearly and perfect as that of her face. When almost every woman he knew practically bathed in fake tan it was a novelty to see a woman so pale he could see the faint tracery of blue veins beneath her skin. Indeed the more he studied her, the more aware he became of her unusual delicate beauty and the tightening fullness at his groin was his natural masculine reaction to her allure. She had that leggy pure-bred look but those big pale eyes and that wickedly suggestive mouth etched buckets of raw sex appeal into her fragile features. That she could look that good even without make-up was unparalleled in his experience of her sex. In the right clothes with that amazing hair loose she would probably be a complete knockout. What a shame she was a humble chambermaid about to be charged with petty theft, he reflected impatiently, returning his thoughts to reality while marvelling at the detour into fantasy that they had briefly and bizarrely taken.

Jacques reappeared and shook his head in response to his employer's enquiring glance. Something akin to panic gripped Tawny. Evidently Julie wasn't still in the storage room ready and able to make an explanation. Until that instant Tawny had not appreciated just how much she had been depending on her friend coming through that door and immediately sorting out the misunderstanding.

'Julie must have heard you come back and she's gone back downstairs to Reception,' Tawny reasoned in dismay.

'I'm calling the police,' Navarre breathed, turning to lift the phone.

'No, let me call Reception and ask Julie to come up and explain first,' Tawny urged in a frantic rush. *'Please,* Mr Cazier!'

For a split second Navarre scanned her pleading eyes, marvelling at their rare colour, and then he swept up the phone and, while she held her breath in fear and watched, he stabbed the button for Reception and requested her friend by name.

Colour slowly returning to her drawn cheeks, Tawny drew in a tremulous breath. 'I'm not lying to you, I swear I'm not… I didn't even get the chance to open your laptop—'

'Naturally you will say that,' Navarre derided. 'You

could well have been in the act of returning it to the room when I surprised you—'

'But I *wasn't!*' Tawny exclaimed in horror when she registered the depth of his suspicion. 'I had only just lifted it when you returned. I'm telling you the truth!'

'That I had some kinky one-night stand with a camera and a receptionist?' Navarre queried with stinging scorn. 'Do I strike you as that desperate for entertainment in London?'

Suffering her very first moment of doubt as to his guilt in that quarter, Tawny shrugged a slight shoulder in an awkward gesture while her heart sank at the possibility that she could be wrong. 'How would I know? You're a guest here. I know nothing about you aside of what my friend told me.'

'Your friend lied to you,' Navarre declared.

After a tense two minutes of complete silence a soft knock sounded on the door and Julie entered, looking unusually meek. 'How can I help you, Mr Cazier?'

'*Julie...*' Tawny interposed, leaping straight into speech. 'I want you to explain about you asking me to take the laptop so that we can get this all sorted out—'

'What about the laptop? Take *whose* laptop?' Julie enquired sharply, widening her brown eyes in apparent confusion and annoyance. 'What the hell are you trying to accuse me of doing?'

In receipt of that aggressive comeback, Tawny was bewildered. She could feel the blood draining from her cheeks in shock and the sick churning in the pit of her stomach started up afresh. 'Julie, please explain...look, what's going on here? You and Mr Cazier know each other—'

Julie's brow pleated. 'If you mean by that that Mr Cazier is a regular and much respected guest here—'

'You told me that he took photos of you—'

'I have no idea what you're talking about. Photos? I'm sorry about this, Mr Cazier. Possibly this member of staff has been drinking or something because she's talking nonsense. I should call the penthouse manager to deal with this situation.'

'Thank you, Miss Chivers, but that won't be necessary. You may leave,' Navarre cut in with clear impatience. 'I've heard quite enough.'

Navarre motioned his security chief back to his side with the movement of one finger and addressed the older man in an undertone.

In disbelief, Tawny watched her erstwhile friend leave the suite with her head held high. Julie had lied. Julie had actually pretended not to know her on a personal basis. Her friend had *lied*, turned her back on Tawny and let her take the fall for attempted theft. Tawny was not only stunned by that betrayal, but also no longer convinced that Julie had ever spent the night with Navarre Cazier. But if that suspicion was true, why had Julie told her that convoluted story about the nude photography session? Why else would Julie have wanted access to the billionaire's laptop? What had she wanted to find out from it and why?

As Tawny turned white and swayed Navarre thought she might be about to faint. Instead, demonstrating a surprising amount of inner strength for so young a woman, she leant back against the wall for support and breathed in slow and deep to steady herself. Even so, he recognised an attack of gut-deep fear when he saw one but he had not the slightest pity for her. Navarre always hit back hard against those who tried to injure him. At the same time, however, he also reasoned at the speed of light, an ability that had dug him out of some very tight corners while growing up.

If he called the police, what recompense would he receive for the possible crime committed against him? There would be no guarantee that the maid would be punished and even if this was not a first offence she would be released, possibly even to take advantage of selling a copy of his hard drive to either his business competitors or the paparazzi, who had long sought proof of the precise nature of his relationship with Tia. Either prospect promised far reaching repercussions, not just to his extensive business empire, but even more importantly to Tia, her marriage and her reputation. He owed Tia his protection, he reflected grimly. But it might already be too late to prevent revealing private correspondence entering the public domain.

On the other hand, if he were to prevent the maid from contacting anyone to pass on confidential information for at least the next seven days, he could considerably minimise the risks to all concerned. Granted a week's grace the business deal with the Coulter Centax Corporation, CCC, could be tied up and, should his fear with regard to the emails prove correct, Tia's world-class PR advisors would have the chance to practise damage limitation on her behalf. In the event of the worst-case scenario isolating the maid was the most effective action he could currently take.

And, even more to the point, if he was forced to keep the maid around he might well be able to make use of her presence, Navarre decided thoughtfully. She was young and beautiful. And, crucially, he already knew that her loyalty could be bought. Why should he not pay her to fill the role that presently stood empty? With a movement of his hand he dismissed Jacques and his companion. The older man left the suite with clear reluctance.

Tawny gazed back at Navarre, her triangular face taut with strain. 'I really wasn't trying to steal from you—'

'The camera recording in here won't lie,' Navarre murmured without any expression at all, lush black lashes low over intent green eyes.

'There's a camera operating in here?' Tawny exclaimed in horror, immediately recognising that if there was he would have unquestionable proof of her entering the suite and taking his laptop.

'My protection team set up a camera as a standard safeguard wherever I'm staying,' Navarre stated smooth as glass. 'It means that I will have pictorial evidence of your attempt to steal from me.'

Her narrow shoulders slumped and her face fell. Shame gutted her for, whatever her motivation had been, theft was theft and neither the police nor a judge would distinguish between what she had believed she was doing and a crime. She marvelled that she had foolishly got herself into such a predicament. Caught red-handed as she had been, it no longer seemed a good idea to continue to insist that she had not been stealing. 'Yes...'

'Having you sacked and arrested, however, will be of no advantage to me,' Navarre Cazier asserted and she glanced up in surprise. 'But if you were to accept my terms in the proposition I am about to make you, I will not contact the police and in addition I will pay you for your time.'

Genuinely stunned by the content of that speech, Tawny lifted her head and speared him with an ice-blue look of scorn. 'Pay me for my time? I'm not that kind of girl—'

Navarre laughed out loud, grim amusement lightening the gravity on his face as her eyes flashed and her chin came up in challenge. 'My proposition doesn't entail taking your clothes off or, indeed, doing anything of an illegal or sexual nature,' he extended very drily. 'Make your mind up—this is very much your decision. Do I call the police or are you going to be sensible and reach for the lifebelt I'm offering?'

CHAPTER TWO

TAWNY straightened her shoulders. Her mind was in a fog torn between panic and irrational hope while she tried to work out if the exclusion of either illegal or sexual acts would offer her sufficient protection. 'You'll have to tell me first what grabbing the lifebelt would entail.'

'*Rien à faire*…nothing doing. I can't trust you with that information until I know that I have your agreement,' Navarre Cazier fielded without hesitation.

'I can't agree to something when I don't know what it is…you can't expect that.'

His stunning eyes narrowed to biting chips of emerald. '*Merde alors*…I'm the party in the position of power here. I can ask whatever I like. After all, you have the right of refusal.'

'I don't want to be accused of theft. I don't want a police record,' Tawny admitted through gritted teeth of resentment. 'I am not a thief, Mr Cazier—'

Navarre Cazier expelled his breath in a weary sigh that suggested he was not convinced of that claim. Tawny went red and her slender hands closed into fists. She was in a daze of desperation, trapped and fighting a dangerous urge to lose her temper. 'This proposition—would I be able to accept it and keep my job on here?' she pressed.

'Not unless the hotel was prepared to allow you a leave of absence of at least two weeks.'

'I don't have that kind of flexibility,' Tawny said heavily.

'But I did say that I'd pay you for your time,' Navarre reminded her drily.

That salient reminder, when Tawny was worrying about how the loss of her job would impact on her ability to pay her grandmother's mortgage, was timely. 'What's the proposition?'

'Are you agreeing?'

Her even white teeth snapped together. 'Like I have a choice?' she flashed back at him. 'Yes. Assuming there's nothing illegal, sexual or offensive about what you're asking me to do.'

'How would I know what you find offensive? Give me a final answer. Right now you're wasting my valuable time.'

Rigid with resentment, Tawny looked at him, scanning the pure hard lines of his bronzed face. His eyes piercing with the weight of his intelligence, he wore an impenetrable mask of impassivity. He was incredibly handsome and incredibly unemotional. What could the proposition be? She was a lowly chambermaid whom he believed to be a thief. In what possible way could she be of use to such a wealthy, powerful man? Even more to the point, how could she put herself in such a man's power? Logic reminded her that as long as that unseen camera of his held an image of her apparently stealing she was in his power whether she liked it or not.

'How much would you pay me?' Tawny prompted drymouthed, her face burning as she tried to weigh up her single option.

Realising that they were finally dealing in business

terms, Navarre's emerald-green gaze glittered with renewed energy. He estimated what she most probably earned in a year and doubled it in the sum he came back to her with. Although it went against the grain with him to reward criminal behaviour, he was aware that if she was to lose her job in meeting his demands he had to make it worth her financial while. She went pale, her eyes widening in shock, and in the same moment he knew he had her exactly where he wanted her. Everyone had their price and he had, it seemed, accurately assessed hers.

That amount of money would cover any future period of unemployment she might suffer as well as her grandmother's mortgage for the rest of the year and more, Tawny registered in wonderment. But the truth that he had her pinned between a rock and a hard place was still a bitter pill to swallow. She would accept the money, but then any alternative was better than being arrested and charged with theft. She jerked her chin in affirmation. 'I'll do whatever it is as long as you promise to wipe that camera once it's done.'

'And I will accept that arrangement as long as you sign a confidentiality agreement, guaranteeing not to discuss anything you see or hear while you're in my company.'

'No problem. I'm not a chatterbox,' Tawny traded flatly. 'May I return to work now?'

Navarre dealt her an impatient look. 'I'm afraid not. You can't leave this hotel room without an escort. I want to be sure that any intel you may have gleaned from my laptop stays within these four walls.'

It finally dawned on Tawny that he had to have some highly sensitive information on that laptop when he was prepared to go to such lengths to protect it from the rest of the world. A knock sounded on the door and Navarre strode across the room, his tall, well-built body emanating

aggressive male power, to pull it open. Tawny went pale
when she saw the penthouse manager, Lesley Morgan, in
the doorway.

'Excuse me, Mr Cazier. Reception mentioned that there
might be a problem—'

'There is not a problem.'

'Tawny?' Lesley queried quietly. 'I'm sure you must
have work to take care of—'

'Tawny is resigning from her job, effective immediately,' Navarre Cazier slotted in without hesitation.

Across the room Tawny went rigid but she neither confirmed nor protested his declaration. In receipt of a wildly
curious glance from the attractive brunette, Tawny flushed
uncomfortably. So, she was going to be unemployed while
she fulfilled his mysterious mission. It was an obvious
first step. Whatever he wanted from her she could hardly
continue to work a daily shift at the hotel at the same time.
On the other hand, she would be virtually unemployable
with a criminal record for theft hanging over her head,
and, if she could emerge from the agreement with the
French industrialist with her good name still intact, losing her current job would be a worthwhile sacrifice.

'There are certain formalities to be taken care of in the
case of termination of employment,' Lesley replied with
an apologetic compression of her lips.

'Which my staff will deal with on Tawny's behalf,'
Navarre retorted in a tone of finality.

Beneath Tawny's bemused gaze, the penthouse manager took her leave. Navarre left Tawny hovering in the
centre of the carpet while he made a brisk phone call to
an employee to instruct her to organise appointments for
him. A frown divided Tawny's fine brows when she heard
him mention her name. He spoke in French too fast for

her to follow to a couple of other people and then finally tossed the phone down. A knock sounded on the door.

'Answer that,' Navarre told her.

'Say please,' Tawny specified, bravely challenging him. 'You may be paying me but you can still be polite.'

Navarre stiffened in disbelief. 'I have excellent manners.'

'No, you don't...I've seen you operating with your staff,' Tawny countered with a suggestive wince. 'It's all, *do* this, *do* that...why haven't you done it already? Please and thank you don't figure—'

'Open the damn door!' Navarre raked at her, out of all patience.

'You're not just rude, you're a bully,' Tawny declared, stalking over to the door to tug it open with a twist of a slender hand.

'Don't answer me back like that,' Navarre warned her as his security chief walked in and, having caught that last exchange, directed an astonished look of curiosity at his employer.

'You're far too tempting a target,' Tawny warned him.

Icy green eyes caught her amused gaze and chilled her. 'Control the temptation. If you can't do as you're told you're of no use to me at all.'

'Is that the sound of a whip cracking over my head?' Tawny looked skyward.

'Do you hear anyone laughing?' Navarre derided.

'You've got your staff too scared.'

'Jacques, take Tawny to collect her belongings and bring her back up without giving her the chance to talk to anyone,' Navarre instructed.

'Men aren't allowed in the female locker room,' Tawny told him gently.

'I will ask Elise to join us.' Jacques unfurled his phone.

Navarre studied Tawny, far from impervious to the amusement glimmering in her pale eyes combined with the voluptuous pout of her sexy mouth. Desire, sudden and piercing as a blade, gripped him. All of a sudden as he met those eyes he was picturing her on a bed with rumpled sheets, hair fanned out in a wild colourful torrent of curls, that pale slender body displayed for his pleasure. His teeth clenched on the shot of stark hunger that evocative image released. He was consoled by the near certainty that she would give him that pleasure before their association ended, for no woman had ever denied him.

Gazing back at Navarre Cazier, Tawny momentarily felt as though someone had, without the smallest warning, dropped her off the side of a cliff. Her body felt as if it had gone into panic mode, her heartbeat thundering far too fast, her mouth suddenly dry, her nipples tight and swollen, an excited fluttering low in her belly. And just as quickly Tawny realised what was *really* happening to her and she tore her attention guiltily from him, colour burning over her cheekbones at her uncontrollable reaction to all that male testosterone in the air. It was desire he had awakened, not fear. Yes, he was gorgeous, but under no circumstances was she going to go there.

Rich, handsome men didn't attract her. Her mother and her sisters' experiences had taught Tawny not to crave wealth and status for the sake of it, for neither brought lasting happiness. Her father, a noted hotelier, was rich and miserable and, according to her older half-sisters, Bee and Zara, he was always pleading dissatisfaction with his life or latest business deal. Nothing was ever enough for Monty Blake. Bee and Zara might also be married to wealthy men, but they were both very much in love with their husbands. At the end of the day love was all that really mattered, Tawny reflected thoughtfully, and substituting sex for love and hoping it would bridge the gap didn't work.

That was why Tawny didn't sleep around. She had grown up with her mother's bitterness over a sexual affair that had never amounted to anything more. She had also seen too many friends hurt by their efforts to found a lasting relationship on a basis of casual sex. She wanted more commitment before she risked her heart; she had always wanted and demanded *more*. That was the main reason why she had avoided the advances of the wealthy men introduced to her by her matchmaking sisters, both of whom had married 'well' in her mother's parlance. What could she possibly have in common with such men with their flash lives in which only materialistic success truly mattered? She had no wish to end up with a vain, shallow and selfish man like her father, who was solely interested in her for her looks.

'Are you going to tell me what this proposition entails?' Tawny prompted in the simmering silence.

'I want you to pretend to be my fiancée,' Navarre spelt out grimly.

Her eyes widened to their fullest, for that had to be almost the very last thing she might have expected. 'But why?' she exclaimed.

'You have no need of that information,' Navarre fielded drily.

'But you must know loads of women who would—'

'Perhaps I prefer to pay. Think of yourself as a professional escort. I'll be buying you a new wardrobe to wear while you're with me. When this is over you get to keep the clothes, but not the jewellery,' he specified.

No expense spared, she thought in growing bewilderment. She had read about him in the newspapers, for he made regular appearances in the gossip columns. He had a penchant for incredibly beautiful supermodels and the reputation of being a legendary lover, but none of the ladies in his life seemed to last very long. 'Nobody's going to believe you're engaged to someone as ordinary as me,' she told him baldly.

'Ce fut le coup de foudre...' It was love at first sight French-style, he was telling her with sardonic cool. 'And nobody will be surprised when the relationship quickly bites the dust again.'

Well, she could certainly agree with that final forecast, but she reckoned that he had to be desperate to be considering her for such a role. How on earth would she ever be able to compare to the glamorous model types he usually had on his arm? Jacques ushered a statuesque blonde in a dark trouser suit into the room. 'Elise will escort you down to the locker room,' he explained.

'So you're a bodyguard,' Tawny remarked in French as the two women waited in the lift.

'I'm usually the driver,' Elise admitted.

'What's Mr Cazier like to work for?'

'Tough but fair and I get to travel,' Elise told her with satisfaction.

Elise hovered nearby while Tawny changed out of her uniform into her own clothes and cleared her locker. The Frenchwoman's mobile phone rang and she dug it out, glancing awkwardly at Tawny, who was busily packing a carrier bag full of belongings before moving to the other side of the room to talk in a low-pitched voice. That it was a man Elise cared about at the other end of the line was obvious, and Tawny reckoned that at that instant she could have smuggled an elephant past the Frenchwoman without attracting her attention.

'What's going on?' another voice enquired tautly of Tawny.

Tawny glanced up and focused on Julie, who stood only a couple of feet away from her. 'I'm quitting my job.'

'I heard that but why didn't he report you?'

Tawny shrugged non-committally. 'You didn't spent the night with him, did you? What's the real story?'

'A journalist offered me a lot of money to dig out some personal information for him. Accessing Cazier's laptop was worth a try. I've got credit cards to clear,' Julie admitted calmly, shockingly unembarrassed at having her lies exposed.

'Mademoiselle Baxter?' Elise queried anxiously, her attention suddenly closely trained on the two women.

Tawny lifted her laden bags and walked away without another word or look. So much for friendship! She was furious but also very hurt by her former friend's treachery. She had liked Julie, she had automatically trusted her, but she could now see her whole relationship with the other woman in quite a different light. It was likely that Julie had deliberately targeted her once she realised that Tawny would be the new maid in charge of Navarre Cazier's usual suite. Having befriended Tawny and put her under obligation by helping her to move into her bedsit, Julie had then conned the younger woman into trying to take Navarre's laptop. What a stupid, trusting fool Tawny now felt like! How could she have been dumb enough to swallow that improbable tale of sex and compromising photos? Julie had known exactly which buttons to press to engage Tawny's sympathies and it would have worked a treat had Navarre Cazier not returned unexpectedly to catch her in the act.

'You have an appointment with a stylist,' Navarre informed Tawny when she reappeared in his suite and set down her bags.

'Where?'

He named a famous department store. He scanned the jeans and checked shirt she wore with faded blue plimsolls and his wide sensual mouth twisted, for in such casual clothing she looked little older than a teenager. 'What age are you?'

'Twenty-three...you?'

'Thirty.'

'Speak French,' he urged.

'I'm a little rusty. I only get to see my grandmother about once a month now,' Tawny told him.

'Give me your mobile phone,' he instructed.

'My phone?' Tawny exclaimed in dismay.

'I can't trust you with access to a phone when I need to ensure that you don't pass information to anyone,' he retorted levelly and extended a slim brown hand. 'Your phone, please...'

The silence simmered. Tawny worried at her lower lip, reckoned that she could not fault his reasoning and reluctantly dug her phone out of her pocket. 'You're not allowed to go through it. There's private stuff on there.'

'Just like my laptop,' Navarre quipped with a hard look, watching her redden and marvelling that she could still blush so easily.

He ushered her out of the suite and into the lift. She leant back against the wall.

'Don't slouch,' he told her immediately.

With an exaggerated sigh, Tawny straightened. 'We mix like oil and water.'

'We only have to impress as a couple in company. Practise looking adoring,' Navarre advised witheringly.

Tawny wrinkled her nose. 'That's not really my style—'

'*Try,*' he told her.

She preceded him out into the foyer, striving not to notice the heads craning at the reception desk to follow their progress out of the hotel. A limousine was waiting by the kerb and she climbed in, noting Elise's neat blonde head behind the steering wheel.

'Tell me about yourself…a potted history,' Navarre instructed.

'I'm an only child although I have two half-sisters through my father's two marriages. He didn't marry my mother, though, and he has never been involved in my life. I got my degree at art college and for a couple of years managed to make a living designing greeting cards. Unfortunately that wasn't lucrative enough to pay the bills and I signed up as a maid so that I would have a regular wage coming in,' she told him grudgingly. 'I want to be a cartoonist but so far I haven't managed to sell a single cartoon.'

'A cartoonist,' Navarre repeated, his interest caught by that unexpected ambition.

'What about you? Were you born rich?'

'No. I grew up in the back streets of Paris but I acquired a first-class degree at the Sorbonne. I was an investment banker until I became interested in telecommunications and set up my first business.'

'Parents?' she pressed.

His face tensed. 'I was a foster child and lived in many homes. I have no relatives that I acknowledge.'

'I know how we can tell people we met,' Tawny said with a playful light in her eyes. 'I was changing your bed *when*—'

Navarre was not amused by the suggestion but his attention lingered on her astonishingly vivid little face in which every expression was easily read. 'I don't think we need to admit that you were working as a hotel maid.'

'Honesty is always the best policy.'

'Says the woman whom I caught thieving.'

Her face froze as though he had slapped her, reality biting again. 'I wasn't thieving,' she muttered tightly.

'It really doesn't matter as long as you keep your light fingers strictly to your own belongings while you're with me,' Navarre responded drily. 'I hope the desire to steal is an impulse that you can resist as we will be mingling with some very wealthy people.'

Mortified by the comment, Tawny bent her bright head. 'Yes, you don't have to worry on that score.'

While Navarre took a comfortable seat in a private room in the store, Tawny was ushered off to try on evening gowns, and each one seemed more elaborate than the last. When the selection had been reduced to two she was propelled out to the waiting area, where Navarre was perusing the financial papers, for a second opinion.

'That's too old for her,' he commented of the purple ball gown that she felt would not have looked out of place on Marie Antoinette.

When she walked out in the grey lace that fitted like a glove to below hip line before flaring out in a romantic arc of fullness round her knees, he actually set his newspaper down, the better to view her slender, shapely figure. '*Sensationnel,*' he declared with crowd-pleasing enthusiasm while his shrewd green eyes scanned her with as much emotion as a wooden clothes horse might have inspired.

Yet for all that lack of feeling they were such unexpectedly beautiful eyes, she reflected helplessly, as cool and mysterious as the depths of the sea, set in that strong handsome face. Bemused by the unusually fanciful thought, Tawny was whisked back into the spacious changing room where two assistants were hanging up outfits for the stylist to choose from. There were trousers, skirts, dresses, tops and jackets as well as lingerie and a large selection of shoes and accessories. Every item was designer and classic and nothing was colourful enough or edgy enough to appeal to her personal taste. She would only be in the role of fake fiancée for a maximum of two weeks, she reminded herself with relief. Could such a vast number of garments really be necessary or was the stylist taking advantage of a buyer with famously deep pockets? She wondered what event the French industrialist was taking her to that required the over-the-top evening gown. She was not required to model any other clothing for his inspection. That was a relief for, stripped of her usual image and denied her streetwise fashion, she felt strangely naked and vulnerable clad in items that did not belong to her.

Navarre was on the phone talking in English when she returned to his side. As they walked back through the store he continued the conversation, his deep drawl a low-pitched sexy purr, and she guessed that he was chatting to a woman. They returned to the hotel in silence. She wanted to go home and collect some of her own things but was trying to pick the right moment in which to make that request. Navarre vanished into the bedroom, reappearing in a light grey suit ten minutes later and walking past her.

'I'm going out. I'll see you tomorrow,' he told her silkily.

Her smooth brow furrowed. 'Do I have to stay here?'

'That's the deal,' he confirmed with a dismissive lack of interest that set her teeth on edge.

It was after midnight when Navarre came back to his suite with Jacques still at his heels. He had forgotten about Tawny so it was a surprise to walk in and see the lounge softly lit. Three heads turned from the table between them to glance at him, three of the individuals, members of his security team, instantly rising upright to greet him with an air of discomfiture beneath Jacques's censorious appraisal.

From the debris it was clear there had been takeout food eaten, and from the cards and small heaps of coins visible several games of poker. Tawny didn't stand up. She stayed where she was curled up barefoot on the sofa.

Navarre shifted a hand in dismissal of his guards. Tawny had yet to break into her new wardrobe, for she wore faded skinny jeans with slits over the knee and a tee with a skeleton motif. Her hair fell in a torrent of spiralling curls halfway down her back, much longer than he had appreciated and providing a frame for her youthful piquant face that gave her an almost fey quality.

'Where did you get those clothes from?' he asked bluntly.

'I gave Elise a list of things that I needed along with my keys and she was kind enough to go and pack a bag for me. I didn't think that what I wore behind closed doors would matter.' Tawny gazed back at him in silent challenge, striving not to react in any way to the fact that he was drop-dead gorgeous, particularly with that dark shadow of stubble roughening his masculine jawline and accentuating the sensual curve of his beautifully shaped mouth.

Navarre bent to lift the open sketch pad resting on the arm of the sofa. It was an amusing caricature of Elise and instantly recognisable as such. He flicked it back and found another, registering that she had drawn each of her companions. 'You did these? They're good.'

Tawny shifted a narrow shoulder in dismissal. 'Not good enough to pay the bills,' she said wryly, thinking of how often her mother had criticised her for choosing to study art rather than a subject that the older woman had deemed to be of more practical use.

'A talent nonetheless.'

'Where am I supposed to sleep tonight?' Tawny asked flatly, in no mood to debate the topic.

'You can sleep on the sofa,' Navarre told her without hesitation, irritated that he had not thought of her requirements soon enough to ask for a suite with an extra bedroom. 'It will only be for two nights and then we'll be leaving London.'

'To go where?'

'Further north.' With that guarded reply, he walked into the bedroom and a couple of minutes later he reappeared with a bedspread and a pillow in his arms. He deposited them on a chair nearby and then with a nod departed again. He moved with the fluid grace of a dancer and he emanated sex appeal like a force field, she acknowledged tautly, her eyes veiling as she struggled to suppress a tiny little twisting flicker of response to him.

'You know…a real gentleman would offer a lady the bed,' Tawny called in his wake.

Navarre shot her a sardonic glance, green eyes bright as jewels between the thick luxuriance of his black lashes as he drawled, 'I've never been a gentleman and I very much doubt that you're a lady in the original sense of the word.'

CHAPTER THREE

THE next morning, Navarre watched Tawny sleep, curls that melded from bright red to copper tipped with strawberry-blonde ends spilling out across the pale smooth skin of her narrow shoulders, dark lashes low over delicate cheek-bones, her plump pink pouting mouth incredibly sexy. He brushed a colourful strand of hair away from her face. 'Wake up,' he urged.

Tawny woke with a start, eyes shooting wide as she half sat up. 'What?'

Navarre had retreated several feet to give her space. 'Time to rise. You have a busy day ahead of you.'

Tawny rubbed her eyes like a child and hugged her pyjama-clad knees before muttering, 'Doing what?'

'A beautician and a hairstylist will be here this after-noon to help you to prepare for this evening's event. A jeweller will be here in an hour. The bathroom's free,' he informed her coolly. 'What do you want for breakfast?'

'The full works—I'm always starving first thing,' she told him, scrambling off the sofa and folding the spread with efficient hands, a lithe figure clad in cotton pyjama pants and a camisole top. 'Where are you taking me this evening?'

'A movie awards ceremony.'

Her eyes widened. 'Wow…fancy, so that's what the boring grey dress is for—'

'It isn't boring—'

'Take it from me, it was boring enough that my mother would have admired it,' she declared unimpressed, heading off to the bathroom, pert buttocks swaying above long slim legs.

'Wear one of your new outfits,' he told her before she vanished from view.

'But if we're not going out until this evening—'

'You need a practice run. Get into role for the jeweller's benefit,' Navarre advised.

Tawny rummaged through the huge pile of garment bags, carriers and boxes that had been delivered to the suite the night before. She had hung the bags on the door of the wardrobe but had felt uneasy about the prospect of stowing away the clothing in a room that he was using. She set out a narrow check skirt and a silk top. It was a dull conventional outfit but, for what he had promised to pay her for her services as a fake fiancée, she was willing to make an effort. She took the undies into the bathroom and went for a shower, using his shower gel but keeping her hair out of the water because she did not want the hassle of drying it.

Navarre watched her walk back across the carpet to join him at the breakfast table, her heart-shaped face composed, her bright curls bouncing like tongues of flame across her silk-clad shoulders. His masculine gaze took in the pouting curve of her breasts, her tiny waist and the long tight line of the skirt, below which her shapely legs were very much in evidence. *'Tu es belle…y*ou are beautiful, *mignonne.'*

Tawny rolled her eyes, unconvinced, recognising the

sophisticated and highly experienced charm of a womaniser in his coolly measuring appraisal. 'I clean up well.'

Navarre liked her deprecating manner and admired the
more telling fact that she had walked right past a mirror
without even pausing to admire her own reflection. The
waiter arrived with a breakfast trolley. Although Tawny
knew him the young man studiously avoided looking at
her even while she was making her selections from the hot
food on offer. Her cheeks burned as she realised that the
staff would naturally have assumed that she was sleeping
with Navarre.

Navarre had never seen a woman put away that much
food at one sitting. Tawny ate daintily but she had a very
healthy appetite. After her second cup of coffee and final
slice of toast she pushed away her plate, relaxed back in
her chair and smiled. 'Now I can face the day.'

'Do you think you've eaten enough to keep you going
until lunchtime?' Navarre could not resist that teasing
comment.

Her eyes widened in suggestive dismay. 'Are you saying that I can't have a snack before then?'

The biter bit, Navarre laughed out loud, very much
amused. In that instant, eyes glittering with brilliance between dense black lashes that reminded her very much of
lace, he was so charismatic he just took her breath away
and left her staring at his handsome face. It was impossible to look away and as his gaze narrowed in intensity
her tummy flipped as if she had gone down in a lift too
fast.

Navarre thrust back his chair and sprang upright to extend a hand down to her. Breathless and bemused, Tawny
took his hand without thought and stood up as well. Long
fingers framed her cheekbone and he lowered his arrogant dark head to allow the tip of his tongue to barely

skim along the fullness of her lower lip. She opened her mouth instinctively, her entire body tingling with an electric awareness that raised every tiny hair on her skin. His tongue darted into the moist interior of her mouth in a light teasing flicker that skimmed the inner surface of her lip. It was so *incredibly* sexy it made her shiver as if she were standing in a force-ten gale. Desire rose in her in an uncontrollable wave, screaming through her, spreading heat and hunger into every erotic part of her body. Helplessly she leant forwards, longing to be closer to him, insanely conscious of the tight fullness of her breasts and the hot, damp sting of awareness pulsing between her thighs. With a masculine growl vibrating deep in his throat, he finally kissed her with sweet sensual force, giving her the exact level of strength and urgency that her entire being craved from him.

When in the midst of that passionate embrace Navarre suddenly stopped kissing her and angled his head back, Tawny was utterly bewildered.

'*C'est parfait!* You're really good at this.' Navarre gazed down at her with eyes as ice-cold as running water. 'Anyone seeing such a kiss would believe we were lovers. That pretence of intimacy is all that is required to make us convincing.'

Tawny turned white and then suddenly red as a tide of mortification gripped her but she contrived to veil her eyes and stand her ground. 'Thank you,' she replied as if she had known all along what he was doing and had responded accordingly.

She was mentally kicking herself hard for having responded to his advances as if she were his newest girlfriend. How could she have done that? How could she have lost all control and forgotten who he was and who she was and exactly why they were together? He was paying her, for goodness sake! There was nothing else between them, no intimate relationship of any kind, she reminded herself brutally. On his terms she was something between an employee and a paid escort and not at all the sort of woman he would normally spend time with. Yet she had found that kiss more exciting than any she had ever experienced and would probably have still been in his arms had he not chosen to end that embarrassing little experiment. He had given his fake fiancée a fake kiss and she had fallen for it as though it were real.

Why on earth did she find Navarre Cazier so attractive? He might be extraordinarily good-looking but surely it took more than cheap physical chemistry to break down her barriers? As a rule she was standoffish with men and a man had to work at engaging her interest. All Navarre had done was insult her, so how could she possibly be attracted to him? Infuriated by her weakness, she took a seat as far away from him as she could get.

A warning knock sounded on the door before it opened to show Jacques shepherding in two men, one carrying a large case. It was the jeweller, complete with his own bodyguard. Navarre brought her forwards to sit beside him. Stiff as a doll and wearing a fixed smile, she sat down and looked on in silence as the older man displayed a range of fabulous rings featuring different stones.

'What do you like?' Navarre prompted.

'Aren't diamonds supposed to be a girl's best friend?' Tawny quipped and the diamond tray immediately rose uppermost.

Navarre took her small hand in his. 'Choose the one you like best.'

His hand was so much larger than hers, darker, stronger, and all she could think about for an horrific few moments was how that hand would feel if it were to touch her body, stroking...*caressing.* What the heck was the matter with her brain? Hungry hormones and heated embarrassment mushrooming inside her, Tawny bent her head over the diamond display and pointed blindly. 'May I try that one?'

'A pink diamond...a superb choice,' the jeweller remarked, passing the ring to Navarre, who eased the ring onto Tawny's finger. It was a surprisingly good fit.

'I like it,' Navarre declared.

'It is just *unbelievably* gorgeous!' Tawny gushed, batting her lashes like fly swats in response to the squeeze hold he had on her wrist.

Navarre shot her a quelling look in punishment for that vocal eruption while the purchase was being made. Several shallow jewel cases were removed from the case and opened to display an array of matching diamond pieces. Without recourse to her, Navarre selected a pair of drop earrings, a slender bracelet and a brooch, which she gathered were being offered on loan for her to wear that evening.

'Try not to behave like an airhead,' Navarre advised when they were alone again. 'It irritates me.'

Tawny resisted the urge to admit even to herself that awakening his irritation was preferable to receiving no reaction from him at all, for that made her sound childish. Had he not been hovering, however, she would have reached for her sketch pad, for his unmistakeably French character traits amused her. Regardless of the apparent passion of that kiss, she was convinced that Navarre Cazier rarely lost control or focus. He was arrogant, cool, reserved and extremely sure of himself.

'My English lawyer will be calling in shortly with the confidentiality agreement which you have to sign,' Navarre informed her, shrugging back a pristine shirt cuff to check the time. 'I have business to take care of this afternoon. I will see you later.'

'Can I go out? I'm going stir crazy in here,' she confided.

'If you go out or contact anyone our agreement will be null and void,' Navarre spelt out coldly. 'Elise will be keeping you company while I'm out.'

Elise arrived and he had barely left the room before Tawny's sketch pad was in her hand and she was drawing. Capturing Navarre on paper with strong dark lines, she drew him as she had seen him while she modelled evening gowns for him at the department store the day before. *'Sensationnel,'* he had purred with his charismatic smile, but she had known meeting his detached gaze that the compliment was essentially meaningless for she meant nothing to him beyond being a means to an end. In the cartoon she depicted the stylist as a curvaceous man killer, standing behind her and the true focus of his masculine admiration. It was artistic licence but it expressed Tawny's growing distrust of Navarre Cazier's astute intelligence, for she would have given much to understand why he felt the need to *hire* a woman to pretend to be his fiancée. What was he hiding from her or from the rest of the world? What were the secrets that he was so determined to keep from public view on that laptop? Secrets of such importance that he was willing to hold Tawny incommunicado and a virtual prisoner within his hotel suite to ensure that she could not share them…

'May I see what you have drawn?' Elise asked.

Tawny grimaced.

'If it's the boss I won't tell anyone,' she promised, and Tawny extended her pad.

Elise laughed. 'You have caught him well but he is not a lech.'

'A cartoon is a joke, Elise, not a character reference,' Tawny explained. 'You're very loyal to him.'

'I was in lust with him for the first year I worked for him.' Elise wrinkled her nose in an expression of chagrin. 'It hurts my pride to remember how I was. He seemed so beautiful I couldn't take my eyes off him.'

'And then he *speaks*,' Tawny slotted in flatly.

'No, no!' Elise laughed at that crack. 'No, I realised what a fool I was being once I saw him with his ladies. Only the most beautiful catch his eye and even they cannot hold him longer than a few weeks, particularly if they demand too much of his time and attention. He would never get involved with an employee, but he is very much a single guy, who wants to keep it that way.'

'I can't fault him for that. Who is the current lady in his life?'

Elise winced and suddenly scrambled upright again as if she had just remembered who Tawny was and what she was supposed to be doing with her. 'I'm sorry, I can't tell you. That is confidential information.'

Tawny went pink. 'No problem. I understand.'

A suave well-dressed lawyer arrived with the confidentiality agreement soon afterwards. He explained the basics of the document and gave it to her to read. When she had finished reading what seemed to be a fairly standard contract she borrowed his pen to sign it and, satisfied, he departed. Elise ordered a room-service lunch for them and when it was delivered Tawny noticed the waiter flicking his eyes repeatedly to the napkin on her lap. She ran her fingers through the folds and felt the stiffness of paper. As she withdrew what she assumed to be a note she pushed it into the pocket of her jeans for reading when she was alone and then shook out the napkin, her heart thumping. A note? But from whom? And about what? Julie was the only member of staff she had got close to and why would Julie be trying to communicate with her again?

As if to apologise for her caginess about her employer's private life, Elise told Tawny about her boyfriend, Michel, who was a chef in Paris and how difficult the couple found it to see each other with Michel usually working nights when Elise was most often free. After a light meal, Tawny went off to the bathroom to unfurl the note and felt terribly guilty about doing so, knowing that her companion was supposed to be ensuring that no such communications were taking place. Unfortunately for Navarre, Elise just wasn't observant enough to be an effective guard.

'If you call…' the note ran and a London phone number followed. 'Information about Navarre Cazier is worth a lot of money.'

It was typed and unsigned. Tawny thrust the note back into her pocket with a frown of discomfiture. Was this a direct approach from the journalist who had tried to bribe Julie into doing his dirty work for him by stealing Navarre's laptop? If it was the same journalist he was certainly persistent in his underhand methods. Was he hoping that Tawny would make use of her current seemingly privileged position to spy for him and gather information about Navarre Cazier?

Distaste filled her. She felt slightly soiled at having even read the note. Navarre Cazier might think she had no standards because she had agreed to let him pay her to act as his fiancée, but Tawny had only agreed to that role because she was determined to ensure her grandmother Celestine's continuing security in her retirement home. If it had only been a matter of personal enrichment, if Navarre had not had the power to force Tawny to give up her employment, she would have refused his offer outright, she reflected unhappily. She would never forget the lesson of how her own mother's financial greed had badly hurt Celestine. Even family affection had proved insufficient to avert that tragedy and Tawny did not think she would ever find it possible to fully forgive her mother for what she had done to the old lady.

When she returned to the lounge Elise was taking delivery of a substantial set of designer luggage. 'For your new clothes,' she explained. 'You'll be travelling tomorrow.'

Feeling uncomfortable with the other woman after secretly reading that forbidden note, Tawny used the delivery as an excuse to return to the bedroom and pack the contents of all the bags, boxes and garment carriers into the cases instead. By the time she had finished doing that the beautician and her assistant had arrived with a case of tools and cosmetics and Tawny had to wrap herself in a towel to let them start work. What followed was a whirlwind of activity in the bedroom, which was taken over, and the afternoon wore on while she was waxed and plucked and massaged and moisturised and painted. By the time it was over she was convinced that there was not an inch of her body that had not been treated and enhanced in some way. As a woman who devoted very little time to her looks she found it something of a revelation to appreciate how much stuff she could have been doing to add polish to her appearance.

By the time the hairdresser arrived, Tawny was climbing the walls with boredom, a mood that was not helped by the stylist's visible dismay when confronted by Tawny's tempestuous mane of spiralling ringlets. When her hair was done, she was made up, and only when that was over could she finally don the grey lace evening gown. She was looking at herself in the mirror and grimacing at how old-fashioned she thought she looked when Elise brought in the diamond jewellery and Tawny put on the ring, the drop earrings and the bracelet. Studying the brooch, she suddenly had an idea and she bent down and pulled up the skirt to hold it above the knee, where it cascaded down in ruffles to her ankles. Ignoring Elise's dropped jaw, she anchored the skirt there with the brooch, straightened, pushed up the long tight sleeves of her dress to her elbow and bared her shoulders as well. The dress, magically, acquired a totally different vibe.

Navarre, waiting impatiently in the lounge to shower and change, glanced up as the bedroom door swung open and there she was, framed in the doorway. The classic elegant image he had expected was nowhere to be seen. There she stood, her magnificent hair tumbling in a rather wild torrent round her shoulders, her face glowing with subtle make-up, dominated by eyes bright as stars and a soft ripe mouth tinted the colour of raspberries. She looked so beautiful that he was stunned. That the dress he had chosen had been mysteriously transformed into sexy saloon girl-style went right past him because he was much too busy appreciating her satin smooth white shoulders and the slender, shapely perfection of her knees and ankles.

The silence filled the room and stretched as Tawny studied him expectantly.

'Is the shower free?' Navarre enquired smoothly, compressing his stubborn mouth on any comment relating to her appearance. She was working for him. He was paying for the entire display. Any remark, after all, would be both superfluous and inappropriate.

CHAPTER FOUR

TAWNY knew she had never looked so good and while she waited for Navarre to get ready she tried not to feel offended by his silence on that score. What was the matter with her? He was not a date, he was not required to pay her compliments and at least he hadn't complained about the liberties she had taken with the grey lace shroud he had picked for her to wear. Shouldn't she be grateful that he was maintaining a polite distance? Did she want the boundary lines between them to blur again? She certainly didn't want another kiss that made her feel as if she were burning up like a flame inside her own skin. Well, actually she *did* want one but that was not a prompting powered by her brain, it was more of a deeply mortifying craving. She told herself that there was no way that she would be stupid enough to succumb to his magnetic sexual allure a second time. Forewarned was forearmed.

'Let's go,' Navarre urged, joining her in an exquisitely tailored dinner jacket, the smooth planes of his freshly shaven features as beautiful as a dark angel's.

In the lift she found it a challenge to drag her eyes from the flawless perfection of his visage. 'Don't you think you should finally tell me where we're going?' she pressed.

'The Golden Awards and the showbiz party afterwards,' he revealed.

Her eyes widened in shock. She struggled to be cool and not reveal the fact that she was impressed to death. A huge number of well-known international celebrities would be attending the opulent Golden Movie Awards ceremony. The GMAs were a famous annual event, beloved of the glitterati. 'All the press will be there,' she said weakly, suddenly grasping why she was wearing a very expensive designer dress and a striking array of diamonds.

Acutely aware of the abnormal number of staff at Reception waiting to watch their departure, Tawny had to struggle to keep her head held high, but there was nothing that she could do to stop her face burning. Everybody would think she was sleeping with him; of course they would think that! People always went for the sleaziest explanation of the seemingly incomprehensible and why else would a chambermaid be dolled up in a designer frock and walking with a billionaire? Navarre escorted her out to the limousine.

'You've got some nerve taking someone like me with you to the Golden Awards,' Tawny dared to comment as the luxury car pulled away from the kerb.

Navarre studied her with amusement gleaming in his eyes. '*Mais non.* No man who looks at you will wonder why I am with you.'

'You mean they'll all think that I have to be absolutely amazing in bed!' Tawny retorted unimpressed.

Navarre shifted a broad shoulder in a tiny shrug that was very Gallic, understated and somehow deeply cool. 'I have no objection to inspiring envy.'

Tawny swallowed the angry words brimming on her tongue and breathed in slow and deep, while staunchly reminding herself of Celestine's need for her financial assistance.

'You're wearing an engagement ring,' Navarre reminded her drily. 'That puts you into a very different category, *ma petite*.'

'Don't call me that— I'm not *that* small!' Tawny censured.

A grin as unexpected as it was charismatic momentarily slashed his wide sensual mouth. 'You are considerably smaller than I am and very slim—'

'Skinny,' Tawny traded argumentatively. 'Don't dress it up. I eat like a horse but I've always been skinny.'

'We met at an art gallery...our fake first meeting,' Navarre extended when she frowned at him in bewilderment. 'If you are asked you will say that we met at an art showing here in London.'

'If I must.'

'You must. I refuse to say that I met the woman I intend to marry while she was changing my bed,' Navarre told her unapologetically.

'Snob,' Tawny told him roundly, crossing her legs and suddenly aware of the sweep of his gaze finally resting on the long length of thigh she had unintentionally exposed as the skirt of her gown slid back from her legs. As she lifted her head and encountered those spectacular eyes of his there was a knot of tension at the tender heart of her where she was unaccustomed to feeling anything.

Hard as a rock as he scrutinised that silken expanse of thigh, Navarre was exasperated enough by his body's indiscipline and her false impression of him to give a sardonic laugh of disagreement. 'I am not a snob. I worked in hotel kitchens to pay my way as a schoolboy. Survival was never a walk in the park when I was growing up and I have never forgotten how hard I had to work for low pay.'

Filled with all the embarrassment of someone labelled a thief and the new knowledge that he did have experience of working long hours for a small wage, Tawny evaded his gaze and smoothed down her skirt. She thought of the very generous tips he had left for her on his previous stays at the hotel and shame washed over her in a choking wave of regret. She wished she had never met Julie and never listened to her clever lies, for she had betrayed Navarre's trust. His generosity should have been rewarded by the attention of honest, dependable staff.

The car was slowing down in the heavy flow of traffic, gliding past crowded pavements to come to a halt outside the brightly lit theatre where the Goldens were to be held. As Tawny glimpsed the crush of sightseers behind the crash barriers, the stand of journalists, a presenter standing talking beside men with television cameras and the red carpet stretching to the entrance, something akin to panic closed her throat over.

'Don't stop to answer questions. Let me do the talking if there are any. Just smile,' Navarre instructed.

Tawny found it a challenge to breathe as she climbed out of the car. As cameras flashed she saw spots in front of her eyes and Navarre's steadying hand at her elbow was appreciated. He exchanged a light word with the attractive presenter who appeared to know him and steered her on smoothly into the building. An usher showed them to their seats inside the theatre. No sooner had they sat down than people began to stop in the aisle to greet Navarre and he made a point of introducing her as his fiancée. Time after time she saw surprise blossom in faces that Navarre should apparently be on the brink of settling down with one woman. That sceptical reaction told her all she needed to know about his reputation as a womaniser, she reflected sourly. Furthermore it seemed to her as though it might take more than diamonds and a designer gown to persuade his friends that she was the genuine article.

She watched as renowned actors and directors walked

up to the stage to collect awards and give speeches. Her hands ached from clapping and her mouth from smiling. It was a strain to feel so much on show and something of a relief when he indicated that it was time to leave.

As they crossed the foyer on their way out of the theatre a musical female voice called breathily, 'Navarre!' and he came to a dead halt.

Tia Castelli, exquisite as a china doll in a stunning blue chiffon dress teamed with a fabulous sapphire pendant, was hurrying down the staircase that led up to the private theatre boxes. Tawny couldn't take her eyes off the beauty, who was very much the screen goddess of her day. Earlier she had watched Tia collect a trophy for her outstanding performance in her most recent film in which she had played a woman being terrorised by a former boyfriend, and she had marvelled that she could be even seated that close to a living legend.

'And you must be Tawny!' Tia exclaimed, bending down with a brilliant smile to kiss Tawny lightly on both cheeks while cameras went crazy all around them as every newshound in their vicinity rushed to capture photos of the celebrated actress. Tawny was knocked sideways by that unexpectedly friendly greeting. Tia was extraordinarily beautiful in the flesh and, confronted by such a very famous figure, Tawny felt tongue-tied.

'Congratulations—I was so happy to hear your news and Navarre's,' Tia continued. 'Join Luke and I in our limo. We're heading to the same party.'

'How on earth did you get so friendly with Tia Castelli?' Tawny hissed as security guards escorted them back out via the red carpet.

'My first boss in private banking took care of her investments. I've known her a long time,' Navarre responded calmly.

Tia paused to greet fans and pose for the TV cameras while her tall, skinny, unshaven husband, clad in tight jeans, a crumpled blue velvet jacket and a black trilby as befitted the image of a hard-living rock star, ignored every attempt to slow down his progress and headed straight for the waiting limousine. With a rueful sigh, Navarre urged Tawny in the same direction and wished, not for the first time, that Tia were less impulsive and more cautious.

'So you're going to marry Navarre,' Luke Convery commented, his Irish accent unexpectedly melodic and soft as he introduced himself carelessly and studied Tawny with assessing brown eyes. 'What have you got that the rest of them haven't?'

'This...' Tawny showed off the opulent pink diamond while finding it impossible not to wonder just how much younger Luke was than his wife. They didn't even look like a couple, for in comparison to her polished Hollywood glamour he dressed like a tramp. She doubted that the musician was out of his twenties while Tia had to be well into her thirties, for her incredibly successful career had spanned Tawny's lifetime. She thought it was good that just for once it was an older woman with a younger man rather than the other way round, and she was warmed by the way Luke immediately reached for his wife's hand when she got into the car and the couple exchanged a mutually affectionate smile.

By all accounts, Tia Castelli deserved a little happiness, for she had led an impossibly eventful life from the moment she was spotted by a film director as a naive schoolgirl in a Florentine street and starred in her first blockbuster movie as the child of a broken marriage. She was a mesmerising actress, whom the camera truly loved. Admittedly Tia was no stranger to emotion or tragedy, for violent and unfaithful husbands, jealous lovers and nervous breakdowns with all the attendant publicity had all featured at one point or another in the star's life. She had suffered divorce, widowhood and a miscarriage during her only pregnancy.

'Let me see the ring,' Tia urged, stretching out a bejewelled hand weighted with diamonds. 'Oh, I *love* it.'

'You haven't got a finger free for another diamond,' Luke told his wife drily. 'How long do we have to stay at this party?'

'A couple of hours?' Tia gave him a pleading look of appeal.

'It'll be really boring,' Luke forecast moodily, his lower lip coming out in a petulant pout.

Beside her Navarre stiffened and Tia looked as though she might be about to burst into tears. Navarre asked Tia's husband about his upcoming European tour with his rock group, the moment of tension ebbed and shortly afterwards they arrived at the glitzy hotel where the party was being held. Tia was mobbed by paparazzi outside the hotel and lingered to give an impromptu interview to a TV presenter. Tawny was startled when Navarre stepped slightly behind her to pose for a photo, mentioning her name and their supposed engagement with the relaxed assurance of a man who might have known her for years rather than mere days. It occurred to her that he was quite an actor in his own right, able to conceal his essential indifference to her behind a convincing façade as though she were indeed precious to him. While he spoke the warmth of his tall, strong physique burned down her slender spine like a taunting lick of flame and the faint scent of some expensive cologne underscored by clean, husky masculinity filled her nostrils and suddenly her body was going haywire with awareness, breasts swelling, legs trembling as she remembered that earth-shattering kiss.

One freakin' kiss, Tawny thought with furious resentment, and she had fallen apart at the seams. He hadn't even made a pass at her. She had to be fair, he wasn't the pawing type, indeed he never laid a finger on her without good reason, but even so, when he got close, every skin cell in her body leapt and dived as if she were a dizzy teenager in the grip of her first crush.

'Are you always this tense?' Navarre enquired.

'Only around you,' she told him, knowing that there was more than one way to read that reply.

Trailing adoring hangers-on like a vibrant kite followed by fluttering ribbons, Tia surged up to them as soon as they entered the function room and complained that Luke had already taken off and abandoned her.

'He hates these things,' she complained ruefully as Navarre immediately took on the task of ushering her to her prominently placed table.

Tia was very much what Tawny would have expected of a beautiful international star. She had to have constant attention and wasn't too fussy about how she went about getting it. She was very familiar with Navarre, touching his arm continually as she talked, smiling sexily up at him, employing every weapon in the considerable armoury of her beauty to keep him by her side and hold his interest. A proper fiancée, Tawny reflected wryly, would have wanted to shoot Tia and bury her deep.

'You should tell him you don't like it,' Luke whispered mockingly in Tawny's ear, making her jump because she had not realised he had come to stand beside her.

'I've got no complaints. Your wife is the life and soul of the party,' Tawny answered lightly, as if she were quite unconcerned when in fact she had felt invisible in Tia's radius.

'No, she likes handsome men around her,' Luke Convery

contradicted, watching the Italian blonde hold court at her table surrounded by attentive males, his demeanour a resentful combination of admiration and annoyance. As if he was determined to defy that view he draped an arm round Tawny's taut shoulders and she stiffened in surprise.

Across the room, Navarre's glittering green gaze narrowed to rest on Tawny, watching her lift her face to look up into Luke Convery's eyes and suddenly laugh. They looked remarkably intimate, he noted in surprise. How had that happened between virtual strangers? Or was the luscious redhead a quick study when it came to impressing rich and famous men? Anger broke like a river bursting its banks through Navarre's usual rock-solid self-discipline and he vaulted upright to take immediate action.

'You should try staying by Tia's side,' Tawny was saying warily to Luke Convery.

'Been there, done that. It doesn't work but you might have more luck with that angle.' The musician shot her a challenging appraisal from brooding dark eyes. 'If you're engaged to the guy, why are you letting Tia take over?'

Reminded of her role, Tawny flushed and headed off to the cloakroom to escape the awkward exchange. How was she supposed to react when a household name with a face that could have given Helen of Troy a run for her money was flirting like mad with her supposed fiancé? When she returned to the party, she was taken aback to see Navarre poised near the doors, evidently awaiting her reappearance. When he saw her, he immediately frowned and jerked his arrogant head to urge her over to him.

'What have you been doing? Where have you been?' he demanded curtly.

Resenting his attitude, Tawny rolled her eyes. 'I was in the cloakroom, trying to discreetly avoid coming between you and the object of your affections.'

He followed her meaningful sidewise glance in the direction of Tia Castelli's table and his strong jawline clenched as though Tawny had insulted him. His eyes narrowed to rake over her with scorn. '*Drôle d'excuse…* what an excuse! Tia and I are old friends, nothing more. But I saw you giggling with Convery—'

'What do you mean by you "*saw*" me with Luke?' Tawny pressed hotly, hostile to both his intonation and his attitude. 'And I'm not the giggly type.'

Navarre flattened his wide sensual mouth into a forbidding line. 'We are supposed to be newly engaged. You are not here to amuse yourself. *Stay by my side.*'

'As long as you appreciate that I'm only doing it for the money,' Tawny shot back at him in an angry hiss, her face stiff with chagrin at his criticism of her behaviour.

'I'm unlikely to forget the fact that I'm paying for the pleasure of your company,' he retorted crushingly. 'That's a first for me!'

'You do surprise me.' Hot pink adorning her cheeks at that cutting retaliation, Tawny stuck to him like glue for the rest of the party. He circulated, one arm attached to Tawny as he made a point of introducing her as his future wife.

Tawny played up to the label, clinging to his arm, smiling up at him, laughing slavishly at the mildest joke or story and generally behaving as if he were the centre of her world. And for what he was paying for the show, she told herself ruefully, he deserved to be.

'Did you have to behave like a bimbo?' Navarre growled as she climbed back into the limousine at the end of the evening, shoulders drooping as exhaustion threatened to claim her.

'In this scenario it works. As you said yourself, if we seem unsuited, nobody will be surprised when the engagement only lasts for five minutes,' Tawny retorted, thoroughly irritated at receiving yet more vilification from his corner. Could she do nothing right in his eyes? What exactly did he want from her? 'Personally, I think I put in a pretty good performance.'

A silence that implied he had been less than impressed stretched between them all the way back to the hotel. In the lift he stabbed the button for a lower floor. 'Elise has offered to share her room with you tonight so that you don't have to use the sofa again,' he informed her glacially. 'I believe she already has had your belongings moved for your convenience.'

Relief filled Tawny as she stepped out of the lift and found the tall blonde bodyguard waiting to greet her. With Elise, she could take off her fancy glad rags, climb into her pjs and relax, which was exactly what she was most longing to do at that instant.

Navarre absorbed the alacrity of Tawny's departure from the lift, frowning at the strangely appealing sound of the giggling she had said she didn't do trilling down the corridor just before the lift doors closed again. He had never had a woman walk away from him before without a word or a glance and his eyes momentarily flashed as though someone had lit a fire behind them. He could not accuse Tawny Baxter of attempting to ensnare him, but he recalled the manner in which she had melted into that kiss and smiled, ego soothed. It was not a very nice smile.

CHAPTER FIVE

'OH...my...goodness!' Tawny squealed in Navarre's ear as she squashed her face up against the window of the helicopter to get a better view of the medieval fortress they were flying over, a sixteenth-century tower house complete with a Victorian gothic extension. It was late afternoon. 'It's a castle, a *real* castle! Are we really going to be staying there?'

'Oui,' Navarre confirmed drily.

'You are *so* spoilt!' Tawny exclaimed loudly, winning Jacques's startled scrutiny from the front seat as she turned briefly to shoot his employer a reproachful look. 'You're going to be staying in a genuine castle and you're not even excited! Not even a little bit excited?'

'You're excited enough for both of us,' Navarre countered. His attention was commanded against his will by the vibrant glow of her heart-shaped face and the anticipation writ large there, eyes starry, lush peachy mouth showing a glimpse of small white teeth. Adults rarely demonstrated that much enthusiasm for anything and, to a man who kept all emotion under strict lock and key, there was something ridiculously appealing about her complete lack of inhibition.

The helicopter, which had carried them north from their private flight to Edinburgh and lunch at a smart hotel there, landed in a paddock within full view of the castle. Navarre sprang out in advance of Tawny and then swung round to lift her out. 'I could've managed!' she told him pointedly, smoothing down her clothing as though he had rumpled her.

'Not without a step in that skirt,' Navarre traded with all the superiority of a male accustomed to disembarking from such craft with a woman in tow.

Tawny had slept like a log the night before in the room she had shared with Elise. Similar in age, the two young women had chattered over a late supper, exchanging innocuous facts about friends and families.

'The boss warned me that I had to be sure to feed you!' Elise had teased, watching, impressed, as Tawny demolished a plate of sandwiches.

Now she was in the Scottish Highlands for the weekend but Navarre had only divulged their destination after he had invited her to join him for breakfast in his suite that morning, when he had also filled her in on a few useful facts about their hosts.

Tawny was rather nervous at the prospect of meeting Sam and Catrina Coulter. Sam was the extremely wealthy owner of the Coulter Centax Corporation. Catrina, whom Navarre had admitted was an ex, was Sam's second, much younger wife and formerly a very successful English model. The couple had no children but Sam had had a son by his first marriage, who had died prematurely in an accident.

'So is this where Sam and Catrina live all the year round?' Tawny asked curiously as they walked towards the Range Rover awaiting them. 'It must be pretty desolate in winter.'

'They don't own Strathmore Castle, they're renting it

for the season,' Navarre told her wryly. 'Sam's very into shooting and fishing.'

Sam Coulter was in his sixties, a trim bespectacled man with grey hair and a keen gaze. Catrina, a beautiful brunette with big brown eyes and an aggressively bright smile, towered over her empire building husband, who made up for what he lacked in height with his large personality. Refreshments were served before the fire in the atmospheric Great Hall that had walls studded with a display of medieval weaponry, fabulous early oak furniture and a tartan carpet. Catrina made a big thing out of cooing over Tawny's engagement ring and tucked a friendly hand into the younger woman's arm to lead her upstairs, but there was neither true warmth nor sincerity in her manner. Only when Catrina left Navarre and Tawny in the same room did it occur to Tawny that they were expected to occupy the same bed.

'We're supposed to share?' she whispered within seconds of the door closing behind their hostess.

'What else would you expect?'

Unfortunately Tawny had not thought about the possibility. Now she scanned the room. There was no sofa, nothing other than the four-poster bed for the two of them to sleep on, and something akin to panic gripped her. 'You could say you snore and keep me awake *and*—'

'You're not that naive. We must share the bed. It is only for two nights,' Navarre drawled.

'I'm shy about sharing beds,' Tawny warned him.

Navarre studied her, intently. 'I'm *not*,' he told her without hesitation, flashing her a wickedly amused smile.

A painful flush lit Tawny's complexion. But the mesmerising charm of his smile at that instant knocked her sideways and her susceptible heart went boom-boom-

boom inside her ribcage. 'I really don't want to share a room with you.'

'You must have expected this set-up,' Navarre said very drily. 'Engaged couples rarely sleep in separate beds these days.'

It was a fair point and Tawny winced in acknowledgement. 'I didn't think about it.'

'We're stuck with the arrangement,' Navarre countered in a tone of finality. 'Or is this a ploy aimed at demanding more money from me? Is that what lies behind these antiquated protests?'

Tawny froze in astonishment, affronted by the suggestion. 'No, it darned well is not! How dare you suggest that? I just haven't shared a bed with a guy before—'

Navarre quirked a sardonic black brow. 'What? *Never?* I don't believe you.'

'Well, I don't care what you believe. You may sleep around but I never have!' Tawny slung back at him in furious self-defence.

'I didn't accuse you of sleeping around,' Navarre pointed out, his innate reserve and censure never more evident than in his hard gaze and the tough stubborn set of his strong jawline. 'Nor will I accept you throwing such impertinent remarks at me.'

'Point taken but I've always believed in calling a spade a spade and exclusive you're not!' Tawny responded, her temper still raw from the idea that he could think she was using the need to share a bed as an excuse to demand more money from him.

'Tonight we're sharing that bed, *ma petite.*' Navarre dealt her an intimidating appraisal, inviting her disagreement.

Tawny opened the case sited on the trunk at the foot of the bed to extract the outfit she had decided to wear for dinner. She loathed his conviction that she was unscrupulous and mercenary but she saw no point in getting into an argument with him. Navarre would probably fight tooth and claw to the death just to come out the winner. A row might be overheard and he would have reason to complain if anything happened to mar their pretence of being a happy couple.

'And by the way, I am exclusive with a woman for the duration of our time together.'

Bending over the case, Tawny reckoned that that would impose no great sacrifice on a man famous for never staying long with one woman and she murmured flatly, 'None of my business.'

Navarre breathed in slow and deep while on another level he drank in the intoxicating glimpses of slim, shapely thigh visible through the split in the back of her skirt. She straightened to shed her cardigan. Hunger uncoiled inside him. Every time she awakened his libido the effects got stronger, he acknowledged grimly, noting the way her bright rippling curls snaked down her slender spine, somehow drawing his attention to the fact that the top she wore was gossamer thin and revealed the pale delicate bra that encased her dainty breasts. *Merde alors,* he was behaving like a schoolboy salivating for his first glimpse of naked female flesh!

The chosen outfit draped over her arm, Tawny moved towards the wardrobe to hang the garment and as she did so she collided with Navarre's intent gaze. It was as if all the oxygen in her lungs were sucked out at once. Her heart went *thud* and she stilled in surprise as she recognised the sexual heat of that brutally masculine appraisal. 'Don't look at me like that,' she told him gruffly.

Navarre reached for her. 'I can't help it,' he purred.

'Yes, you can,' she countered shakily, longing with

every fibre of her rebellious being to be drawn closer to him while her brain screamed at her to slap him down and go into retreat. But there was something incredibly flattering about such a look of desire on a handsome man's face. Navarre had the ability to make her feel impossibly feminine and seductive, two qualities that she had never thought she possessed.

One hand resting on her hip, Navarre skimmed the knuckles of the other gently down the side of her face. 'You're beautiful, *ma petite*.'

Tawny had never seen herself as beautiful before and that single word had a hypnotic effect on her so that she looked up at him with shining ice-blue eyes. Teased for having red hair at school, she had grown into a sporty tomboy who lacked the curves required to attract the opposite sex. Boys had become her mates rather than her boyfriends, many of them using her as a step closer to her then best friend, a curvy little blonde. Curvy and blonde had become Tawny's yardstick of beauty and what Navarre Cazier could see in her was invisible to her own eyes.

Indecent warmth shimmied through Tawny from the caressing touch of his fingers and she wanted to lean into his hand, get closer on every level while that tightening sensation low in her body filled her with a sharp, deep craving. Struggling to control that dangerous sense of weakness, Tawny froze, torn between stepping closer and stepping back. While she was in the midst of that mental fight, Navarre bent his arrogant dark head and kissed her.

And it wasn't like that first teasing, tender kiss in London, it was a kiss full of an unashamed passion that shot through her bloodstream like an adrenalin rush. One kiss was nowhere near enough either. As his hungry, demanding mouth moved urgently on hers her fingers delved into his luxuriant black hair to hold him to her and she felt light-headed. His tongue delved and unleashed such acute hunger inside her that she gasped and instinctively pushed her taut, aching breasts into the inflexible wall of his broad chest. Gathering her closer, his hand splayed across her hips and she was instantly aware of the hard thrust of his erection. Her knees went weak as a dark tingling heat spread through her lower body in urgent response to his arousal.

He lifted her up and brought her down on the bed, still exchanging kiss for feverish kiss and suddenly she was on fire with longing, knowing exactly what she wanted and shocked by it. She wanted his weight on top of her to sate the ache at the core of her. She wanted to open her legs to cradle him but, ridiculously, her skirt was too tight.

In a sudden movement driven by that last idiotic thought, Tawny tore her lips from his. 'No, I don't want this!' she gasped, planting her hands on his wide shoulders to impose space between them.

Navarre immediately lifted back, face rigid with self-discipline. He vaulted back off the bed to stare down at her with scorching green eyes. 'Yes, you do want me as much as I want you. Together we're like a fire raging out of control and I don't know why you're imposing limits, unless it's because—'

'No, don't say it!' Tawny cut in, sitting up in a hurry and raking her tumbled hair off her brow with an impatient hand. 'Don't you dare say it!'

Navarre frowned in bewilderment. 'Say what?'

'Offer me more money to sleep with you...*don't you dare!*' she launched at him warningly.

Navarre elevated a sardonic black brow and stood straight and tall to gaze broodingly down at her. *'Mais c'est insensé*...that's crazy. I have not the slightest intention of offering you money for sex. I don't pay for it, never have, never will. Perhaps you're angling for me to make you that kind of an offer before you deliver between the sheets. But I'm afraid you've picked the wrong guy to work that ploy on.'

As that derisive little speech sank in Tawny went white with rage and sprang off the bed, the wild flare of her hot temper giving her a strong urge to slap him. But Navarre snapped hands like bands of steel round her wrists to hold her arms still by her side and prevent any other contact. *'No,'* he said succinctly. 'I won't tolerate that from any woman.'

High spots of colour bloomed in Tawny's cheeks as she jerked back from him, his icy intervention having doused her anger like a bucket of cold water. It didn't prevent her from still wanting to kill him though. 'I wasn't trying to put the idea in your head…OK? It's just I know what guys like you are like—'

'Like you know so many guys like me,' Navarre fielded witheringly.

'You're used to getting exactly what you want when you want and not taking no for an answer.'

'Not my problem,' Navarre countered glacially.

Tawny got changed in the bathroom. Her mouth was still swollen from his kisses, her body still all of a shiver and on edge from the sexual charge he put out. She mouthed a rude word at herself in the mirror, furious that she had lost control in his arms. She had genuinely feared that he might offer her money to include sex in their masquerade and she had tried to avert the risk of him uttering those fatal humiliating words, which would have reduced her to the level of a call girl. Unfortunately for her Navarre had actually suspected that she was sneakily making it clear to him that the offer of more money might make her amenable to sex.

Rage at that recollection threatening to engulf her in a rising red mist, Tawny anchored her towel tighter round her slim body and wrenched open the bathroom door in a sudden movement. 'I'm a virgin!' she launched across the room at him in stark condemnation. 'How many virgins do you know who sell themselves for money?'

I am not having this crazy argument, Navarre's clever brain told him soothingly as he cast down the remote control he had used to switch on the business news. She's a lunatic. I've hired a thief and a lunatic…

'I don't know any virgins,' Navarre told her truthfully. 'But that's probably because most of them keep quiet about their inexperience.'

'I don't see why I should keep quiet!' Tawny snapped, tilting her chin in challenge. 'You seem to be convinced that I would do anything for money…but I'm not like that.'

'We're not having this conversation,' Navarre informed her resolutely, stonily centring his attention back on the television screen.

But a flickering image of her entrancing slender profile in a towel with damp ringlets rioting round her small face still stayed inside his head. He didn't pay for sex. That was true. But there had definitely been a moment on that bed when, if he was equally honest, he would have given her just about anything to stay there warm and willing to fulfil his every fantasy. The ache of frustrated desire was with him still. Taking the moral high ground had never felt less satisfying. Even so his naturally suspicious mind kept on ticking. Why was she telling him that she was a virgin? Hadn't he read about some woman selling her virginity on the Internet to the highest bidder? Could Tawny believe that virgins had more sex appeal and value to the average male? Surely she didn't think that he would actually believe that a woman of twenty-three years of age was a total innocent? Did he look that naive and trusting?

Clad in a modestly styled green cocktail dress and impossibly high heels, Tawny descended the stairs by Navarre's side. They pretty much weren't speaking, which felt weird when he insisted on holding her hand. She was looking eagerly around her when Sam came to greet them, ushering them to the fire and the drinks waiting in the Great Hall. Having answered her questions about the old property, he offered them a tour.

The tower house was not as large as it had looked from the air and many of the rooms were rather pokey or awkwardly shaped. But Tawny adored the atmosphere created by the ancient stone walls and fireplaces and she looked at Catrina in surprise when she complained about the difficulty of heating the rooms and the remote location while her husband talked with single-minded enthusiasm about the outdoor pursuits available on the estate. The Victorian extension to the rear of the castle had been recently restored and contained a fabulous ballroom used for parties, modern utilities and staff quarters.

'You haven't been with Navarre long, have you?' Catrina remarked while the men were talking business over by the tall windows. The sun was going down for the day over the views of rolling heathland banded by distant mountains that had a purple hue in the fast-fading light.

Tawny smiled. 'I suppose it shows.'

Catrina sat down beside her. 'It does rather. He's obsessed with his work.'

'Successful men tend to be,' Tawny answered lightly, recalling that her half-sisters often complained about how preoccupied their husbands were with their business interests.

'Navarre will always be more excited about his latest deal than about you,' Catrina opined cattily.

'Oh, I don't think so.' Quite deliberately, Tawny flexed the fingers of the hand that bore the opulent diamond ring and glanced across the room at Navarre, admiring that bold bronzed masculine profile silhouetted against the window. As she turned back to Catrina she caught the other woman treating Navarre to a voracious look of longing. Navarre, she registered belatedly, had lit a fire in the other woman that even her marriage had yet to put out.

'Navarre won't change,' the beautiful brunette forecast thinly. 'He gets bored very easily. No woman ever lasts more than a few weeks in his bed.'

Tawny dealt her companion a calm appraisal. 'I don't begrudge Navarre his years of freedom. Most men eventually settle down with one woman just as he has,' she murmured sweetly. 'What we have together is special.'

'In what way?' Catrina enquired baldly and then she laughed and raised her voice, 'Navarre…what do you find most special about Tawny?'

Sam Coulter frowned, not best pleased to have his discussion interrupted by his wife's facetious question.

'Tawny's joie de vivre is without compare, and her face?' Navarre moved his shapely hands with an elegant eloquence that was unmistakeably French. 'Ca suffit… enough said. How can one quantify such an elusive quality?'

Unexpectedly, Sam gave his wife a fond smile that softened his craggy features. 'I couldn't have said it better myself. The secret of attraction is that it's impossible to put into words.'

Tawny was hardened to her hostess's little gibes by the end of the evening and grateful that other people would be joining them the following day. Catrina might have been married to Sam Coulter for two years but the brunette was very dissatisfied with her life.

Clad in a silk nightdress rather than her usual pjs, for she was making an effort to stay in her role, Tawny climbed into the wide four-poster bed. 'I used to dream of having a bed like this when I was a child,' she said to combat her discomfiture at Navarre's emergence from the bathroom, his tall, well-built physique bare but for a pair of trendy cotton pyjama bottoms.

He looked absolutely spectacular with his black hair spiky with dampness and a faint shadow of stubble highlighting his carved cheekbones and wide, mobile mouth. He also had an amazing set of pecs and obviously worked out regularly. Her attention skimmed over the cluster of dark curls on his torso and the arrowing line of hair bisecting the flat corrugated muscle of his stomach to disappear below his waistband, and her tummy flipped.

'Full marks for all the questions you asked Sam about the history of Strathmore,' Navarre remarked with stunning cynicism. 'He was charmed by your interest.'

Tawny stiffened. 'I wasn't putting on an act. History was my favourite subject next to art and I've always been fascinated by old buildings. Are you always this distrustful of women?'

Brilliant eyes veiled, Navarre shrugged and got into the other side of the bed. 'Let's say that experience has made me wary.'

'Catrina's still keen on you, isn't she? Is that why you wanted a fake fiancée to bring with you?' she asked abruptly.

'One of the reasons,' Navarre conceded evenly. 'And your presence does at least preclude her from making indiscreet remarks.'

Tawny was suffering from an indisputable need to keep on talking to lessen her discomfiture. 'I have to make a phone call some time tomorrow—'

'No,' Navarre responded immediately.

'I'll go behind your back to make the call if you try to prevent me. It's to my grandmother. I always ring her on Saturdays and she'll worry if she doesn't hear from me,' Tawny told him with spirit. 'You can listen to our conversation if you like.'

Navarre punched a pillow and rested his dark head down. 'I'll consider it.'

Tawny flipped round and leant over him. 'See that you do,' she warned combatively.

Navarre reached out and entwined his long brown fingers into the curling spirals of red hair that were brushing his chest. For a timeless moment his eyes held her as fast as manacles. 'Don't tease—'

Her bosom swelled as her temper surged over the rebuke. 'I *wasn't* teasing!'

'You mean that you didn't tell me you were a virgin to whet my appetite for you?' Navarre derided.

'No, I darned well didn't!' Tawny snapped furiously. 'I only told you in the first place because I thought it would make you understand why I was offended by your assumption that my body has a price tag attached to it!'

Navarre was engaged in studying the pulse flickering at the base of the slim column of her throat and the sweet swelling mounds of her breasts visible through the gaping neckline of the nightdress as she bent over him. Hard as a rock, he was still trying to work out what the price tag might encompass so that he could meet the terms and get much better acquainted with that truly exquisite little body of hers.

'I also thought that my inexperience would be more

likely to put you off,' Tawny admitted, her voice trailing away breathily as she connected with his eyes. 'Let go of my hair, Navarre...'

'Non, ma petite. I'm enjoying the view too much.'

Only then did Tawny register where his attention was resting and, hot with embarrassment, she lifted the hand she had braced on the pillow by his head to press the neckline of her nightdress flat against her chest.

Navarre laughed with rich appreciation. 'Spoilsport!'

Off-balanced by the rapidity of her own movement, Tawny struggled to pull back from him but he tipped her down instead and encircled her mouth with his own, claiming her full lips with a harsh masculine groan of satisfaction. That sensual mouth on hers was an unimaginable pleasure and it awakened a hunger she could not control. Without her quite knowing how it had happened, she found herself lying back against the pillows with a long masculine thigh pinning her in place. Her hands smoothed over his wide brown shoulders, revelling in the muscles flexing taut below his skin. His fingers flexed over the swell of her breast and her spine arched as his thumb rubbed over the straining nipple. Her response was so powerful that it scared her and she jerked away from him.

'This is not happening!' she gasped in consternation. 'We can't—'

'What do I have to do to make it happen?' Navarre asked huskily.

Tawny tensed and then rolled back, ice blue eyes shooting uncertainly to his face. 'What's that supposed to mean?'

Navarre shifted against her hip, making no attempt to conceal the extent of his arousal. 'Whatever it needs to mean to bring about the desired result, *ma petite.* I want you.'

Tawny flushed and imposed space between them. 'Let's forget about this and go to sleep. I'm working for you. And this situation is exactly why working for you should not include the two of us sharing a bed half naked.'

Navarre toyed with the idea of offering her all the diamonds. Just at that moment no price seemed too high. But that would be treating her like a hooker ready to trade sex for profit. She had got her feelings on that message home, he conceded in growling frustration. He scanned her taut little face and then noticed that she was trembling: there was an almost imperceptible shake in her slight body as she lay there. He compressed his stubborn mouth, rolled back to his own side of the bed and switched out the light. She played hot and then cold but he was beginning to consider the idea that it might not be a deliberate policy to fan his desire to even greater heights. What if she really was a virgin? *As if...*

In the darkness tears inched a slow stinging trail down Tawny's cheeks. She felt out of control and out of her depth and she hated it. She had never understood why people made such a fuss about sex until Navarre had kissed her and if he had tried he probably could have taken her to bed right there and then. Unhappily for him he had missed the boat when she was at her most vulnerable and now she knew that Navarre Cazier somehow had that magical something that reduced her usual defences to rubble. Her breasts ached, the area between her legs seemed to ache as well and even blinking back tears she was within an ace of turning back to him and just surrendering to the powerful forces tormenting her body. Stupid hormones, that was what the problem was!

Tawny was still a virgin purely because the right man

had failed to come along. She had never had a serious relationship, had never known the wild highs and lows of emotional attachment aside of an unrequited crush in her schooldays. She had had several boyfriends at college. There had been loads of kisses and laughs and fun outings but nobody who had made her heart stop with a smile or a kiss. She tensed as Navarre thrust back the sheet with a stifled curse and headed into the bathroom. She listened to the shower running and felt guilty, knowing she had responded, knowing she had encouraged him, but finally deciding that he was not suffering any more from the anticlimax of their lovemaking than she was herself. Restraint physically *hurt*.

Early the following morning she wakened and opened her eyes in the dim room to centre them on Navarre. He was poised at the foot of the bed looking gorgeous and incredibly masculine in shooting clothes that fitted his tall, broad-shouldered and lean-hipped physique so well they were probably tailor made. 'What time is it?' she whispered sleepily.

'Go back to sleep—unless you've changed your mind and decided to come shooting?' As Tawny grimaced at the prospect he laughed softly. *'Peut-être pas*...perhaps not. What was that about you not wanting to kill little fluffy birds, *ma petite*?'

'Not my thing,' she agreed, recalling Sam Coulter's dismay at grouse being given such an emotive description.

'Are you joining us for the shooting lunch?'

'I have no idea. I'll be at Catrina's disposal. She mentioned something about a local spa,' Tawny told him ruefully.

'You'll enjoy that.'

'I hate all that grooming stuff. It's so boring. If I was

here on my own I'd be out horse riding or hiking, doing something active—'

'You can ride?' Navarre made no attempt to hide his surprise.

Watching him intently, Tawny nodded. She decided it was that fabulous bone structure that moved him beyond handsome to stunning. 'My grandparents used to live next door to a riding school and I spent several summers working as a groom.'

Navarre sank down on her side of the bed, stretching out long powerful legs. 'You can phone your grandmother this evening before the party.'

'Thank you.' Her soft pink mouth folded into a blinding smile and he gazed down at her animated face in brooding silence.

Navarre ran a forefinger across the back of the pale hand lying on top of the sheet. 'I've been thinking. I may be willing to extend our association.'

Her brow furrowed. 'Meaning?'

'When our business arrangement is complete I may still want to see you.'

His expression told her nothing and she suppressed the leap of hope inside her that told her more than she wanted to know about her own feelings. 'There's no future in us seeing each other,' she replied flatly.

'When I find it a challenge to stay away from a woman, there is definitely a future, *ma petite*.'

'But that future doesn't extend further than the nearest bed.'

'Don't all affairs begin the same way?' Navarre traded.

And he was *so* right that once again she was tempted to slap him. She didn't want to want him the way she did because such treacherous feelings offended her pride and her intelligence. Yet here she was already imagining how she might lie back in readiness as he pushed aside the sheet and shed his clothes to join her in the bed. Her mind was out of her control. Desire was like a scream buried deep inside her, longing and frantically searching for an escape. Her brain might want to wonder where the relationship could possibly go after fulfillment, but her body cared only that the fulfilment took place.

'Tonight, *ma petite*…I would like to make you mine and you will have no regrets,' Navarre purred, stroking his fingertips delicately along the taut line of her full lower lip, sending wicked little markers of heat travelling to every secret part of her as she thought helplessly of that mouth on hers, those sure, skilled hands, that strong, hard body. She couldn't breathe for excitement.

The shooting lunch was delivered to the men on the moors while those women who had no taste for the sport joined Catrina and Tawny for a more civilised repast at the castle. During that meal, liberally accompanied by fine wine, celebrity and designer names were dropped repeatedly as well as descriptions of fabulous gifts, insanely expensive shopping trips and impossibly luxurious holidays with each woman clearly determined to outdo the next. It was all highly competitive stuff and Tawny hated it, finding the trip to the spa something of a relief, for at least everyone was in separate cubicles and she no longer had to try to fit in by putting on an act.

'You and Navarre won't last,' Catrina informed Tawny confidently as they were driven back to Strathmore.

'Why do you think that?'

'Navarre will get bored and move on, just as he did with me,' Catrina warned. 'I was once in love with him too. I've seen your eyes follow him round the room. When he ditches you, I warn you…it'll hurt like hell.'

'He's not going to ditch me,' Tawny declared between

clenched teeth, wondering if her eyes did follow Navarre round the room. It was an image that mortified her. It was also unnerving that she could be unconscious of her own behaviour around him.

When she entered the bedroom it was a shock to glance through the open bathroom door and see Navarre already standing there naked as he towelled his hair dry. Her face burning, she averted her eyes from that thought-provoking view and went over to the wardrobe to extract the evening dress she planned to wear—a shimmering gold gown that complimented her auburn hair and fair complexion. Her palms were damp. He was gorgeous, stripped he was even more gorgeous. *Tonight...I would like to make you mine.* She shivered at the memory of the words that had burned at the back of her mind throughout the day, full of seductive promise and threatening her self-discipline. For never before had Tawny wanted a man as she wanted Navarre Cazier—with a deep visceral need as primitive as it was fierce.

The towel looped round his narrow hips Navarre strolled out and tossed her mobile phone down on the bed. 'Ring your grandmother,' he told her.

She switched on her phone but there was no reception and after a fruitless moment or two of pacing in an attempt to pick up a signal at the window, Navarre handed her his phone. 'Use mine.'

Celestine answered the call immediately. 'I tried to ring you yesterday but I couldn't get through. I thought you might be too busy to ring, *ma chérie*. And on a Friday evening that would be good news,' the old lady told her chirpily. 'It would mean you had a date which would please me enormously.'

'I am going to a party tonight,' Tawny told her, knowing how much her grandmother would enjoy that news. 'Why were you trying to ring me?'

'A friend of yours called me, said she was trying desperately to get in touch but that you weren't answering your phone. It was that work friend of yours, Julie.'

'Oh…forget about it, it wouldn't have been important.' Tawny felt her skin turn clammy as she wondered what Julie was after now. How dared she disturb her grandmother's peace by phoning her? And where on earth had she got Celestine's number from? It could only have been from Tawny's personnel file, which also meant that Julie had used her computer skills to go snooping again. Had her calculating former friend hoped that the old lady might have information about where Tawny and Navarre had gone after leaving the hotel?

'What are you wearing to the party?' Celestine asked, eager for a description.

And Tawny really pushed the boat out with the details, for the old lady adored finery. Indeed Tawny would have loved to tell Celestine about the Golden Movie Awards and Tia Castelli and her husband, not to mention the castle she was currently staying in, but she did not dare to breathe a word of what Navarre probably considered to be confidential information. Instead she caught up with her grandmother's small daily doings and she slowly began to relax in the reassuring warmth of the old lady's chatter. Unlike her daughter, Susan, Celestine was a very happy personality, who always looked on the bright side of life.

'You seem very close to your grandmother,' Navarre commented as Tawny returned his phone to him.

'She's a darling,' Tawny said fondly, gathering up stuff to take into the en suite with her, mindful of the fact she had been accused of being a tease and determined not to give him further cause to believe that she was actively encouraging his interest.

'What about your mother?'

Tawny paused with her back still turned to him and tried not to wince. 'Relations are a little cool between us at present,' she admitted, opting for honesty.

Mother and daughter were still speaking but things had been said during that last confrontation that would probably never be forgotten, Tawny reflected painfully. Tawny could not forget being told what a drastic disappointment she was to her mother. But then mother and child had always rubbed each other up the wrong way. Tawny had refused to dye her red hair brown when her mother suggested it and had sulked when a padded bra was helpfully presented to her. She had done well in the wrong subjects at school. She had declined to train for a business career and as a result had failed to attain the salary or status that her mother equated with success. And finally and unforgivably on Susan's terms, Tawny had failed to make the most of her entrée into her half-sisters' wealthy world where with some effort she might have met the sort of man her mother would have viewed as an eligible partner. Her recent work as a chambermaid had been the proverbial last straw in her dissatisfied mother's eyes. No, Tawny would never be a daughter whom Susan felt she could boast about with her cronies.

Supressing those unhappy memories of her continuing inability to measure up to parental expectations, Tawny set about doing her make-up. She had watched the make-up artist who had done her face for the Golden Awards carefully and she used eyeliner and gold sparkly shadow with a heavier hand than usual, outlining her lips with a rich strawberry-coloured gloss. The dress had an inner corset for shape and support and she had to breathe in hard and swivel it round to put it on without help. Toting her cosmetic bag, she emerged from the bathroom.

Navarre fell still to look at her and it was one of those very rare occasions when he spoke without forethought. 'Your skin and hair look amazing in that colour.'

'Thank you.' Suddenly shy of him but with a warm feeling coiled up inside her, Tawny turned to the dressing table to put on the diamond earrings and bracelet. Even while she did so she searched out his reflection in the mirror, savouring the sight of him in a contemporary charcoal-grey designer suit. So tall, dark and sophisticated, so wonderfully handsome, Navarre Cazier was the ultimate fantasy male…at that point her thoughts screeched to a sudden stricken halt.

Why was she thinking of him like that? It was past time that she reminded herself that absolutely everything, from the fancy clothes she wore to her supposed relationship with Navarre Cazier, was a giant sham. She felt her upbeat spirits dive bomb. After all, she was not living the fairy tale in a romantic castle with a rich handsome man, she was *faking* it every step of the way. It was a timely recollection.

CHAPTER SIX

Towards midnight, Navarre strode into the ballroom, his keen gaze skimming through the knots of guests until it came to rest on Tawny.

In the subdued light Tawny shimmered like a golden goddess, red hair vibrant, diamonds sparkling, her lovely face full of animation as she looked up at the tall blond man talking to her with a hand clamped to her waist. Navarre recognised her companion immediately: Tor Henson, a wealthy banker very popular with women. Although Navarre had been absent for most of the evening while he talked business with Sam Coulter and had left Tawny very much to her own devices, he was not pleased to see her looking so well entertained. She had not gone without amusement; she had, it seemed, simply *replaced* him. A rare burst of anger ripped through Navarre's big frame, cutting through his powerful self-discipline with disorientating speed and efficiency. His strong white teeth ground together as he crossed the floor to join them.

'*Je suis désolé...*' Navarre began to apologise to Tawny for his prolonged absence.

At the sound of his voice, Tawny whirled round, her expression telegraphing equal amounts of relief and annoyance. 'Where have you been all this time?'

'I gather you don't read the business papers,' Tor Henson

remarked with a knowing glance in Navarre's direction for recent revealing movements on the stock market had hinted that major change could be in store for Sam Coulter's business empire.

Navarre captured a slender white hand in his and held it fast. He wanted to haul her away from Henson and take her upstairs to spread her across their bed, a primal prompting that he dimly understood was born of a rage unlike anything he had ever experienced. 'Thank you for looking after her for me, Tor,' he murmured with glacial courtesy.

'I'm not a child you left behind in need of care and protection!' Tawny objected, ice-blue eyes stormy as he ignored the comment and virtually dragged her onto the dance floor with him. 'Why are you behaving like this, Navarre? Why are you acting like I've done something wrong?'

'Haven't you? If I leave you alone for five minutes I come back to find you flirting with another man!' he censured with icy derision, splaying long sure fingers to her spine to draw her closer to his hard, powerful body than she wanted to be at that moment.

The scent of him, clean, warm and male, was in her nostrils and she fought the aphrodisiac effect that proximity awakened in her treacherous body. 'You left me alone for *two hours*!'

'Was it too much for me to expect you to be waiting quietly where I left you?' Navarre prompted shortly, in no mood to be reasonable.

'Yes, I'm not an umbrella you overlooked and I *wasn't* flirting with Tor! We were simply talking. He knows I'm engaged,' Tawny snapped up at him, tempestuous in her own self-defence.

'Tor would get a kick out of bedding another man's fiancée, *n'est-ce pas?*'

She saw the genuine anger in his gaze and the hard-edged tension in his superb bone structure. 'You're jealous,' she registered in wide-eyed surprise, astonished that she could have that much power over him.

His beautiful mouth took on a contemptuous curve. 'Of course I'm not jealous. Why would I be jealous? We're not really engaged,' he reminded her very drily.

But Tawny was not so easily deflected from an opinion once she had formed it. 'Maybe you're naturally the possessive type in relationships… You definitely didn't like seeing me enjoy myself in another man's company. But have you any idea how insulting it is for you to insinuate that I might go off and shag some guy I hardly know?'

'I'd have bedded you within five minutes of meeting you, *ma petite,*' Navarre confided with a roughened edge to his voice, holding her so close to his body that she could feel the effect her closeness was having on him and warmth pooled in the pit of her tummy in response to his urgent male sexuality.

'I'm not like you—I would never have agreed to that!' Tawny proclaimed heatedly, stretching up on tiptoe to deliver that news as close to his ear as she could reach.

'*Mais non…*I can be very persuasive.' Navarre laced long deft fingers into her tumbling curls to hold her steady while he bent his mouth to hers, his breath fanning her cheek. He was no fan of public displays but in that instant he was controlled by a driving atavistic need to mark her as his so that no other man would dare to approach her again. He crushed her succulent lips apart and tasted her with uninhibited hunger, not once but over and over again until she shuddered against him, her slight body vibrating like a tuning fork in response to his passion.

With reluctance, Navarre dragged his mouth from hers, scanned her rapt face and urged her towards the exit. 'Let's go.'

Go where? she almost asked, even though she knew where. She could not find the breath or the will to argue. After all, she *wanted* to be alone with him. She wanted him to kiss her again, she had never wanted anything more, and where once the presence of others might have acted as a welcome control exercise, this time around it was an annoyance. Objections lay low in the back of her mind, crushed out of existence by the fierce longing rippling through her in seductive waves.

'This has to be a beginning, not an end,' Navarre declared, thrusting shut the door of the bedroom.

Tawny didn't want him to talk, she only wanted him to kiss her. As long as he was kissing her she didn't have to think and wonder about whether or not she was making a mistake. Even worse, the wanting was so visceral that she could not stand against the force of it.

He unzipped her gown, ran his fingers smoothly down her slender spine and flipped loose her bra. She shivered, electrified with anticipation, knees turning to water as his hands rose to cup the swelling mounds of her breasts and massage the achingly sensitive nipples. He touched her exactly as she wanted to be touched. She had never dreamt that desire might leave her so weak that it was a challenge to stay upright, but now as she leant back against him and struggled simply to get oxygen into her lungs she was learning the lesson. She turned round in the circle of his arms and kissed him, hands closing into his jacket and pushing it off his broad shoulders. For an instant he stepped back, shedding the jacket, freeing his shirt from his waistband to unbutton it.

Just looking at him made her mouth run dry. A muscular bronzed section of hair-roughened torso was visible between the parted edges of his shirt and she wanted to touch, explore, *taste*...it was as though he had got under her skin and changed her from inside out, teaching her to crave what she had never even thought of before. Now she didn't just think, she acted. She raised her hands to that hard flat abdomen and let her palms glide up over the corrugated muscles to discover the warm skin and revel shamelessly in the way that her touch made him tense and roughly snatch his breath in.

Navarre lifted her free of her gown and she stood there, feeling alarmingly naked in only her high heels and a flimsy pair of white silk knickers. He sank down on the side of the bed and drew her down between his spread thighs, nibbling sensuously at her swollen lower lip while he eased his hand beneath the silk and rubbed the most sensitive spot of all with a skill and rhythm that provoked a series of gasps from her throat.

'I want you naked, *ma petite*...' he breathed thickly as he slid down her knickers and removed them, flipping off her shoes with the careless casual skill of a man practised at undressing women. 'And then I want you every way I can have you.'

Navarre bent her back over his arm and brought his mouth down hungrily on the proud pouting tip of an engorged nipple, drawing on the sensitised bud while his hand continued to explore the most sensitive part of her. Her fingers dug into his black cropped hair as he caressed her, a sharp arrow of need slivering through her. 'You're wearing too many clothes,' she told him shakily.

He settled her down on the bed and stood over her stripping. The shirt and the trousers were followed by his boxers. She had never seen a man naked and aroused before and she couldn't take her eyes off the long thick steel of his bold length. She was both intimidated and aroused by the size of him. Her face hot with self-consciousness, she scrabbled below the covers, her entire body tingling with extra-sensory awareness. He tossed foil-wrapped condoms down on top of the bedside cabinet and slid in beside her, so hot and hard and strong that he sent a wave of energising desire through her the instant she came into contact with his very male physique.

He detached the diamond earrings still dangling from her ears and set them aside, brilliant green eyes locked to her anxious face. 'What's wrong?'

As he leant down to her she closed her arms round his neck and kissed him, needing the oblivion of passion to feel secure, trembling as the hot hardness of his muscular body connected with hers. He lowered his tousled dark head and kissed her breasts, teasing her straining nipples with his tongue and pulling on the oversensitive buds until her hips squirmed in frustration on the mattress. Only then did he touch her where she most needed to be touched. He explored the silken warmth between her thighs with deft fingers and then he subjected that tender flesh to his mouth. She was unprepared for that ultimate intimacy and she jerked away in shock and tried to withdraw from it, but he closed his hands on her hips and held her fast until sensation spread like wildfire at the heart of her and entrapped her as surely as a prison cell. She wanted more of that wild, intoxicating feeling, she couldn't help wanting *more;* she was a slave to sensation. The hunger rose like a great white roar inside her, bypassing her every attempt to control it. Her body was shaking and the constricted knot at her core was notching tighter and tighter until the pleasure just rose in a huge overwhelming tide and engulfed her, leaving her shuddering and crying out in reaction.

'Navarre...' she whispered jaggedly.

'You liked that, *ma petite,*' he husked with all the satisfaction of a man who knew he had given a woman unimaginable pleasure.

Numbly she nodded, every reaction slowed down. It had never occurred to her that her body could feel anything that intensely and in the stunned aftermath of that climax she was only dimly aware that he was reaching for a condom, and then he was reaching for her again. Her body was pliant with obedience, already trained to expect pleasure from him, and as he pushed back her thighs and rose over her she quivered with the awareness of him hard and bold and alien at her tiny entrance, but there was a sense of trust as well.

'You're so tight,' he groaned with pleasure as he sank into her tender channel with controlled care.

A startled sound somewhere between a gasp and a cry was wrenched from her as he broke through the fragile barrier of her inexperience. Her body flinched and he stilled in the act of possession, staring down at her with scorching green eyes fringed by black, recognising in that heightened instant of awareness that he was the only lover she had ever had. 'You were telling me the truth...'

'Women aren't all liars,' Tawny breathed, shuddering as he drove all the way home to the heart of her body.

Immersed in the molten heat of her, Navarre was fighting for control, leaning down to crush her mouth under his again and breathe in the luscious scent of her skin. She felt so good, she smelt even better. He shifted his lean hips and thrust, wanting to take it slow and easy but struggling against his explosive level of arousal with every second that passed. Tawny arched up into him with a whimper of encouragement and he sank deeper, harder and suddenly he couldn't hold back any more against the elemental storm of need riding him. Holding her firmly, he eased back until he had almost withdrawn and then he thrust back into her with seductive force. The pleasure was building inside Tawny again in a wild surge of sensation that scooped her up and left her defenceless. His provocative rhythm heightened every feeling to an unbearable level and then all of a sudden it was as if a blinding white light exploded inside her, heat and hunger coalescing in a fierce fiery orgasm.

In the heady, dizzy aftermath she thought she might never move again, for her limbs felt weighted to the bed. She was incredibly grateful that she had chosen him as her lover, for he had made it extraordinary and she knew that was rare for a first experience. She hugged him tight, pressed her lips to a smooth brown shoulder, able to reason in only the most simplistic of ways, her brain on shutdown. He rolled back from her and headed for the bathroom.

It crossed her mind that barely a week earlier he had been a billionaire businessman and hotel guest to her. Now what was he? A very desirable lover who could also be absolutely infuriating and the guy who was *paying* her to fake being his fiancée. As cruel reality kicked in Tawny flinched from it, alarmed that she could have forgotten the financial nature of their agreement. It was a complication, but not one that couldn't be handled with the right attitude on both sides, she reasoned frantically, determined to stay optimistic rather than lash herself with pointless regrets. What was done was done. He was her lover now.

Navarre reappeared from the bathroom and strolled back to the bed. She had fallen sound asleep, a tangle of rich red curls lying partially across her perfect profile, a hand tucked childishly below her cheek. That fast he wanted her again and the strength of that desire disturbed him. Desire was wonderful as long as it stayed within certain acceptable bounds. Uninhibited hunger that threatened his control was not his style at all, for it was more likely to add complications to a life he preferred to keep smooth and untrammelled, a soothing contrast to his troubled and changeable childhood years. At heart he would always be an unrepentant loner and he thought it unlikely that he would change, for everything from his birth to his challenging adolescence had conspired to make him what he was. He had seduced her, though, he knew he had, and taking her virginity had roused the strangest protective instinct inside him. Even so he was equally aware that he could not afford to forget that she was a thief whose loyalty was for sale to the highest bidder...

Tawny wakened while it was still dark, immediately conscious of the new tenderness between her thighs and the ache of unfamiliar muscles. Instantly memory flooded back and she slid quiet as a wraith from the bed, padding across the carpet to the bathroom. Although it was almost four in the morning she ran a warm bath and settled into the soothing water to hug her knees and regroup. She had slept with Navarre Cazier and it had been amazing.

She didn't want to get all introspective and female about what had happened between them, for common sense told her that such powerful physical attraction as theirs generally only led to one conclusion. She especially didn't want to think about the feelings he was beginning to awaken inside her: the stab of intense satisfaction she had felt once she had registered that he was jealous of that banker's interest in her, the sense of achievement when he listened to her and laughed, the walking-on-air sensation when he admired her appearance, her unreserved delight in discovering that unashamed passion of his, which was so at variance with his cool, unemotional façade.

She knew without being told that she was walking a dangerous line. She had abandoned her defences and taken the kind of risk she had never taken before. Yet wouldn't she do it again given the chance to feel what he had made her feel? It wasn't just physical either. It was more that astonishing sense of feeling insanely alive for the first time ever, that wondrous sense of connection to another human being. Still lost in her thoughts, Tawny patted herself dry with a fleecy towel. She decided that she wasn't going to act the coward and bail on the experience just because it was unlikely to give her a happy ending. She was only twenty-three years old, she reminded herself doggedly, way too young to be worrying about needing a happy ending with a man. She tiptoed back to bed, eased below the cool sheets, and when a long masculine arm stretched out as though to retrieve her and tugged her close she went willingly into that embrace.

She loved the scent of his skin, clean and male laced with an evocative hint of designer cologne. She breathed in that already familiar scent as though it were an addictive drug, her fingers fanning out across his flat stomach as she shifted position. She adored being so close to him because she was very much aware that when he was awake he was not a physically or verbally demonstrative man likely to make her feel secure with displays of affection or appreciation. Her hand smoothed possessively down a hair-roughened thigh and he released a drowsy groan of approval.

In the darkness a cheeky smile curved her generous mouth when she discovered that even asleep he was aroused and ready for action. Wide awake now and unashamedly keen to experiment she became a little more daring and her fingertips carefully traced the steely length of his shaft. With a muffled sound of appreciation Navarre

shifted position and began to carry out his own reconnais-
sance. She was stunned by how fast her body reacted to
his sleepy caresses with her nipples stiffening into instant
tingling life while heat and moisture surged between her
legs. Muttering a driven French imprecation, he pinned
her beneath him, his hands suddenly hard with urgency as
he pushed between her slender thighs and drove hungrily
into her yielding body again. Instinctively she arched up
to him to ease the angle of his entrance and he ground his
body deeper into hers with a guttural sound of pleasure.
He moved slowly and provocatively in a strong sensual
rhythm. Her lips parted as she breathed in urgent gasps,
clinging to his broad shoulders as the glorious pressure
began to build and build within her. She came apart in an
explosive climax as his magnificent body shuddered to
the same crest with her. A glorious tide of exquisite sensation cascaded through her spent body.

In an abrupt movement, Navarre freed himself of her
hands and rolled away from her to switch on the lights.
Blinded by the sudden illumination, Tawny blinked in
bewilderment.

'Merde alors! Was this a planned seduction?' Navarre
flung at her furiously, a powerfully intimidating figure
against the pale bedding as she peered at him from narrowed eyes. 'To be followed by a meticulously planned
conception?'

Utterly bemused by that accusation, Tawny pushed herself up against the tumbled pillows with frantic hands. 'What
on earth are you talking about? Seduction, for heaven's
sake?'

'We just had sex without a condom!' Navarre fired at
her in condemnation.

'Oh…my…goodness,' Tawny framed in sudden comprehension, her skin turning clammy in shock. 'I didn't think of that—'

'Didn't you? You woke me out of a sound sleep to make love to you. A lot of men would overlook precautions in the excitement of the moment!'

'You can't seriously think I deliberately tempted you into sex while you were half asleep in the hope that you would forget to use a condom?' Tawny told him roundly, colour burnishing her cheeks.

'Why wouldn't I think that? I once caught a woman in the act of puncturing a condom in the hope of conceiving a child without my knowledge!' Navarre ground out in contemptuous rebuttal. 'Why should you be any different? Wealthy men are always targets for a fertile woman. When a man fathers a child by a woman he's bound to support her and her offspring for a couple of decades!'

'I feel sorry for you,' Tawny breathed tightly, her small face stony with self-control. 'It must be crippling to be as suspicious of other human beings as you are. Everybody is not out to con you or make money out of you, Navarre!'

'I've already caught you thieving from me,' Navarre reminded her icily. 'So forgive me for not being impressed by your claim to be morally superior.'

In the wake of that exchange, Tawny had lost every scrap of her natural colour. She had not required that final lowering reminder of how she had attempted to make off with his laptop. Lying there naked with her body still damp and aching from his lovemaking, she felt like the worst kind of whore. He had to despise her to be so suspicious of her motives that even an act of lovemaking could be regarded as a potential attempt to rip him off. It was a brutal wake-up call to the reality that, while she had moved on from the humiliation of their first meeting, his opinion of her was still that of a calculating little thief without morals. Sleeping with her had not changed his outlook and what a fool she had been to believe otherwise. Had he really caught a woman damaging contraception in the hope of falling pregnant by him? She was appalled. No wonder he was such a cynic if that was the sort of woman he was accustomed to having in his bed.

'We'll discuss this tomorrow,' Navarre breathed curtly as he doused the lights again.

'Let's not,' she said woodenly, turning on her side so that her back was turned to him. 'My system's very irregular—I'm pretty sure we won't have anything to worry about.'

But in spite of that breezy assurance she was still lying wide awake and worrying long after the deep even sound of his breathing had alerted her to the fact that he had gone back to sleep. Why, oh, why had she chosen to overlook the fact that he was paying her thousands of pounds to pretend to be his fiancée? Money problems always changed the nature of relationships, she thought wretchedly. The cash angle had put a wall between them. It was the single biggest difference between them, that reminder that he was rich and she was poor, never mind the truth that he had found her apparently stealing from him. Why had she believed that she could handle sex in such an unequal relationship? He had just proven how wrong that conviction could be.

By the time that dawn was lightening the darkness behind the curtains, Tawny had had enough of lying in the bed as still as a corpse. She got up again as quietly as she could and decided that she could go out for a walk without disturbing the entire household. The only clothes of her own that she had packed were her skinny jeans and skeleton tee. She put them on, teaming them with a woollen jacket with a velvet collar and a pair of laced boots. She crept out of the room and downstairs and was soon out in the fresh air experiencing a deep abiding sense of relief and a desperate need to reclaim her freedom.

The charade of their engagement would shortly be over, she told herself soothingly. Soon she would be back home and out searching for another job. Hopefully the turmoil of overexcited feelings that she was currently feeling would vanish along with Navarre Cazier...

CHAPTER SEVEN

'TAWNY! I saw you walking up the drive from the window. Navarre will be relieved—he's been looking everywhere for you!' Catrina told her brightly as Tawny mounted the front steps, muddy and windblown and embarrassed by her long absence and untidy appearance. It occurred to her that her hostess had never smiled at her with such welcoming warmth before but she was in too troubled a state of mind to be suspicious.

'I went out for a walk and got a bit lost,' Tawny muttered apologetically. 'Have I missed breakfast?'

'No. Navarre was worried that you had seen that story in the newspapers and been upset by it...it's so embarrassing when these things happen when you're away from home,' Catrina commented with unconvincing sympathy.

Tawny had frozen in the hallway. 'What newspaper story?'

Catrina helpfully passed her the tabloid newspaper she was already clutching in readiness. 'I'll have breakfast sent up to your room if you like.'

Tawny opened the paper and there it was: *Billionaire and Maid?* There was a beaming picture of Julie, her self-elected best friend, who she could only assume had spilled her guts to a reporter for cash. She supposed that in the absence of any more colourful story about Navarre going with an engagement that had to be a fake must have seemed worthwhile. Almost everything she had ever told Julie that could be given the right twist was there in black and white from Tawny's brief time in foster care as a child to the recent mysterious breakdown in family relations. Oh, yes, *and* what Julie described as Tawny's frantic determination to meet and marry a rich man through her work…*yes,* Julie had had to find an angle to make Tawny sound more interesting and that was the angle she had chosen. Tawny was a rampant gold-digger in search of a meal ticket. According to Julie Tawny had used her employment as a chambermaid to sleep with several wealthy guests in a search for one who would offer to take her away from cleaning and spoil her to death with his money for ever. What insane rubbish! Tawny thought furiously, wondering who on earth would believe such nonsense.

'Wouldn't you prefer to have your breakfast in your room?' Catrina Coulter prompted expectantly.

'Have all the guests seen this?' Tawny enquired.

Catrina gave her a sympathetic glance as unconvincing as her earlier smile. 'Probably…'

'I'll be eating downstairs,' Tawny announced, folding the paper and tucking it casually below one arm to march into the lofty-ceilinged dining room with her bright head held high and a martial glint in her gaze. A moment too late she recalled that her hair was in a wild tangle and her jeans spattered with mud, but she had to tough out that knowledge because her fellow guests turned as one to watch her progress down the length of the long table towards the empty chair beside Navarre.

Navarre, sleek and sexy in a striped shirt and a pair of designer chinos, stood up as she approached and spun out the chair for her. Inside, her body hummed as if an engine had been switched on. Her eyes, with an alacrity all their own, darted over him, taking in the cropped black hair, the brilliant green eyes and the dark shadow that told her he hadn't shaved since the night before. And it was no use, in spite of the fact that she was furious with him the fact that he was drop-dead gorgeous triumphed and she blushed with awareness, her heartbeat quickening in time with her pulse as she sank down into the seat.

'I'll get you something to eat,' Navarre offered, vaulting upright to stride across to the side table laden with lidded dishes laid out on hot plates for guests to serve themselves.

Surprised that he was giving her that amount of attention, Tawny watched him heap a dining plate as high as if he were feeding half the table instead of just one skinny redhead and bring it back to her with positive ceremony.

'You must've walked miles…you have to be starving,' he pointed out when she gaped at the amount of food he had put on the plate.

Trying not to laugh at the shocked appraisal of the blonde with a health conscious plate of fresh fruit opposite, Tawny began to butter her first slice of toast. 'I walked miles more than I planned. I'm afraid I found myself on boggy ground and got lost and very muddy. I ended up having to walk along the road to find my way back here. I shouldn't have gone so far without a map,' she confided breathlessly as he poured her coffee for her.

Tawny sugared her coffee while wondering why Navarre, who had hurt her so much just hours earlier, was now being so kind and attentive. Had he not read the same newspaper spread? Didn't he realise that she could only have tried to steal his laptop to grab his attention and then bonk his brains out in the hope that great sex would make him her meal ticket for life? It was obvious that the rest of the guests had read the newspaper. She was painfully conscious that everyone else at the table was watching her and Navarre closely, clearly hoping for some gossipy titbit or some sign that he was going to dump her right there and then. Thanks to her erstwhile friend she had been depicted in print as a mercenary chambermaid who had seduced innocent hotel guests in an effort to entrap a wealthy husband.

Navarre watched Tawny eat a cooked breakfast with the enthusiasm of a woman who had not seen food for a month. He was relieved to see that a scurrilous article in a downmarket newspaper had not detracted from her appetite. Above all things Navarre admired courage and the courage she had displayed in choosing to take her breakfast as normal in front of an inquisitive audience hugely impressed him. Few women would have kept their cool in such an embarrassing situation.

'I have to pack,' she told him prosaically once she had finished her second cup of coffee.

In the mood Tawny was in the packing did not take long. Ten minutes and it was done. Navarre walked into the room just as she lowered the case to the floor. She would have offered to do his packing as well just to keep busy but he had already taken care of the task. She folded her arms defensively.

'We should talk before the helicopter arrives,' Navarre imparted flatly. 'We'll be staying in another hotel for the next couple of days, after which I will let you return to your life. I'll be tied up with business once we return to London.'

Tawny said nothing. Another hotel, mercifully not the one where she had once been employed. It was clear that their arrangement would soon have run its course. So much for his declaration the night before that their intimacy was to be a beginning and not an end! She had fallen for a line, it seemed.

Navarre studied her with sardonic cool. 'I hope you won't prove to be pregnant.'

Tawny stiffened. 'I hope so too, particularly because it would be my life which would be majorly screwed up by that development.'

'It would screw up *both* our lives,' Navarre countered grimly.

Tawny resisted the urge to challenge that statement. She was too well aware as a child born to a single mother that her birth had made little impact on her own father's life. Monty Blake had paid the court-ordered minimum towards Tawny's upkeep and that was all. He had not taken an interest in her. He had not invited her to visit him, his second wife and their family. Indeed he had deliberately excluded Tawny from family occasions. When her mother had chosen to continue her pregnancy against his wishes he had hit back by doing everything he could to ignore Tawny's existence. Had her older half-sisters not chosen to look her up when she was a teenaged schoolgirl, Tawny would never have got to know them either. Certainly she would never have had the confidence to approach either Bee or Zara on her own behalf when their father had made her feel so very unworthy of his affection. And that hurtful feeling of not being good enough to be an acceptable daughter had dogged her all her life.

That evening, Tawny was once again ensconced in a hotel suite with only Elise for company. Navarre had chatted at length in Italian to someone on the phone while the car travelled slowly through the London traffic and as soon as they checked into the hotel he had gone out again. This time around, however, the suite Navarre had taken had *two* bedrooms. She was not expected to sleep on the sofa or share his bed. Their little fling was over. She reminded herself of the unjust accusation he had made before dawn that same day, relived her fury and hurt at that charge and told herself that it was only sensible to avoid further intimacy and misunderstanding. While Elise watched television Tawny worked through her emotions with the help of her sketch pad, drawing little cartoon vignettes of her rocky relationship with Navarre.

Navarre came back just after midnight, exchanging a word or two with Elise as she raised herself sleepily from the sofa, switched off the television and bid him goodnight. Left alone, he lifted Tawny's sketch pad. The Frenchman, it said on the first page, and there he was in all his cartoon glory, leching at the stylist while pretending to admire Tawny in her evening dress. He leafed through page after page of caricatures and laughter shook him, for she had a quirky sense of humour and he could only hope that the one depicting Catrina as a man-eating piranha fish never made it into the public eye, for Sam would be mortally offended at the insult to his wife. His supreme indifference to the newspaper revelations about her background as a maid was immortalised in print as she showed him choosing to fret instead about how much fried food the English ate at breakfast time. Did she really see him as that insensitive? Admittedly he avoided getting up close and personal on an emotional front with women, for time and experience had taught him that that was unwise if he had no long-term intentions.

'Oh, you're back...' Tawny emerged from her bedroom, clad in her pyjamas, which had little monkeys etched all over the trousers and a big monkey on the front of the camisole, none of which detracted in the slightest from his awareness of the firm swell of her breasts and the lush prominence of her nipples pushing against the thin clinging cotton. 'I'm thirsty.'

He watched as she padded drowsily over to the kitchenette in one corner to run the cold tap and extract a glass from a cupboard. He was entranced by the smallness of her waist and the generous fullness of her derriere beneath the cotton: she was *all* woman in the curve department in spite of her slender build. His groin tightened as he remembered the feel of her hips in his hands and the hot tight grip of her beneath him. He crushed that lingering memory, fought to rise above it and concentrate instead on the divisive issues that kept his desire within acceptable boundaries.

'Why did you take my laptop that day?' he demanded without warning.

Tawny almost dropped the moisture-beaded glass she was holding. 'I told you why. I thought you'd taken nude photos of my friend and refused to delete them. She told me that if I got it for her she would wipe them. I believed her—at the time I trusted her as a good friend but I realised afterwards that she was lying to me and hoping to make money out of it. She was working for a journalist who wanted information on you and your activities.'

'I know,' Navarre volunteered, startling her. 'I had Julie checked out—'

'And you didn't think to mention that to me?'

'I have no proof that you weren't in it for a profit with her, *ma petite*.'

'No, obviously I would think that it would be much more profitable to get pregnant with a child you don't want so that I could be lumbered with its sole care for the next twenty years!' Tawny sizzled back.

'I didn't realise that you'd once been in a foster home as well,' Navarre remarked, carefully sidestepping her emotive comeback, believing it to be the wrong time for that conversation. 'You didn't mention it when I admitted my own experiences.'

'Obviously you read every line of that newspaper article,' Tawny snapped defensively. 'But I was only in foster care for a few months and as soon as my grandparents found out where I was they offered to take me. When I was a toddler my mother hit a rough patch when she was drinking too much and I was put into care. But she overcame her problems so that I was able to live with her again.'

'Clearly you respect your mother for that achievement, so why are you at odds with her now?'

At that blunt question, Tawny paled, for the newspaper article had not clarified that situation. 'My grandfather's will,' she explained with a rueful jerk of a slim shoulder that betrayed her eagerness to forget that unpleasant reality. 'My grandparents owned and lived in a cottage in a village where my grandmother was very happy. When my grandfather died he left half of it to his wife and the other half to his only child, my mother. My mother made my grandmother sell her home so that she could collect on her share.'

Navarre was frowning. 'And you disapproved?'

'Of course I did. My grandmother was devastated by the loss of her home so soon after she had lost her husband. It was cruel. I understood that my mother has always had a struggle to survive and had never owned her own home but still think what she did was wrong. I tried to dissuade her from forcing Gran to sell up but she wouldn't listen. Her boyfriend had more influence over her than I had,' Tawny admitted unhappily. 'As far as Mum was concerned Grandad might have been Gran's husband but he had also been her father and she had rights too. She put her own rights first, so the house was sold and Gran, who had always been so good to us both, moved into a retirement village where—I have to admit—she's quite happy.'

'Your mother gave way to temptation and she has to live with that. At least your grandmother had sufficient funds left after the division of property to move somewhere she liked.'

Tawny said nothing. She had seen no sign that her mother was suffering from an uneasy conscience and, having put all that she possessed into purchasing her new apartment, Celestine's current lifestyle was seriously underfunded. But Tawny believed that subjecting the old lady to the stress of changing to more affordable accommodation would be downright dangerous, for Celestine had already suffered one heart attack. The upheaval of another house move might well kill her.

'I'd better get back to bed.' But instead Tawny hovered, her gaze welded to the stunning eyes above his well-defined cheekbones, the beautiful wilful line of his passionate mouth.

'I want to go there with you, *ma petite,*' Navarre admitted in his dark, distinctively accented drawl.

As if a naked flame had burned her skin, Tawny spun on her heel and went straight back into her bedroom, closing the door with a definitive little snap behind her. She flung herself back below the duvet, tears of frustration stinging her eyes, her body switching onto all systems go at the very thought of him in the same bed again. Stupid, silly woman that she was, she craved the chance to be with him again!

Navarre had just emerged from a long cooling shower when Tia phoned him. She wanted him to bring Tawny to a weekend party she and Luke were staging on a yacht in the Med. He rarely said no to the beautiful actress but he said it this time, knowing that it would be wiser to sever all ties with his pretend fiancée rather than draw her deeper into Tia's glitzy world. Mixing business, pleasure and dark secrets could not work for long. He would pay Tawny for her time and draw a line under the episode: it was the safest option. He refused to consider the possibility that she might fall pregnant. If it happened he would deal with it, but he wouldn't lose sleep worrying about it beforehand.

Navarre had left the hotel by the time Tawny was ready for breakfast the next morning. She was bored silly and not even her sketch pad could prevent her from feeling restless. 'Where's your boss?' she pressed Elise.

'He's in business meetings all day,' the blonde confided. 'We're returning home tomorrow...I can't wait.'

'You'll see your boyfriend,' Tawny gathered, reckoning that it had to be the strongest sign yet of her unimportance on Navarre's scale that even his employees knew he was leaving the UK before she did.

But life would soon return to normal, she told herself firmly. She had had a one-night stand and she wasn't very proud of the fact. The next day, however, she would be out job-hunting again as well as getting in touch with her agent to see if she had picked up any new illustrating commissions. She would also catch the train down to visit Celestine at the weekend. Elise got her the local papers so that she could study the jobs available and she decided to look for a waitressing position rather than applying to become a maid again. A waitress would have more customer contact. It would be livelier, more demanding, and wasn't distraction exactly what her troubled mind needed?

No way did she need to be wondering how she would cope if she had conceived a child by Navarre! There was even less excuse for her to be wondering whether she would prefer a boy or a girl and whether the baby might look like her or take more after Navarre, with his dramatic black hair and green eyes. If she turned out to be pregnant, she had no doubt that she would have much more serious concerns. Her mother had once admitted that she had been thrilled when she first realised that she was carrying Tawny. Back then, of course, Susan Baxter had naively assumed that a child on the way would cement her relationship with her child's father instead of which it had destroyed it. At least, Tawny reflected ruefully, she cherished no such romantic illusions where Navarre Cazier was concerned.

About ten that evening, Tawny ran a bath to soak in and emerged pink and wrinkled from her submersion, engulfed in the folds of a large hotel dressing gown. At that point and quite unexpectedly, for Elise had believed him out for the evening, Navarre strode in, clad in a dark, faultlessly tailored business suit with a heavy growth of stubble darkening his handsome features. He acknowledged Elise with barely a glance, for his attention remained on Tawny with her vibrant curls rioting untidily round her flushed face and her slender body lost in the depths of the oversized robe she wore. Hunger pierced him as sharply as a knife, a hunger he didn't understand because it had not started at the groin. That lingering annoying sense that something was lacking, something lost, infuriated him on a day when he had more reason than most to be in an excellent mood to celebrate. He was the triumphant new owner of CCC. The deal had been agreed at Strathmore after weeks of pre-contract discussions between their lawyers and various consultants and now it was signed, sealed and delivered.

'Goodnight, Navarre,' Tawny said flatly.

Elise slipped out of the door unnoticed by either of them. 'I'm leaving tomorrow,' he told Tawny without any expression at all.

Tawny smiled as brightly as if she had won an Olympic race. 'Elise mentioned it.'

'I'll drop you off at home on the way to the airport. I have your phone number and I'll stay in touch…obviously,' he added curtly.

'It's not going to happen,' Tawny responded soothingly, guessing what he meant. 'My egg and your sperm are more likely to have a fight than get together and throw a party for three!'

His face darkened. 'I hope you're right, *ma petite*. A child should be planned and wanted and cherished.'

Her eyes stung as she thought of how much truth there was in that statement. Her own life might have been very different had her parents respected that example. Struggling to suppress the over emotional tears threatening, she was only capable of nodding agreement, but she was grateful that he wasn't approaching the thorny subject with hypocrisy or polite and empty lies. He didn't want to have a child with her and she appreciated his honesty. She shed the robe and got into bed where the tears simply overflowed. She sniffed and coughed, furious with herself. He might have lousy square taste in women's clothes, but he was fantastic in bed and that was the *sole* source of her regret where Navarre Cazier was concerned. He would have made a great casual lover, she told herself doggedly, refusing to examine her feelings in any greater depth.

About twenty minutes later, a light knock sounded on her door and she called out, 'Come in!' and sat up to put on the light by the bed.

She was stunned when Navarre appeared in the doorway, his only covering a towel loosely knotted round his narrow hips. 'May I stay with you tonight?'

Her mouth ran dry, her throat closed over, but her body

went off on a roller-coaster ride of instant sit-up-and-beg response. 'Er...'

'I've tried but I can't stop wanting you,' Navarre admitted harshly.

And she admired that frankness and the streak of humility it had taken for him to approach her again after he had attempted to close that door and move their relationship into more platonic channels. He was not so different from her, after all, and it was a realisation that softened her resentment when she couldn't stop wanting him either. 'Stay,' she told him gruffly, switching out the light in the hope it would hide her discomfiture.

That she was too weak to send him packing still offended Tawny's pride. He had suspected that she might be in league with Julie to plunder his life for profitable information that could be sold to the press. He even believed she might have deliberately tried to get pregnant by him because he was a wealthy man. He did not see her as a trustworthy woman with moral scruples. He was rich, she was poor and a gulf of suspicion separated them. She ought to hate him, but when the muscle packed heat and power of Navarre eased up against her in the dimness, a healthy dose of blood cooling hatred was nowhere to be found. Instead a snaking coil of heat uncurled and burned hot in her and she quivered, every nerve ending energised by anticipation.

Navarre had spent the day in an ever more painful state of arousal, which had steadily eaten away at his self-discipline. Throughout he had remained hugely aware that this was the last night he could be with Tawny and the temptation of having her so close had finally overpowered every other consideration. He might be violating his principles, but when had he ever pretended that he was perfect? In any case, he reasoned impatiently, sex was just sex and it would be an even worse mistake to get emotional about a wholly physical prompting. She turned him on hard and fast, she had made sex exciting for him again. What was a moral dilemma in comparison to what she could make him feel?

Having divided his attention hungrily between the large pink nipples that adorned her small firm breasts and discovered that she was even more deliciously responsive than he recalled, Navarre slowly worked his way down her slender body, utilising every expert skill he had ever learned in the bedroom. If she could make him want her to such an extent, that power had to cut both ways and he was not content until she was writhing and whimpering in abandon, pleading for that final fix of fulfilment.

He sank deep into her and an aching wave of pleasure engulfed her, the little shivers and shakes of yet another approaching climax overwhelming her until she was sobbing out her satisfaction into a hard brown shoulder and falling back against the pillows again, weak as a kitten, emptied of everything.

Still struggling to recapture his breath after that wild bout of sex, Navarre threw himself back out of the bed before he could succumb to the need to reach for her again. Once was never enough with her, but he was suddenly in the grip of a fierce need to prove to himself that he *could* turn away from the powerful temptation she offered. In the darkness he searched for his towel in the heap of clothing discarded by the bed. He shook a couple of garments with unconcealed impatience and Tawny stretched up to put on the bedside light.

'Where are you going?' Clutching the sheet to her chest, frowning below the tumbled curls on her brow, Tawny studied him, unable to believe that he could already be leaving her again. A quick tumble and that was that? Was that all the consideration he now had for her? Did familiarity breed contempt that fast?

Navarre snatched up the towel and at the same time what he took for a screwed up banknote on the floor, assuming it had fallen out of an item of her clothing when he shook it. As he smoothed the item out to give it to her he caught a glimpse of his own name and he withdrew his hand and stepped back from the bed to read the block printed words on the piece of paper.

'If you call...' the note ran and a London phone number followed. 'Information about Navarre Cazier is worth a lot of money.'

Seeing that scrap of paper in his hand, Tawny almost had a heart attack on the spot and she lunged towards him with a stricken gasp. 'Give me that!'

His face set like a mask, Navarre crumpled the note in a powerful fist and dropped it down on her lap. *'Merde alors!* What information about me are you planning to sell?' he enquired silkily.

After their intimacy mere minutes earlier it was like a punch in the stomach for Tawny to be asked that brutal question. He had simply assumed that, in spite of the fact that he had already offered her a very large sum of money to help him out, she would think nothing of going behind his back to the press and selling confidential information about him. It was a blow that Navarre could still think so little of her morals. She lost so much colour that her hair looked unnaturally bright against her pallor.

'News of my successful buyout of CCC was in the evening papers so you've missed the boat on the business front,' Navarre derided, winding the towel round his narrow hips with apparently calm hands. 'What else have you got to sell?'

Tawny breathed in deep and gave him a wide sizzling

smile that hurt lips still swollen from his kisses. 'Basically the story of what you're like in bed. You know, the usual sleaze that makes up a kiss-and-tell, how you treated me like a royal princess and put a ring on my finger for a few days, had the sex and then got bored and dumped me again.'

Still as a bronzed statue, Navarre focused contemptuous green eyes on her and ground out the reminder, 'You signed a confidentiality agreement.'

'I know I did, but somehow I don't think you'll lower yourself to the task of dragging me into a courtroom just because I tell the world that you're a five-times-a night guy!' Tawny slung back with deliberate vulgarity, determined to tough out the confrontation so that he would never, ever suspect how much he had hurt her.

Navarre could barely conceal his distaste.

'You still owe me proof that that camera that recorded my supposed theft of your laptop has been wiped,' Tawny remarked less aggressively as that recollection returned to haunt her.

His sardonic mouth curled. 'There was no camera, no recording. That was a little white lie voiced to guarantee your good behaviour.'

'You're such a ruthless bastard,' Tawny quipped shakily, fighting a red tide of rage at how easily she had been taken in. Why had she not insisted on seeing that recording the instant he'd mentioned it?

'It got you off the theft hook,' he reminded her without hesitation.

'And you'll never forget that, will you?' But it wasn't really a question because she already knew the answer. She would *always* be a thief in Navarre Cazier's eyes and a woman he could buy for a certain price.

'Will you change your mind about the kiss-and-tell?'

Navarre asked harshly, willing her to surrender to his demand.

'Sorry, no…I want my five minutes of fame. Why shouldn't I have it? Have a safe journey home,' Tawny urged breezily.

'*Tu a un bon coup*…you're a good lay,' he breathed with cutting cool, and seconds later the door mercifully shut on his departure.

There was no hiding from the obvious fact that making love with him again had been a serious mistake and she mentally beat herself up for that misjudgement to such an extent that she did not sleep a wink for what remained of the night. Around seven in the morning she heard Jacques arrive to collect his employer's cases and later the sound of Navarre leaving the suite. Only when she was sure that he was gone did she finally emerge, pale and with shadowed eyes, from her room. She was shocked to find a bank draft for the sum of money he had agreed to pay her waiting on the table alongside her mobile phone. Was he making the point that, unlike her, once he had given his word he stuck to his agreements? He had ordered breakfast for eight o'clock as well and it arrived, the full works just as she liked, but the lump in her throat and the nausea in her tummy prevented her from eating anything. In the end she tucked the bank draft into her bag. Well, she couldn't just leave it lying there, could she? In the same way she packed the clothes he had bought her into the designer luggage and departed, acknowledging that in the space of a week he had turned her inside out.

CHAPTER EIGHT

'IF Tawny doesn't tell Cazier soon, I intend to do it for her,' Sergios Demonides decreed, watching his sister-in-law, Tawny, play ball in the sunshine with his older children, Paris, Milo and Eleni. Tawny's naturally slender figure made the swelling of her pregnant stomach blatantly obvious in a swimsuit.

'We can't interfere like that,' his wife, Bee, told him vehemently. 'He hurt her. She needs time to adapt to this new development—'

'How much time? Is she planning to wait until the baby is born and then tell him that he's a father?' Sergios reasoned, unimpressed. 'A man has a right to know that he has a child coming *before* its birth. Surely he cannot be as irresponsible as she is—'

'She's not irresponsible!' Bee argued, lifting their daughter, Angeli, into her arms as the black-haired toddler clasped her mother's knees to steady her still-clumsy toddler steps. 'She's just very independent. Have you any idea of how much persuasion I had to use to get her out here for a holiday?'

Outside Tawny glanced uneasily indoors to where her sister and her brother-in-law stood talking intently. She could tell that their attention was centred on her again and she flushed, wishing that Sergios would mind his own business and stop making her feel like such a nuisance. It was typical of the strong-willed Greek to regard his un-married sister-in-law's pregnancy as a problem that was his duty to solve.

But that was the only cloud on her horizon in the wake of the wonderful week of luxurious relaxation she had enjoyed on Sergios's private island, Orestos. London had been cold and wintry when she flew out and she was re-turning there the following day, flying back to bad weather and her very ordinary job as a waitress in a restaurant. She felt well rested and more grounded after the break she had had with her sister and her lively family though. Sergios had become the guardian of his cousin's three orphaned children and with the recent addition of their own first child to the mix—the adorable Angeli—Bee was a very busy wife and mother. She was also very happy with her life, although that was an admission that went against the grain for Tawny, who was convinced that she could never have remained as even tempered and easy going as Bee in the radius of Sergios's domineering nature. Sergios was one of those men who knew the right way to do everything and it was always *his* way. And yet Bee had this magical knack of just looking at him sometimes when he was in full extrovert flood and he would suddenly shut up and smile at her as if she had waved a magic wand across his forbidding countenance.

'I can't bear to think of you going back to work such long hours. You should have rested more while you were here.' Bee sighed after dinner that evening as the two women sat out on the terrace watching the sun go down.

'The way you did?' Tawny teased, recalling how in-credibly hectic her half-sister's schedule had been while she was carrying her first child.

'I had Sergios for support…and my mother,' Bee reminded her.

Bee's disabled mother, Emilia, lived in a cottage in the grounds of their Greek home and was very much a member of their family. In comparison, Tawny's mother was living with her divorced boyfriend and his children in the house she had purchased with her inheritance from Tawny's grandfather. She was aghast that her daughter had fallen pregnant outside a relationship and had urged her to have a termination, an attitude that had driven yet another wedge into the already troubled relationship between mother and daughter. No, Tawny could not look for support from that quarter, and while her grandmother, Celestine, was considerably more tolerant when it came to babies, the older woman lived quite a long way from her and with the hours Tawny had to work she only saw the little Frenchwoman about once a month.

'It's a shame that you told Navarre that you *weren't* pregnant when he phoned you a couple of months ago,' Bee said awkwardly.

'I honestly thought it was the truth when I told him that. That first test I did *was* negative!' Tawny reminded the brunette ruefully. 'Do you really think I should have phoned him three weeks later and told him I'd been mistaken?'

'Yes.' Bee stayed firm in the face of the younger woman's look of reproach. 'It's Navarre's baby too. You have to deal with it. The longer you try to ignore the situation, the more complicated it will become.'

Tawny's eyes stung and she blinked furiously, turning her face away to conceal the turbulent emotions that seemed so much closer to the surface since she had fallen pregnant. She was fourteen weeks along now and she was changing shape rapidly with her tummy protruding, her waist thickening and her breasts almost doubling in size. Ever since she had learned that she had conceived she had felt horribly vulnerable and out of control of her body and her life. All too well did she remember her mother's distressing tales of how Tawny's father had humiliated her with his angry scornful attitude to her conception of a child he didn't want. Tawny had cringed at the prospect of putting herself in the same position with a man who was already suspicious of her motives.

'I know that Navarre hurt you,' her half-sister murmured unhappily. 'But you should still tell him.'

'Somehow I fell for him like a ton of bricks,' Tawny admitted abruptly, her voice shaking because it was the very first time she had openly acknowledged that unhappy truth, and Bee immediately covered her hand with hers in a gesture of quiet understanding. 'I never thought I could feel like that about a man and he was back out of my life again before I even realised how much he had got to me. But there was nothing I could do to make things better between us—'

'How about just keeping your temper and talking to him?' Bee suggested. 'That would be a good place to make a start.'

Tawny didn't trust herself to do that either. How could she talk to a man who would almost certainly want her to go for a termination? Why should she have to justify her desire to bring her baby into the world just because it didn't suit him? So, she decided to text him the news late that night, saving them both from the awkwardness of a direct confrontation when it was all too likely that either or both of them might say the wrong things.

The first test I did was wrong. I am now 14 weeks pregnant,' she informed him and added, utilising block capitals lest he cherish any doubts, *'It is YOURS.'*

Pressing the send button before she could lose her nerve, she slept that night soothed by the conviction that she had finally bitten the bullet and done what she had to do. Bee was shocked that her sister had decided to break the news in a text but Sergios believed that even that was preferable to keeping her condition a secret.

Navarre was already at work in his imposing office in Paris when Tawny's text came through and shock and disbelief roared through him like a hurricane-force storm. He wanted to disorder his immaculate cropped hair and shout to the heavens to release the steam building inside him as he read that text. *Merde alors!* She would be the death of him. How could she make such an announcement by text? How could she text 'YOURS' like that as if he were likely to argue the fact when she had been a virgin? He tried to phone her immediately but could not get an answer, for by then Tawny was already on board a flight to London. Within an hour Navarre had cancelled his appointments and organised a trip there as well.

Tawny stopped off at her bedsit only long enough to change for her evening shift at the restaurant and drop off her case. As she had decided that only actual starvation would persuade her to accept money from a man who had called her a good lay to her face, she had not cashed Navarre's bank draft and had had to work extremely hard to keep on top of all her financial obligations. Luckily some weeks back she had had the good fortune to sell a set of greeting card designs, which had ensured that Celestine's rent was covered for the immediate future. Tawny's work as a waitress paid her own expenses and, as her agent had been enthusiastic enough to send a selection of her Frenchman cartoons to several publications, she was even moderately hopeful that her cartoons might soon give her the break she had long dreamt of achieving.

Navarre seated himself in a distant corner of the self-service restaurant where Tawny worked and nursed a cup of the most disgusting black coffee he had ever tasted. Consumed by frustration over the situation she had created by keeping him out of the loop for so long, he watched her emerge from behind the counter to clear tables. And that fast his anger rose. Her streaming torrent of hair was tied back at the nape of her neck, her slender coltish figure lithe in an overall and leggings. At first glance she looked thinner but otherwise unchanged, he decided, subjecting her to a close scrutiny and noting the fined-down line of her jaw. Only when she straightened did he see the rounded swell of her stomach briefly moulded by the fabric of her tunic.

She was expecting his baby and even though she clearly needed to engage in hard menial work to survive, he reflected with brooding resentment and disapproval, she had still not made use of that bank draft he had left in the hotel for her. He had told his bank to inform him the instant the money was drawn and the weeks had passed and he had waited and waited, much as he had waited in vain for some sleazy kiss-and-tell about their affair to be published somewhere. When nothing happened, when his lowest expectations went totally unfulfilled, it had finally dawned on him that this was payback time Tawny-style. In refusing to accept that money from him, in disdaining selling 'their' story as she had threatened to do, she was taking her revenge, making her point that he had got her wrong and that she didn't need him for anything. Navarre understood blunt messages of a challenging nature, although she was the very first woman in his life to try and communicate with him on that aggressive level.

In addition, he had really not needed a shock phone call from her bossy sister Bee to tell him how *not* to handle her fiery half-sister. Bee Demonides had phoned him out of the blue just after his private jet landed in London and had introduced herself with aplomb. Tawny, he now appreciated, had kept secrets that he had never dreamt might exist in her background, secrets that sadly might have helped him to understand her better. Her sibling was married to one of the richest men in the world and Tawny had not breathed a word of that fact, had indeed 'oohed' and 'ahhed' over Sam Coulter's rented castle and the Golden Awards party as if she had no comparable connections or experiences. In fact, from what he had since established from Jacques's more wide-reaching enquiries, Tawny's other half-sister, Zara, was married to an Italian banker, who was also pretty wealthy. So, how likely was it that Tawny had ever planned to enrich herself by stealing Navarre's laptop to sell his secrets to the gutter press? On the other hand why did she feel the need to work in such lowly jobs when she had rich relatives who would surely have been willing to help her find more suitable employment? That was a complete mystery and only the first of several concerning Tawny Baxter, Navarre acknowledged impatiently.

Tawny was unloading a tray into a dishwasher in the kitchen when her boss approached her. 'There's a man waiting over by the far window for you...says he's a friend and he's here to tell you about a family crisis. I said that you could leave early—we're quiet this evening. I hope it's nothing serious.'

Tawny's first thought was that something awful had happened to her mother and that her mother's boyfriend, Rob, had come to tell her. Fear clenching her stomach, she grabbed her coat and bag and hurried back out into the restaurant, only to come to a shaken halt when she looked across the tables and saw Navarre seated in the far corner. His dark hair gleamed blue-black below the down lights that accentuated the stunning angles and hollows of his darkly handsome features. He threw back his head and she collided with brilliant bottle-green eyes and somehow she was moving towards him without ever recalling how she had reached that decision.

'Let's get out of here,' Navarre urged, striding forwards to greet her before she even got halfway to his table.

Still reeling in consternation from his sudden appearance, Tawny let him guide her outside and into the limousine pulling up at the kerb to collect them. Her hand trembled in the sudden firm hold of his, for their three months apart had felt like a lifetime and she could have done with advance warning of his visit. Thrown into his presence again without the opportunity to dress for the occasion and form a defensive shell, she felt horribly naked and unprepared. Once again, though, he had surprised her in a uniform that underlined the yawning gulf in their status.

'I wasn't expecting you—'

'You thought you could chuck a text bombshell at me and I was so thick-skinned that I would simply carry on as normal?' Navarre questioned with sardonic emphasis. 'Even I am not that insensitive.'

Tawny reddened. 'You took me by surprise.'

'Just as your text took me, *ma petite*.'

'Not so *petite* any longer,' she quipped.

'I noticed,' Navarre admitted flatly, his attention dropping briefly to the tummy clearly visible when she was sitting down. 'I'm still in shock.'

'Even after three months I'm still in shock.'

'Why did you tell me you weren't pregnant?'

'I did a test and it was negative. I think I did it too early. A few weeks later when I wasn't feeling well I bought another test and that one was positive. I didn't know how to tell you that I'd got it wrong—'

'*Exactement!* So, instead you took the easy way out and told me nothing.'

His sarcasm cut like the sudden slash of a knife against tender skin. 'Well, actually there was nothing easy about anything I've gone through since then, Navarre!' Tawny fired back at him in a sudden surge of spitfire temper. 'I've had all the worry without having anyone to turn to! I've had to work even though I was feeling as sick as a dog most mornings and the smell of cooking food made me worse, so working in a restaurant was not a pleasant experience. My hormones were all over the place and I've never felt so horribly tired in my life as I did those first weeks!'

'If only you had accepted the bank draft I gave you. We had an agreement and you earned that money by pretending to be my fiancée,' he reminded her grittily. 'But I understand why you refused to touch it.'

Her glacier blue eyes widened in disconcertion. 'You... *do?*'

'That last night we were together I was offensive, inexcusably so,' Navarre framed in a taut undertone, every word roughened by the effort it demanded of his pride to acknowledge such a fault to a woman.

That unexpected admission made it easier for Tawny to unbend in her turn. 'I made things worse. I shouldn't have pretended that I was planning to sell a story about you.'

'I made an incorrect assumption...time has proven me wrong, for no story appeared in the papers.'

'That note was smuggled in to me before we flew up to

Scotland. Julie would've been behind it. She even phoned my gran to try and find out where you and I had gone. I put the note in my pocket and forgot about it. I never intended to use that phone number.'

'Let the matter rest there. We have more important concerns at the moment.'

'How on earth did you find out where I was working?'

'You can thank your sister Bee for that information.'

Her exclamation of surprise was met by his description of the phone call he had received at the airport. Tawny winced and squirmed, loving Bee but deeply embarrassed by her interference. 'Bee hates people being at odds with each other. She's a tremendous peace maker but I do wish she had trusted me to handle this on my own.'

'She meant well. You're lucky to have a sister who cares so much about your welfare.'

'Zara is less pushy but equally opinionated.' At that point Tawny recalled Navarre telling her that he had no family he acknowledged and that memory filled her heart with regret and sympathy on his behalf. She might sometimes disagree with her relatives' opinions but she was still glad to have them in her life. People willing to tell her the truth and look out for her no matter what were a precious gift.

'Where are we heading?'

'Your sister and brother-in-law have kindly offered us the use of their home here in London for our meeting. We need somewhere to talk in private and I am tired of hotels,' he admitted curtly. 'It's time that I bought a property in this city.'

Tawny was pleased that Bee had offered the use of her luxury home in Chelsea and relieved not to have to take him back to her dreary bedsit to chat. Navarre, with his classy custom-made suits and shoes would never relax against such a grungy backdrop and she did want him to relax. If they were going to share a child it was vitally important that they establish a more harmonious relationship, she reasoned ruefully.

Ushered into the elegant drawing room of Bee and Sergios's mansion home by their welcoming housekeeper, Tawny was grateful to just kick off her shoes and curl up on a well-upholstered sofa in comfort. All of a sudden she didn't care any more that she was looking less than her best in a work tunic with a touch of mascara being her only concession to cosmetic enhancement. After all, what did such things matter now? He was no longer interested in her in that way. Three months had passed since he had walked away from her without a backwards glance—she didn't count that single brief phone call made out of duty to ask if she was pregnant—and for such diametrically opposed personalities as they it had probably been a wise move.

Navarre marvelled at the manner in which she instantly shed all formality and made herself comfortable. She made no attempt to pose or impress him, had not even dashed a lipstick across her lush full mouth. He was used to women who employed a great deal more artifice and her casual approach intrigued him. In any case the lipstick would only have come off, he thought hungrily, appreciation snaking through him as he noted the purity of her fine-boned profile, the natural elegance of her slender body in relaxation. And that hint of a bump that had changed her shape was *his* child. It struck Navarre as quite bizarre at that moment that that thought should turn him on hard and fast.

Tawny was now thinking hard about their predicament, trying to be fair to both of them. Their baby was a complication of an affair that was already over and done with, she conceded unhappily, and the more honest she was with him now, the more likely they were to reach an agreement that suited both of them.

'I want to have this baby,' she told Navarre straight off, keen to avoid any exchange with him in regard to the choices she might choose to make for their child. 'My mother thinks I'm being an idiot because she believes that giving birth to me and becoming a single parent ruined her life. I've heard all the arguments on that score since I was old enough to understand what she was talking about but I don't feel the same way. This baby may not be planned but I love it already and we'll manage.'

'I like your positive attitude.'

'Do you?' She was warmed by the comment and a tremulous smile softened the stressful line of her pink mouth.

'But it does seem that we are both approaching this situation with a lot of baggage from our own childhoods.' Navarre compressed his hard sensual mouth as he voiced that comment. 'Neither of us had a father and we suffered from that lack. It is hard for a child to have only one parent.'

'Yes,' she agreed ruefully.

'And it also puts a huge burden on the single parent's shoulders. Your mother struggled to cope and became bitter while my mother could not cope with parenting me at all. Our experiences have taught us how hard it is to raise a child alone and I don't want to stand back and watch you and our child go through that same process.'

The extent of his understanding of the problems she might have took Tawny aback at the same time as his thoughtfulness and willingness to take responsibility impressed her. 'I'm not belittling my mother's efforts as a parent because she did the very best she could, but she was very bitter and I do think I'm more practical in my expectations than she was.'

'I don't think you should have to lower your expectations at your age simply because you will have a child's needs to consider.'

Tawny pulled a wry face. 'But we have to be realistic.'

'It is exactly because I am realistic about what life would be like for you that I've come here to ask you to marry me. Only marriage would allow me to take my full share of the responsibility,' Navarre told her levelly, his strong jawline squaring with resolve. 'Together we will be able to offer our child much more than we could offer as parents living apart.'

Tawny was totally stunned for she had not seen that option hovering on her horizon at all. She stared back at Navarre, noting how grave his face was, grasping by his composed demeanour that he had given the matter a great deal of thought. 'You're not joking, are you?'

'I want to be there for you from the moment this child is born,' Navarre admitted with tough conviction. 'I don't want another man to take my place in my child's life either. The best way forwards for both of us is marriage.'

'But we know so little about each other—'

'Is that important? Is it likely to make our relationship more successful? I think not,' he declared with assurance. 'I believe it is infinitely more important that we are strongly attracted to each other and both willing to make a firm commitment to raise our child together.'

Tawny was mesmerised by his rock solid conviction. She felt slightly guilty that she had not appreciated that he might feel as responsible for her well-being and for that of their child as he evidently did. Too late did she grasp that she had expected him to treat her exactly as her absent father had treated her mother—with disdain and resentment. He was not running away from the burden of childcare, he was moving closer to accept it. Tears of relief stung her eyes and she blinked rapidly, turning her face away in the hope he had not noticed.

But Navarre was too observant to be fooled. 'What's wrong, *chérie*? What did I say?'

Tawny smiled through the tears. 'It's all right, it's not you. It's just I cry over the silliest things at the minute—I think it's the hormones doing it. My father was absolutely horrible to my mum when she told him she was pregnant and I think I sort of subconsciously assumed you would be the same. So, you see, we're both guilty of making wrong assumptions.'

Navarre had tried to move on from his cynical suspicions about her, she reasoned with a feeling of warmth inside her that felt remarkably like hope. She had not cashed the bank draft, she had not talked to the press about him and as a result he was willing to reward her with his trust. He treated her now with respect. He was no longer questioning the manner of their baby's conception or even mentioning a cynical need for DNA testing to check paternity. In short he had cut through all the rubbish that had once littered their relationship and offered her a wedding ring as a pledge of commitment to a new future. And she knew immediately that she would say yes to his proposal, indeed that it would feel like a sin not to at least try to see if they could make a marriage work for the sake of their child.

This was the guy whom against all the odds she had fallen madly in love with. He was the guy who ordered her magnificent breakfasts and admired her appetite and constantly checked that she wasn't hungry, the guy who had batted not a single magnificent eyelash over those embarrassing newspaper revelations about her background in spite of the presence of a bunch of snobbish socialite guests, who had undoubtedly looked down on his bargain basement taste in fiancées. He was also the guy who was endearingly, ridiculously jealous and possessive if another man so much as looked at her, an attitude which had made her feel irresistible for the first time in her life.

'Do you like children?' she asked him abruptly.

Navarre laughed. 'I've never really thought about it, but, yes, I believe that I do.'

When he smiled like that the power of his charisma rocketed, throwing him into the totally gorgeous bracket, and he made her heart hammer and her breath catch in her throat. 'Yes, I'll marry you,' she told him in French.

'You're an artist. I believe you will like living in Paris.'

He made it all seem so simple. That first visit he insisted on meeting her mother and her partner over dinner the following night at a very smart hotel. At first mother and daughter were a little stiff with each other, but at the end of the evening Susan Baxter took Tawny to one side to speak to her in private and said, 'I'm so happy it's all working out for you that I don't really know what to say,' she confided, tears shining in her anxious gaze. 'I know you were annoyed with the solution I suggested but I just didn't want your life to go wrong while you were still so young. I was afraid that you were repeating my mistakes and it felt like that had to be my fault—'

'Navarre's not like my father,' Tawny cut in with perceptible pride.

'No, he seems to be very mature and responsible.'

The word 'responsible' stung, although Tawny knew that no insult had been intended. She was too sensitive, she acknowledged ruefully. Navarre would not walk away from his child because he had grown up without the support of either a father or a mother and only he knew what that handicap had cost him. For that reason he would not abandon the mother of his child to struggle with parenthood alone. Acknowledging that undeniable fact made Tawny feel just a little like a charity case or an exercise in which Navarre would prove to his own satisfaction that he had the commitment gene, which his own parents had sadly lacked. It was an impression that could have been dissolved overnight had Navarre made the smallest attempt to become intimate with his intended bride again... but he did not. The pink diamond was placed on her engagement finger again, for real this time around, but his detached attitude, his concentration on the practical rather than the personal, left Tawny feeling deeply insecure and vulnerable.

Bee and Sergios offered to stage Navarre and Tawny's wedding at their London home and under pressure from Tawny, after initially refusing that offer Navarre agreed to it. He then rented a serviced apartment for Tawny's use and at his request she immediately gave up her job as a waitress and moved into the apartment while he returned to Paris. From there he hired a property firm to find them an ideal home in London and she spent her time doing viewings of the kind of luxury property she had never dreamt she might one day call home.

Only days after Tawny told her other half-sister, Zara, that she was getting married, Zara arrived in London for an unexpected visit, having left her children, Donata and her infant son, Piero, at home with her husband outside Florence.

'Does this visit now mean you aren't able to come to the wedding next week?' Tawny asked, surprised by the timing of her sister's trip to London. 'I know it was short notice but—'

'No, I just wanted the chance to talk to you alone *before* the wedding,' Zara completed with rather tense emphasis.

Drawing back from her half-sibling's hug, Tawny frowned. 'What's up? Oh, my goodness, you and Vitale aren't having trouble, are you?' she prompted in dismay, for the other couple had always seemed blissfully happy together.

Her dainty blonde sister went pink with discomfiture. 'Oh, no...no, nothing like that!' she exclaimed, although her eyes remained evasive.

The two young women settled in the comfortable lounge with coffee and biscuits. Tawny looked at Zara expectantly. 'So, tell me...'

Zara grimaced. 'I truly didn't know whether to come and talk to you or not. Bee said I should mind my own business and keep my mouth shut, so I discussed it with Vitale, but he thought I should be more honest with you.'

Tawny was frowning. 'R-right...I'm sorry, I don't understand.'

'It's something about Navarre, just rumours, but they've been around a long time and I don't know whether you know about them or even *should* know about them.' Her tongue tying her into increasingly tight knots, Zara was openly uncomfortable. 'I wouldn't usually repeat gossip—'

Tawny's spine went rigid with tension. Zara was a gentle kind person, never bitchy or mean. If Zara felt there were rumours about Navarre that Tawny ought to hear, she reckoned that they would very probably be a genuine source of concern for her. 'I'd like to say that I don't listen to gossip, but I'm not sure I could live without knowing now that you've told me there's something you think I should know about my future husband.'

'Now remember that I'm married to an Italian,' Zara reminded her uneasily. 'And for many years in Italy there have been strong rumours to the effect that Navarre Cazier is engaged in a long-running secret affair with Tia Castelli…you know the Italian movie star…?'

CHAPTER NINE

TAWNY who had literally stopped breathing while Zara spoke, relocated her lungs at the sound of that name and started to breathe again.

'My goodness, is there anyone on this planet who hasn't heard of Tia Castelli?' Tawny asked with her easy laugh. 'Are there rumours about Navarre and Tia having an affair? *Truthfully?* When I saw them together—'

Zara leant forwards in astonishment. 'You've already met Tia Castelli? You've actually seen her with Navarre? The word is that they're in constant contact.'

Tawny told her sister about her appearance by Navarre's side at the Golden Awards and her encounter with Tia and her husband, Luke.

'Surprising,' Zara remarked thoughtfully. 'I should think if that there had been anything sneaky going on Navarre would have avoided their company like the plague.'

'Navarre has known Tia for years and years. He worked for the banker that handled Tia's investments—that's how they first met,' Tawny explained frankly. 'Tia is very flirtatious. She expects to be the centre of attention but she's perfectly pleasant otherwise. I think you'd best describe her as being very much a man's woman.'

'So, you didn't notice anything strange between her

and Navarre? Anything that made you uncomfortable?'
Zara checked.

All Tawny felt uncomfortable about at that moment was
that she did not feel she could tell Zara the truth of how
she had met Navarre and become his fiancée, because she
and Navarre had already agreed that now their relationship
had become official nobody else had any need to know
about their previous arrangement. But it did occur to her
just then that the night she had met Tia Castelli, she had
been no more than a hired companion on Navarre's terms
and he had had less reason to hide anything from her. He
had been very attentive towards Tia, almost protective,
she recalled, struggling to think back and recapture what
she had seen. And Tia *was* an extraordinarily beautiful
and appealing woman. Tawny wondered if she was being
ridiculously naive about their relationship and could not
help recalling Luke Convery's annoyance at his wife's
friendship with Navarre. No smoke without fire, she reasoned ruefully. It was perfectly possible that Navarre and
Tia *had* been lovers at some point in the past.

'Now I've got you all worked up and worried! I
should've kept quiet! Why is Bee always right?' Zara exclaimed guiltily as she tracked the fast changing expres-
sions on the younger woman's face. 'She would never ever
have mentioned those stupid rumours to you.'

Ironically, what Tawny was thinking about then was
the number of times she had heard Navarre talking on
the phone in Italian, a language that he seemed to speak
with the fluency of a native. Could he have been speaking to Tia? Surely not every time she had heard him using
Italian, though, she told herself irritably, for that would
have meant that he talked to the gorgeous blonde almost
every day.

At the end of the afternoon, when Zara departed assuring Tawny that she and her husband would attend her wedding, Tawny was conscious that there was now a tiny little seed of doubt planted inside her that was more than ready to sprout into a sturdy sapling of suspicion.

Prior to her pregnancy, Navarre had seemed so hungry for Tawny, but not so hungry that he had made any attempt to get her back into bed in advance of the wedding. Who had been satisfying that hot libido of his during the three months of their separation? And why was she thinking that him having wanted her automatically meant he could not have also wanted Tia Castelli? Was she really that unsophisticated? After all, Tia was married and the sort of catch many men would kill to possess even briefly. Even if Tia and Navarre were having an affair Tia must surely accept that there would also be other women in Navarre's life. Her peace of mind shattered by that depressing conclusion, Tawny went to bed to toss and turn, troubled by her thoughts but determined not to share what she still deemed might be ridiculous suspicions with Navarre. Revealing such concerns when she had no proof would make her look foolish and put her at a disadvantage.

In the middle of the night she got up and performed an Internet search of Tia and Navarre's names together to discover any links that there might be. An hour later she had still not got to the end of the references, but had discovered nothing definitive, nothing that could not be explained by honest friendship. There were several pictures of Tia and Navarre chatting in public places, not a single one of anything more revealing—no holding of hands, no embraces, *nothing*. And if the paparazzi had failed to establish a more intimate link, the likelihood was that there wasn't one, for Tia Castelli's every move was recorded by the paps. But ironically for the first time Tawny was now wondering what had been on Navarre's laptop that he had so feared having exposed. What had Julie's high-paying journalist really hoped to find out from that computer? About the buyout of CCC? Her worst fears assuaged by that idea, for she recalled Navarre's comment about the deal already being in the news, Tawny went back to bed.

It was a wonderful wedding dress, fashioned by a designer to conceal the growing evidence of the bride's pregnancy. Tawny looked at her reflection in the mirror with her sisters standing anxiously by her side and then hugged Zara, who had located the glorious dress, which bared her shoulders and her newly impressive chest in a style that removed attention from her abdomen.

'You've sure got boobs now, babe,' Zara pronounced with a giggle.

Tawny grinned, her lovely face lighting up for it was true: for the first time ever she had the bosom bounty that she had always lacked and no padding was required.

'Are you happy?' Bee prompted worriedly. 'You're sure Navarre is the right man for you?'

Tawny lifted a hand to brush a wondering finger across the magnificent diamond tiara that anchored her veil and added height to her slim figure. 'Well, it's either him or the diamonds he's just given me,' she teased. 'But it all feels incredibly right.'

An offer had been made and accepted on a town house with a garden in the same area in which Bee and Sergios lived. In a few weeks' time it would provide a very comfortable base for her and Navarre when they were in London, ensuring that she need never feel that she was being taken away from absolutely everything she had ever known. She was on a high because everything in her world seemed to be blossoming. After all, she had just sold her first cartoons as well. One of the publications

that her agent had sent her work to had shared them with
a French sister magazine and the French editor had offered Tawny a contract to create more of her Frenchman
drawings. Ecstatic at the news, Tawny had still to share it
with Navarre because she wanted to surprise him by putting the magazine in front of him when the first cartoon
appeared in print.

'You should've let me twist Dad's arm to give you
away,' Zara lamented. 'He would have done it if I'd pushed
him.'

'I don't know our father, Zara. I wouldn't have wanted
him to do it just to please you and Bee. I much prefer
Sergios. At least he genuinely wishes Navarre and I well,'
Tawny pointed out.

Her opinion of Sergios had recently warmed up, for
it was thanks to Sergios and his managing ways that her
grandmother, Celestine, was being whisked to London in
a limousine for the wedding and put up that night in Bee's
home so that the extended celebration was not too much
of a strain for the old lady.

At the church, Tawny breathed in deep, her hand resting
lightly on Sergios's arm before she moved down the aisle,
her sisters following her clad in black and cream outfits.
All her attention locked to Navarre, who had flown back
to France within days of his proposal, she moved slowly
towards the altar. Devastatingly handsome in a tailored
silver-grey suit teamed with a smart waistcoat and cravat,
Navarre took her breath away just as he had the very first
time she saw him and she hugged the knowledge to herself that he would soon be her husband. As she reached
the altar Celestine, a tiny lady with a mop of white curls,
turned her head to beam at her granddaughter.

Although Tawny's head told her that she was entering
a shotgun marriage of the utmost practicality, it didn't feel

like one. She loved the ceremony, the sure way Navarre made his responses, the firm hold of the hand on hers as he slid on the wedding ring. In her heart she felt that he was making a proper commitment to her and their child. Before they left the church Navarre took the time to stop and greet her grandmother, whom he had not had time to meet beforehand.

'Do you like the dress?' she asked him once they were alone in the limo conveying them back to her sister's home.

'I like what's in it even better, *ma petite,*' Navarre confided, his attention ensnared by the luminosity of her beautiful eyes, and momentarily a pang of regret touched him for the parts of his life that he could never share with her. He had always believed that as long as he kept his life simple nothing could go wrong, but from the instant Tawny had walked into his life to try to steal his laptop his every plan had gone awry and things had stopped happening the way he had assumed they would. He didn't like that, he had learned to prefer the predictable and the safe, but he told himself that now that they were married his daily life would return to its normal routine. Why should anything have to change?

Tawny gazed dizzily into beautiful emerald-green eyes framed by black spiky lashes and her heart hammered. Her breasts swelled beneath her bodice, the pointed tips straining into sudden tingling life. His attention was on her mouth. The tip of her tongue slid out to moisten her lower lip and he tensed, his sleek strong face hard and taut. The silence lay heavy, thick like the sensual spell flooding her treacherous body, and she leant closer, propelled by promptings much stronger than she was.

'I'll wreck your make-up,' Navarre growled, but a hard hand closed into the back of her veil to hold her still while his mouth plundered hers with fierce heat and hunger, the delving of his tongue sending every skin cell she possessed mad with excitement.

Tawny wanted to push him flat on the back seat and have her wicked way with him. That fast her body was aching with need and ready for him. Her fingers flexed on a long powerful masculine thigh and then slid upwards to establish that the response was not one-sided. He was hard and thick and as eager as she was and even as he pushed back from her, surprise at her boldness etched in his intent gaze, she was content to have discovered that the exact same desire powered them both. Her face was flushed as she eased away from him, her body quivering with the will power it took to do so.

'*Mon Dieu, ma belle*...you make me ache like a boy again,' he confessed raggedly.

And the gloss on Tawny's day was complete. Happy at the response she had received, reassured by his desire, she sailed into her wedding reception in the ballroom of her sister's magnificent home. Perhaps he had only restrained himself sexually with her out of some outmoded idea of respecting her as his future wife, she thought buoyantly, for she had noticed that Navarre could sometimes be a shade old-fashioned in his outlook. Whatever, her insecurity was gone, her awareness of her pregnancy as a source of embarrassment banished while she held her head high and stood by his side to welcome the wealthy powerful guests whom Navarre counted as friends and business connections. Only recently she would only have got close to such people by waiting on them in some menial capacity, but now she met with them as an equal. Tia Castelli kissed her cheek with cool courtesy, her previous warmth muted, while her husband, Luke, gave Tawny a lazy smile. Tawny perfectly understood and forgave Tia for that dash of coolness in her manner, for the actress had to be aware that a married man would be far less available to her than a single guy.

Later that afternoon, it did her heart good when Bee drew her attention to the fact that Navarre was sitting with her grandmother, Celestine. 'They've been talking for ages,' her half-sister informed her.

Tawny drifted over to Navarre's side and he laced long fingers with hers to tug her down into a seat beside him. 'You've been holding out on me, *chérie*.'

'And me,' Celestine added. 'All these months I had no idea you were paying my rent.'

Tawny froze. 'What on earth are you talking about?'

'One of the other residents spoke to me about his problems meeting the maintenance costs and when certain sums were mentioned I knew that I did not have enough money to meet such enormous bills either,' the old lady told her quietly. 'I spoke to my solicitor and although he didn't break your confidence, I soon worked out for myself that there was only one way that my costs could be being met. I felt very guilty for not realising what was going on sooner.'

'Don't be daft, Gran…I've managed fine!' Tawny protested, upset that the older woman had finally registered the level to which her expenses had exceeded her means.

'By slaving away as a chambermaid and waiting on tables,' Celestine responded unhappily. 'That was not right and I would never have agreed to it.'

'I've reassured Celestine that as a member of the family I will be taking care of any problems from now on and that I hope she will be a regular visitor to our home.'

Tawny sat down beside him to soothe the old lady's worries and with Navarre's support Celestine's distress gradually faded away. Soon after that her grandmother admitted that she was tired and Tawny saw her up to the room she was to use until her departure the next morning.

'Navarre is...*très sympathique*,' her grandmother pronounced with approval. 'He is kind and understanding. You will be very happy with him.'

Having helped her grandmother unpack her overnight bag and locate all the facilities, Tawny hurried back downstairs to find Navarre waiting for her at the foot. 'Why didn't you tell me what you needed the money for months ago?' he demanded in a driven undertone, his incredulity at her silence on that score unhidden.

'It was nothing to do with you. She's my granny.'

'And now she's mine as well and you will change no more beds on her behalf!' Navarre asserted fierily.

'It's not a problem. I never had a burning desire to be a maid but it was easy work to find and it allowed me to do my illustration projects in the evenings.'

He tilted up her chin. His gaze was stern. 'Couldn't you have trusted me enough to tell me the truth for yourself?' he pressed. 'I assumed your loyalty could be bought—I thought less of you for being willing to take that money from me in payment.'

'Only because you've forgotten what it's like to be poor and in need of cash,' Tawny told him tartly. 'Poverty has no pride. When I was a child, my grandparents were very good to me. I'd do just about anything to keep Celestine safe, secure and happy.'

'And I honour you for it and for all your hard work for her benefit, *ma petite*. You also took on that responsibility without any expectation of ever receiving her gratitude, for you tried to hide your contributions to her income. I'm hugely impressed,' Navarre admitted, his stunning gaze warm with pride and approval on her blushing face. 'But why didn't you approach your sisters for help?'

'Celestine isn't related to them in any way. I wouldn't dream of bothering them for money,' Tawny argued in consternation.

'I suspect Bee would have liked to help—'

'Maybe so, Navarre,' his bride responded. 'But I've always believed in standing on my own two feet.'

An hour later when Tawny was chatting to her mother and her partner, Susan commented on how effective her daughter's dress was at concealing her swelling stomach. Amused, Tawny splayed her hand to her abdomen, momentarily moulding the fabric to the definite bulge of her pregnancy. 'My bump's still there beneath the fancy trappings!' she joked.

A few feet away, she glimpsed Tia Castelli staring at her fixedly, big blue eyes wide, her flawless face oddly frozen and expressionless before, just as quickly, the actress spun round and vanished into the crush of guests. As Tawny frowned in incomprehension Bee signalled her by pointing at her watch: it was time for Tawny to change out of her finery, and she followed her sibling upstairs because she and Navarre were leaving for France in little more than an hour. Twenty minutes later, Tawny descended a rear staircase a couple of steps in Bee's wake. She was wearing a very flattering blue skirt with floral silk tee and a long flirty jacket teamed with impossibly high heels.

Bee stopped dead so suddenly at the foot of the stairs that Tawny almost tripped over her. 'Let's go back up...I forgot something!' she exclaimed in a peculiar whisper.

But Tawny was not that easily distracted and Bee, unfortunately, was not a very good actress when she was surprised and upset by something. Correctly guessing that her sister had seen something she did not want her to see, Tawny ignored Bee's attempt to catch her arm and prevent her from stepping into the corridor at the bottom of the stairs. Tawny moved past and caught a good view of the scene that Bee had sought to protect her from. Tia Castelli was sobbing on Navarre's chest as if her heart were breaking and he was looking down at the tiny blonde with that highly revealing mixture of concern and tenderness that only existed in the most intimate of relationships. Certainly one look at the manner in which her bridegroom was comforting Tia was sufficient to freeze Tawny in her tracks and cut through her heart like a knife. It was a little vignette of her worst nightmares for, while she had from the outset accepted that Navarre did not love her, she had never been prepared for the reality that he might love another woman instead.

Abruptly registering that they had acquired an audience, Navarre stepped back and Tia flipped round to make a whirlwind recovery, eyes damp but enquiring, famous face merely anxious. 'I had a stupid row with Luke, I'm afraid, and Navarre swept me off to save me from making a fool of myself about it in public.'

It was a wry and deft explanation voiced as convincingly as only a skilled actress could make it. It sounded honest and it might even have been true, Tawny reckoned numbly, but she just didn't believe it. What she had seen was something more, something full of stronger, darker emotions on both sides. Tia's distress had been genuine even though it was hidden now, the blonde's perfect face tear-stained but composed in a light apologetic smile.

'I understand,' Tawny said flatly, for she had too much pride and common sense to challenge either of them when she had no evidence of wrongdoing. But in the space of a moment fleeting suspicion had turned into very real apprehension and insecurity.

'You look charming, *chèrie,*' Navarre murmured smoothly, scanning her shuttered face with astute cool.

He would give nothing away for free. No information, no secrets, no apologies. He would not put himself on the defensive. She knew that. She had married a master tactician, a guy to whom manipulation was a challenging game, which his intelligence and courage ensured he would always excel at playing.

Pale though she was, Tawny smiled as if she had not a worry in the world either. She hoped he would not notice that the smile didn't reach her eyes. She suspected that he was probably more relieved that she did not speak Italian and therefore was quite unable to translate the flood of words Tia had been sobbing at the moment they were disturbed. But at that instant Tawny also realised that someone had been present who could speak Tia's native tongue and she glanced at her linguistically talented sister Bee, who was noticeably pale as well, and resolved to question her as to what she had overheard before they parted.

When they returned to the ballroom, there was no sign of Tia or Luke and Tawny was not surprised by that strategic retreat. Promising Navarre she would be back within minutes, Tawny set off to find her sister again. She was even less surprised to find Bee talking to Zara, both their faces tense and troubled.

'OK…I'm the unlucky woman who just married a guy and caught a famous film star hanging round his neck like an albatross!' Tawny mocked. 'Bee, tell me what Tia was saying.'

Her sisters exchanged a conspiratorial glance.

'No, it's not fair to keep it from me. I have a right to know what you heard.'

Bee parted her lips with obvious reluctance. 'Tia was upset about the baby. I don't think she had realised that you were pregnant.'

'She was probably jealous. She's never been able to have a child of her own,' Zara commented.

'But the normal person to share that grief with would be her own husband, not *mine,*' Tawny completed with gentle emphasis. 'Don't worry about me. This isn't a love match. I've always known that. This marriage may not work out…not if that woman owns a slice of Navarre. I couldn't live with that, I couldn't *share* him—'

'I don't think that you have anything to worry about. Now if you'd caught them in a clinch that would've been a different matter,' Bee offered quietly. 'But you *didn't*. Don't let that colourful imagination of yours take over, Tawny. Be sensible about this. I think all you witnessed was a gorgeous drama queen demanding attention from a handsome man. I suspect that Tia is an old hand at that ruse and Navarre looked a little out of his depth. I also think that from now on he will be more careful with his boundaries when he's around Tia Castelli. He's no fool.'

Tawny struggled to take Bee's advice fully on board while she and Navarre were conveyed to the airport. He chatted calmly about their day and she endeavoured to make appropriate responses but she could not deny that the joy of the day had been snuffed out for her the instant she saw Navarre comforting Tia. She felt overwhelmed by the competition. What woman could possibly compete with such a fascinating femme fatale? Tia Castelli was a hugely talented international star with a colossal number of fans, an extraordinary beauty who truly lived a gilded life that belonged only in the glossiest of magazines. And Navarre *cared* about Tia. Tawny had seen the expression on his face as he looked down at the tiny distressed woman and that glimpse had shaken her and wounded her for she would have given ten years of her life to have her bridegroom look at her like that even once. That, she thought painfully, was what really lay at the heart of her suffering. Seeing him with Tia had only underlined what Tawny did not have with him.

But she would still have to man up and handle it, Tawny told herself in an urgent pep talk while they flew to Paris on Navarre's sleek private jet. She could not run away on the very first day of married life. She would only get one chance to make their marriage work so that they could give their son or daughter a proper loving home with a mother *and* a father. It was what she had always longed for and always lacked on her own account, but perhaps she had been naive as well not to face the truth that any relationship between two people would at times hurt her and demand that she compromise her ideals.

By the time they were in a limousine travelling to his home on Ile de France, several miles west of Paris, Navarre had borne the silence long enough. It was not a sulk—a sulk he could have dealt with. No, Tawny spoke when spoken to, even smiled when forced, but her vibrant spirit and quirky sense of fun were nowhere to be seen and it spooked him.

'I don't know you like this…what's wrong?' he asked, although it was a question that on principle he never, ever asked a woman, but now he was asking even though he feared that he already knew the answer.

Tawny shot him another fake smile. 'I'm just a bit tired, that's all. It's been a very long day.'

'D'accord. I constantly forget that you're pregnant and I'm making no allowances for that,' Navarre responded smoothly. 'Of course you're tired.'

It was on the tip of her tongue to tell him that it was their wedding night and she wasn't *that* tired but that would have been like issuing an invitation and she no longer possessed the confidence to do that.

The awkward silence was broken by her gasp as she looked out of the window and saw that the car was travelling through elaborate gardens and heading straight for a multi-turreted chateau of such stupendous splendour that she could only stare. 'Where on earth are we?'

'This is my home in Paris.'

'You're sure it's not a hotel?' Tawny asked stupidly, aghast at the size and magnificence of the property.

'It was for a while but it is now my private home. It's within easy reach of my offices and I like green space around me at the end of the day.'

Yes, it was obvious to her that he liked an enormous amount of green space and even more obvious why he had not been unduly impressed by Strathmore Castle, the entirety of which might well have fitted into the front hall of his spectacular chateau. Tawny was gobsmacked by the dimensions of the place. Although they had flown from London in a private jet it had still not occurred to her that Navarre might live like royalty in France. Nor had not it crossed her mind until that very moment what a simply vast gulf divided them as people.

'I feel like Cinderella,' Tawny whispered weakly. 'You live in a castle.'

He was frowning. 'I thought you'd be pleased.'

They were greeted by a manservant in the echoing vastness of the hall and every surface seemed to be gilded or marbled or mirrored so that she could see far too many confusing reflections of her bewildered face. 'It's not really a castle, it's more like a palace,' she muttered when he informed her that refreshments awaited them upstairs.

She mounted the giant staircase. 'So how long have you lived here?'

'Several years. You know, you shouldn't be wearing heels that high in your condition—'

'Navarre?' Tawny interrupted. 'Don't tell me what to wear. I'm not working for you any more.'

'No, we're married now.'

Tawny did not like the tone Navarre had employed to make that statement. She felt that he ought to be over the moon about being married to her, or at least capable of pretending to be. Instead he sounded like a guy who had got to bring the wrong woman home and that was not an idea that she liked at all, for it came all too close to matching her own worst fears.

'I don't want to have an argument with you on our wedding day,' Navarre informed her without any expression at all.

'Did I say that I wanted an argument?' Tawny demanded a touch stridently as he thrust open a heavy door and she stalked into yet another vast room, a bedroom complete with sofas and tables and several exit doors. 'It's too big…it's *all* too big and fancy for me!'

As her voice began to rise in volume Navarre cut in. 'Then we'll sell it and move—'

'But then you wouldn't be happy. This is what you're used to!'

'I grew up in a variety of slums,' he reminded her levelly and somehow the way he looked at her made her feel like a child throwing a tantrum.

Tawny gritted her teeth on another foolish comment. Her brain was all over the place. It certainly wasn't functioning as it should be. She kept on picturing Tia's flawless face and her even more perfect and always immaculately clothed body. She was thinking of the frivolous, frothy, wedding night negligee she had purchased with such joy in her heart and feeling sick at the prospect of having to put the outfit on and appear in it for his benefit. Who was she kidding? It would not hide her overblown breasts or her even more swollen stomach.

'You know...' Tawny mumbled uneasily, succumbing to her sense of insecurity. 'I'm not really in the right mood for a wedding night.'

*'Je sais ce que tu ressens...*I know how you feel.' Navarre stood there like a statue.

Tawny had expected him to argue with her, not agree with her. She wanted him to kiss her, persuade her, make everything magically all right again, but instead he just stood there, six feet plus of inert and unresponsive masculine toughness.

'You're tired, *ma petite.* I'll sleep elsewhere.'

Tawny recognised the absolute control he was exerting not to let her see what he really thought. She suspected that he was annoyed with her, that he had hoped she would continue as though nothing whatsoever had happened, as though nothing at all had changed between them. But how could she do that? How *could* she pretend she had not seen the way he looked at Tia? He had never looked at her like that, but she so badly needed him to and, denied what she most wanted, she refused to settle for being a substitute for Tia. And, to be frank, a very poor second-best at that.

Wishing her goodnight with infuriating courtesy, Navarre left the room. Her legs weak, Tawny sagged down on the sofa at the end of the bed as though she had gone ten rounds with a champion boxer. He was gone and she was no happier. She was at the mercy of as many doubts as a fishing net had holes. Had she done the wrong thing? What was the right thing in such circumstances when all she was conscious of was the level of her disillusionment? She turned her bright head to look at the big bed that they might have shared that night had she been tougher and more practical and she imagined she heard the sound of a sharp painful crack—it was the sound of her heart breaking…

CHAPTER TEN

Tawny signed the cartoon and sat back from it with a sense of accomplishment. She was working in the room that Navarre had had set up as a studio for her. For the first time in her creative life she had the latest in light tables to work at. Her cartoon series now entitled 'The English Wife' and carried in a fashionable weekly magazine, had already attracted a favourable wave of comment from the French press and she had even been interviewed in her capacity as cartoonist and wife of a powerful French industrialist. A knock on the door announced the arrival of Gaspard, who was in charge of the household and the staff, bringing her morning coffee and a snack.

On the surface life was wonderful, Tawny acknowledged, striving to concentrate only on the positive angles. Navarre had been in London the previous night on a business trip, but Tawny had not accompanied him because she had work to complete. Furthermore just as he had forecast she adored Paris: the noble architecture of the buildings, beautiful bridges and cobblestoned streets, the Seine gleaming below the autumn sunlight, the entertaining parade of chic residents. Settling in for someone who spoke French and was married to a Frenchman had not proved much of a challenge. In fact her new life in France was absolutely brilliant now that her career had finally taken off. She had no financial worries, a beautiful roof over her head covered with all the turrets a castle-loving girl could ever want and a staff who ensured that she had to do virtually nothing domestic for herself. The food was amazing as well, Tawny conceded, munching hungrily through the kind of dainty little pastry that Navarre's chef excelled at creating.

In fact after six weeks of being married to Navarre, Tawny was willing to admit that she was a very lucky woman. Cradling her coffee in one hand, Tawny studied herself in a wall mirror. Her hair piled on top of her head in a convenient style that her hairdresser had taught her to do, she was wearing her favourite skinny jeans teamed with an artfully draped jersey tunic that skimmed her growing bump and long suede boots. She had signed up with a Parisian obstetrician and her pregnancy was proceeding well. She had no problems on that front at all: she was ridiculously healthy.

Indeed her only problem was her marriage...or, to be more specific, the marriage that had never got off the ground in the first place. With the calmer frame of mind brought on by the passage of several weeks, she knew that wrecking their wedding night and rejecting Navarre had been the wrong thing to do. An outright argument would have been preferable; a demand for an explanation about that scene with Tia would have been understandable. But refusing to ask questions and hiding behind her wounded pride had not been a good idea at all, for it had imposed a distance between them that was impossible to eradicate in such a very large house. My goodness, he was sleeping two corridors away from her! And she had only found that out by tiptoeing round like a cat burglar in the dark of the night and listening to where he went when he came upstairs at the end of the evening.

There were times, many many times, when Tawny just wanted to *scream* at Navarre in frustration. He did not avoid her but he did work fairly long hours. At the same time she could not accuse him of neglecting her either because he had gone to considerable lengths to make time and space for her presence in his life and show her Paris as only a native could. He would phone and arrange to meet her for lunch or dinner or sweep her off shopping with an alacrity that astonished her. Navarre was a very woman-savvy male. When she was in his company he awarded her his full attention and he was extraordinarily charming, but he still continued to maintain a hands-off approach that was driving her crazy.

Sometimes she wondered if Navarre was very cleverly and with great subtlety punishing her for that rejection on the first night. He took her romantic places and left her as untouched as if she were his ninety-year-old maiden aunt. He had introduced her to Ladurée, an opulently designed French café/ gallery where the beautiful people met early evening for coffee and delicious pastel-coloured macaroons that melted in the mouth. He had shown her the delights of La Hune, a trendy bookshop in the bohemian sixth *arrondissement* of St-Germain. He had taken her shopping on the famous designer rue St—Honoré and spent a fortune on her. She had toured the colourful organic market at boulevard Raspail and eaten pumpkin muffins fresh from a basket. They had dined at Laperouse, a dimly lit ornate restaurant beside the Seine, an experience that had cried out for a more intimate connection and she had sat across the table willing him to make a move on her or even voice a flirtatious comment, only to be disappointed.

And then there were the gifts he brought her, featuring everything from an art book that had sent her into ecstasies to a pair of Louboutin shoes that sparkled like pure gold, not to mention the most gorgeous jewels and flowers. He was never done buying her presents, indeed he rarely came home empty-handed. She had got the message: he was generous, he liked to *give*. But how was she supposed to respond? Her teeth gritted. She really didn't understand the guy she had married because she didn't know what he wanted from her. Was he content with their relationship as it was? A platonic front of a marriage for the sake of their child? Were the constant gifts and entertaining outings a reward for not questioning his relationship with Tia Castelli? Could he possibly be that callous and without scruples?

Yet this was the same man who had gripped her hand in genuine joy and appreciation when he attended a sonogram appointment with her and they saw their child together for the first time on a screen. The warmth of his response had been everything she could have hoped for. Their little girl, the daughter whom Tawny already cherished in her heart, would rejoice in a fully committed and ardent father. She knew enough about Navarre to understand how very important it was for him to do everything for his child that had not been done for him. He might hide his emotions, but she knew they ran deep and true when it came to their baby. It hurt not to inspire an atom of that emotion on her own account.

After a light lunch, she walked round the gardens until a light mist of drizzling rain came on and drove her indoors. She was presented with a package that had been delivered and she carried it upstairs, wondering ruefully what the latest treat was that Navarre had bought her. She extracted an elaborate box and, opening it, worked through layers of tissue paper to extract the most exquisite set of silk lingerie she had ever seen in her life. A dreamy smile softened her full mouth and her pale eyes flared with the thought of the possibilities awakened by that more intimate present. Her fingers dallied with the delicate set. An invitation? Or was that wishful thinking? Was it just one more in a long line of wonderfully special gifts? Maybe she should wear it to meet him off his flight this evening and just ask him what he meant by it. That outrageous thought made her laugh out loud.

But that same thought worked on her throughout the afternoon. Maybe a little plain speaking was all that was required to sort out their marriage. And Navarre was far too tricky and suspicious of women to engage in plain speech without a lot of encouragement. Was she willing to show him the way? Put her money where her mouth was? The concept of putting her mouth anywhere near Navarre was so arousing that she blushed.

Toying with the concept, she went off to shower and rub scented cream all over her mostly slender body before applying loads of mascara and lippy. When she saw herself in that exquisite palest green lingerie she almost got cold feet. The tummy was there, there was no concealing or avoiding it, but it was his baby and he was definitely looking forward to its existence, she reminded herself comfortingly. As long as she wore vertiginous boots and looked at herself face on rather than taking in her less sensually appealing profile, she decided she didn't look silly. Donning a black silky raincoat ornamented with lots of zips that had recently caught her eye for being unusual, she left the bedroom.

At the airport, Navarre was stunned when, engaged in commenting on his reorganisation of CCC to a financial journalist, he glanced across the concourse and saw his wife awaiting him. That was definitely an unexpected development. In truth he had been a little edgy about the latest gift he had sent her. He had worried that it was a step too far, which might upset the marital apple cart even more, and so he had waited until he was out of the country to send it. He could never remember being so unsure with a woman before and he had found it an unnerving experience. As he excused himself to approach her a radiant smile lit up her face and she looked so gorgeous with her spectacular hair tumbling round her fragile features that he almost walked into a woman wheeling a luggage trolley.

'Navarre...' Tawny pronounced, hooking a slender pale hand to his arm.

'I like the coat, *ma petite*,' he murmured, although even with his wide experience he had never before seen a raincoat that appeared to lead a double life as a distinctly sexy garment, for it was short, showing the merest glimpse of long pale thigh and knee above the most incredible pair of long, tight, high-heeled boots.

Luminous pale blue eyes lifted to his face. 'I thought you'd like the boots—'

'*Il n'y a pas de mais*...no buts about that,' Navarre breathed a little thickly, wondering what she was wearing below the coat because from his vantage point no garment was visible at the neck. He watched her climb into the limousine and as the split at the back of the coat parted a tantalising couple of inches along with the movement he froze for a split second at the sight of the pale green knickers riding high on her rounded little bottom.

As the car pulled away, Tawny crossed her legs and asked him about London. His attention was welded to her legs, though, his manner distracted, and when he glanced up to find her watching him, a faint line of colour barred his high cheekbones, highlighting eyes of the most wicked green. 'You have to know that you look amazing,' he stressed unevenly. 'I can't take my eyes off you.'

'That's what I like to hear, but it's been so long since you said anything in that line...or looked,' she pointed out gently.

His lush lashes cloaked his gaze protectively. 'Our wedding day should have been perfect but instead everything went wrong and that was my fault. I didn't feel that I was in a position to make demands. I didn't want to risk driving you away.'

In a sudden movement, Tawny reached for his hand. 'I'm not going anywhere!'

'People said stuff like that to me throughout my childhood and then broke their promises,' he admitted with a stark sincerity that shook her.

'Touching me...I mean,' she said awkwardly, 'it wouldn't have needed a demand.'

Navarre rested a light fingertip below the ripe curve of her raspberry-tinted mouth and said, 'How was I to know that?'

As his hand trailed along her cheekbone Tawny pushed her cheek into his palm, lashes sensually low. 'You know now,' she told him.

'You're so different from the other women I've known. I didn't want to get it wrong with you,' he admitted gruffly, a delicious tension stretching out the moment as she angled her mouth up and he took the invitation with a swift, sure hunger that released a moan of approval from her throat.

Navarre straightened again and a gave her a breathtaking smile. 'I dare not touch you until we get back home. I'm like dynamite waiting on a lit match,' he groaned, studying her with hot, hungry intensity. 'It's been too long and I'm too revved up.'

Alight with all the potency of her feminine power, Tawny grinned and whispered curiously, 'How long?'

His brow indented. 'You know how long it's been.'

'You mean…I was your last lover? When we were together that last time in London?' Tawny specified in open amazement. 'There hasn't been anyone else since then?'

Navarre gave a rueful laugh. 'I've always been more into quality than quantity, *chérie*. I'm past the age where I sleep with women purely for kicks.'

Tawny tacitly understood what he was confirming. Even when their short-lived relationship had appeared to be over he had not taken another lover. Obviously he had not met anyone he wanted enough, which with the choices he had to have was a huge compliment to Tawny. Even more obviously, if she accepted his word on that score, it meant that he could not be engaged in even an occasional affair with Tia Castelli. Perhaps he had once loved Tia and, although it was in the past, he retained a fondness for the beautiful film star, she reasoned feverishly, desperate to explain what she had seen between them on her wedding day.

But she *was* seriously surprised by the news that he had been celibate for months on end. Meeting his level scrutiny, she believed him on that score one hundred per cent and it was as if the weight of the world fell off her shoulders in the same moment. Suddenly she was furious with herself for not asking questions about Tia and demanding answers sooner. She had conserved her pride and remained silent but unhappy and she wasn't proud of the reality that she had behaved like a coward, frightened of what the truth might reveal and of how much it might hurt. Loving a man who could be so reserved might never be easy, but she needed to learn how to handle that side of his nature.

In the vast bedroom that she had become accustomed to occupying alone she let him unzip the coat and part the edges to look down at her scantily clad curves with smouldering appreciation.

'I'm going to have to start buying you stuff,' she began shyly as he laid her down on the bed and started to carefully unzip her boots.

'No, this moment is my gift,' Navarre countered huskily, burying his mouth between her breasts and running a skilful hand along the extended length of her thigh to the taut triangle of fabric between her legs.

Her body was supersensitive after all the months of deprivation. The pulse of need she was struggling to control tightened up an almost painful notch. Sadly the lingerie that had brought them together received precious little attention and was cast aside within minutes while Navarre's shirt got ripped in the storm of Tawny's impatience. She ran her hands over the gloriously hard, flat expanse of his abs and then lower to the blatant thrust of his arousal. His breath hitched in his throat as he protested that he was too aroused to bear her touch.

'You mean you're only good for one go...like a Christmas cracker?' Tawny asked him deadpan.

And, startled by that teasing analogy, Navarre laughed long and hard as he studied her with fascination. 'Where have you been all my life?'

He kissed her passionately again and matters quickly became extremely heated. He tried to make her wait because he wanted to make an occasion of what he saw as a long delayed wedding night, but she was in no mood for ceremony and she refused to wait, holding him to her with possessive hands and locking her slim legs round his waist to entrap him. She had expectations and she was unusually bossy. He was trying for slow and gentle,

she was striving for hard and fast, and with a little art-
ful angling of her hips and caressing and whispered en-
couragements she got exactly what she wanted delivered
with an unrivalled hunger that left her body singing and
dancing with excitement. Desire momentarily quenched,
she lay in his arms, peacefully enjoying the fact that he
was still touching her as if he couldn't quite believe that
he had now reclaimed that intimacy. He stroked her arm
and strung a line of kisses round the base of her throat
while still holding her close to his lean, damp body and
at that instant, with all that appreciation coming her way,
she felt like a queen.

In fact when he got out of bed she almost panicked, a
small hand clamping round his wrist as if he were a flee-
ing prisoner. 'Where are you going?'

Navarre lifted the phone with a flourish. 'I'm ordering
some food, *ma petite*—we both need sustenance to keep
up the pace.'

'And then?' she checked, heat and awareness still rippling through swollen and sensitive places as she looked
at him.

'We share a shower and I stay...all night?' He was looking hopeful and she knew she wouldn't be able to disap-
point him, particularly when she just didn't want him out
of her sight for a minute.

'And if you should feel the need to wake me up and
jump me during the night at any time,' Navarre drawled
silkily over supper, 'you are very welcome.'

'Well, the pregnancy damage is already done.'

'Don't say that even jokingly,' he urged, feeding her
grapes and Parma ham and tiny sweet tomatoes and reminding her all over again why she loved him so much.
'I can't wait to be a father.'

In the secure circle of Navarre's arms for the first time

ever, Tawny slept blissfully well. To his great disappointment she didn't wake him up for anything so that he could
prove all over again that he had nothing in common whatsoever with a Christmas cracker. When she wakened it
was late morning and she blinked drowsily. Stretching a
hand over to the empty space beside her in the bed, she
suppressed a sigh even as she stretched luxuriantly while
lazily considering their marriage, which she was finally
convinced had a real future. He was gone, of course he
was long gone, he left for the office at the crack of dawn
most weekdays. Only when she had stumbled out of bed
to move in the direction of the bathroom did she realise
that Navarre had not even left the room—he was actually
seated in an armchair in the dimness.

'My word, I didn't see you over there…what a fright
you gave me!' She gasped, stooping hurriedly to pick up
her robe from the foot of the bed and dig her arms into the
sleeves because she was still somewhat shy of displaying
her pregnant body to him. 'Why are you still at home?'

'May I open the curtains?' At her nod, he buzzed back
the drapes and light flooded in, illuminating the harsh
lines etched in his taut features. 'I've been waiting for
you to wake up.'

'What's wrong? What's happened?'

'Your cell phone has been ringing on and off for a couple of hours…your sisters, I assume, your family trying to
get in touch with you…I didn't answer the calls.' Navarre
lifted a shoulder in a very Gallic shrug and surveyed her
with brooding regret. 'I switched off your phone because
I wanted to be the one to tell you what has happened—'

'I need to use the bathroom first!' Tawny flung wildly
at him and sped in there like a mouse pursued by a cat,
slamming the door behind her. She didn't want to know;
she didn't want to hear anything bad! She had wakened

feeling happy, safe and insanely optimistic for the first time in a long time. How could that precious hope be taken away from her so quickly?

CHAPTER ELEVEN

ONCE Tawny had freshened up and mentally prepared herself for some sort of disaster, she emerged again, pale and tense.

'Has someone died? My gran—?'

'*Merde alors*...no, it is nothing of that nature!' Navarre hastened to assure her.

Tawny breathed again, slow and deep, striving to remain calm when all she really wanted to do was scream and be hysterical and childish because she had never wanted bad news less, and now she feared that he was about to tell her something or *confess* something that would destroy her and their marriage. If nobody had died or got hurt, what else was there?

'I saw Tia while I was over in London. She took a hotel room and I visited her there. Yesterday an English tabloid newspaper published an account of the fact that we were in that hotel suite alone together for more than an hour and printed photos of us entering and leaving the hotel separately.'

Tawny drew her body up so stiff with her muscles pulled so tight that she stretched at least an inch above her normal height. 'You went to an hotel with her...you're admitting that?'

'I won't lie to you about it.'

'You know a normal man would be rendezvousing with his secretary or a colleague between five and seven in the evening for clandestine sex before he comes home to his wife. That's the norm for a mistress—you're not supposed to be shagging a world-famous film star!' Tawny condemned shakily, throwing words in a wild staccato burst while nausea pooled in her stomach because she immediately grasped the appalling fact that his confession meant that all her worst fears were actually true. She felt as if she had woken up inside a nightmare and did not know what to say or do. She hovered on the priceless Aubusson rug, swallowed alive by her anguish.

Navarre was watching every flicker cross her highly expressive face and he too had lost colour below his bronzed complexion. 'Tia is not and has never been my mistress. We're friends and we lunched in her suite in private, that's *all*,' Navarre declared, shifting an emphatic hand to stress that point. 'The paparazzi never leave her alone. Her every move is recorded by cameras. She has to be very careful of her reputation because of her marriage and her career, which is the only reason why we usually meet up in secret—'

'Never mind her. What about *your* marriage?' Tawny asked him baldly, wondering if he could seriously be expecting her to swallow such an unlikely story. Lunch and no sex? What sort of an idiot did he think she was?

A hasty rat-a-tat-tat sounded on the bedroom door and, with a bitten-off curse that betrayed just how worked up he was as well, Navarre strode past her to answer it. Hearing Gaspard's voice, Tawny rested a hand on a corner of the bed and slowly, carefully sank her weak body down on the comfortable mattress. Her legs felt like wet noodles and she felt dizzy and sick. It was nerves and fear, of course, she told herself impatiently. She wasn't about to faint or throw up like some silly Victorian maiden. Her husband had slept with Tia Castelli. In fact he obviously slept with the actress on a very regular basis, for by the sound of it their meeting arrangements seemed to be set in quite a cosy little routine. That suggested that their private encounters had been taking place for at least a couple of years.

Navarre closed the door and raked long restive fingers through his short black hair. Momentarily he closed his eyes as he was struggling to muster his resources.

'What did Gaspard want?'

Navarre expelled his breath in a hiss and shot her a veiled glance. 'To tell me that Tia has arrived—'

'Here? She's *here*?' Tawny exclaimed in utter disbelief.

'We'll talk downstairs and settle this for once and all,' Navarre pronounced grimly. 'I'm sorry I've involved you in this mess—'

'Tia will be even sorrier if I get my hands on her,' Tawny slammed back strickenly. 'How on earth could she come here? What sort of a woman would do that?'

'Think about it,' Navarre urged tautly. 'Only a woman who is not my lover would come to the home I share with my wife—'

'That might be true of most women, but not necessarily when the woman concerned is a drama queen like Tia Castelli! I'll get dressed and come down…but don't you dare go near her without me there!' Tawny warned him fierily while she dug frantically through drawers and wardrobes to gather up an outfit to take into the bathroom.

He's having an affair and his lover has got the brass neck to come to the home he shares with his pregnant wife, she thought in shock and horror. Yet last night they had been so close, so happy together. How could she have been prepared for such a development? In a daze she pulled on her jeans and a loose silk geometric print top. She couldn't even *try* to compete with an international star in the looks department.

He had belonged to Tia first, Tawny reasoned wretchedly, only choosing to marry Tawny because she was pregnant and possibly because he had wanted to make his own life away from Tia's. After all, Tia was married as well. And she could have forgiven him for the affair if he had broken off his liaison with the blonde beauty to concentrate on his marriage instead. But he had not done that. Indeed Navarre appeared to believe that he could somehow have both of them in his life. Did he aspire to enjoying both a mistress *and* a wife?

'What is she doing here in France?' Tawny pressed Navarre on the way downstairs.

'We'll find out soon enough,' Navarre forecast flatly.

A very large set of ornate pale blue leather cases sat in the hall and Tawny was aghast at that less than subtle message. Tia had not only come to visit but also, it seemed, to stay. Tia, sheathed in a black form-fitting dress that hugged her curves, broke into a tumbling flood of Italian as soon as Navarre and Tawny entered the drawing room.

'Speak in English, please,' Navarre urged the overwrought woman. 'Let us be calm.'

Tawny dealt him a pained appraisal. 'Only a man would suggest that in this situation.'

'Luke's thrown me out—he won't listen to anything I say!' Tia cried in English and she threw herself at Navarre like a homing pigeon. 'What am I going to do? What the hell am I going to do now?'

Standing there as superfluous as a third wheel on a bicycle and being totally ignored, Tawny ground her teeth together. 'Well, you *can't* stay here,' she told Tia loudly, reckoning that it would take a raised voice to penetrate the blonde's shell of self-interest.

Slowly, Tia lifted her golden head from Navarre's chest and focused incredulous big blue eyes on Tawny. 'Are you speaking to me?'

'You're not welcome under this roof,' Tawny delivered with quiet dignity.

Ironically, in spite of all that had happened, Tia seemed aghast at that assurance. She backed off a step from Navarre, her full attention locking to him. 'Are you going to allow her to speak to me like that?'

'Tawny is my wife and this is her home. If she doesn't want you staying here in the wake of that scandal in London, which affects me as much as you, I'm afraid you will have to listen to her,' he spelt out.

A little of Tawny's rigid tension eased.

'You should be putting me first—what's the matter with you?' Tia yelled at him accusingly, golden hair bouncing on her shoulders, slender arms spread in dramatic emphasis.

'I'm putting my marriage first but I should have done that sooner,' Navarre murmured levelly and, although he spoke quietly, his deep dark drawl carried. 'Allow me to tell Tawny the truth about our relationship, Tia—'

Tia stalked back towards him, her beautiful face flushed with furious disbelief. 'Absolutely not...you can't tell her...not under *any* circumstances!'

'We don't have a choice,' Navarre declared, his impatience patent while strain and something else Tawny couldn't distinguish warred in his set features as he looked expectantly at the older woman.

Tia shot Tawny a fulminating appraisal. 'Don't tell her. I don't trust her—'

'But I do...' Navarre reached out to Tawny and after

a moment of surprise and hesitation she moved closer to accept his hand and let him draw her beneath one arm. 'Tawny is part of my life now. You can't ignore her, you can't treat her as if she is of no account.'

'If you tell her, if you risk my marriage and my career just to please her, I'll never forgive you for it!' Tia sobbed in a growing rage.

'Your marriage is already at risk but that's not an excuse to put mine in jeopardy as well.' Navarre's arm tightened round Tawny's taut shoulders. 'Tawny...Tia is my mother, but that is a very big secret which you can't share with anyone at all outside this room—'

'Your m-mother?' Tawny stammered, completely disconcerted by that shattering claim and twisting her head to stare at him. 'For goodness' sake, she's not old enough to be your mother!'

Navarre was wryly amused. 'Tia is a good deal older than she looks.'

Tia went rigid with resentment at that statement. 'I was only a child when I gave birth to you—'

'She was twenty-one but pretending to be a teenager at the time,' Navarre extended wearily. 'I'll tell you the rest of the story some other time but right now the fact that she is my mother and that we like to stay in regular contact is really all that's relevant.'

'His...mother,' Tawny framed weakly, still studying the glamorous older woman in disbelief, for, according to what Navarre had just told her, Tia had to be into her fifties yet she could still comfortably pass for being a woman in her late thirties. Shock was still gripping Tawny so hard that she could hardly think straight.

'But that can never come out in public,' Tia proclaimed, angrily defensive. 'I've told lies. I've kept secrets. It would destroy my reputation and I don't want Luke to know that his own mother is younger than I am—'

'I bet she's not a beauty like you, though,' Tawny commented thoughtfully and earned an almost appreciative glance from the woman whom she had just discovered to be her mother-in-law.

'I think Luke could adapt,' Navarre interposed soothingly. 'You're still the same woman he loved and married.'

Tia shuddered. 'He would never forgive me for lying to him.'

'Why were you crying on our wedding day?' Tawny enquired to combat the simple fact that she was still dizzily thinking, She can't be his mother, she *can't* be!

'Do I *look* like I want to be a grandmother?' Tia demanded in a tone of horror. 'Do I look that old?'

'I don't think you'll ever be asked to carry out that role,' Tawny responded drily, weary of the woman's enormous vanity and concern about her age while she instinctively continued to study those famous features in search of a likeness between mother and son. And she realised that when she removed their very different colouring from the comparison there was quite a definite similarity in bone structure. He was so good-looking because his mother was gorgeous, she registered numbly.

'Right now I only want to lie down and rest. I'm exhausted,' Tia complained petulantly, treating both her son and his wife to an accusing look as though that were their fault. 'I assume I can stay now that I've shown my credentials.'

'Yes, of course,' Tawny confirmed, marvelling that such a selfish personality had ever contrived to win Navarre's loyalty and tenderness. And yet, without a shadow of a doubt, Tia had. Tawny had not been mistaken over what she had thought she had seen in Navarre when he was with his mother on their wedding day. He cared for the volatile woman.

'If you want to sort this out with Luke you will have to let him into the secret,' Navarre warned his mother levelly.

Tia told him to mind his own business with a tartness that was very maternal, but which would have been more suited to a little boy than an adult male. Gaspard was summoned to show Tia to her room. Tawny had offered but was imperiously waved away, Tia clearly not yet prepared to accept a friendly gesture from her corner. Tawny grasped that she had a possessive mother-in-law to deal with, for Tia undoubtedly resented Navarre's loyalty to his wife.

Tia swept out and the door closed. Navarre looked at Tawny.

Tawny winced and said limply, 'Wow, your mother's quite a character.'

'She's temperamental when she gets upset. I wanted to tell you but a long time ago I swore never to tell anyone that I was her son and she held me to my promise.'

'Your mother...' Tawny shook her head very slowly. 'I never would have guessed that in a million years.'

Over breakfast and only after Tawny had phoned her sisters to tell them that, *no,* she really wasn't concerned about silly stories in the papers, Navarre explained the intricacies of his birth, which had been buried deep and concealed behind a wall of lies to protect Tia's star power. According to Tia's official history she had been discovered as a fifteen year old schoolgirl in the street by a famous director. Her first film had won so many awards it had gone global and shot her to stardom. In fact the pretence that she was much younger had simply been a publicity exercise and her kid sister's birth certificate had been used for proof when Tia was actually twenty-one years old. Soon after her discovery she had fallen pregnant by the famous director. A scandalous affair with a married man threatened to destroy her pristine reputation and her embryo career, so Navarre's birth had taken place in secrecy. Tia had travelled to Paris with her older sister and had pretended to be her so that her baby could be registered as her sister's child. That cover up achieved, Tia had returned to show business while paying her sister and her boyfriend to raise Navarre in a Paris flat.

Tawny was frowning. 'Then how come you ended up in foster care?'

'I have no memory of my aunt at all. She only kept me for a couple of years. The money Tia used to buy her sister's silence was spent on drugs and when my aunt died of an overdose I joined the care system. I had no idea I had a mother alive until I was eighteen and at university,' Navarre extended wryly. 'I was approached by a lawyer first, carefully sworn to silence—'

'And then you met your mother. Must've been a shock,' Tia remarked.

An almost boyish expression briefly crossed his lean taut face as he looked back into the past and his handsome mouth took on a wry cast. 'I was in complete awe of her.'

Tawny could hardly imagine the full effect of Tia Castelli on a teenager who had been totally alone in the world all his life. Naturally his mother had walked straight into his heart when he had never had anyone of his own before. 'She's very beautiful.'

'Tia may not be showing it right now but she does also have tremendous charm. Ever since then we've been meeting up at least once a month and we often talk on the phone and email. That's one of the reasons I was so concerned that someone might have accessed my laptop,' he confided. 'I've seen her through many, many crises and have become her rock in every storm. I'm very fond of her.'

Tawny nodded. 'Even though she won't own up to you in public?'

'What would that mean to me at my age? I know she's far from perfect,' Navarre acknowledged with a dismissive lift of an ebony brow. 'But what else does she know? She was an abused child from a very poor home.'

Tawny was not as understanding of his mother's flaws as he was. 'But what did she ever do for you? You had a miserable childhood.'

'But it made me strong, *chérie*. As for Tia, even after decades of fame she still lives in terror of losing everything she has. She did what she thought best for me at the time. She helped me find my first job, invested in my first company, undoubtedly helped me to become the success that I am today.'

'That's just the power of money you're talking about and I doubt if it meant much to someone as rich as she must be.' Her eyes glittered silver with moisture, the tightening of her throat muscles as she fought back tears lending her voice a hoarse edge. 'I'm thinking of the child you were, growing up without a mother or love or anyone of your own…I can't bear the thought of that.'

In an abrupt movement that lacked his normal measured grace, Navarre vaulted upright and walked round the table to lift Tawny up out of her seat. *Je vais bien…* I'm OK. But I admit that I didn't know what love was until I met you.'

Assuming that he had guessed how she felt about him, Tawny reddened. 'Am I that obvious?'

A gentle fingertip traced the silvery trail of a tear on her cheek.

'There is nothing obvious about you. In fact you defied my understanding from the first moment we met and, the more I saw of you, the more desperately I wanted to know what it was about you which got to me when other women never had.'

Her lashes flicked up on curious eyes. 'I...got to you? In what way?'

'In every way a woman can appeal to a man. First to my body, then to my brain and finally to my heart,' Navarre specified. 'And you dug in so deep in my heart, I was wretched without you when we were apart but far too proud to come looking for you again.'

Tawny rested a hand on a broad shoulder to steady herself. 'Wretched?' she repeated doubtfully, unable to associate such a word with him.

A rueful smile shadowed Navarre's wide eloquent mouth. 'I was very unhappy and unsettled for weeks on end. I thought I was infatuated with you. I tried so hard to fight it and forget about you but it didn't work.'

'Navarre...' Tawny breathed uncertainly. 'Are you trying to tell me that you love me?'

'Obviously not doing a very good job of it. I think it was love at first sight.' His eyes gazed down into hers full of warmth and tenderness. 'I've been in love with you for months. I knew I loved you long before I married you. Why do you think I was so keen to put that wedding ring on your hand?'

'The b-baby.'

Navarre drew her back against him and splayed a possessive hand across the firm swell of her stomach. 'I have very good intentions towards our baby but I married you because I loved you and wanted to share my life with you, *n'est ce pas?*'

'But you said you were strongly attracted to me and that that was enough.'

'I said what I had to say to get that ring on your finger for real,' Navarre breathed, pressing his mouth to the sensitive nape of her neck and making her shiver with sudden awareness. 'I'm a ruthless man. I would have said whatever it took to achieve that goal because I believed the end result would be worth it. I was determined that you would be mine for ever, *ma petite.*'

Overjoyed by that admission, Tawny twisted round and pressed her hands to his strong cheekbones to align their mouths and kiss him with slow, sweet brevity as more questions that had to be answered bubbled up in her brain. 'What on earth was on that laptop of yours?'

'CCC buyout stuff and some very personal emails from Tia. She tells me everything.'

'No wonder Luke's jealous of you.'

'As long as Tia refuses to tell him the truth I am powerless to alter that situation.'

Tawny treated him to a shrewd appraisal. 'She's part of the reason you wanted a fake fiancée for the Golden Awards, isn't she?'

'I promised Tia that I would bring a girlfriend and I too believed it to be a sensible precaution where Luke was concerned. Unfortunately the lady backed out at the last minute and—'

'And you hired me instead,' Tawny slotted in. 'What happened to the lady who backed out?'

'I told her that I'd met someone else when I got back to Paris.'

'But that wasn't true…you had already left me.'

His eyes glimmered. 'But I still didn't want anyone else. You had me on a chain by then. Don't you remember that last night in London when I came to your door?'

Tawny stiffened. 'I also recall how it ended with you telling me I was a good—'

Navarre pulled her up against him and gazed down at her in reproof. 'Wasn't that in response to you threatening to tell the world what I was like in bed?'

A sensual shimmer of response wafted through Tawny and she pressed closer, tucking her head into his shoulder to breathe in the deliriously addictive scent of his skin. 'Well, now that you mention it, it might have been,' she teased, acknowledging that she had met her match while relishing the claim she had had him on a chain by that stage. A chain of love and commitment he refused to give to a woman who was a failed thief threating to tell all to the newspapers? She didn't blame him for that, she couldn't blame him for walking away at that point, for one thing she did appreciate about the man she loved was his very strong moral compass.

'When I saw you with Tia at the wedding I feared the worst,' she confided as his arms tightened round her.

'I was desperate to tell you the truth and relieved when you didn't force a scene because I didn't want to break my promise to my mother,' he admitted grimly. 'But I should have broken the promise and told you then. Unfortunately it took me a few weeks to appreciate that as my wife you have to have the strongest claim to my loyalty.'

'Sorry about the wedding night that never was,' she mumbled ruefully. 'I felt so insecure after seeing how close you were to her. I could *see* that there was a connection between you and I love you so much...'

Navarre pushed up her chin and stared down at her searchingly. 'Since when?' he demanded and his beautiful mouth quirked. 'Since you saw my beautiful castle in France?'

His wife dealt him a reproving look. 'I shall treat that

suggestion with the contempt it deserves! No, I fell for you long before that. Remember that breakfast in Scotland after that nasty newspaper spread which revealed that I was a maid? When you brought me my food and stood by me in front of everyone as though nothing had happened, I really *loved* you for it…'

'Snap. I loved you for your dignity and cool, *ma petite.*' A tender smile softened the often hard line of his shapely mouth. Long fingers stroked her spine as he crushed her to him and kissed her with a breathless hunger that made her knees weak.

For once, Tawny had a small breakfast because the conversation and what followed were too entertaining to take a rain check on. He urged her upstairs to the bed they had only shared once and they lost themselves in the passion they had both restrained for so long.

In the lazy aftermath of quenching their desire, Tawny stared at her handsome husband and said, 'What on earth game have you been playing with me all these weeks we've been married?'

'It was no game.' Navarre laughed. 'We had no courtship—we never dated. I was trying to go back to the beginning and do everything differently in the hope that you would start feeling for me what I felt for you.'

In dismay at that simple exclamation and touched that he had gone to that amount of idealistic effort without receiving the appreciation he had undoubtedly deserved, Tawny clamped a hand to her lips. 'Oh, my goodness, how stupid am I that I didn't see that?'

Navarre looked a touch superior and stretched luxuriantly against the tumbled sheets while regarding her with intense appreciation. 'Of the two of us, I'm the romantic one. Don't forget that reality when you next draw a cartoon in which I figure merely as a skirt-chasing Frenchman!'

Tawny smoothed a possessive hand over his spectacular abs and smiled down at him with unusual humility. 'I won't,' she promised happily. 'I love you just the way you are.'

EPILOGUE

JOIE, named for the joy she had brought her adoring parents, toddled across the floor and presented Luke Convery with a toy brick.

'She's cute but I wouldn't want one of my own,' the rock musician said with an apologetic grimace as he dropped down on his knees to place the brick where Navarre and Tawny's daughter, with her fantastically curly black hair and pale blue eyes, wanted it placed. 'I grew up the youngest of nine kids and I've never wanted that kind of hassle for myself.'

'Kids aren't for everyone,' Tawny agreed, thinking of how much her mother had resented being a parent, yet Susan Baxter had proved to be a much more interested grandmother than her daughter had expected. In fact mother and daughter had become a good deal closer since Joie's birth in London eighteen months earlier.

Tawny often spent weekends in London to meet up with her sisters and her mother before travelling down to see her grandmother. She had been married to Navarre for two years and had never been happier or more content. She and Navarre seemed to fit like two halves of a whole. Her liveliness had lightened his character and brought out his sense of humour, while his cooler reserve had quietened her down just a tiny bit. Through her cartoons, Tawny had become quite a familiar face in Parisian society, and when 'The English Wife' cartoons had run out of steam she had come up with a cartoon strip based on an average family, which had done even more for her career.

A peal of laughter sounded in the hall of Navarre and Tawny's spacious London home followed by an animated burst of Italian, and Luke grinned and sprang upright. 'Tia's back...'

Tawny's mother-in-law, swathed in a spectacular crimson dress and looking ravishingly beautiful, posed like the Hollywood star she was in the doorway, and her husband grinned and pulled her into his arms with scant concern for their audience. Within the space of thirty seconds they had vanished upstairs. Tia had just finished filming in Croatia and Luke was about to set off on tour round the USA. As they had been apart for weeks and Luke had a stopover in the city Tia had invited herself and her husband to dinner and to spend the night.

From the moment that Tia had finally faced reality and persuaded Navarre to take care of the challenging task of telling Luke who he really was, all unease between the two couples had vanished. Luke had been very shocked, but relieved by the news that he had no reason to feel threatened by Navarre's bond with Tia, and certainly the revelation did not seem to have dented Luke's devotion to his demanding wife. Navarre would be Tia's big dark secret until the day he died but that didn't bother him and if the paparazzi were still chasing around trying to make a scandal out of his encounters with his mother, it no longer worried him or her. The people that mattered knew the truth and Navarre had no further need to keep secrets from Tawny.

Tia was a fairly uninterested grandmother, freezing with dismay if Joie and her not always perfectly clean hands got too close to her finery. Tia's life revolved round her latest movie, her most recent reviews and Luke, whom she uncritically adored. She had initially taken a step back from her son but that hadn't lasted for long, Tawny thought wryly, for Tia rejoiced in a strong manly shoulder to lean on and Navarre was very good at fulfilling that role when Luke was unavailable. Tia's marriage had become rather more stable and fortunately the passionate disputes had died down a little, so Navarre was much less in demand in that field. Tawny, who had nursed certain fears, also had to admit that Tia never interfered as a mother-in-law. She had become friendlier, but at heart Tia Castelli would always be a larger-than-life star and she didn't really 'do' normal family relationships or even understand them.

Navarre, who had flown Tia back from Europe in his private jet, appeared in the doorway.

'Where have our guests gone?' Tawny's tall, darkly handsome husband enquired, bending down to scoop up the toddler shouting with excitement at his appearance.

Tawny watched with amusement as Navarre's immaculate appearance was destroyed by his daughter's enthusiastic welcome. His black hair was ruffled, his tie yanked and he was almost strangled by the little arms tightening round his neck, but he handled his livewire child with loving amusement.

'Our guests are staging their reunion…we just may find ourselves dining alone tonight,' Tawny warned him, her easy smile illuminating her face.

'That would be perfect,' Navarre confided as he set Joie down to run to her nanny, who had appeared in the hall. *'Merci,* Antoinette.'

'I don't really want company either when you've been away for a couple of days,' Navarre admitted bluntly once the door closed on their nanny's exit with their daughter. 'Whose idea was this set-up anyway?'

'You need to ask? Tia's, of course. You're so posses-sive, Monsieur Cazier,' Tawny teased, but when those in-tent green eyes looked at her like that she knew she was loved and she adored that sensation of warm acceptance.

'And with you getting more beautiful every day that's not going to change any time soon, *ma petite*.'

'How do I know you haven't simply become less picky since you met me?' Tawny teased.

'Because every month that I have you and Joie in my life I love you even more,' he murmured with roughened sincerity as he drew her into his arms. 'My life would be so empty, so bleak without you both.'

'I missed you,' she admitted in reward.

'So much,' Navarre growled, leaning in for a hungry, demanding kiss. 'What time's dinner?'

'I thought, since our guests have made themselves scarce, we could go out…later,' Tawny whispered en-couragingly.

'This is why I love you so much,' Navarre swore with passionate admiration. 'You've worked out what I want before I even speak.'

Tawny knotted his tie in one hand and laughed. 'And sometimes I even give you what I want because I love you…'

'And I love you,' Navarre husked, making no attempt to conceal his appreciation.

* * * * *

**Fall under the spell of *New York Times*
bestselling author**

Nora Roberts

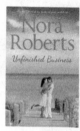 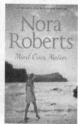 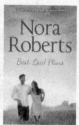 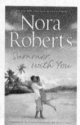

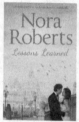 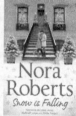 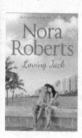

**450 million of her books in
print worldwide**

www.millsandboon.co.uk